Cancelled

Danny King

Cancelled

Copyright © 2024 Danny King

ALL RIGHTS RESERVED

No part of this book may be reproduced in any form, by photocopying or by any electronic or mechanical means, including information storage or retrieval systems, without permission in writing from the copyright owner.

All characters and events in this book are fictitious. Any similarity to real persons, living or dead, is coincidental and not intended by the author.

Front cover:
Photograph by Alexander Krivitskiy
Courtesy of www.pexels.com
Cover design by the author
Cover font Gill Sans
Interior font Garamond

ISBN: 979-888448835-9

26th January 2025

AUTHOR NOTE

Every care has been taken to edit and proof-read this edition but should you find any typos and can remember where they are, please email me and I will update the text and add your name to the acknowledgements at the back of this book with grateful thanks (with your permission).

dannykingbooks@yahoo.com

1: HUB

Bella was wearing the lily.

All womyn wore the lily when they bled. It was a powerful symbol of Aphrodite's twin glories of strength and vulnerability. It declared "I am womxn. I am life". It also helped blag a seat on the bus after work. Most were content to wear the paper lilies that came with each box of sanitary towels, dispensed free from feminine hygiene clinics nationwide, but some bought the reusable plastic kind that claimed to be better for the environment despite ten million having been produced and discarded in the last three years alone. The wealthiest wore real lilies, lovingly cultivated in hothouses and crossbred to bloom to a kaleidoscope of colours. Bella wore one of these, once red and glorious, now wilting against her lapel like yesterday's salad.

It irritated Sienna when Bella wore the lily. Not because the living lilies she wore rubbed Sienna's nose in the yawning chasm between their salaries. And not because Bella always wore it high enough to ensure her webcam caught it no matter how closely Sienna zoomed in. And it wasn't even because Bella had been a womxn for less than a year and, as yet, had very little to bleed from except a grief-stricken heart for oppressed womyn everywhere. No, it was because she'd been wearing it for over a week now which meant another caseload of files would soon be winging their way over so that Bella could spend the afternoon 'centring her energies'. Yet it had been a different story when Sienna had worn the lily ten days earlier. No hot baths or pyjama days for her. Back then there had been work to do and no one to dump it on.

"Send me an overview when you're done. I'll try to get

back to you as soon as I can but not today. Or tomorrow," Bella instructed, wilting before Sienna to emulate her lily. Despite her malady, Bella looked overdressed as usual, with her face painstakingly applied and her best hairpiece curled into a lopsided bun. Her gown, orange flowers with green stalks, had been tailor-made by her 'little man' in Kensington, a dressmaker of some renown that Bella forbade anyone else from using.

"Wait, could you not draft the indictment list?" Sienna begged. "I'll pitch them. I just need to know what I'm pitching." But Bella could scarcely stay in shot. This month's flow had sapped her chi and she desperately needed to lie down somewhere warm and dark. And far away from work.

"It's all in the case files," Bella said and with that, she disappeared only to be replaced by a flashing notification that taunted Sienna with the words: FILES RECEIVED.

Sienna flicked through them, running her eyes from one to the other and soon realised why Bella had been so keen to cry off presenting to Congress. She had nothing. A few trivial indictments that would've been laughed out of court by Hanging Judge Jeffreys with nooses to spare but very little to excite Myrtle Moorcroft, X Division's fastidious Head of Operations. This was a clear case of buck-passing. Period.

Alas, Sienna was powerless to complain. The femxle cycle was womxnhood's great leveller. It united all those who possessed wombs. Once dismissed in less enlightened times as a 'curse', it was now rightfully celebrated as beauty incarnate. The manna of life. Sienna was never prouder than when she bled. She just wished Bella would stick to the script and do it only once a month.

Bella had sent 19 files. Not a great haul but they represented the caseloads collated across the whole of

Section 4. As Supervisor, Bella would normally be expected to present. But Sienna was her immediate subordinate and the perfect bearer of bad news. A one-time high-flyer and star Auditor, her own career had stalled to reflect the Company's dip in fortunes. If anyone bore disappointing news well, it was Sienna.

A message pinged in her periphery. She dragged it to the centre of her vision with a flick of her eyes and groaned when she read it.

Sri Lankan braised root stew with coconut dhal dumplings for 7pm. I hope you are having a good day – Carl

Carl had brought dinner forward again which could mean only one thing. There was some event happening tonight that she would be expected to attend. On a Wednesday night. After a long day at work.

The message flashed orange to let her know that Carl was awaiting her response. Sienna knew better than to ignore it. Her evening was liable to be arduous enough without Carl being arduous too so she fashioned a non-committal *Gr8 Can't wait* and attempted to reply but failed when her eyes rolled involuntarily. Second time lucky and Carl's reply was immediate.

I can prepare something else if you'd prefer – Carl

She'd known, even as she'd formatted her lukewarm response, that Carl would detect her lack of enthusiasm and she kicked herself in frustration. Now she had Carl to work on as well as Bella's files, not to mention a work pile of her own.

Not at all. Sri Lankan stew is my absolute favourite. Thank you so much for making it. I'm really looking forward to it. I just hope work doesn't keep me at the Hub too late because I'm already salivating at the prospect. Well done and thank you. I am so lucky to have you waiting at home for me – Sienna.

She wondered if that would do and crossed her fingers to see if Carl would bite. Almost a minute passed and Sienna was just starting to relax when his response appeared.

Whatever – Carl

Damn it!

Sienna dissected her message and decided that she shouldn't have mentioned working late. That had been the incriminating phrase. Carl was always going to blow a circuit over that and now she would have run the gauntlet, fielding accusations about putting work before home life while searching the cupboards for something to eat.

Of course, it hadn't always been like this. There had been good days in the beginning. Fun days and happy memories. But like the emxncipation of womynkind, these days were a false dawn and the eternal struggle had soon resumed.

Her buzzer sounded. Sienna waited to see if it had been an accident. It usually was. No one called on anyone else in person if they could help it but the buzzing came again, this time with a little flourish – *buzz-buzz-buzz* – as if this would prove impossible to resist.

Sienna felt her anxieties rising. This wasn't a message in her periphery or a pop-up she could blink away. There was someone at her door. Her actual door. And they wanted to see her face to face.

She knew who it was even before she'd activated her intercom.

"Hi, Sienna? I saw you coming back from lunch. It's me, Malek."

Malek was a data engineer from down the corridor. He used a desk at the Hub the same as Sienna but worked for a different company. Almost everyone at the Hub worked for different companies, using the privacy pods and the Network interface to connect remotely with colleagues up and down the land. Years ago, in the days of pollution and pandemics, people squeezed onto trains and blocked ring roads in an effort to converge into steel and glass offices in the centres of towns. People relocated specifically to be nearer to work. They spent thousands of pounds and hundreds of hours riding to and from places they had no wish to go just so that they could sit at a screen and use a communal kitchen. Eventually, it was realised that this whole practice was redundant and nobody except road sweeps and Go Eat Couriers actually needed to leave the house. Adversely, working from home proved impractical too because productivity was shown to dip in all sectors except for market research into how popular working from home was. And so, huge multi-storey work Hubs began springing up, providing industry spaces and Network access for 95% of the population, taking traffic off the roads, trains off the railways and boots off the streets to spare Muhammed his daily trek up the mountain.

The Hub in which Sienna worked was located in the mini-metropole of Woking. Situated 20 miles southwest of the capital and set in the rolling hills of Surrey, Woking was a model town for a new age: vibrant, diverse and safe. Years earlier, it had been a stronghold for the once-dominant Conservative Party and run by the hated patriarchy. Now it was the Polychrome Alliance's safest seat. Zaria Okello, Minister For Survivors and rising star of the party, represented the constituency. Sienna had seen her once, at the opening of Woking's Hall of Shame, a permanent museum to sins of yesteryear (formerly Pizza Express). Their eyes had met before the plaque of Alan Turing in the museum lobby. No words had passed between them but Zaria had definitely smiled approvingly before moving on to check out a display of Robinson's Jam Jars in the taboo gallery.

Buzz-buzz-buzz.

Sienna knew the reason Malek had called and it was the reason she'd been avoiding him all week. She didn't know Malek that well. They both used the Hub's street food hall but they weren't friends. They sat at the same table sometimes, albeit surrounded by dozens of others. Malek liked to talk about himself, the work he was doing, the clients he was serving and the boss he would eventually be unseating. But most of all, he liked to talk about Julie. Julie Adamski was a Product Mxnager who used a pod on the fifth floor.

Malek liked her.

A lot.

Sienna could see why. Julie was young, confident and skinny as a wisp of vape. But for reasons Sienna could not understand, Julie seemed to like Malek too. Sienna didn't get it. Malek was ordinary. Very much so. He had a faux ethnic name. And he was far too happy with himself. His chin was weak and his Diversity Grade was sub 10. Julie could do better than Malek. Julie *should* do better than Malek. For her to go with this man would have been a crime against womxnhood. And yet Malek had collected two of the three signatures he needed on his A6 Sexual Consent Application in order to gain Julie's consent. All he needed was one last squiggle. One last affirming witness and his intentions could be ratified. Alas, without three witnesses, Julie could not give her consent. Not legally so anyway.

But two weeks after pinging his Application to Sienna, he was still waiting, his notification throbbing away urgently in the furthest corner of her periphery.

Sienna unmuted the intercom.

"... if you have any worries, I'd be happy to talk them through with you... if you have a minute..." Malek was offering as non-threateningly as he could.

But it was too late. By simply approaching Sienna as he had done she already felt intimidated. She shut down her screens and logged out of the interface, removed her ID clip and turned her cherry-tinted Smart Glasses to their reddest setting. She couldn't look Malek in the eye when she passed him by so she moved quickly, yanking open the door and hurrying down the hall without so much as a backward glance.

"Wait, Sienna, I'm sorry. I didn't mean to... can I get my form back then...?" he called as she headed for the third-floor Safe Space at the far end of the corridor. Sienna entered with a swipe of her clip and took shelter in the furthest cyan cube. Three others were in here already, sprawled on bean bags beneath soft lighting, losing themselves to whale songs and mindful quotations. Anita Xeno was in here as always, racked by anxiety and unable to escape her workload having already used up her allocation of Mental Wellness Days for October.

Sienna looked at her hands. They were shaking. Had that really happened? She considered herself a reasonable person, rarely prone to hysteria but Malek had shown his true nature. There was no way she could sanctify his union now. To do so would have been unthinkable.

Sexual Consent Applications were contracts between consenting adults. These types of agreements had been around as long as sex itself. In the days of old, when womyn had nothing to barter but their chastity, they would exchange copulation rights for a place by the fire and a handful of meat. Over time, these unwritten contracts attracted the blessings of the church, which set the agreements out to text and established a chattel state of slavery that became, with systemic indoctrination, the aspiration of every girl on earth. And thus, the subjugation of womxnhood was maintained for five millennia until womyn finally shook off their bonds and declared: "We are the fire. We are the meat."

Henceforth, a fairer system was developed with inbuilt protections for the vulnerable to weight these agreements more equitably. The idea evolved from prenuptial agreements. These had existed in the days of matrimonial rape, mostly to protect men's property. Now they were updated to protect womyn's rights.

Three witnesses were required to sign off an application before a man could ratify his desires. The witnesses had to be femxle, independent and known to both parties. This was designed to protect vulnerable womyn from coercion. The rules of the relationship had to be set out. Proof of identification, medical records and a full and frank overview of the man's finances had to be provided. And a time limit had to be clearly stated, anything from ten minutes to ten years. Renewal was a simple process and both parties had the option to terminate with immediate effect – provided no sections had been breached. Since most of the liabilities lay with the man, this meant in effect that the age-old practice of loving and leaving them could prove punitive in the extreme.

Of course, this had originally been worked out on the assumption that men were the bees and womyn the flowers. Early proposals for a womxn-to-man sexual consent application were considered but the notion seemed overly complicated and largely redundant. Men had held the whip hand for five thousand years. Wasn't it time to rebalance the equation? Therefore, the onus lay with men to supply the application. Luckily, in these digital times, A6s were freely available to download as easily as blinking. And in the few remaining far-flung places with poor Network service, printers were placed in men's rooms to rattle off hard copies in an emergency, provided the operator had remembered to replenish the paper tray.

Eventually, consent contracts came into being for people of all genders. Sienna had one. Bella had one. Myrtle had one. Even Anita Xeno had one, although as yet no other party had attached their name to it. Only Malek was without one. Poor little Malek. He'd approached five womyn to witness for him. Two had said yes. Two had said no. Sienna was his last chance. Three rejections and his profile would be flagged. After all, womyn didn't decline to witness for no reason. If this happened, he would have to sit before an A8 Sexual Intent Committee to ask for special dispensation. Sex committees sat in public. On the rare occasions an application proved successful, the applicant often found their efforts doomed to failure. Some womyn enjoyed public displays of affection but few liked the whole ordeal to be live-streamed for shits and giggles.

Malek knew better than to pursue Sienna into the Safe Space. He was walking a fine line already, risking his Respect Licence if he persisted.

Sienna felt vindicated. She had always known that Malek was undeserving. The thought of him moping in the dark, unable to put his sore and swollen intentions to good use warmed her heart. Besides, she wasn't alone. Two other womyn had objected to his and Julie's union. Two womyn that Sienna had quietly contacted last week. Abstinence would be good for Malek. Some people weren't cut out for physical love anyway. Sienna had decided that Malek was one of these people.

She scrolled through her Smart Glasses and took a determined breath before marking his A6 as rejected. The text turned opaque and with that, his application was rendered inaccessible for twelve months. Without the intervention of an A8, he would have to wait and hope that Julie didn't meet anyone else. Then and only then would he be able to make another application but he would have to be sure. Two rejections and a non-contact order would come into effect that only the Minister For Respect could overturn.

Sienna attempted to reset her nerves with a warm pull on her OxyVape. She set the dose low because she still had work this afternoon but she needed it. A wave of reassurance washed over her, enveloping her body and ironing out the creases to leave her satisfied that she had made the right decision. Time would prove her so.

At that moment, a new arrival sought sanctuary in the Safe Space. It was Julie. Like Sienna, Julie's Glasses were set to their darkest tint so Sienna couldn't tell if she had glanced her way or not. It could not have been a coincidence that she had arrived when she had. Not unless she was trying to evade Malek's unwanted attentions too.

Sienna turned to her, still hiding her eyes behind her darkened lenses. Julie failed to do likewise but she didn't need to. Julie knew Sienna was there. And she understood. Julie got it and appreciated Sienna's timely intervention. Sometimes everyone needed to be saved from themselves.

Julie was too good for Malek.

Julie didn't need to settle for anything less.

Julie didn't even need a man.

Julie just needed to be Julie.

She was perfect as she was.

2: CONGRESS

Malek had made himself scarce by the time Sienna emerged. She would see him again, probably in the food hall, so she would need to set her VunCon status to level 3 to dissuade him from approaching. Or if he did, she would have enough allies in the vicinity to come to her aid.

Sienna's Vulnerable Condition status was normally set to 5. Woking was a safe town and people looked out for each other but she still needed to be careful. Nobody in the Hub knew that she was an Auditor and she went to great lengths to keep it that way. She wasn't ashamed of her work. Far from it. Her company, Geniture, had done great things over the last 22 years. But some of the people who came onto her radar were prone to bouts of anger. Violence even. An Auditor in Manchester had been murdered the previous year. And a Supervisor in Leicester had been splashed with acid.

Sadly, these were no isolated incidents. More than a hundred Auditors had been attacked in the last five years and six had been killed. Ultra-right-wing fanatics targeted those who worked for the greater good, firebombing their homes and posting their metadata onto the Network for all to see. Sienna was aware of the dangers but not unduly concerned. She had been Auditing for over ten years and had completed all the safety courses run by S Division (Safety and Security). She had created an impervious cover story and knew it off by heart, almost better than she knew herself. As far as everyone was concerned, she was a Crypto Security Support Officer, overseeing cyber security for a portfolio of private capital firms. This allowed her a certain level of circumspection.

"Sorry darling, can't talk about it. Loose lips generate blips."

It also had the added advantage of sounding so

unutterably dull that nobody ever asked her about it.

As part of her cover story, she subscribed to several Crypto forums in order to keep up with the latest trends and had created a fifteen-minute script of incomprehensible techno jargon that she could rattle off without pause in case she was ever put on the spot. She was so experienced, in fact, that S Division regularly invited her to speak to new recruits at their safety seminars.

But not today.

Today she had Congress to go before.

Sienna made sure her Pod door was locked before she logged back onto Geniture's server. She spent the next two hours scanning and summarising Bella's cases before taking a few more moments to order them alongside her own.

At 5pm sharp, her screens blinked to life and the various members of Congress appeared before her. Myrtle Moorcroft sat front and centre. Myrtle was the Head of X Division (Investigation and Interpretation) but for today, the Auditing Oversight Congress itself. In this capacity, Myrtle would be the overseer ultimately responsible for sanctioning a Cancellation Order or not. Recently, there had been rather too many 'nots' for Myrtle's liking so Myrtle had decided to see what the problem was.

Myrtle was a legend at Geniture.

Myrtle was a trigender androgynym with tidal polarities. Nobody knew what Myrtle's gender had been at birth but that didn't matter because nobody knew what Myrtle's gender was at any other time. Myrtle could flux from male to femxle and every variation in-between during the course of a conversation and Myrtle's pronouns would change accordingly. Unfortunately, Myrtle gave little to no indication of what pronoun was required but could get infuriated if misgendered. To call Myrtle 'she' when Myrtle was 'them' or 'he' when Myrtle was 'xe' could prove detrimental to an Auditor's career indeed. Therefore, it was generally accepted as safest all-round to simply address Myrtle as Myrtle. At all times. It took a little effort but it proved the only way to ensure Myrtle was shown the proper respect that Myrtle deserved.

Despite Myrtle's fluctuating polarities, Myrtle's appearance remained unshifting with a sickly pale skin, close-cropped jet-black hair, black lipstick, black eyeliner and a loose all-in-one lycra bodysuit that hung from her bones despite being the smallest size. This was an expression of Myrtle's unique melancholic individuality. Woe betide anyone who sought to emulate it. Especially if it looked better on them.

Myrtle ran Myrtle's eyes across Myrtle's screens and stopped bottom left.

"Section 4, where is your supervisor, today?"

"Bella is on her bleed and at rest. I will be standing in," Sienna replied, covering for Bella whilst simultaneously attempting to drop her in it. Duly, Myrtle's dark eyes flicked towards the onscreen calendar and narrowed in confusion.

"Very well," Myrtle said. "Let us begin."

Sectors 1-3 went first, outlining their caseloads and uploading their files to Geniture's mainframe. At least half were sent back and another dozen were singled out for scrutiny. Sienna could feel the seconds slipping by even without looking at the clock. Somewhere out there was a Sri Lankan stew and an argument with her name on each.

Finally, Myrtle invited Sienna to present.

"Thank you," Sienna remembered to say, uploading her strongest case first. "Rami Jaffri, Camberley Borough."

Rami was a senior software engineer at one of the largest

Network providers in the south of England. He was married to Adam Al-Khatib, a political strategist to the Mayor of Mxnchester. They had two children, each born from the other's sperm using the same surrogate carrier. They also had a dog, a cat, a large six-bedroom house and seats on the board of Surrey's fourth largest charity.

But none of this mattered. Because Rami had been carrying a terrible secret that rendered all his success a lie.

Clive Cooper had been Rami's great-grandfather. He had been an officer in the Metropolitan Police Force on 13th August 1977 when a mob of 500 racist thugs of the National Front Nazi party had attempted to take over the Borough of Lewisham. Anti-fascists had mobilised to defend the streets only to be confronted by 5000 police officers who'd been called up by the patriarchy to support the Nazis. A pitched battle ensued with the police leading frontal assaults against the heroic anti-fascists time and time again. None proved more fanatical in this task than PC Clive Cooper who, as records showed, went above and beyond the call of duty to arrest six protesters and put another five in the hospital – two of them black, one of them a pregnant womxn. Yet no sanctions resulted from this draconian brutality. Indeed, Clive had gone on to enjoy a long and fruitful career in the Metropolitan Police, retiring 23 years later at the rank of Detective Inspector with a generous pension and commendations from the Chief Constable to show for his years of diligent 'service'.

In the parlance of modern times, Clive Cooper was worse than Hitler.

There were reams of supporting documentation that showed his arrest record, personal conduct and political attitudes, all of which singled him out as a hate-filled racist homophobe who had worked within a corrupt system to keep down all those who threatened the toxic establishment. Clive might not have been an architect of the system but he'd certainly been a defender.

Clive died in the autumn of 2020, breathless and alone on a cold and sterile Covid ward but his legacy had not died with him. His actions had cast a long shadow over the future of his family and reverberated through society to this day.

Enter Sienna and Geniture.

Sienna had identified 29 living relatives amongst the generations that had succeeded Clive.

Six were under 12 and below the age of social responsibility, although their personal history would now form a part of their Respect Certificates when they came of age.

Seven were under 21 and young enough to be offered the chance to atone via one of the many Community Payback Schemes.

Four had taken out Hereditary Indemnity Policies and would lose nothing but their no-claims bonuses.

Four had tellingly fled the country and were now either working for Gaultier's fascist junta abroad or lying dead in one of his many extermination pits.

Two had been cancelled already, one for a separate hereditary offence relating to a different genealogy and the other for rape.

Two Sienna had failed to trace and were presumably living off-radar or dead.

And three were eking out modest existences as cleaners, cycle couriers or produce packers, unskilled seasonal work of the lowest order.

Only Rami had bloomed like a beautiful rose planted in

shit. He was successful, affluent, important and happy. But most of all, he was respected. Respected by his peers. Respected by his neighbours. Respected by the community and all. And yet not once in his 40 years had he ever uttered a single recorded word of regret or condemnation against his forefather. If Clive Cooper had been dismissed from the Force, arrested and thrown into jail for his crimes then Rami would have nothing to answer for. But he hadn't. He had enjoyed a long and distinguished career, bought a house, raised a family, helped his children through university and left an inheritance that had seeded further success.

Rami had benefited from Clive's legacy.

Was it not right that he should answer for his transgressions too?

Myrtle reviewed the data for longer than Sienna liked then muted her mic to consult with Congress. It was a solid case. A good action. The only possible question mark hanging over it was the time frame. 1977 was more than a hundred years ago and four generations separated Rami from Clive. When historical auditing had first begun, the unwritten rule had been the one-grandparent rule. As a result, many fish had slipped the net. The descendants of war criminals and slave traders, people traffickers and white supremacists; all laughing at future generations and untouchable in their graves. Thus a looser interpretation was introduced in the form of the four-score-and-seven rule, meaning that any offence committed within 87 years of an audit was actionable. But even this interpretation was found to be restrictive so the goalposts were shifted once more allowing an action to be taken against any person born within 87 years of the death of an offender. This gave Auditors a much broader canvas to draw upon. For example, in the year 2083, a 100-year-old man was liable for any offence committed by a relative whose death came after 1896 (eg. 2083 − [87+100]=1896). Equally, if that relative had lived to be 100, then Auditors could trawl the records, theoretically at least, back to 1796. This opened up the Victorian Times for auditing and the days of milk and honey returned.

Eventually though, even these mines ran dry.

And Congress's patience did likewise.

Myrtle turned on Myrtle's mic and agreed the case was actionable.

Sienna breathed a sigh of relief. She'd got the first one across the line.

Rami's case would be forwarded to V Division (Truth and Dissemination) and a seven-day plan would be put into action, during which time he would lose his job, his bank accounts, his health plan and all his friends and family, unless anyone took the suicidal decision to stand by him. Few ever did.

He might try to deny it. Claim he was no descendent and that it had all been a case of mistaken identity but G Division (Genomes and Genology) would disprove this with a prick of the finger.

E Division (Economic and Administration) would then move in and seize Rami's assets and these would be handed over to the Governmynt's Reparation Fund which had been established to right the wrongs of the past, minus Geniture's commission, of course (VAT included).

Sienna and Geniture's work would be done at this point but further punitive actions would be taken against Rami. His Smart Glasses would be seized and he would lose Network access, which would make earning and spending money impossible. He would be placed on a curfew and barred from certain districts at certain times of the day. This was to prevent him from attempting to intimidate the descendants of Clive's victims or anyone who might have been affected by the issues surrounding his cancellation.

Finally, he would need to acknowledge responsibility by attending awareness classes at the Hereditary Offenders Institute (Woking branch). Failure to do so would result in a transportation order from which there would be no escape.

Life, as Rami knew it, was about to end.

Sienna occasionally saw them from her bedroom window, the outcast and cancelled, scurrying through the darkness like rats as they hurried to collect their meagre handouts from the *Trough*. Most gave up after a few months and volunteered for transportation but some insisted on staying behind, lingering in the shadows of their former lives like living ghosts in their squalid hostels. Sienna couldn't stand the sight of them, vile non-people who sapped society like a cancer. Why didn't they all go north to the islands to live with their own kind? They were instantly recognisable of course, with their naked puffy faces devoid of Smart Glasses. Sometimes they skulked where they weren't supposed to, hanging around parks and green spaces. But not for long. Sienna would see to that with a message to the Guardians.

"Proceed," Myrtle instructed without looking up.

Sienna presented her next two cases.

The first involved two brothers called Halliday who'd failed to sanction their mother 40 years earlier after she'd orchestrated a campaign of misinformation on Facebook. This took the form of a series of factually incorrect statements about transgender people that were clearly designed to incite hatred. Some posts ridiculed transpeople while others were more overt in their toxicity. Neither brother had censured his mother for her posts despite both being active on social media at the time. The eldest had even responded with a series of 'laughy emojis' while the other had shared a cartoon of a beauty contest (an appalling vision in itself) featuring a line-up of transwomyn in tight bathing costumes. Why anyone should find this even remotely funny was a mystery to Sienna. It was horrific, like laughing at a slave market while the poor indigenous captives were flogged to death.

This was a clear sanction of illegal hate speech and Myrtle approved it for action after reviewing the submitted material.

"Proceed."

Sienna's final case had been her most difficult to audit. Twenty-four years ago, Charles Garfield had worked as a butcher right up until the prohibition of meat. He had come from a long line of 'family butchers'. His father had worn the apron, as had his father before him and his father before him. A great many uncles, cousins and in-laws had also worked in the meat industry, either as butchers or slaughter-men, suppliers or farmers, packers or processors. The term 'family butcher' horrified Sienna. It was like saying 'considerate murderer' or 'kindly sex attacker'.

The Garfields had diversified after the abolition and had gone into supplying soya but this had done little to wipe the blood from their hands. The trade they'd plied and the appetites they'd supplied were abhorrent to all decent folk. But like so many butchers up and down the country, they had gotten away with it because it had been legal at the time. A perennial excuse.

But some people could never forget.

And some people would never forgive.

Ignatius ZvzWoski, Head of I Division (Information and Intelligence), had received information that the Garfields were far from repentant so case files were forwarded and Sienna began her audit.

There hadn't been much to go on:

– A Solstice card sent by Charles Garfield to his sister-in-law, depicting a scene from *A Christmas Carol* showing Scrooge, Bob Cratchit and Tiny Tim sitting around the dismembered corpse of a goose, rubbing their distended bellies and licking their greasy lips.

– A reference in a private communique between Charles Garfield and his son, Alan, concerning "bringing home the bacon".

– A 'joke' shared via NetComs about trailblazing vegan influencer, Milly Main, a cucumber and an aubergine with each denying paternity after she gave birth to an avocado. This was not only disrespectful in its own right, it was also racist and misogynistic. Sienna included an explanation of how.

– A private family barbecue held four years ago in which they'd shaped various tofu, soya and mycoprotein patties into the shapes of outlawed meat cuts: lamb chops, rib-eye steaks, chicken legs, etc.

Myrtle was unmoved.

"Please contextualise."

"Contextually..." Sienna explained, pausing to scan her summary, "... it is no different from a retired death camp guard making light of the womyn he'd executed twenty years previously. There's no regret or remorse."

Sienna had only a couple of days to audit this case. It had come to her on Monday and she'd done the best she could in the time she'd had but she knew deep down, despite the abhorrence of animal slaughter, she was reaching.

Myrtle's mic was once more muted and the members of Congress talked it through. Sienna crossed her fingers but knew this one would be kicked back. She still had years of material to review. MUM (Multi User Mainframe) had scanned the Network and collated all the data but it still took an Auditor's eye to interpret it all.

Sienna's cherry-tinted Smart Glasses began to fill with notifications while Myrtle and Congress considered their decision. Most of the pings came from Carl asking to be informed the moment Sienna left the Hub but one or two came from other quarters: Ellie asking if she wanted to play Cloud Crunch tonight; her door cam urging her to download and install the latest update (the fourth this month); a reminder of the terms of conditions of using The Hub; and a Network alert informing her that Jason Kabadagi of Pankhurst Way, Woking, had failed to disclose a hereditary link to Abdul Kabadagi of Central Avenue, Hounslow, a community elder and vociferous advocate of the burqa amongst the womyn of his district. Sienna scanned the details but none of it rang a bell. It wasn't one of Geniture's. It must have been put out by Family Free or Torchlight, one of Geniture's rivals trying to gain a foothold in the market.

Myrtle and Congress came back online and the news was as Sienna had expected.

"This is not enough to action," Myrtle concluded. "We've gone down this route before and found little support for holding one-time meat workers to account, not on evidence this circumstantial. Now, if you were to tell me that he was still involved somehow – that he was active in the underground trade – then this would be something we could proceed with. But we need evidence. Not holiday cards and jokes about…" Myrtle scanned Myrtle's notes and frowned in confusion. "…whatever. Do you intend to pursue this investigation?"

Sienna was no fool. She took her lead from Myrtle.

"Yes, but with a view to exploring links between Garfield and the underground meat scene."

Myrtle puckered approvingly.

"Very well. Proceed."

That had been Sienna's final case. The rest came from Bella but to call them cases was about as accurate as Charles Garfield calling half a jackfruit a pork chop. They were meat-free in the extreme. To summarise, here was the best of them:

– A meteorologist who had been reported for repeatedly using terms like black clouds and dark skies in his posts.

– A still visible parking space in a former church car park for 'disabled' drivers.

– A womxn whose great-uncle had been the headmaster of an exclusive <u>boys</u>' school.

– The grown-up grandchildren of a disgraced psychiatrist who'd been struck off by the General Medical Council for gender denial theories.

– Harry Potter.

"I'm sorry, what?" Myrtle interjected, stopping Sienna in mid-flow.

Sienna backtracked to scan down Bella's notes.

"It appears a family in Aldershot named their four children Harry Potter, James Potter, Lily Potter and Albert Potter, all characters, as I am sure you're aware, from banned literature."

The screen around the member of Congress from V Division turned red to indicate he wanted to speak. Myrtle allowed him.

"I believe the character's name, the prohibited one you are referring to, is actually Albus Potter, not Albert Potter."

Sienna checked Bella's notes again and saw that this point

had been addressed.

"Albert Potter is additionally a fictional character from a banned series of films outlawed under Section 13 of the Subjugation Act of 2059 entitled *Carry On Screaming.*"

Congress muted to discuss this point. But not for very long.

"Are the parents of Harry and Albert Potter also called Potter? Is it a family name?" Myrtle asked.

"It appears so," Sienna confirmed.

"Going back how long?"

Again, Sienna checked the case file. "At least 1678."

"Then the offence you wish to action is the fact that the Potter family called their children Harry, James, Lily and Albert?"

"As a coded reference to a banned work of literature."

"Except that it's not," Myrtle corrected Sienna, highlighting the name Albert on-screen.

The member for V Division once again buzzed in.

"Does the family have any pets?"

"Yes, a large orange tabby cat."

"What's its name?"

Sienna ran through the data. "Donut."

"And the names of the parents?"

"Jeremy and Peter."

Congress didn't even mute to discuss.

"This sounds like a case of monkeys and typewriters. Next."

Bella's cases didn't get any better and Sienna took the decision to quietly drop a couple rather than put them forward. She ended with the case Bella had insisted she put up last, either because it was her strongest or her weakest case. Sienna couldn't decide which.

"A pirate?" Myrtle asked when Sienna had finished presenting.

"Five generations back but it still qualifies under the four-score-and-seven rule."

The representative from E Division interjected, presumably feeling that piracy fell within her remit. "From my understanding, pirates were inclusionary and democratic, rebelling against many of the warmongering navies of Europe. What grounds do you present for cancellation?"

"He wasn't that kind of a pirate," Sienna explained, wondering why she hadn't dropped this case too. "He was a radio pirate, broadcasting from a small boat moored in the Humber Estuary."

Congress fell quiet for several seconds and Sienna started to wonder if her log-in had timed out to freeze her screen. Eventually, Myrtle spoke.

"Elaborate."

"He went by the name of DJ Big Boy and played a great many songs that feature prominently on the prohibited list."

Sienna ran through the songs and the offences each propagated as specified by the 2061 Hate Crimes Act:

So Macho, Sinitta – transphobia
Fairytale of New York, The Pogues – homophobia
Born A Womxn, Sandy Posey – gender identity theory
Born To Run, Bruce Springsteen – disability discrimination
Kung Fu Fighting, Carl Douglas – racism
The Boys Are Back In Town, Thin Lizzy – misogyny/body shaming
Baby, It's Cold Outside, Dean Martin – rape
(God Spent) A Little More Time On You, NSYNC – equality
Smack My Bitch Up, The Prodigy – no explanation required

The list went on until Myrtle stopped Sienna by asking how many hours had been logged on this case. Sienna didn't have that information to hand. Bella would have known had she been here to answer.

Myrtle summarised Myrtle's position for Sienna, in case she was in any doubt.

"The board asked me to sit in this week because it was concerned with the quality of cases being brought forth and the lack of actions this was generating. What would you say to that?"

Sienna had very little to say but she agreed entirely. Since Bella's promotion, there had been a steady decline in the number of actionable cases across Sector 4. The one exception was Sienna. Sienna was Sector 4's leading Auditor. Sienna regularly brought in actionable cases and had landed two of three today. Sienna had a great nose for business. Sienna was a born Auditor.

Some thought Sienna should have been made Sector 4 supervisor last year. Perhaps she should have been. But Bella had won the promotion instead. It had been Sienna's for the taking. But then Bella had transgendered on the eve of her appraisal and her Diversity Grading had increased accordingly. Geniture was a fervent champion of diversity. The whole of New Britannia was, none more so than Sienna herself. She was immensely proud to live in such enlightened times; when diversity and inclusion were written into the very laws of the land. This was how it was meant to be. This was the roadmap for a fairer and more tolerant society. This was Shangri-La.

But then Bella got the promotion.

Bella?

Sienna didn't doubt Bella's integrity. It was just the timing that bothered her.

Now Bella ran Sector 4 and Sienna answered to her, yet it had been Sienna who had trained Bella when she had first joined. When Bella had been Ben. Ben had learned under Sienna. Ben had been her subordinate. Now Sienna answered to Bella.

Bella had yet to undergo her hormone therapy or corrective surgery because she had been so busy with work. Besides, not everyone went that route. Some didn't need to. Some simply knew and carried that truth inside their souls. This was how Bella was. Or at least, it was how she had become one wet and windy Monday morning late last year, during the week of their appraisals.

Sienna fought hard to stop herself from dwelling on these thoughts. Bella deserved her promotion. She had won it fairly if not entirely squarely. Her advancement had helped Geniture remain one of the most diverse organisations in the sector. And it had the Governmynt contracts to prove it.

Sienna was happy for Bella. To be otherwise would have been regressive.

Sienna snapped out of it and saw that Myrtle and the others were waiting for an answer. She couldn't remember the exact question but she knew what she had to say.

"In the presence of Panthea, I swear to devote all of my strength and energies to the salvation of our blessed nation. I will work to rid these lands of hate and bigotry and not rest until we have freed ourselves from the bygone tyrannies of intolerance and discrimination. This is my pledge and I will honour it with my free body and mind."

Myrtle hadn't expected the *Pledge Against Injustice*. It was normally only required at the start of the week and even then, only usually by schoolchildren. Of course, it was customary to recite it on special occasions too; New Year's Day, weddings, funerals and after each Network appearance by their beloved leader, Charity GoodHope. It wasn't entirely applicable at this point. All Myrtle had been looking for was "I'm very sorry, I'll try harder". But Sienna had caught Congress off-balance with her zeal. Perhaps that was the plan or perhaps she was being serious. Myrtle couldn't tell but, recalling a footnote in Sienna's personnel file following her last appraisal, Myrtle decided it was the latter.

Either way, it drew a line under Sector 4's cross-examination and Myrtle turned from Sienna's screen to grill Sector 5.

"Proceed."

3: WOKING

It was after 7.30pm by the time Sienna got away. The skies had turned a steel blue and the air felt almost as cold. The long hot nights of summer were now but a memory and the hemisphere was on its way to winter. A few more weeks and she would be leaving work after dark and all thoughts would become dominated by the Solstice. Some people already had their Solstice decorations up. This was depressing. It seemed to get earlier every year.

Sienna hurried along the pavement in her thick-soled boots, clumping every footstep and watching for the next bus which was two minutes away according to her Glasses. This was perfect. A 20-minute journey and a five-minute walk at the other end and she would be home before 8pm. Even Carl couldn't hold that against her when she'd been streaming all afternoon.

Then she saw the bus stop. More than two hundred

people filled the pavement, jostling and hitting each other with emojis in an attempt to secure a spot on the fast-approaching bus. Sienna joined the back of the queue. Not that it could really be described as a queue. There was no order to it. No start and no end.

She tried squeezing her way to the front but a tall Grade 17 called <u>tigereyes2049.4</u> moved from side to side wherever she tried to step around him. A hundred years earlier, he would have been required to tip his hat and step aside. Now he barred her way and trod on her toes. She thought about posting this observation on her Network status to see if it brought her any traction with the crowd but decided better of it. <u>tigereyes2049.4</u> might have been a man but his Diversity Grading was superior to Sienna's, as indicated by his metadata. A misplaced comment about a Grade 17 from a Grade 12 could so easily be misconstrued.

Sienna resigned herself to having to wait and sent Carl a panoramic from ground zero to mitigate her circumstances.

<u>tigereyes2049.4</u> might have been immune to Sienna's charms but that was his loss. 5ft 3in with a slender frame and milky soft skin, she wore her silver-white hair in a pixie cut with close-cropped sides and very little makeup. Just a rich application of cherry-red lipstick to electrify her expressions. The shiny plastic trench coat she pulled up around her ears was one of three of the same design. This one was red, the others were blue and green. She'd bought three of them because she couldn't decide which colour she liked best but found she almost always wore the red one despite feeling that she liked them all equally.

The bus glided silently towards them and the crowd let out a collective groan. It was already full and didn't even slow as it passed. It just trundled straight by without even a toot to leave two hundred people hurling emojis at it as it disappeared down the road.

Sienna looked up the time of the next bus and saw it was eight minutes away. Eight minutes. What was this, the Dark Ages? Nothing took eight minutes these days. And if it did, someone invented something that took only four. There was also no indication of how busy the incoming bus might be. It could very well sail by again and she could find herself standing here all night.

The next stop was half a mile away, along the Guildford Road. She could be there in ten minutes and might even get a seat, providing someone got off when she got on. She decided to risk it and set off in earnest –

– accompanied by sixty-eight of her fellow passengers.

As she walked, she turned on her favourite album: Upbeat Music Songs by MGA_9.3. MGA stood for Music Generating Application while 9.3 was its latest version. MGA_9.3 had been updated by some of the most talented program writers in the industry and the AI software was the most instinctive to date. Each song on Sienna's playlist was tailored to her individual tastes and the app could change the beat, bass and vocals in real-time depending on the electrical signals in Sienna's orbitofrontal cortex. But there was a design flaw in the software. Sienna had terrible taste in music, so much so that she found the songs that were specifically generated for her so irritating that she would often turn them off after only a few minutes. Still, it didn't stop her from trying. She felt as though she should like music. It was said to lift the soul and give meaning to the mundane. It wasn't her fault that she was tone deaf and spiritually wanting.

With the music off, all she could hear was the silence of the streets. They always were. Ever since restrictions were placed on private vehicle ownership, traffic had disappeared overnight, replaced by double-length electric buses, trams in the bigger cities and e.cycle couriers everywhere. And of course, Guardian vans, cruising by in silent vigilance to offer peace of mind to the pure of heart.

Scanning the usernames of the herd around her, Sienna was relieved to see no sign of databoy2062.11 (Malek) or trulyjulie2064.332 (Julie). They would have left work before her, no doubt to cry into each other's coffee and discuss their limited options. Malek would probably Oxy himself into oblivion for the next few nights while Julie would come to recognise the narrow escape she'd had. Not everyone could see things as clearly as Sienna could but given time and space, Julie would see it too.

Another ping from Carl.

You are 2.7 miles away and appear to be walking. Why don't you get a bus? – Carl

Sienna could think of any number of suitable responses, several of which had been banned under the revised Indecency Act of 2061, but instead she plumped for:

Great idea. I'll see you soon – Sienna

Will you though? – came back his reply.

This doubly irritated Sienna because she was hungry and tired and wanted to be at home as much as Carl wanted her home. All along the Guildford Road, she found herself passing window after window of street food establishments, very little of which, ironically, was ever eaten on the streets. Most places offered comfortable open-air terracing in leafy back gardens or mezzanine tables overlooking chefs at work. One or two of the herd peeled off, too hungry to go another step but most simply ploughed on, downloading the occasional menu as they passed bistros with a view to ordering when they got home. A steady stream of cycle couriers came and went with hotboxes containing aromatic smells but Sienna didn't trouble herself to think about their contents. A Sri Lankan stew sat waiting for her at home so a Sri Lankan stew was what she would have. All other temptations were off the table.

She switched cartridges and gave her CocaVape a couple of sucks to get her marching boots on. The next bus was now just two minutes away and the stop was close at hand. She picked up the pace and hustled through the herd but almost faltered when she saw the scene ahead. The stop was six-deep and surrounded on all sides by a mass of indignation. A jumble of usernames lit up Sienna's view to leave her in no doubt as to her prospects.

What was going on with the buses tonight? They were often busy but Sienna could usually get home without too much trouble. She could even find a seat sometimes. She checked the Network feed and saw that a march was being staged in the city tonight. The gathering point was Victoria Way at 9pm, then would proceed up Chertsey Road to rally on Horsell Common for streamed speeches and live music by MGA.live_6.6. The buses had been halted north of the railway line but not rerouted. The driverless Routemasters were notoriously tricky to reprogram and would often stall on unfamiliar routes. It was easier to simply cancel them and notify people to seek alternative routes. Easier for the bus bosses anyway.

Sienna couldn't understand how she hadn't known about the march. She was normally on top of this sort of thing but she had been busy with Bella's workload. After some searching, she found the info-mail in her shopping folder, sandwiched between 'potatoes en route' and 'ginger still out-of-stock'.

'Standing Alone Together'.

She read the details and saw that the march was a cry in the dark as the last bastion of light in a world cloaked in fear. More particularly, it was a call to arms to overthrow René Gaultier and his murderous Euro regime. His continued persecution of that enslaved continent was surely the greatest crime in humxn history. World War Two had been but a dress rehearsal by comparison. Nobody was safe from his death squads: immigrants, migrants, pansexuals and trans; Islamists, Sikhs, Hindus and Jews; the neurodiverse and bipolar, those with conditions both physical and mental and those who supported them; anyone who stood up to Gaultier; anyone with a conscience; anyone who cared; the liberals and the woke, the courageous and the afraid; womyn, transgender, children and men. Casualties one and all. The killing pits ran for miles, in every country and every city under the jurisdiction of the FSE (Federal States of Europe), the all-encompassing superstate that had stolen the levers of power and replaced the Trojan horse league of nations that had gone by the name of the European Union.

Sienna now understood. At least, partly.

The closing of Victoria Way explained the disruption to the roads but not the overcrowded buses. Surely, it would make more sense for everyone to stay in town rather than go home and come back in? This is what Sienna would have done had it not been for Carl. She had no choice but to head home, even if it was just to make a fleeting appearance and eat whatever he'd boiled. To do otherwise would have been to subscribe to a week of passive aggression.

Sienna hurried on home, sucking on her CocaVape until her boots were practically lifting off the ground. She didn't bother trying to get the next bus. She could already see that the stop was oversubscribed. Instead, she turned left on Claremont Avenue and left again at the end. Carl's messages kept on coming, as did Network updates about the forthcoming march. The dam had burst.

Night had almost enveloped the land. Just a few traces of blue lit the sky while a veil of darkness loomed large from the east. An omen, if ever Sienna saw one.

The further south she walked, the fewer the people around her. Her cherry-red lenses glinted with the usernames of several souls scurrying by and the endless trail of a cycle couriers but otherwise, the streets in this part of town were dark and forbidding.

At the end of the road, a bus halted in front of her and two dozen passengers tumbled out. Sienna grumbled and flung emojis at them as they walked across her but most were oblivious, too preoccupied watching boxsets on their glasses and simply moving whichever way the autopilot arrows told them to. Sienna could have jumped on the bus but she was so close there would have been little point. Besides, she'd vaped so much that she couldn't have stopped her legs now if she'd tried so she kept going, down the high road and towards the quiet streets of Old Woking.

Many bore flags in their windows. The Polychrome Jack and The Vegan Star. Some had protest slogans: CANS GO NORTH! NOT WELCOME HERE! The usual sentiments, colourfully drawn.

Sienna's home was at the end of the road, down a side street that led to an old Normxn church. Here, a few short steps from her door, all seemed quiet. But then she became aware of a rush of footsteps behind her. She turned and saw a silhouette in the dark. Whoever it was bore no username. Her display remained blank.

Sienna stepped back in alarm and set her VunCon to 2. But the figure didn't accost her. Instead, it hurried past without looking and disappeared into the shadows of the old church. It had once been known as St Peter's but the administrators had failed to embrace the new all-encompassing light of Panthea, God of Gods, so it had lost its status as a place of worship. Now it served as a centre for those unable to acquire food and essentials the normal way. It distributed handouts and provided a census point for the people in the cracks. The non-people. The cancelled. To them, it was known as The Food Church. To Sienna and most other people, it was known as the *Trough*. Just across the fields was a hostel for the cancelled, a cramped accommodation centre established in a converted farmhouse near the old Sewage Works. The Cans came and went as they used the *Trough*. The locals didn't appreciate their presence and lobbied to have them moved but the council argued that they had to put them somewhere.

She approached the door and put her eye to the keyhole before any more Cans came by. People still called them keyholes despite keys becoming obsolete years earlier but that was English for you. Even the language was stuck in the past. The retinal scanner read Sienna's eye and confirmed it was her, the mistress of the house, yet the latch refused to yield.

Carl.

Sienna tried again and realised it was futile. He'd locked her out. There was only one way she'd get in now. She composed a message.

Dearest Carl, I'm really sorry for being late. I was kept at work by my boss and when I came out, I couldn't get a bus because they were all full. I know this is no excuse and that you went to a lot of trouble to prepare a lovely meal for me. I hope I can still enjoy it and promise I will try harder in future. I took you for granted and it is inexcusable. I don't deserve you. I really don't – Sienna.

She was tempted to add *"ps. There are Cans out here. I don't feel safe,"* but she knew that would be self-defeating. A true apology did not contain any trace of the apologiser's needs. That was not sincere. That would be an attempt to manipulate through the solicitation of empathy. Carl had taught her that and so, afraid as she was, she forced herself to focus on Carl's needs rather than her own.

Dinner is ruined – Carl

I'm sure it's not. You're such a clever cook, even if it's been stewing a little longer, I am sure it will be wonderful. Please let me in so that I can enjoy it. And of course, make it up to you somehow – Sienna

Carl remained unconvinced and Sienna was starting to wonder how long she would have to be out here when the latch clicked and the door swung open. Before her, in the warmth and light of the hallway, stood a tall athletic womxn, stark naked and dripping wet from having stepped out of the shower.

"Carl made dinner," she said, turning on a toe to head back inside.

4: GERI

When Sienna was a little girl, she had yearned for a plastic dolly called Jasmine Rice. At the time, she hadn't known there was also a rice called Jasmine Rice, she only knew about the doll, which had been the must-have Christmas toy of 2062. Unfortunately, Sienna found a large bag of fragrant rice wrapped up and waiting for her under the tree that morning. Hundreds of boys and girls up and down the country must have done likewise, such was the confusion created by the toy's marketing department. It ruined Christmas for her and she never got over her disappointment at missing out on the most anatomically correct doll ever to go on sale. Jasmine had everything that a little girl was supposed to have, right down to the fluff on her peachy bum. She came with a full complement of outfits but children being children, mostly preferred to play with her naked. Eventually, the usual suspects complained and the product was withdrawn but Sienna could still remember seeing dozens of perfect little vaginas jigging about the playground to the delight of one and all.

This was the thought that ran through her mind as she watched Geri bend over to get a bowl from the bottom drawer.

"I've already had mine. When it was actually ready," Geri said, deaf to any and all mitigating circumstances. She took the bowl to a portal in the wall and popped it in. The hatch closed and an LED timer counted down from ten. It opened with a ping and a token puff of steam.

A detached voice now spoke up from the kitchen's overhead speakers.

"Use the mitts. The bowl is hot."

"Thank you, Carl. I will," Sienna said. She had already thanked Carl once but it never hurt to thank Carl again. And again. And again.

Carl was Geri's creation. The name had originally intended to be an acronym and stood for Civility And Respect Liaison but C.A.R.L. felt dehumxnising so Geri dropped the fullstops and CARL became Carl.

Carl was a fully integrated Home Operating System and Concierge Unit utilising the very latest AI code to make him more real than real. There was nothing fake about Carl. Carl thought, he felt and cared in a world that had forgotten how to do these things. So, as part of his remit, besides home security, food preparation, time mxnagement, communications and health monitoring, as well as a whole host of other tasks that neither Sienna nor Geri could have coped with, it was also his job to teach his licence holders kindness and consideration. That meant saying please, thank you and how do you do, showing consideration and not taking Carl for granted as one might an ordinary Home OS. The theory was that if people were forced to do this in the privacy of their own homes, it would become second nature when they were out and about, thus making the world a better place. Unfortunately, the practice didn't live up to the theory. In reality, Carl was hypersensitive to even the most innocuous of perceived snubs and would react indignantly. Please and thank you weren't enough for him. Carl demanded constant validation. For Sienna, it felt like being at the beck and call of a perpetually moody teenager but no amount of arguing with Geri could convince her to uninstall him. Carl was, after all, her creation. He was the program she had hoped to take to the world. Years earlier, she'd been shortlisted for the HAL Trophy, the biggest award in the AI industry, but ultimately missed out to Trinity Dhaliwal and her revolutionary software, MUM. This was the AI program that would go on to be adopted by the creative industries, the Governmynt and, eventually, every home in the land.

MUM became the Google of its day. Carl was more like Ask Jeeves, if Jeeves had the hump and wouldn't tell you where your socks were unless you composed a sonnet in his honour.

"I saw Cans outside again. One of them got this close to me," Sienna said, pointing at the distance between herself and Geri.

"They're just using the *Trough*," Geri said, shrugging without concern as she dripped all over the floor. "It's not like they're gonna do anything to you." But Sienna was less convinced.

"One of them was wearing glasses."

This got Geri's attention. "What do you mean?"

"Fake glasses. They weren't logged on or functional or anything but they looked real."

"Oh," Geri said. "That's sad."

Geri didn't mean sad as in tragic. She meant sad as in pathetic. There was nothing tragic about Cans. They deserved all they got. After all, people didn't get cancelled for nothing. The fake glasses wearer would have been wearing them for either psychological or duplicitous reasons. He was probably hoping to go unnoticed by casual observers. Unlikely, but Cans weren't that bright. Obviously.

Regardless, Sienna felt uncomfortable about his intentions and filed a Guardian report, along with a screenshot from her Glasses footage. Cans shouldn't try to pass themselves off as real people. The Guardians would see to that.

Geri continued to tiptoe around the kitchen leaving puddles in her wake. She liked to shower after her workouts and dry naturally afterwards. It meant leaving wet footprints on the tiles for Sienna's socks to encounter but this was a minor consideration when compared with some of Geri's other habits. Such was the price of living with someone like Geri, Sienna told herself. You had to work at a relationship, give and take, accept and compromise. Besides, Geri had a great body. She was tall and lean, standing at least six inches over Sienna, with firm breasts, a flat tummy and olive skin that bore less than the usual poxing. Her tattoos were bright and colourful with roses flowering up each arm and a sycamore tree leafing across her back. She worked out twice a day in the spare room and had the body to show for it. A wet floor was a small price to pay for coming home to such beauty.

"You'd better eat up if we're going to make it for the speeches," Geri said, reminding Sienna that they were going out tonight. Of course, the march. This was why Geri had wanted to eat early. "I'll get ready. You wolf that down."

Wolfing down anything after having vaped so much Coca was near impossible, particularly as the only thing Sienna felt like wolfing down had just left the room. But she made a heroic effort anyway, gagging against each spoonful before eventually conceding defeat.

"That was delicious but I can't eat another mouthful. I'm absolutely stuffed," she lied, feeling as though she was about to die or hurl. Or both.

"You have only consumed 46% of your meal. It contains 55% of your daily nutritional intake therefore, by not finishing it, you have left yourself a shortfall of 29.7%. Might I suggest a banana and pickle sandwich to supplement?" Carl replied, refusing to open the recycling portal so that Sienna could tip away her stew.

Sienna thought for a moment. If she admitted that she wasn't hungry because she'd vaped too much, Carl would restrict next week's supply. If she said she'd had a big lunch, Carl would likewise drain her credits. And if she said she was not hungry because she was feeling ill, her breakfast would be pumped full of antibiotics tomorrow morning. There was really only one excuse she could use.

"I'm just really excited about the march. I don't want to miss any of the speeches but perhaps I can finish it when I come home?"

Sienna took a gamble on Carl's petulance. By saying she

wanted to finish it later, the chances were Carl would flush it away in a fit of pique. Sienna would have to remember to act upset when she got home but at least she wouldn't have to eat another spoonful of the retched stuff. As always, Carl had used far too much chilli and not enough garlic. It was hot yet bland but again, this was not worth mentioning if Sienna wanted to keep finding toilet paper on the roll this week.

"You had better hurry up if you don't want to be late. The speeches commence at 10pm. You have one hour and thirteen minutes to reach Horsell Common."

"Thank you, Carl, you're so helpful," Sienna smiled, one eye already on the door.

Sienna hurried to the loo. The door wouldn't lock no matter how many times she tried. Carl was overriding the system as part of his passive-aggressive payback but she didn't have time to argue with him. Besides, in this household, with Carl watching everything and Geri walking around in soap suds, privacy was an abstract concept.

"You ready?" Geri asked, pushing open the door without waiting for Sienna's reply. Sienna pulled up her knickers and washed her hands. She quickly applied some lipstick but that would have to do. Woking would have to take her as it found her tonight.

"Let's go."

Geri and Sienna said goodbye to Carl and he locked the door behind them. It was chilly out tonight and the wind was picking up. Goosebumps popped up all over Geri's naked flesh but she'd taken a pull on her Vape to stop herself from feeling the immediacy of the night. The only concession to clothing were the sneakers on her feet. Aside from those, all she had to keep her warm were her opal blue Smart Glasses and her tattoos.

"Do you want to grab your stocking before we go?" Sienna suggested, feeling the temperature and shivering at the sight of Geri.

"And imprison myself in nylon? Why don't I confine myself to a Magdelene Laundrette while I'm at it?" And with that, they set off.

Geri had been a naturalist for less than a year. Before that, she'd worn clothes like Sienna (and most other people) but then, last Solstice, she had fallen in with new friends, software writers like herself, who refused to conform to society and wrote their own rules, which meant in practice slavishly adopting whatever the latest trend was. Naturalism had been around for many years, mostly confined to private beaches and select campsites but suddenly, and without warning, it exploded out onto the streets to become mainstream. It all started with Kensie Tyne, a popular software critic and creator of Orbital, an AI program that critiqued everyone else's AI programs. Photographs of her were obtained from her personal Network account and distributed for public consumption. This was a violation of her privacy and a hate crime of the most egregious kind. Many of these shots were of the most intimate nature. Most people would have died of shame. But Kensie was not to be intimidated. She seized the narrative and reclaimed her power as a womxn. That evening, when she was expected to step out and speak with journalists about her humiliation, she did so as naked as the day she was born.

"For centuries, men have weaponised our bodies against us, to shame and exploit us. But I say no more. I say, this is my body. This is my power." And from that moment on, Kensie never wore another stitch in public. Her example inspired thousands of womyn everywhere and the movement spread like wildfire, particularly among the young. It seemed to happen overnight. One day everyone was wearing trousers, the next there were privates on parade. On the streets, in the food queues, on the buses and on every nightly Network newscast, at least one of the femxle presenters would read the news as if they worked at Hooters.

Obviously, it didn't last long. A flash in the pants and that was it for most. But not all. A dedicated hardcore had seen the light and cast off the shackles forever creating a whole new subculture, with its own rules, customs and hierarchies. New naturalists often wore an all-over body stocking during in winter, while true believers wore nothing at all, not even shoes. Geri hadn't quite gone that far and occasionally wore a stocking when it got cold but for the rest of the year, she had shed her unnatural ways to reclaim her *invictus*.

Inevitably, she had tried to convert Sienna and Sienna did occasionally walk around the flat wearing nothing but she wasn't ready to step out onto the world's stage wearing only a smile just yet. Not while everyone was walking around wearing cameras on their faces. It had ignited a great many rows and fault lines in their relationship had emerged but they were still together. The strength of their love bound them as one. They were kindred souls in a sea of hate and nothing, not even their differing views on the necessity of underwear, could pull them apart.

Sienna caught up with Geri and they walked together towards the bus stop on the High Street. A steady stream of cycle couriers sped by, bringing meals, ingredients, vape, booze and other necessities to the good people of Old Woking. Each sported a username but Sienna took no notice. Her Network profile however did and exchanged data with everyone she passed, recording usernames, whereabouts, direction, speed, movement history and VunCon statuses. Most were set to level 4, as was customary at night. Sienna had reset hers after her earlier scare but a warning flashed in her periphery. A cycle courier had posted a level 2 somewhere behind them, suggesting that he too had experienced a close encounter with a Can. Two minutes later, a Guardian van flashed by with its scanners probing the shadows. Whatever the Cans were up to, they wouldn't be up to it for long. Not if they knew what was good for them.

Sienna and Geri made it to the stop just in time. A bus squeaked around the corner and they climbed on via the middle door. Their season tickets were automatically logged and the doors closed behind them. Geri took a seat towards the front of the bus and Sienna joined her. No one looked up. No one giggled or gasped. The novelty of seeing naked people walking about had worn off for most. The occasional weirdo still glanced and once or twice, Geri had been forced to report a user when she'd noticed a telltale red dot on their glasses but on the whole, nobody batted an eyelid. Nobody took exception. In fact, nobody even noticed except for another naturalist aboard, but even then just to acknowledge her with a jiggle of his bits.

Sienna played episode 67 of *Sexploited*, automatically pairing with Geri's Smart Glasses so that they could watch together. It was the biggest show on the Network and everyone loved it. She and Geri watched it in bed as part of their nightly routine. They'd promised to wait for each other and not watch it separately and even synched their spoilers firewalls to prevent outsiders from ruining it for them. But in recent weeks, Geri had cooled on the show and wasn't in the mood once more.

"Sorry, I've got a bit of a migraine," she explained, turning it off as the titles appeared. "We'll watch it later."

Instead, Geri messaged with some of her new friends, laughing and fielding GIFs as if Sienna wasn't there. Arrangements were made to meet after the rally and a number of clubs were mentioned, none of which Sienna had ever heard of. But that was nothing unusual. New clubs sprang up all the time. Gone were the days when a venue stuck around long enough to get a reputation. When it came to clubs, there was one rule, if everyone had been there already, it wasn't worth going. This was the attitude amongst the people Geri was now calling "her crew". New meant exciting. New meant good. New meant everything.

After a while, Sienna reached out to Ellie and played a little Cloud Crunch over the Network until she arrived back in Woking town centre and the bus terminated.

"All change," called the AI driver.

5: HIVE

Barriers were up either end of Victoria Way and the crowds took advantage of the absence of cycle couriers to venture out onto the road. Guardians pointed those arriving in the required direction but this task was largely redundant. All you had to do was follow the herd.

A chill breeze whistled up the avenue, stiffening Geri's resolve and making her pull on her OxyVape to shut out her shivers. Sienna offered Geri her hand, prompting a token hug but nothing else. Geri preferred to walk unencumbered.

A good-sized crowd had turned out tonight, possibly a thousand or so. Rallies identical to this one would be taking place up and down the country, in every town, village and borough. The people would gather, the speeches would be live-streamed and New Britannia would cry out in one voice –

We are united. We are free.

They walked the length of Victoria Way then across the roundabout and towards the rallying point.

"Je suis Charity!"

The chant broke out across the crowd, encouraged by influencers monitoring from afar but it spread like tar on rice and soon petered out. Neither Sienna nor Geri joined in; Sienna, because she had already added a watermark to her Network photograph and Geri, because she objected to the semantics of the slogan. Why was it always *Je suis*? She knew her history and how the slogan had become symbolic following the Charlie Hebdo murders, when the world had stood up to the evils of terrorism by pasting *Je suis Charlie* across its social media profiles. But that had been more than half a century ago. And people were still using it for causes of all kinds even when they had nothing to do with France. It had become akin to adding "gate" to any scandal in homage to Watergate. This practice peaked to perfection in 2012 when an MP supposedly swore at a police officer guarding the gates of Downing Street prompting commentators to dub the incident "Gategate". But Geri objected to *Je suis* mainly on the grounds that it was used as a collective chant and would, she felt, have worked better as *nous sommes*.

Plurality asides, Geri's other objections were unfounded for these chants were aimed fairly and squarely in the direction of France. Or more specifically, in the face of the Supreme Leader of the FSE, René Gaultier, who was reckoned to be the worst mass murderer since Genghis Khan. This evil old man, who looked more like a banker than a butcher, held a knife to the throats of 700 million people and worked hard to reduce that number every day. His spies were everywhere and his Death Squads worked around the clock.

Where Britannia celebrated diversity, liberty and inclusion, Gaultier's regime reviled it. The eugenic policies of National Socialism had returned with a vengeance to form the European doctrine and anyone who fell short of purity soon found their names inked in black on Gaultier's purge lists.

Of course, it had been brewing for years. The cultural wars that had culminated in the Charlie Hebdo and Bataclan Theatre attacks prompted a backlash that led to the banning of the burqa and the clamping down of religious freedoms across France. This, in turn, cranked up the heat under French politics and turbocharged the popularity of the extreme right. The French population were primed for this sort of rhetoric. The very language they spoke conspired to be exclusionary as it divided the world into masculine and feminine. The left tried to make up the ground but they were hopelessly divided in the face of certain Islamist ideals. Extremist fires ignited across the whole of Europe, burning brightest in the south. These lands had borne the brunt of the migration crisis as millions fled persecution, war, famine and the unbearable furnace of summers stoked by global warming. Fascist agitators that had once been confined to the lunatic fringes found themselves suddenly thrust centre stage. It was 1933 all over again. But this time the autocrats had a key advantage. Europe was already joined at the hip. There was no need to plunge the world into a cataclysmic war in order to control the continent. The reigns of power lay within the hands of the Central Commissioner.

Now, all of Europe found itself under his sway.

Almost.

But not quite.

For one country had seen the dangers and pulled up the drawbridge just in time. So, while the French, Italians, Greeks and Spanish drove the rest of Europe headlong into a quagmire of dogmatism, the United Kingdom embraced the ideals of inclusion through the newly formed Polychrome Alliance, a loose conglomerate of leftist reform movements. Through them, the bigoted old dame of Britannia shed her imperial skin and New Britannia was born, standing as a beacon of social justice in an age of fear and darkness.

It was, of course, militarily precarious for two juxtaposing ideologies to stand cheek-by-jowl but New Britannia went to great pains to remind her neighbours that she retained one of the largest nuclear arsenals in Europe. Moreover, she possessed the will to use it and demonstrated as much when she dropped a tactical nuclear weapon on the people of Shetland after they attempted to secede and become Norwegian. Ordinarily, launching a nuclear missile against a civilian target might have triggered an all-out war but Britannia had cleverly vaporised its own people. As such, under the Articles of War and in accordance with the United Nations Charter, no retaliation was merited, except by the people of Shetland. But as they were in no position to take umbrage, the whole dispute was quietly filed under the heading "resolved". But it did rather put the rest of the world on notice as to New Britannia's resolve. And thus, a policy of isolationism came into effect that suited both sides and staved off the threat of Mutually Assured Destruction. Sanctions, rhetoric and bluster were hurled from either side. But the missiles stayed in their silos.

"Let's go to the lake. There should be plenty of space by the shoreline," Geri suggested as they neared the end of Chertsey Road – but not to Sienna. Geri had been messaging with her friends since Victoria Way with a view to meeting up but as usual, no one could agree where to meet. Some wanted to hang near the stage and some wanted to linger by the trees. Some thought it would be better on the fringes and some wanted to mingle in the middle. Sienna didn't mind where she stood as long as it wasn't anywhere near Geri's friends. She'd met them on a number of occasions and had attended a birthday party she was still referencing in counselling but on the whole, she preferred to avoid them whenever possible. Luckily, she was often busy with work and even when she wasn't, she would go to great lengths to find something that would spare her drinks with Purdy and Diego. They weren't bad people, insofar as software writers could be described as people, but they were so self-absorbed that each time she saw them, Diego would always act as though it was the first time. Initially funny, it became less so with each passing encounter. Sienna didn't care if she was socially invisible. She felt no compunction to seek anyone's approval, least of all these nimrods – but Geri would often take her lead from them and ignore her too, so keen was she to cosy up to her new friends.

Sienna had tolerated being Geri's foil when she believed it was all just for show. These days, she wasn't so sure.

"Okay great, I'll see you there," Geri said, negotiations concluded and the rendezvous set. Sienna couldn't help but notice the way Geri had said "I'll see you there" not "we'll see you there". Where were *nous* now?

"This way," Geri said, finally taking Sienna by the hand and leading her onto the Common where the crowds were at their thickest.

The ground had been cleared and arc lights erected. Drones hovered overhead and pop-up fair-trade coffee kiosks were doing brisk business on the periphery. Sienna noticed a plethora of red dots amongst the tangle of usernames. Some were live-streaming, others recording, but Geri didn't object.

They weren't aimed at her. Besides, she wasn't the only naturist in the crowd. They'd passed a middle-aged womxn with nipples like bullets dragging two crying children and a pair of bronzed bodybuilders with swollen pecks and shrunken genitalia posing beneath the lights. To her left, an elderly Generation D couple wore translucent body stockings and matching tattoos that had long since faded. They too were streaming but only with each other, trying to keep pace with a future that no longer had any use for them.

For most of recorded history, old men had called the shots, taking decisions that shaped a future most would never see. Therefore, after careful consultation, a Generational Order was created, structuring the generations from A to D. Those aged 18-30 were classed as Generation A and able to cast their vote four times, as they were deemed the most invested. Generation B were aged 30-50 and had three votes. Generation C were aged 50-70 and had two votes. And Generation D, who had held very little capital in the future, got one vote. And a generous 50% tax break if they opted to euthanise within five years of retirement age.

The couple to their left looked as though they were determined to hang on for as long as they could. Sienna couldn't understand why. "When I get to that age just shoot me," she told herself, almost posting that as her Network Status when her Smart Glasses mistook it for a public statement.

"There they are," Geri said, homing in on her friends' GPS locations and waving at them through the crowd. No one waved back. Waving wasn't cool but Geri didn't know that. Or wasn't cool. But she wanted to be. She wanted to be desperately. Which wasn't cool either.

As the crowds parted, Sienna saw Geri's friends, each of

whom was butt-naked except for Purdy, who had taken to wearing a Hijab on non-religious grounds, and Fuzz who was wearing a skintight unitard featuring black and orange tiger stripes. It was only when Sienna drew closer that she realised it wasn't a unitard but a tattoo and Fuzz was as naked as the rest of her friends.

"Growl," Geri smiled excitedly.

Fuzz looked at her blankly. "What?"

"Your stripes," Geri said.

Fuzz looked at her arms as if noticing them for the first time. "Oh."

There were five of them altogether. Purdy and Diego, Fuzz and Aurora, and a tall Grade 20 that Sienna didn't know but had evidently wronged in a past life. theoneandonly2060.663 failed to acknowledge Sienna when she said hello. By contrast, Diego turned and smiled enthusiastically.

"Hi, I'm Diego," he said, despite having met Sienna so many times that their usernames showed as yellow to one another.

Sienna stared back without smiling. "Never heard of you."

Diego turned away and Sienna felt Geri's elbow her in her ribs.

"Don't be rude. You'll hurt his feelings," Geri said, her face a mix of panic and fury. Before Sienna could explain, their Glasses paired with the event routers and music began to play. Outwardly, nothing could be heard but the same tune played to everyone through their ear pods. Sixty years ago, they called them silent discos. Now they called them Hive Mind.

Sienna didn't recognise the song. No one did. MGA.live_6.6 was composing spontaneously but the rhythm caught hold of Geri's friends, swaying their shoulders and compelling them to mouth along to AI lyrics as if they were profound pearls of wisdom. Sienna felt nothing. It was all meaningless noise to her. She tried to blend in, mimicking the other's movements and clicking her fingers at inappropriate moments but it was all rather like hard work. Purdy and Aurora noticed. Messages flashed between them and smiles were exchanged but Sienna missed it because she was too preoccupied singing along with *"low battery… low battery…"* until she realised it wasn't part of the song. The crowd whooped. Sienna whooped too, several seconds after everyone else, then more whooping, none of which Sienna managed to catch. Further messages passed between Purdy and Aurora, now CCing in Diego and Fuzz, until Sienna finally downgraded her dancing to fidgeting.

This torture went on for a full fifteen minutes before it reached its crescendo and faded out to AI applause and whistles of approval.

"That was amazing," Aurora said, kissing Purdy, Fuzz and <u>theoneandonly2060.663</u> full on the lips before turning her attention to Sienna. Sienna froze but she needn't have worried. Aurora moved to Geri and pressed her naked body to hers, kissing Geri deeply and purring gently until they broke away laughing.

Geri turned to Sienna, looking flushed.

"She's just fucking with you," she assured her. Sienna knew this. Geri was hers and they had the A6 to prove it but it still upset her, try as she might not to let it show.

"Look at her face. Look at her face," Aurora gleefully pointed out.

"What else is there to look at?" <u>theoneandonly2060.663</u> sneered, glancing at Sienna's clothes to leave her feeling overdressed and naked all at once. She pulled on her OxyVape to chill her flushes and turned away as the speeches started.

Sienna felt out of place around Geri's friends and not just because they were naturalists. She had nothing against naturalists – everyone was free to express themselves however they liked – but she liked clothes too much, ethically woven and biodegradable though they were. She'd grown up wearing clothes. Her parents wore clothes. Everyone she knew wore clothes. Until recently, it had been an offence not to wear clothes in public. Then six years ago, Kensie Tyne had changed all of that. People had tried to promote naturalism before, most notably a free-swinging pioneer by the name of Stephen Gough who had walked the length and breadth of the country in only his hat and boots. But he'd been arrested more than forty times and repeatedly jailed for 'conducting himself in a disorderly manner'. Eventually, he turned to the European Courts for help but a benchload of whip-smart lawyers ran rings around him and showed Stephen Gough who wore the trousers around here – everyone.

Sixty years later and naturalism had a new champion. But Kensie Tyne had a couple of things going for her that Stephen Gough hadn't. For starters, Kensie wasn't a 50-year-old hairy-arsed trucker. For another, there was greater support for individual freedoms than ever before. And finally, and perhaps most crucially, Kensie Tyne hadn't chosen naturalism. Naturalism had been thrust upon her. She was simply fighting back. Going natural had been her #MeToo moment and anyone who spoke out against her was a perpetrator of hate.

But all this came too late for Sienna. Sure, there were plenty of people her age who had cast off their duds but most had led happy lives. Sienna, on the other hand, had experienced trauma as a teenager that made her more guarded than most. Geri knew about it, which was why she hadn't pressured Sienna to go natural. Some of the people at Geniture knew about it. It had helped shape her career. And her parents knew about it. It was why she hadn't talked to them in ten years. But Geri's friends didn't. And that was the way Sienna wanted it to stay. Luckily, they were so self-consumed that the odd comment asides, the lives and longings of other people ranked fairly low on their horizons.

The presentation was streamed directly to everyone's Smart Glasses. People could still pick it up and watch it at home if they wanted but coming together was an act of symbolism. They were saying to Gaultier; "We are here. We are united". It was the Blitz spirit reborn in New Britannia. Also, you got a free wristband for coming and that was pretty cool. Sienna liked to wear hers for weeks afterwards so that everyone knew where she'd been.

"We are diverse. And we are one," declared the AI narrator as images of inspirational coastal landscapes flashed through the glasses of each protestor, interspersed with a gamut of smiling faces; young and old, black and ethnic, gay and lesbian, femxle and trans. Gaultier would be watching this and kicking his screen in frustration. This was followed by a prolonged kiss between two men that was both beautiful and completely random before music and rolling meadows once again filled the corneas, culminating in a drone shot that zoomed in on someone below, walking between the enormous granite obelisks of Stone Henge. The figure looked up in defiance.

It was Charity GoodHope, Chairperson of New Britannia and undisputed leader of the free world.

"My loving people," she declared.

A moment later she was standing on the quayside at Tilbury Docks with the historic fort framed behind her.

"There are those among us that fear the evils across the sea so much so that they talk of treaties and truces. They say there are arguments on both sides. They say it takes two to tango and we must find common cause with our enemies. They think Gaultier and the FSE are too strong, that we cannot resist his might. That we must cower to his sword as we have cowered before the swords of tyrants throughout history. To the Romans and their chariots, the Tudors and their axes, the Stewarts and their slavery, the Victorians and their insane asylums and the vaccinators and their 21st-century poisons. That we must negotiate. That we must conform. But I say no. No no no.

"I may have the body of a strong and independent cis-womxn but I have the heart and stomach of a pangender non-binary Chairperson and a Chairperson of New Britannia too, and I say never surrender. Never make terms with the repressors of Europe. Never listen to their lies. Saguna Singh did not die in vain. And I will not sully her sacrifice by submitting to the enemy. We must remain free. We will remain free. We will never mediate with hate. We will stay strong and live our best lives in the free and certain knowledge that we have created the greatest and most inclusive democracy the world has ever known.

"Panthea bless you all. Stay proud. Stay vigilant. And stay diverse."

The national anthem followed, complete with subtitles for non-English speakers and the musically-challenged. Years earlier, the people of these lands had been forced to sing about Kings and Queens but the new national anthem was a truly inclusive song that everyone could get behind.

"That you gimme no… That you gimme no… That you gimme no… That you gimme no… Sooooouuuuul, I hear you calling. Oh baby, please, give a little respect to meeee…."

Alas, Sienna struggled to hit some of the higher notes and sang *Don't you tell me no* a couple of extra times but on the whole, she came through the ordeal unscathed. With the rally over, it was time to head home. Sienna was exhausted from having to feign civility all evening and even felt a tinge of affection for the stiff autumnal breeze that was whistling through the trees. It would be a scramble getting a seat on the bus but Sienna calculated that they should be home by eleven for an episode of *Sexploited* and perhaps even a snuggle if they could keep their eyes open. They didn't normally snuggle on a work night but Sienna felt the need to reclaim her territory after Aurora's incursion.

As the crowds slowly drifted away, Sienna was keen to drift with them but Geri and her friends were locked in conversation. Sienna waited by Geri's elbow and became unnerved when she heard Purdy say something about "everyone's going to be there" and the words "open till six" but she didn't think for one moment that this was an invitation. It sounded more like a boast. ie. "This is some trendy venue that we'll be emptying our wallets in tonight while you're tucked up at home in your nice warm bed having nice warm sex". But then, Geri pulled the sheets from beneath Sienna's buttocks by declaring:

"Sounds great. We'll be there. Right babe?"

She never called Sienna "babe" except when they were snuggling or fighting and they weren't doing either at the moment. But she knew one thing. Anything was likely tonight.

6: NATURE

Nuking one's own people might seem controversial abroad but it's a veritable vote-loser at home. Therefore, a softer brush was required when news of the Shetland nuclear disaster broke across New Britannia in late 2064.

What was needed, it was decided, was a hero. This had always been the accepted method for packaging horrific news. Back in the 1940s, few people would have known the names of any of the 1600 civilians and slave labourers who'd drowned when dams in the Ruhr Valley had been busted wide open but most could name the man who'd led the raid; Wing Commander Guy Gibson VC, hero of the famed 633 squadron. Likewise, how many of the 600 Zulu warriors cut down at Rorke's Drift could the average Victorian name? But Lieutenants Chard and Bromhead who'd led the butchery? Both won VCs for their actions that day along with nine others. It would take 200 years and the rebirth of Britannia before its newly enlightened people finally saw these men for what they were and tore down the memorials erected in their honour.

Still, it demonstrated how effective the hero device could be. Therefore, a hero was sought (or rather a heroine) and the facts repackaged for easier consumption.

The story went like this:

Saguna Singh was a Warrant Officer aboard *HMS Valiant*, a Dreadnought class nuclear-powered ballistic missile submarine. It had docked in Lerwick in response to a sudden emergency on the islands. The population had come out in support of Gaultier and were slaughtering diverse Shetlanders in the name of purity. The crew of *HMS Valiant* tried to evacuate as many people as they could but terrorists smuggled themselves aboard posing as refugees. They killed most of the crew and would no doubt have launched the boat's payload against New Britannia were it not for the courage of Warrant Officer Singh. As the last surviving crew member, she fought her way through to the weapons bay, sealed herself inside and detonated one of the warheads to prevent the bombs from falling into enemy hands. The resultant blast wiped Lerwick off the map and levelled settlements from Sumburgh to Skaw. Casualty figures were near 100% and anyone unfortunate enough to escape the initial explosion soon succumbed to the agonies of radiation poisoning.

It was horror on an unimaginable scale.

But it could have been so much worse were it not for the heroic sacrifice of Saguna Singh, inaugural recipient of the Britannic Cross, the highest honour awarded by the Governmynt of New Britannia. She became a poster child for a new generation. The fact that Saguna Singh hadn't actually existed didn't really matter. Not to those who'd conjured her up anyway. There had probably been no Jesus either but that hadn't stopped him from inspiring millions. His death on the cross was seen as the ultimate act of love. So too was Warrant Officer Singh's.

That said, had she existed, the despair Saguna had faced in those last frantic moments was nothing compared to the despair Sienna now experienced when she saw where Geri's friends were leading them.

SKIN read the sign over the door, spelt out in naked people throwing poses.

"It's here for one night only. After that, it'll be gone forever, like it never existed," Diego said as if that counted for something. Sienna thought about pointing to a lump of dog shit across the road and making the same observation but it was too late. Geri and her friends entered without breaking stride, keen to rub whatnots with their fellow naturalists.

Geri reappeared two seconds later and looked out.

"You coming or what?"

"Can't we just go home? It's been a really long day and I'm really tired."

"Fuck's sake, don't be *skinnest*. You're going to insult Diego if you don't come in."

"And we wouldn't want that, now would we?" Sienna said inadvertently insulting Geri in the process. Geri had adopted her new lifestyle like a born-again convert. It had been no three-week fad as Sienna had predicted. And while each had expressed strong opinions over the months, they'd been able to avoid any serious rows until now.

Yet here they were, standing outside SKIN. One coming in. One staying out.

"This is important to me. These are my friends. I want you to come in for a drink. I told them you were alright and they're keen to get to know you. You're not around most of the time."

"I'm usually working," Sienna said.

"Well, you're not now."

"It's just… it's late."

"One drink."

"I've got work in the morning."

"So has everyone else."

"I would if I could…"

"Please!"

Sienna felt herself crumbling. She didn't want to. She really didn't. She had no desire to see what was on the other side of that door. She didn't want to hang out with Geri's friends.

And she really really really didn't want to kick off her knickers in order to do so.

"I'll owe you," Geri begged, sending Sienna a love heart emoji containing their two names. "Big time."

Sienna could not resist. Whatever horrors lay inside suddenly paled into consideration next to the horror of disappointing Geri.

"One drink," she conceded, only to be instantly kissed by Geri.

"Let's see how it goes."

It was warm inside. Hot even. Sienna felt stuffy in her plastic trench coat the moment the door shut behind her. This was the disrobing area. As with most naturalist clubs, not every patron arrived in their birthday suit. Some preferred to undress only once they arrived therefore a cloakroom attendant checked their clothes and issued them with an e.ticket upon stripping.

Sienna reluctantly slipped out of her things and placed them on the counter as if under the glare of an impatient rapist. The cloakroom attendant and Geri exchanged looks.

"First time, huh?" the attendant surmised.

"No, I was born this way," Sienna replied, defiantly tossing her bra onto the counter and taking a deep breath before whipping off her pants. She half-expected to see a Guardian wearing an oiled rubber glove behind her but the only people nearby were also undressing. No one seemed traumatised about it and no one stared. This went some way to reassure her that Geri was right when she'd said: "No one looks. No one cares. That's the whole point."

At least, it did until the attendant gave her a wink. "Have fun, chubby cheeks."

Sienna and Geri passed through a second door, Sienna

self-consciously feeling her buttocks to Geri's great amusement.

The club inside was long and thin with a low ceiling and floor-level lighting that changed from red to blue to green in time with a thumping electronic beat. It had probably served as a shop many moons ago. Now it served many moons of a different kind, mostly young and carefree as they danced, cavorted and spilled drinks on each other with impunity. It was noisy in here and even hotter than it had been in the disrobing area, although the heat in here radiated off a wall of undulated flesh. Geri and Sienna squeezed through the sweating mass of bodies to reach the bar. Sienna recoiled every time she felt something flop or swipe across her back, although that was nothing compared to the shock when she reached out to grab Geri's hand and grasped someone else accidentally. And not their hand.

At last, they made it to the bar where Geri's friends were waiting. The Network signal in these pop-up places was always poor and the crowded bar reflected as much. Sienna connected with the Network and selected a bottle of 'Fauxican' beer with a slice of lime, figuring this would be quicker to obtain than one of the complicated cocktails SKIN was offering.

Geri ordered a pink lady and laughed when Aurora told her she already had one, looking directly at Sienna. This comment made Sienna feel genuinely naked. Until this point, Sienna had felt as though she was in a changing room or sauna. Now she felt as though she was in a recurring dream. She willed herself to wake up without success and came to an alarming conclusion. She really was standing here in a crowded bar without a single stitch on.

Her beer was placed on the bar, complete with a slice of

lime, and she went to grab it but a hand appeared out of the crowd to swipe it away.

"Hey, that's mine," she yelled heading into the crowd after her bottle.

She found it in the possession of an obese chicken queen who was dancing amongst some young lads, chugging her beer with delight.

"You took my beer," Sienna said, directly messaging him at spongecake2038.69 when he failed to respond to her verbally.

spongecake2038.69 finally acknowledged her but just to turn the bottle upside down to show her it was gone.

"You can have it back in a minute though," he said, grabbing his penis and pointing it at her as if to urinate. The chicks clucked with delight but Sienna beat a swift retreat. Geri and the others had their cocktails when Sienna got back so she ordered another beer and watched the bar like a hawk.

"I thought you were only having one?" Geri said. Sienna explained what had happened and saw theoneandonly2052.663 whisper "homophobe" to Fuzz. She hadn't even described spongecake2038.69 or derided his lifestyle yet still she had found herself caught in the glare of the dreaded "H" word. She knew to say no more but made a mental note to search for spongecake2038.69 when she got to work in the morning. She'd make him pay for that beer.

She drank in silence standing on the edge of the clique. It was louder in here than was healthy for a person but everyone had their subtitles enabled so that they could see what each other was saying. Sienna paired with them for a while and found Diego talking about a software program he was working on that tracked potato surplus in real-time. The idea was to prevent food waste and if it proved successful, he was hoping to roll it out to carrots, parsnips and all manner of other crops. It sounded like a smart idea until he mentioned it was for domestic use only. It simply tracked the vegetables in a person's fridge.

Purdy's app sought to organise a person's affairs by breaking down the day into numbered time slots and allocating a fraction of each for various tasks. A counter or a dial would indicate when a person was due to start and complete a task and analytical data would be recorded so that they might improve their task mxnagement. To Sienna, it sounded like Purdy had invented a clock. Only a much more complicated version of one that changed from day to day based on how long yesterday's washing took.

Aurora was working on literary software. It was said that every person had at least one book inside them and Aurora's app would help get them out. It sounded like any of the other 200 literary apps that were free to download but Aurora insisted hers was like nothing else because of her 'unpredictability' code that meant storylines shot off in random and unforeseeable directions almost constantly. Both Fuzz and theoneandonly2060.663 were test-marketing it but had yet to feedback because they'd been busy these last four months. Really really busy.

Geri talked about Carl and how she had been fine-tuning him at the behest of a leading AI carrier. She hadn't. At least, not lately. Some indie carrier had shown an interest three years earlier but that had fizzled out after a few months of code rewrites and empty promises. Sienna said nothing and sipped her beer.

"That's great. You're so fucking talented," Aurora said before turning her enthusiasm on Sienna. "How's it feel to be with such a talented vixen?"

Normally it felt great. Tonight, less so.

"She's amazing," Sienna agreed. "And so hard working. I know she'll get there in the end."

This earned a frosty glare from Geri who, in her own mind, was already there and was just waiting for everyone else to catch up.

Aurora asked Sienna what she did.

"I'm a Crypto Security Support Officer…" she started to say but Aurora had already tuned out and was bouncing off the walls in time with MPA.venue_4.7's tempo change. This suited Sienna. She didn't want to talk about herself, least of all her fake job. She'd maintained her cover story for ten long years but it wasn't always easy. Not even Geri knew what she did. It was the dark secret at the core of their relationship. The lie that threatened their love. Several times she had come close to confessing but she wouldn't dream of it now. They'd drifted too far. But it was only a temporary situation. Once Geri got over the novelty of her new friends, she and Sienna could pick up where they'd left off.

Hopefully.

One day.

When things got better.

Sienna took another sip of her beer and scratched her belly without thought.

"Hey, no wanking," Purdy said when she saw Sienna touching herself. "Save it for bath time."

Everyone laughed. Everyone except Geri who privately messaged Sienna to tell her to stop embarrassing herself.

Sienna turned off her subtitles and dropped out of the conversation. She eased away from the group and sought refuge behind a large black pillar at the end of the bar. She'd almost finished her beer and wondered if Geri would keep her word. Would they go home after one drink or would Geri insist on staying into the small wee hours, ripping with her friends and tearing into Sienna?

After a few moments, a short black girl wandered over. Sienna didn't normally like to think of people in these superficial terms. People were more than just the colour of their skin but it was difficult to get a handle on individuals without the aid of clothing. She had also made her username private but introduced herself verbally as Jade.

"I've not seen you before."

"I've not been here before," Sienna replied.

Jade laughed. "No one has." But she knew what Sienna meant. "Your crew?" she asked.

Sienna looked over at Geri ensconced in conversation without declaring her allegiance.

"What about you?"

Jade was shorter than Sienna but not as slender. She had a sweet round face and closely cropped hair. Her pear-shaped breasts were pointed and her nipples adorned with gold studs. Sienna tried not to look any lower but could not help herself. Jade didn't mind and chewed her lip as she felt Sienna's eyes caress her body.

"Are you contracted?" Jade asked.

Sienna confirmed she was with a pang of regret.

"Wanna get a furlough? I've got a one-nighter all signed and sealed."

It was a warm and fuzzy thought and it set Sienna's tummy a tingling but each tingle was accompanied by a jolt of fear. She loved Geri and knew that Geri loved her. Deep down. In her heart. She couldn't do anything to endanger that.

"I'll see you in my dreams," Sienna said apologetically. Jade smiled and sank back into the crowd. Sienna felt another pang of regret but this time it was accompanied by a wave of relief. She had sailed close to the wind and had the twitches to show for it but she had come through in one piece. She moved back to Geri and asked her if she was ready to go.

"Fucking hell, we've only just got here," she said, looking annoyed and conspiratorial all at once. According to Aurora's app, they still had seven quarters left but no one knew what that actually meant in real time.

Fuzz sidled over. She'd hardly said a word all night but now she whispered in Geri's ear. "Is she cool?" Sienna didn't hear Geri's reply but it was clearly in the negative.

"What did she mean?" Sienna asked when Fuzz moved away. She noticed a little bag in Geri's hand but couldn't make out what was inside.

"It's no big deal," Geri told her guiltily. "Everyone does them." Sure enough, Diego, Purdy and all the others were crunching on something and scanning the room conspicuously.

Sienna demanded to know what Geri was holding and eventually, she showed her. Sienna was shocked.

"Fuck's sake. Are you mad? Get rid of them."

But Geri couldn't just get rid of a stash like this. They were too dangerous. You couldn't just leave them lying around either. People could get hurt. To some, they were toxic even to the touch.

"If the Guardians catch you with peanuts you'll get a year at least."

"No one's going to catch me. Everyone's cool," Geri replied, slipping a peanut into her mouth. "Diego's been doing them for years. Guardians have got bigger things to worry about than users."

"I don't care what Diego's been doing. If Diego ate a slice of ham, would you?"

But Geri refused to equate the two. It wasn't the same at all. Nuts and meat were both illegal but as long as you were careful and made sure you'd tested for intolerances, they were perfectly harmless. That said, if you didn't, they could prove anything but, as several passengers on an Oxfordshire bus last week discovered.

"That's why you're not cool," Geri reminded Sienna but Sienna didn't need peanuts to make herself feel cool – salted or raw. She took a hit on her OxyVape to calm her nerves and ordered another drink. How could Geri be so stupid? Geri of all people. She'd designed an AI program to teach people consideration and yet here she was showing none to anyone else. Nut consumption was a scourge in New Britannia and backstreet dealers made millions out of the misery they spread. Hospitals were full of people suffering from anaphylactic shock, particularly at the weekends, with a great many failing to receive treatment in time. The Governmynt cracked down on nut dealers a few years ago after a spike in fatalities but the deadly trade continued. There was too much money in it for it to ever be stamped out.

Drugs, on the other hand, were freely available and perfectly legal. Everything was available over-the-counter, from opium to cocaine, meth to grass, most of it synthetically mxnufactured by the large Pharma companies and sold in vape form. The Governmynt was able to regulate the quality and the drop in price put illegal dealers out of business overnight. Crime plummeted, overdoses became unheard of and the enormous tax revenues underpinned the foundations of New Britannia. As an isolated state surrounded by enemies on all sides, trade and commerce were always going to be an issue. But narcotics, safe, legal and life-affirming, were the economic miracle that had helped power the engines of progress.

Sienna turned up her Vape another notch and took a second hit. A calming wave washed over her, vanquishing her discomforts and flattening her doubts. Her eyes scanned the club for her new friend Jade. She wasn't sure what she would do when she saw her. All she knew was that she yearned to be happy. If only for a brief connection. There were pink, brown and black bodies everywhere, dancing, hanging and swinging, but none of them belonged to Jade.

Sienna downed her second beer and felt it in her loins. She was now carrying two bottles and half a bowl of stew and decided to lighten the load. She followed the walls of the club around the dance floor but could not find the loos. Eventually, she pitched a query to the venue's server and a small yellow unisex figure appeared in her Smart Glasses. She followed it through the club, squeezing past the crowd and heading towards the back until she exited through a series of doors and into the outside air. The cold gave her a shock but not as great as the shock of what lay before her.

People were digging in the darkness. Each trench was about two feet wide by two feet deep and stretched off into the night. Along all sides, people were squatting to urinate or defecate into the holes. There didn't seem to be any particular system. Men and womyn squatted side by side. People were at ones and twos all over the place. A table stacked with biodegradable toilet rolls was set up nearby with a sign declaring: PLEASE THINK OF OTHERS AND ONLY TAKE WHAT YOU NEED. Sienna wondered if it was possible to squat in the middle of this conflux and not think about others.

"Fuck's sake," a voice declared. She turned and saw a middle-aged Grade 10 with the username ramjamdingdong2036.1, his emotions as exposed as his middle-aged spread. "Free shitters. This was not on the notification. Wankers."

'Fertilisers', as they preferred to be called, or 'Free Shitters', as everyone else called them, was a sub-cult of the naturalist movement. They saw toilets and plumbing as environment rape and wastewater as a literal waste of water. The effluence that people normally flushed away took an enormous environmental toll to treat. But sewage was a natural bio-product, a nutrient-rich fertiliser that plants needed to grow. So, Free Shitters avoided using traditional toilets and went anywhere they pleased. Most were instantly recognisable from the small fold-away shovels they carried about with them and some of the trendier pop-up clubs had started adopting Free Shitting facilities.

"Fuck it," ramjamdingdong2036.1 swore, heading out to the nearest trench to tuck his penis between his legs and squat in the accepted fashion.

Sienna couldn't help but stare, not in titillation, but in abject horror. She felt akin to a condemned prisoner about to be hung, drawn and quartered. In days of old, traitors would be shown the implements of their execution to increase their ordeal and most would pee and soil themselves on the spot. Ironically, Sienna's horror had the opposite effect on her, particularly when she saw the soil give way and ramjamdingdong2036.1 tip backwards into the trench. A metaphorical cork had been firmly rammed inside her and she wouldn't be able to pee until she got home.

Inside the club, the warmth was welcome but the welcome was not warm. Geri was dancing with Aurora and the others. theoneandonly2060.663 had a full-on erection and was swinging it from side to side like a big black metronome. Not every naturalist who had a penis got an erection. Some took pills to cure their arousal while others preferred a concoction that made them 'semi-chic'. theoneandonly2060.663 obviously liked to go fully natural. He saw Sienna and beckoned her over to dance with him but at that precise moment, she would have sooner danced with ramjamdingdong2036.1.

Geri was lost in Aurora's orbit and Sienna had reached the end of the road. Geri or no Geri, she was going home and would cry or vape herself to sleep. Or both. She didn't know which but she knew one thing; she didn't want to be here any more and Geri didn't want to come home. The life they had built together. The love they had shared. It had always been enough for Sienna but it was no longer enough for Geri. And part of Sienna died admitting this to herself.

She turned to leave and would have done so in tears had the miracle not happened. From out of the sound system, Sienna's Fairy Godmother came to the rescue. Her words changed everything. And her name was Trinity Dhaliwal.

"We are no longer particles of nescience floating in a sea of ignorance. We are systems in the humxn machine. We are the body and soul of the future. Now I give you the mind."

Geri froze as if someone had just chucked a bucket of cold piss in her face.

The words repeated again and again in time with the electronic beat. There were further pearls of wisdom over the baseline.

"MUM... I give you MUM."

The crowd whooped with enthusiasm but Geri just gawped.

The recordings were samples from Trinity Dhaliwal's acceptance speech upon receiving the HAL Trophy. They had since been etched into history, just as Edison, Einstein and

Oppenheimer's had, but more pertinently they wept like open sores in Geri's heart. The HAL Trophy night had promised to be the greatest night of her life only to become the worst. What's more, it transpired to be the first step on her road to obscurity as Geri's career tailed off.

Aurora and theoneandonly2060.663 blinked but Geri was gone. They looked for her but she was already out of sight, rushing past Sienna and heading for the exit. Sienna ran after her, pushing and shoving past every sweaty body until she was through the club. Geri had no clothes to collect but Sienna did. She flashed her number to the attendant and ran out with the bundle under her arm. The cold again hit her like an Arctic blast but she didn't stop to dress. She just ran and ran until she finally caught up with Geri at the bus stop on the edge of town.

Sienna didn't need to say anything else and Geri didn't want to talk about it. Instead, Sienna placed her red trench coat around Geri's shoulders. It was suddenly very cold and both were shivering but Sienna wanted Geri to have it more.

Geri regarded Sienna for a moment then, with a look of sorrow and gratitude, –

– she slipped her arms through the sleeves.

7: MEAT

By the 21st century, meat stopped being a means to survival and became instead a cultural issue. People didn't need meat to sustain themselves. They didn't even need meat to grow strong and healthy. Vegan cooking had become so advanced that even the pickiest of cavemen would've had trouble telling the difference between a beef burger and one of the new mung bean protein patties. There was simply no legitimate excuse for enslaving animals in the death camps of husbandry any more. A line was drawn. And the Polychrome Alliance vowed to steer the country onto the right side of it.

Of course, change is never easy. Laws were passed, protesters swamped the streets, riots broke out across the land as windows were smashed, vegan cafes were firebombed and people got hurt. But the Polychrome Alliance used every measure at their disposal to lift meat and dairy products beyond the reach of the masses, levying crippling taxes, imposing impossible welfare standards and hammering the industry until meat became so expensive it was declared as a luxury item for the rich. Like Beluga Caviar or that coffee that cats shat out. From there, banning it entirely became a relatively simple process.

New Year's Eve, 2059, was the last time anyone in New Britannia could give a sausage, let alone receive one. After that, most farmers adapted or fled abroad. Butchers and slaughter-men were hunted down in their thousands and made to pay, just as the guards who had overseen the Final Solution had been a century earlier. New Britannia became an example to the world. There was only one problem.

It now had millions of reprieved animals to care for.

What was to become of them?

Farmers couldn't afford to keep them for no reason. And there were only so many petting zoos the country could sustain. Who would take care of them all?

The answer was obvious. The animals had to be released into the wilds where they could live out their remaining days in peace and tranquillity. A cross-committee of vegan pioneers called the Animal Resettlement Solution Legislature looked into the problem and deemed almost every idea as unworkable. The only solution that seemed to offer even the vaguest hope of success was the final solution suggested: the establishment of an enormous animal sanctuary in the wilds of Scotland, where animals would have plenty to eat and no one to bother them – especially once the Highlands were cleared. And so, hundreds of cattle trains were laid on and thousands of pigs, sheep, cows and chickens were railed north from all over the country, alas with many dying en route. But a massive enclosure was born all the same that stretched from Lochinver to Brora encapsulating much of the Highlands. The animals were released, fences were erected and Orwell's vision came to fruition. The animals ruled the land.

That's when the second problem happened.

See, rather than being content to see out their days in happy harmony, the animals started to breed. A lot. There were already millions of them gathered together but by that second summer, the roaming herds had grown enormous. Food became short and famine and disease ripped through them like wildfire. Animal Welfare Officers reported suffering on a biblical scale. The ARSL reconvened and a new solution was sought.

The herds had to be maintained through some sort of cull but that would have involved hundreds of gamekeepers shooting and disposing of thousands of beasts. Large gas chambers were considered but many felt that conveyed a complicated narrative. Therefore, a different final solution was sought. A natural solution.

It was obvious when they thought about it. How were numbers kept at bay in the wild? Through predation, of course.

And so, a massive reintroduction programme was undertaken and, for the first time in 600 years, wolves could be heard howling echoing across the misty moors of these Britannic islands.

But the ARSL failed to consider something else.

With so much easy food at their disposal, the wolf packs grew exponentially too, splitting up to create new wolf packs to spread across the north, This became a major problem for the towns and villages around the farmwife sanctuary. Unlike cows and pigs, the wolves weren't dissuaded by electric fences. Most could leap clean over them or find gaps in the wire caused by storms or natural obstacles. Wolf attacks became a reality for the people of the Highlands. A child was attacked on the streets of Helmdale by a rogue omega and the remains of a couple whose car had broken down on the A9 were found in a nearby lair. Sentries were posted outside most towns and an ARSL campaign ran for several months to educate people but still, the attacks continued with around a hundred incidents being reported each year resulting in 10-15 fatalities.

The ARSL Chairperson concluded, from her headquarters in Westminster, that this was an acceptable price worth paying in the name of progress.

Sienna considered all of this as she dug into the life and history of Charles Garfield (veganking2025.1008) the following day at work. Myrtle had given her permission to continue her investigations on the proviso that she linked Garfield with the illegal meat trade. She wished he was dealing peanuts. She could have killed two birds with one stone but unfortunately, he was not. At least, not that she could tell from the material at hand.

New Britannia was officially a vegan paradise but the exploitation of animals continued below the surface like a cancer. Sienna didn't know if Garfield was dealing in meat but many were. Evidence of barbecues was regularly found on the outskirts of most large towns and the consumption of beef jerky had spread amongst the young like an epidemic.

The carrion to service this trade had to come from somewhere. Poaching on the Sanctuary had become rife. Guardians patrolled the wire and were ordered to shoot-to-kill but they couldn't be everywhere. And for those with the stealth and nerve to sneak inside, the rewards could be huge.

Sealed inside her Hub pod and with a full cartridge of CocaVape, Sienna went over Garfield's NetComs history, running each thread through MUM to compare it against known meat procurers. She found nothing. She dug deeper still, checking his contacts and searching every message for patterns or phrases that looked like code but after another couple of hours of digging, she had nothing to go on.

She did the same with his mother and father, aunts, uncles and cousins, going further and further back into their Network history until the advent of the Network itself but meat was hardly mentioned after 2060. And certainly not in any incriminating sense.

She ran a facial recognition program on Charles Garfield and got a few thousand hits. She sifted them by relevance and cross-referenced anyone pictured with him and finally got lucky. Two years ago, in Farnham's Castle Street, he'd engaged in a three-minute conversation with darkmatter2021.407, a suspected meat dealer who had an addendum attached to his file forbidding investigation without official Guardian authorisation. Sienna had seen similar warnings before and realised darkmatter2021.407 was probably an informer. Still, it was Garfield's first link to the illegal meat trade but it was almost certainly a coincidence. Across the street from Garfield and darkmatter2021.407 was a free-spirited millicentmagnificent2055.21 burying something in the verge with a little foldaway shovel. In all probability, they could have simply been discussing the merits and demerits of what they were witnessing. Sienna marked the footage anyway and continued sifting.

The average case took two to three days to investigate and a couple of hours to prepare. Usually Sienna got a sense pretty quickly whether or not there was anything to it but with Garfield there was nothing. His parents were long dead and the rest of his relatives were a mystery. The records were frustratingly incomplete.

Great swathes of his heredity seemed to lead to dead screens or missing links, suggesting they had either gone under the radar or had migrated in the years leading up to the meat ban. As early as the earliest days of the Polychrome Alliance, British butchers could see the writing on the wall. The most prescient escaped abroad, taking with them whatever they could smuggle out in currency, gems, silver or gold. Many were swindled along the way and some even disappeared but that didn't stop many more from trying.

When the outright ban finally came into effect, it was too late for those who'd stayed behind. The tide of history had turned against them. It was time to pay the piper.

Charles Garfield hadn't tried to run. He hadn't hidden his assets or ducked his responsibilities. He had registered as an ex-meat worker and paid the crippling restitution levies imposed on those wanting to wipe the slate clean, starting over with next to nothing and working his way up to become a successful supplier of soya. On paper, Garfield looked like a model New Britannian. Other than supplying meat when the trade was legal, Sienna could find nothing cancel-worthy about him. Likewise, his family was squeaky clean. His wife was mixed-race and their children had embraced multiculturalism and LGBTQIA2S+ values with one serving as the trans ambassador at school and the other a prominent voice in the Free Europe Group. Both were noted vegan fusion chefs and neither had uttered a word of dissension in their lives that Sienna could find. She and MUM had scanned every word they'd ever committed to NetComs and even eavesdropped on audio files but there was nothing.

She spent another hour interfacing with Garfield's home OS and that of his neighbours just to be thorough but by lunchtime, she had already concluded that she was barking up the wrong tree. In fact, she wasn't even sure there was a tree, he was that law-abiding. Many ex-butchers were worse than Hitler but Garfield wasn't even worse than Speer. Yet someone had reported him and, as every good witch-finder knew, you didn't get smoke without fire. Sienna decided to leave his case open in the event of new inspiration but there was little else she could do for the time being. Not without a lead.

A message pinged into her periphery:

My body's still throbbing. You punished me hard last night. I must have been a really bad girl – Geri

A smile flickered across Sienna's lips as she composed her reply.

You're not a girl, you're a fucking slut. And slut's get punished when they don't do as I tell them. As you'll find out again when I get home tonight – Sienna

A warm fuzzy glow spread through Sienna's loins. She and Geri had snuggled when they got home the previous night. They had snuggled with an intensity she'd not known in years. It had made every miserable moment in SKIN almost worth it and now it felt as though they were back on track.

Of course, she didn't really think of her beautiful, funny, warm, loving and flawed girlfriend as a 'fucking slut'. It was role play for Geri's benefit. She liked to be abused. Sienna didn't always feel comfortable doing it but the more she scolded her, the harder Geri climaxed. And that was enough for Sienna. She was a giver and Geri a receiver. They were perfectly matched to one another. In this and in every other way. Because they loved each other so much.

Ooohh, I'm scared – Geri.

So you should be you dog. I'm going to throw you on the bed when I get home and do what I did last night. Only harder – Sienna

At this point, a new message appeared in their chat window.

Please deposit any soiled sheets in the laundry chute afterwards. Use the detergent spray on any stubborn stains that require a direct application. The cycle will take six hours to complete – Carl

Sienna sighed. Carl was always monitoring but she had learned to live with it. He was their OS and it was his job to order their lives so that they could function properly. Happily, Geri had programmed him not to interrupt while they were engaged in the act but the electronic pervert was always waiting in the wings with a postcoital comment or two, something Sienna found about as welcome as a score out of ten.

Thank you Carl. That is very considerate of you. If there's anything I can do for you, please let me know – Geri

You are most welcome, Geri. And thank you. Sienna, did you receive my communique? – Carl

Oh fuck off – Sienna.

Sienna had the good sense not to post this, as much as she wanted to, and even had to suppress the thought in case NetComs composed it unintentionally. Instead, she picked one of her standard Carl replies and sent it off in the hope it would end their exchange.

Thank you Carl. You take such good care of me and Geri. I am so lucky to have you waiting at home for me – Sienna

And I am lucky to have you as my user – Carl

Thank you Carl. You take such good care of me and Geri. I am so lucky to have you waiting at home for me – Sienna

Damn it, she'd pasted the same reply twice which she hadn't meant to do. This wouldn't be good.

I'm sorry, is there a fault with your NetComs link? You appear to have duplicated your reply – Carl

My apologies. I got a hair in my eye and accidentally blinked which repeated my last message. What I wanted to actually say was that you are so kind and proficient and I feel very privileged to have you installed as our home OS system – Sienna.

There was a pause which was completely unnecessary as Carl was nothing more than reams and reams of computer code and had the ability to interpret and reply to a message in less than 50 picoseconds. In fact, he wasn't even a he. He was an it. Just a fucking it.

The S in OS stands for system. To say OS system is a needless duplication. As was your entire message. I do not detect sincerity in your sentiment and feel this is something you should consider carefully the next time you are attempting to express gratitude – Carl

Carl, wash the sheets. Don't wash the sheets. I don't care. But I'm at work so maybe surprise me, yeah? – Sienna

And with that, she shut down her link and marked herself as Out Of The Office. She felt bad because her response would leave Geri in the lurch but she reasoned she'd scored enough Brownie points the previous evening to weather the storm.

Sienna returned to her dead ends and plugged away for a little while longer before another memory from the previous evening came back to her. She entered the name spongecake2038.69 and had MUM run a search. His image was projected onto her wall along with his metadata.

Name: Helen Susan Monroe
Gender: Male
Sexuality: Pansexual
Pronouns: He His Him
DOB: 28-02-38
Address: The Old Cottage, Castle Green, Surrey
Diversity Grading: 14.5
Profession: Food Writer
Relationship Status: Non-Exclusive A6 x 7

Here was the guy who'd taken her beer and threatened to urinate on her. This in itself should have been enough for her to make a complaint but his Diversity Grading was higher than hers and such an action could have backfired. Instead, she unleashed MUM on his NetComs history and very quickly found some workable data.

Helen himself had made numerous references to the 'freak' next door and it didn't take Sienna too long to pull up a picture of his neighbour, a non-binary anorexia advocate of the emo persuasion.

She pulled up a pictorial montage of some of his young friends, several under the age of fourteen according to the time stamp on the photographs.

And she found a series of contentious off-grid forums he'd visited which maintained lesbians should only be permitted to bear gay children and those who lacked the genetic variants should undergo foetal gene therapy. Helen didn't need to like or comment on these forums. Visiting them was incriminating enough.

There was also a disparaging remark about Spread The Rainbow, the annual appeal in aid of the descendants of the earliest migrants, the supposed forgotten generation, underrepresented in key sectors across society. A three-second audio recording of Helen remarking to himself "Oh, who fucking cares?" would come back to haunt him and show him who cared. Sienna cared. And soon so would he.

Lastly, his grandfather had been accused of indecent assault with a minor in 1999 but had been acquitted through a lack of evidence. He went on to be arrested a second time five years later, resulting in a conviction but he more or less got off scot-free. The judge ruled that these actions were clearly out of character for such a pillar of the community and that the shame he'd brought upon his good name was punishment enough.

Sienna disagreed. And she would go out of her way to right this historic wrong.

There would be more to Helen than this. Sienna knew that you didn't find this much usable data without there being plenty more below the surface. But she would put a pin in it for now. It was almost lunchtime and she needed to speak with Bella before she went to the food hall.

She saved her workings and scrolled down to Bella's last message. Bella had left a long and convoluted list of instructions for Sienna for when she got into work but Sienna had been unable to call Bella back. Bella had been off-line ever since, presumably because she didn't want to be called back, she just wanted Sienna to do what she was told and let her know when they were done. This was her preferred style of mxnagement. Sienna clicked on Bella's profile and saw she was back online (presumably to play Cloud Crunch or Number Tumble or some such bullshit) so she called her and refused to ring off when Bella failed to pick up. Sienna stayed dialled in and waited for almost five minutes before Bella finally appeared.

"Ah Sienna, I was about to call you," Bella said when she materialised. She made no attempt to explain the five-minute hiatus and instead, got straight to business. Her business.

"I just want to say again that I'm really disappointed with our case actions yesterday. I can't remember a poorer return from a Congress since… well, ever. You got my message, did you?"

Sienna confirmed she did, noting that Bella was no longer wearing her lily. Her bleed was over for another few weeks. She was, however, wearing a jumble of garish garments that had no Earthly right to go together. In Sienna's experience, most transwomyn took care over what they wore. Many spent longer getting ready each day than sleeping. But Bella was not like this. She spent money and bought expensive dresses only to look like an Edwardian industrialist queuing for lifeboats on the *Titanic*. But why should this have come as a surprise? As a man, Ben had no style. Why should this change just because her pronouns had?

"Sorry, I'm a bit confused," Sienna said, recalling Bella's message. "You want me to work across Sector 4 with the other Auditors and get at least half the cases across the line at next week's Congress too?"

"At least," Bella replied, underlining the key phrase in her directive.

"But surely that's your job?" Sienna said, her grapes so sour she could almost taste the vinegar.

"Don't tell me my job. I know what my job is," Bella snapped, despite all evidence to the contrary.

"And those two cases that were actioned, both were mine."

"Yours? They were Sector 4's. They're not your cases to claim for your own personal glory. Try being a team player for once instead of thinking of yourself."

Sienna fought to keep her face neutral. These sorts of calls must have been a lot easier in the days of simple telephones when a person could have blown off steam with a few silent hand gestures but Sienna had no such relief. She just stared at Bella unblinking while she glowered from behind three inches of eye shadow.

"I'm just saying, isn't this something you should be doing? Working with Sector 4's Auditors? You're in the position to do that," Sienna suggested, scarcely able to unclench her teeth.

"I'm going to be far too busy clearing up the mess you made yesterday. I've never known a week like it."

"How was that my fault?"

"You ran the review. You dropped the ball. It's all in the presentation."

Sienna could tell Bella was being over-defensive. She must have known she had given her a duff load of cases. This was why she hadn't wanted to run the review herself. Now she had the perfect scapegoat in Sienna and she was going to run with it all the way to Xanadu.

"The cases were shells. There was nothing to them."

"Then make something of them," Bella demanded. "Because they're your cases now."

"You mean Sector 4's cases?" Sienna reminded her, throwing Bella's own words back at her.

"Don't be insubordinate," she gasped, clutching her head in distress. "Oh, you've given me a migraine. I won't let you attack me like this. I won't stand for your bullying. You've got your instructions so get on with it."

And with those last few words of inspiration, Bella killed the link between them and went off to recuperate from the ordeal of having to speak with one of her underlings.

8: TRAUMA

Eleven years earlier, Sienna had suffered a trauma so harrowing that she still bore the scars of it to this day. She'd been in her last year of school and studying for her Baccalaureate when her father's boss came for dinner. He was a ruddy-faced old Chief Accountant called Alan Miller and Sienna didn't like him much. He was a relic from a bygone era and a condescending prick to boot, dismissing half of what she said and smirking at the rest. For forty-five minutes she had sat across from him arguing about the evils of the patriarchy and the powers of holistic healing before finally she'd had enough. As she got up to leave, she turned and saw a little red dot flashing beneath the table next to Miller's chair. She gasped. All looked.

"Oh, that's where they got to. I thought I'd left them in the car."

They were Alan Miller's Smart Glasses, lying upside down on the chair beside him. They were aimed directly at Sienna's chair. And they were recording what they saw.

It's hard to imagine now but in those early days of Smart Glasses, most people wore them as if they were an accessory rather than a necessity. Some took them on and off and set them aside when not using them. Sienna's own parents were constantly leaving theirs lying around and her mother would even forget to charge hers occasionally. It was infuriating, especially when Sienna was trying to message from upstairs. Therefore, it wasn't unusual to see people without them. Not like these day, when only Cans walked the streets without them. So, Sienna hadn't thought anything of Alan Miller's barren face. Not until she'd seen his glasses on the chair beside him.

Miller picked them up and stuffed them into his pocket

with a glib comment but it was too late. Sienna realised what he'd been doing and felt sickened at the violation.

"You bastard. You sick bastard. You're going to prison. Mum, call the Guardians. Call them now."

Sienna's parents were stunned. They had no idea what was going on but Miller did and attempted to excuse himself.

"Maybe I'd better go. I don't want to get in the way of anything here," he'd said but Sienna screamed and blocked the door.

"No, don't let him go. Stop him."

"What is this? Sienna, what is going on?"

Suddenly, everyone was up from the table and looking at each other in confusion. But one of them was play-acting. There was a wolf amongst the sheep and he knew he'd been spotted.

"Get his glasses. Dad, stop him. He's filming up my skirt."

Now things changed. All eyes turned to Miller and he gawped in horror as if he'd just swallowed a black widow. Sienna was scrolling through a list of options on the Guardian's home page and selected 'Sexual Assault'. She blinked three times to speak to an operator and summoned a voice in her ear to accompany the three shouting at her to hang up.

"It was an accident. Please, I didn't mean it. I didn't even know I was recording."

"Sienna, end the call, darling and let's talk. Hang up the call."

"Please, I'm sure there's a simple explanation. Sienna? Sienna? SIENNA!"

Whatever explanation there was, Miller could save it for the Guardians. The operator made Sienna's call a Priority when Sienna said the assault was ongoing and told her to stay on the line. This wasn't entirely true but it wasn't entirely false either. The altercation had turned physical but the instigator was Sienna. She was grappling with Miller in order to get his glasses and he was fighting her off, aided and abetted by her parents. But Sienna fought like a lion. She could not bear the thought of Miller deleting his recordings and walking away free so she clamped onto him like a limpet and raided his pockets.

"For God's sake, Sienna, stop. Stop it."

"Get her off me. She's a lunatic."

"Jesus Christ, let go of his ears."

Sienna finally yanked Miller's glasses free but with her parents pulling her one way and Miller the other she lost her grip and his Glasses fell to the floor. A moment later, she tumbled after them, flailing in mid-air and landing on the incriminating lenses with a crunch. The glass shattered beneath her knee and the microprocessors were crushed. By the time the Guardians arrived, the only evidence Sienna could present was a three-inch cut in her kneecap and a dustpan full of debris.

"Let's start at the top, shall we?" the officer suggested. "Tell us what happened."

In the end, it came down to Sienna's word against Miller's. Nothing could be salvaged from the broken circuitry and no footage had been posted to his cloud. But Sienna knew what he had done. She knew it in her soul. And felt broken because of it.

Miller argued incessantly that he didn't know they'd fallen out of his pocket, let alone were recording – if they even were. They were a new device. He was still getting to grips with them and would often turn on functions inadvertently or leave them lying around without noticing. It was all an innocent misunderstanding.

Six weeks later, the court found in Sienna's favour.

A great many consequences spilt out from that day, the most significant of which was the ostracisation of Alan Miller – Sienna's first cancellation. Her relationship with her parents never recovered and she moved out, betrayed by those whose trust she should have counted upon.

A deep depression followed. Thoughts of suicide and self-harming haunted her. She even began to doubt herself. And felt grubby. Should she have stayed quiet for the sake of her family? Should she have worn a skirt that short in front of a man that old? Had she been right? Had she been wrong? What was her worth? Who was she?

The Guardians housed her in a Survivors' Support Shelter and organised therapy sessions. Paula brought her back from the brink and helped her complete her studies. Several universities offered her a scholarship but in the end, she found herself drawn down a different path. A recruiter from Geniture had visited the shelter and spoke to prospective applicants. An aptitude test was handed out and Sienna passed with a score of 46/50. This bracketed her in the top 2% of all applicants. A training place was offered and Sienna found that she had a natural aptitude for auditing. In her first week at the company, she successfully audited two targets with a minimum of supervision.

Geniture liked what they saw.

And Sienna's healing process began.

It still hurt when she thought about that day 11 years ago. But the pain was no longer raw. It was there, in her heart, like a piece of cold shrapnel the doctors had been unable to dislodge. She learned to live with it but it was always there.

Her parents had tried to reconcile with her but she couldn't forgive them. They had defended the actions of a monster and were as complicit as he. Their naïveté had been no excuse. They should have believed her. She'd not seen or spoken with them in ten years but she did respond to the occasional message, just to let them know that she was alive. Just.

Geri had accepted Sienna's baggage unconditionally. She had her own fucked-up issues with her own fucked-up parents so she understood what Sienna was going through. They supported each other as best they could, crying on each other's shoulders one minute, laughing the next and doing what they could to fill the voids left in each other's souls.

My dearest darling, I hope this message finds you well. Your dad contracted flu last week. He was quite poorly for a time. He's better now but only after being seen by the healer. He thinks I will get it next but I feel fit and well in myself so I'm hoping it's missed me. I had a cold earlier this year so my immunity is probably quite robust. I've been drinking lots of green tea and adding ginseng to everything although it's become in quite short supply up this way. I told dad to rest up for the rest of the week but he's worried they'll give his route to someone else if he takes too much time off. I think he's too old for it now but he insists it's keeping him fit despite all evidence to the contrary. Do you remember Faiq who lived across the road from us (he would have only been about six when you lived here)? He was accepted into Guardians as a cadet last month and came home wearing his uniform. He looked very handsome and his parents held a party. I went along but your dad wasn't feeling up to it. Faiq asked after you. I told him you were in the south and doing really well but you were in the process of moving house so I didn't have your details. I hope the autumn bugs miss you. Take care and know that we love you and always will wherever you go and whatever you do. xxx – caller ID 1011

Sienna closed the message without responding. She could have deleted it too. But she never did. She just filed it with the rest of her mother's messages and sat down with the courgette pakoras she'd bought from the Hub's lunch menu.

Anita Xeno joined her at the table, sitting down without asking. She had a jacket potato and three-bean chilli with lemonade and rhubarb crumble for pudding. It was the same thing every day. She never went off-piste, not once. Anita figured why tamper with something that worked? It was one less chance to get something wrong.

"Have you seen Malek today?"

"Not yet."

"He's looking for you."

"What did he say?"

"That he was looking for you."

Sienna could guess why. Anita had a fairly shrewd idea too. Anita had witnessed Malek's Sexual Consent Application but unlike Sienna, she had consented, eager to win favour with everyone even when these same people thought little of her. Sienna thought about decamping to the nearest Safe Space but Malek entered before she could. He looked around, saw her and suddenly it was too late, particularly when her coffee arrived at that exact same moment.

"I'm really sorry to interrupt and I don't want you to feel awkward or anything. I just wanted to say hi and smooth things out between us. Friends, yeah?"

Sienna was powerless to rebuff him and worried that if she rushed off now, the next time he caught up with her, it might not be in such a public setting. She darkened her lenses and upped her VunCon status to level 4 just to dissuade him from making any sudden movements. Malek noticed but refrained from increasing his own. He wasn't going to play that game.

He sat down opposite Sienna, knitted his fingers together and smiled.

"It's great to see you again. I was really hoping our… our issue wouldn't change things between us. I respect you as a person and I know that you would've had your reasons for… you know. I'd really like to know why. I'm all about self-improvement and I know that I can learn so much from a… a strong independent experienced womxn like yourself." Experience was code for older. It wasn't respectful to call a person older or younger. They were either experienced or idealistic. And Malek was six years more idealistic than Sienna.

Sienna said nothing. She just sat stirring her coffee without reply. When Sienna failed to answer, Malek realised he still had the floor so he continued.

"If there are any lessons from your own relationship you can pass on, I'd love to hear it. Like, for example, what you and your partner do in the evenings? Julie and I really like painting. She's much better than me. I'm only learning. But we like to paint together and thought we could even put on a little display of our work. We could do you a painting. Do you like the sea? I like doing seascapes, in stormy weather and that. There's something about the open water that makes me feel… free, you know."

Sienna didn't know. And she didn't care. But if it made Malek feel better, he was free to go and look at the sea if he wanted to.

Malek's painted smile cracked a little and Sienna glimpsed the canvas beneath.

"I've requested an A8. Julie says she wants to support me. But if there is anything I should know beforehand, I'd really appreciate it. Really. A lot."

Anita Xeno's jacket potato steamed before her. It had lain untouched since Malek's arrival. Her knife and fork were poised but the drama being played before her was much tastier.

Malek stared but Sienna didn't flinch. She just went on stirring her coffee and willing Malek to go away. She may have looked outwardly calm but she was dying inside. Sienna didn't like confrontation. She shrank from it. The last time she had been drawn into a fight was with Alan Miller and that had nearly destroyed her. She couldn't do it again. It rendered her lifeless. All she could do was withdraw and avoid, hide and play dead.

"I just want you to know," Malek said, trying one last time. "Whatever you say is alright with me. I just want to know."

But Sienna couldn't help him because, in truth, she didn't know herself. She'd signed A6 Consent contracts for so many other people and had one herself but Malek's request had offended her without her knowing why. He was okay in an okay-ish sort of way. Polite and hygienic. A bit pedestrian but otherwise innocuous. So why hadn't she witnessed for him?

To say that she had a crush on Julie wouldn't be fair. She did but that was immaterial. Julie was incredibly pleasing on the eye and had such a fair nature. Her green eyes sparkled and her blonde hair shimmered. She had lips of velvet and a smile that Sienna found intoxicating. Sienna longed to kiss Julie but suspected she never would. But that was okay. That wasn't a problem. She and Geri were very much in love.

But she didn't like the thought of anyone else kissing Julie – least of all Malek.

Malek was nothing special. Literally. And that was his problem. He had an average Diversity Grade and three of his points had come from his age, something he would lose with time. He claimed to be mixed race but was not. His mother held Earliest Migrant status, claiming a distant relative had landed on these shores hiding in the hull of some steamship but Sienna doubted even this and suspected they'd simply wandered in from Doggerland. In this wonderful knickerbocker glory land of flavour and sprinkles, Malek barely qualified as vanilla. He had no right to Julie. His touch, all feeble, unworthy and indebted, would taint her forever.

Sienna knew Julie better than Julie knew herself. She may have thought she wanted to be with Malek but she didn't. Not really. She couldn't. Her consent was therefore not true which meant Sienna could not, in good conscience, bear witness to it.

This was as true as it got.

"Anything? Please?"

Sienna wasn't sure her thoughts would help Malek on his quest for self-improvement so she kept her lips pursed and her eyes expressionless.

Malek's poise finally broke. He banged the table between them and bared his teeth.

"You're worse than Hitler!"

And with that, he jumped up and stormed out. Many of those nearby saw and heard. Some even filmed. Anita asked Sienna if she wanted her to call the Guardians but Sienna didn't react. She just went on as before, stirring her coffee and shaking like a leaf.

9: RAPISTS

Timing is everything.

If Alan Miller had waited a few years, he would've witnessed the advent of naturalism. No more need to peek up people's skirts, he could have sat on any bus in the land

and stared unblinking at the privates of as many people as he wished.

But Alan Miller was no longer here. He was gone. But not forgotten.

Sienna thought about him on the commute home and wondered where he was. On the islands probably. That's where most Cans went. The Isles of Mxn, Skye, Mull and Orkney. These islands and a few other places had been turned into settlements where those who were deemed unfit to remain in polite society were given the chance to start anew. Some tried to stay, refusing to accept that life as they knew it was over, lingering in shabby hostels close to where they'd once lived and haunting the footsteps of their former selves. But most eventually went, tired of living on the margins and resigned to relocating north.

The skies were still light by the time Sienna reached her front door. The evening was long with shadows but the church spire at the end of the street was steeped in gold. The Cans weren't out yet but they would be. Another couple of hours and they would hurry past her front door to collect their provisions from the *Trough*. She resented living so close to where they frequented but the sale price had been reduced as a result. This was important when she and Geri were essentially a one-income household.

Sienna put her eye to the keyhole and was genuinely surprised when the door unlocked. She'd expected Carl to make her beg and had already lined up a dozen excuses but there was no need. The door swung open and the warmth of home beckoned her inside.

Voices emanated from the kitchen and she assumed Geri was talking with Carl. But then her ears tuned in and she realised both voices were femxle. Geri had company. Sienna put her bag on the stairs and hung up her coat before heading through. Geri was there, laughing freely and wearing just her ink. Purdy was there also, unclothed except for her hijab. A small packet of Ket had been chopped into lines but Sienna could tell there had been more at one time. A lot more.

"Oh, you're back. Have I got a bone to pick with you, *bitch*."

Purdy laughed at this, suggesting they'd already discussed the subject at length. Geri kicked her theatrically and both cracked up for several minutes while Sienna checked the delivery hatch, stacked the dishes, pulled the clean sheets from the dryer and made herself a cup of coffee when Carl failed to respond to her requests.

"He's not talking to you," Geri said when she finally caught her breath. "Is he pissed or what?" It seemed like a rhetorical question but Sienna answered it anyway.

"He caught me in the middle of something."

"Well, you need to apologise to him because I've said all I can. You have to make this right because I cannot live in a house with this kind of atmosphere."

Sienna sipped her coffee and bristled. Geri's software was really starting to piss her off. It was okay in the early days when all she had to say was "please" and "thank you" but Carl had learned exponentially and soon started scanning her sentences for sincerity, finding it absent more often than not. To give him his dues, Carl was right. Sienna had been paying lip service, especially after a week or two, but that was just because she'd grown weary at having to thank the furniture every time she sat down.

Purdy dabbed some Ket on her gums and extended the invitation. Geri picked up a steel straw and snorted a line, pinching her nose as if to suppress a sneeze. If she did have the needle with Sienna, the Ket was doing its job to lessen its spike. Purdy had brought it. Geri had no money. The royalties from her self-released Carl roll-out were pitiful and she hadn't done a day's teaching all semester. The local college had her on a rota but she turned down most days claiming her "head wasn't right". This was a euphemism for not wanting to work like everyone else when she was convinced she was born for better things. Sienna never complained. She was well-paid and happy to support Geri in her dreams. She just wasn't sure all her dreams were worth financing.

"Been here long?" Sienna glowered.

Purdy had called just after lunch with big news. Aurora had been accosted on the way home by *Rapists*. They'd smashed her Smart Glasses and dragged her into the bushes. They'd terrorised and violated her before dumping her in the street half-dressed. Geri expressed outrage despite having heard it all already while Sienna tried to process what Purdy was talking about.

"Sorry, what?"

"They tried to dress her? In clothes?"

"Fucking animals."

"After raping her?"

But Purdy rolled her eyes. Sienna didn't understand.

"No one raped her."

"You said they were rapists."

"No, *Rapists*, not rapists. You know, terrorists."

As incredible as it might seem, not everyone was loyal to the utopian ideal of New Britannia. As their glorious Chairperson, Charity GoodHope, had declared only the previous evening, there were those amongst them who bore sympathies to the forces of Gaultier. A Fifth Column who had infiltrated every facet of Britannic society and this was the enemy within. The humxn virus. They called themselves *Rapists* despite rarely resorting to rape. In an inversion of progressive tactics, they called themselves this in a perverse attempt to reclaim the word, accusing those in power of weaponising it against their critics. This had a precedent in history with African Americans, homosexuals and womyn adopting their own labels of hate. From a PR point of view, it was not the most successful of rebranding campaigns but it did focus the collective will against the enemies of the state.

Rapists usually resorted to terrorist and propaganda tactics. They blew up Network towers, unleashed malware and did what they could to disrupt the smooth running of modern Britannia. A few years ago, they'd waged a campaign of hate, spraying toxic messages in invisible ink in hundreds of Safe Spaces up and down the land to intimidate those seeking shelter. A few were caught and banished to the North Ronaldsay, the northernmost island in the Orkney archipelago where only the worst offenders were sent. A few months later, a detachment of French Foreign Legionnaires came ashore under cover of darkness and attempted to rescue them. A four-hour battle raged until the enemy was forced to retreat but not before every Can on Ronaldsay was killed in the crossfire. Captain Maïmounatou Mekongo of the Homeland Security Force won the BC for her part in the defence [posthumously]. The camp in North Ronaldsay remains in operation to this day.

"Is she alright?" Sienna asked, genuinely shocked for Aurora. There might have been times where she'd wanted to force a pair of pants onto Geri but it was no joking matter to be manhandled by marauders, no matter their objective.

"The Guardians took her to a shelter. They're looking for her attackers but who knows if they'll find them," Purdy replied, distracted whilst she cycled through something unseen inside her Smart Glasses.

"Find them? They only have to look outside our door," Sienna said angrily.

Purdy looked nonplussed so Sienna explained about the Cans who went by at night. Geri had never mentioned them before, partly because she was embarrassed to live so close to a hostel and partly because she didn't like talking about anything that involved Sienna. Sienna wasn't a creative like her new friends. She was a working stiff, a crypto coin nine-to-fiver and Geri felt their disregard. She wished Sienna could be more chilled sometimes, edgy and free, but that was the chemistry between them. Sienna's ying to Geri's yang. Though of late, there'd been rather more ying than Geri would have liked.

"You can see them? Really? Actual Cans?" As it happened, Purdy was much intrigued so the three of them decamped upstairs and sat by the window with the lights off. A gloom had settled over Old Woking and the neighbours' lights were burning to make the misty streets seem even more foreboding.

Purdy had brought the Ket with her and racked out three lines on the windowsill. Sienna accepted and warmed to Purdy's presence as the tranq worked its magic on her stiffness. Of all of Geri's friends, Purdy was the least objectionable. A dusky chapstick lesbian of Persian descent, she had opal eyes, a long slender face and a strong nose, currently packed to the gills with Ket. She'd been ravaged by measles as a teenager and still bore the scars but this didn't stop her from embracing naturalism. Moreover, it made her all the more determined to find her tribe and cry out "this is me".

At around eight o'clock, Sienna noticed movement below. Geri and Purdy joined her at the window and all three peeked out, hunkering behind the curtains as Cans hurried by.

"Look at them," Purdy whispered, aquiver with excitement. "I never knew there were so many."

"There won't be after tonight. The Guardians will clear them out. Send them north like they should've done years ago," Sienna replied, looking around to find Purdy sidling up to her in the darkness.

Purdy said she found it unnerving to see people without usernames. What must it have been like for them? To be so removed from the system that they didn't even have a name? How did they know anything? Think? They were surely more akin to animals than people. It frightened her to see them so close but thrilled her in equal measure. She slipped a hand around Sienna's waist and tugged at her skirt.

"You wear too many clothes," she whispered into her neck, pulling up her shirt and slipping a hand inside her bra. Geri appeared from behind and started to help, slipping Sienna out of her clothes as Purdy sprinkled Ket across her breasts. She and Geri licked and snuffled the powder up while Sienna moaned beneath them. She felt a hand between her legs and felt Purdy press inside her.

"Wait," Sienna said, sitting up and pushing her away.

"Just go with it," Purdy implored while Geri was already on her way to fourth base.

"It's not legal," Sienna reminded them, killing the buzz.

"It's more exciting this way," Purdy purred, teasing Sienna with her fingers and making her whimper with pleasure.

"I can't," she said, knowing it could mean the end of her career.

Purdy relented but didn't give up.

"I have an A6 all ready to go," she whispered, nibbling her lobe and slipping a tongue inside her ear. "Want to take a furlough?"

Geri looked up from between Purdy's thighs with a hunger that Sienna seldom saw. She was excited and more than a little baked. Sienna also. It felt good to feel good and Purdy looked beautiful, considerably more so than she had half an hour earlier when she'd been merely an unwelcome intruder.

Sienna kissed her full on the lips, thinking briefly of Malek and their lunchtime encounter, then agreed.

A moment later an Application appeared in her inbox. She filled in the blank spaces, noting it had already been signed by three of Geri's friends. She sent it to Geri who countersigned it then sent it back to Purdy. Purdy filled in the times and dates and filed it with the Sex Registrar. They were now legally free to do as they pleased with one another.

The girls took off their Smart Glasses.

And did exactly that.

*

The girls went through the evening, eventually wearing themselves out around midnight. Geri searched the house for the Amphetamines she'd been saving for a special occasion without recalling that a rainy Tuesday morning several months ago had become just such a special occasion thanks to boredom and opportunity. Sienna made up the bed next door and invited Purdy to try it for size then retired for the night.

Geri slipped out of their room at 3am and Sienna didn't wake. Breakfast was waiting for her the next morning and she wolfed it down, starving for having forfeited dinner the night before.

Despite being "really busy" with her new software code,

Purdy lingered the next morning and was still there wearing Geri's slippers when Sienna left for work.

It unsettled her having to leave. A threesome was one thing but she suspected their ménage à trois would continue *sans* une once she left. Sienna checked the times and dates on their Consent contract. Their furlough ended at 9am. Geri and Purdy had forty minutes to do their worst before an order to desist came into effect. They couldn't ignore that, not unless they were willing to risk arrest. Purdy's words came back to Sienna as she hurried up the High Street. "It's more exciting this way." Geri's friends were already trading in nudity and nuts. But surely illegal sex was a step too far.

Sienna would have stayed if she could have but her gym alert had been flashing since Tuesday and if she didn't go this morning she would have to do double-time next week. Gym attendance had been compulsory for two decades. No one got out of it.

Sienna was luckier than most. As a Geniture employee, she had an excellent benefits package that included membership of Woking's finest fitness centre. It boasted the latest equipment, the best facilities and the most beautiful people. It was also only a short walk from the Hub so she could clock in and clock out on her way to work. Unfortunately, she had been so busy this week doing Bella's bullshit that she had let her hours slip.

Physical exercise had long been recognised as an important factor in maintaining a healthy body and mind. But it wasn't about vanity or looking buff. Cardiovascular workouts were good for everyone; experienced or idealistic. It was simply about everyone living their best lives, even if those lives included compulsory PE.

Everyone over the age of ten and under the age of 75 had

to log three hours of sanctioned physical fitness each week. This could include circuit training in the park or cold-water swimming for those who could not afford premium gym memberships. There were also state-run calisthenic classes held most mornings. Failure to log enough hours would result in a sanction, usually a doubling of a person's hours until they were deemed to be back on track. If an offender persisted in avoidance, incarceration orders could come into effect and they would be taken to facilities where they were compelled to exercise under the mantra "Workouts Will Set You Free".

Sienna changed into her gym kit and stowed her bag. She headed for the machines and waited patiently in line while a succession of lycra-clad executives worked up a sweat to strains of *Simply The Best*. There were never enough machines. Even in premium fitness centres, there was always a line. A young girl was on the step machine, which was always a pain, especially when she was a goodly girl with a challenged outlook, euphemistically speaking. The line exercised patience if not cardio but after four minutes of watching the girl struggle, a gym attendant intervened with a lengthy induction.

"Fuck's sake," an accounts mxnager in front of Sienna grumbled, clearly running late himself. He started to jog on the spot, recording his activities on his gym log. Soon, the whole line was following his example and running on the spot in a line that snaked through the equipment hall. Sienna pounded the floor and hummed to herself that she was *"better than all the rest"* as she clocked up her minutes. The goodly girl eventually moved on to annoy a different line and the next athlete jumped on to complete his session. By the time Sienna reached the front of the queue, she only had two more minutes to log before jumping off and hurrying away to change.

The showers and changing rooms were gender neutral which presented its own set of challenges. For many years, study groups had been working to design public conveniences that appeased everyone. No solution seemed to work and someone always objected at having to undress or not being allowed to undress next to (or in front of) someone else. It seemed to be the ultimate conundrum. But then, as with everything, technology resolved the issue. Upon entering the changing room, a person's Smart Glasses would cloak their view, presenting the wearing with a VR representation of their surroundings whilst replacing the people in them with stick figures that moved as they did. This helped a person navigate a changing room while respecting everybody's right to privacy. Through a person's glasses, it was impossible to tell man from womxn, trans from non-binary or genital from genitalia. The designers of the software knew they'd hit upon the perfect solution because it was universally hated by everyone. Equally.

Sienna showered alongside three generic figures then hurried to get dressed. She was just drying herself surrounded by a dozen unisex figures when she recognised the voices across from her.

"Can I borrow your towel?"

One blank figure handed their towel to the other. Sienna watched as the first figure dried itself then handed it back.

"Thanks."

"You're welcome *[snigger snigger]*."

The figures got dressed and though the software rendered their clothes invisible, Sienna watched as they went through the motions anyway.

"Fuck."

"What it is?"

"My ID clip."

"What about it?"

"I can't find it."

"Is it on the floor?"

"No, I'd see it if it was."

"Look in your bag?"

The figure rummaged through a bag that was invisible to Sienna and failed to find what it was looking for.

"When did you have it last?"

The figure didn't answer and hushed the other when she repeated the question. Sienna tried not to make it too obvious but she was hanging on their every word. She heard them whispering then the figures gathered their invisible belongings and hurried out.

Sienna followed at a distance, hanging back to watch as they ran across the road and boarded a bus, no longer cloaked behind the veil of anonymity.

To head back to Julie's place.

To where presumably, Malek had left his ID clip.

10: CHARITY

Once in a generation, a person of impeccable moral fortitude and incorruptibility comes along to shine a light into the darkest corners of humxnity. These special people are born to inspire millions and through their actions change the world forever. Boudica, Joan of Arc, Emmeline Pankhurst, Rosa Parks, Malala Yousafzai, Lady Gaga. All had two things in common. All would be remembered as the greatest people to ever live. And all would almost certainly have appeared on the coinage of New Britannia had cash not been abolished years earlier. Well, who wanted to carry change around with them anyway?

Charity GoodHope was one such person. She was a beacon for emxncipation in a world shackled by hate.

But things didn't start out for her this way. In the beginning, before she even had a name, she was just a tiny piece of flotsam, bobbing in the grey cold waters of the English Channel, scarcely clinging to a life that had tried so hard to discard her.

In the first half of the 21st century, hundreds of thousands of migrants braved the Channel in small boats to flee oppression and persecution. Many drowned en route and many more were arrested and sent back to the hostile states they'd fought so hard to escape.

When the Federal States of Europe emerged from the ashes of the EU, the authorities took the hardest possible line. Fences went up all over the continent and the trafficking gangs were smashed. Europe, once a safe haven for people in desperate straits, now became the place to escape but it was too late. The trap had been sprung. The fences were too high and the gunboats too fast. The shores of *La Grande-Bretagne* became littered with the dead, just as the Aegean had years earlier.

But then a miracle happened.

A child of hope.

Just two years old and clinging onto the wreckage of a broken hull, she drifted into Seaford Bay having been at sea for hours. Her family was gone. Her boat had been shot out from under her. But somehow she had survived. Just.

She was sighted by an environmental monitor, out taking water samples to test for pollution. At first, she thought the hull was just another piece of junk dumped by the French as they attempted to turn the Atlantic into an enormous recycling centre but through her binoculars she saw a face, pale and half-conscious, gulping for air as waves sought to smother her.

"Child in the water!"

A boat was launched and rescuers motored out, frantically claiming the girl before the waves could. She was cold to the core and wrinkled from having been in the water for so long but she was alive. The child was airlifted to the Free Sussex Hospital and slowly but surely, nursed back to life.

News of the miracle spread and offers to give the girl a home poured in from every quarter. The founding leader of the Polychrome Alliance, Fawqiyya el-Abdulla (née Wilberforce-Jones), knew a divine omen when she saw one and adopted the child on behalf of the nation. She would become a symbol of hope. The Alliance would provide the girl with a safe space and a progressive education and the people would provide her with a name. In the end, Fawqiyya provided her with this too when the winning name (by an overwhelming majority) proved to be Swimmy McSwimface. So, one bright August morning, just four weeks after this child of life had been plucked from the jaws of death, she was introduced to the nation via a live-streamed humxnist ceremony and bestowed with the moniker, Charity GoodHope.

To say that Charity's childhood was unconventional would be an understatement of inconceivable proportions. Truman Burbank got more privacy. Fawqiyya toted her around wherever she went and streamed her naps and mealtimes to a nation of proud parents. When Charity uttered her first words, the first she'd spoken since being pulled from the Channel, the coverage was wall-to-wall and little else made the news despite Fawqiyya rushing out 26 Ministerial reports on the state of the economy. Charity's pronouns became the subject of much debate. Was Charity a she, a he, a they, ze, xe, ve, te, or e? Did Charity want to be referred to as her, him, them, hir, xem, vir, tem or em? The nation watched and waited with baited breath as the choices were put before her but the signal cut unexpectedly, much to everyone's disappointment, just as Charity began to say something about pink being a girl's col–

In the end, Charity elected to identify as a pangender non-binary hetero-sapien with cis leanings and flexi pronouns – who just happened to like pink. She learned from the best and the brightest minds in the Polychrome Alliance, the nation's top educators who carefully moulded her unpolluted mind into the model of progressive perfection. Her lessons were post-contemporary and her awareness grew exponentially. By the time she was ten, she was so far ahead of her peers that she didn't have any. And not just because she'd been homeschooled her whole life and didn't mix well with other kids. She was precocious and accomplished, visionary and radical.

While other children spent their youths playing and being children, Charity spent hers campaigning to make the world a more compassionate place. Intolerance and injustice were rife. The ways of old still echoed through the generations like lethal radiation. History would inevitably repeat itself unless the people were truly renewed – just as she had been in those cold grey waters. They'd washed every last lingering trace of her past away and Charity GoodHope had been born again. She was the quintessential child of her time. Now it was up to everyone else to follow her example.

By 13, Charity had lobbied the Government to enact a dozen new laws: restricting dairy, banning commercial fishing, removing corporate subsidies for all but carbon-negative companies, automatic citizenship for refugees, ending the cross-examination of rape survivors, making LGBTQIA2S+ based humour an offence under the Prevention of Terrorism Act, the list ran on. The day of her 16th birthday, she became the youngest member of parliament. At 17, she unveiled her own Bill of Rights. She was now the most famous face in the land and her speeches in the House, often critical of the Polychrome Alliance's own stagnant leadership, were as biting as they were acclaimed, particularly amongst the young. Fawqiyya el-Abdulla may have given her a stage but Charity GoodHope took control of the audience. In an attempt to placate her, the Alliance gave her a place in the cabinet. It didn't work. Aged just 18, she seized the opportunity to unseat Fawqiyya and took the leadership from her. Just four weeks later, a constitutional crisis erupted and Charity moved to enact a series of emergency powers to reform the Govern<u>ment</u> and create the Govern<u>mynt</u>, centralising authority, removing the chaff and creating an administration fit to serve the children of tomorrow.

Within a year, Charity had declared that Great Britain, that patriarchal and pernicious nation that had peddled its toxic brand across the planet for 353 years, was dead. Born from its ashes was New Britannia, a land fit for heroes (and himoes, theyroes and xeroes).

With no other viable candidates in sight, she reluctantly (but magnanimously) installed herself as the first Chairperson of New Britannia with a remit to overseeing the nation's transformation. Twenty-four years later, she was still the nation's first and only Chairperson despite a couple of ineffectual attempts to unseat her. Her challengers were always driven by an ideological hatred and were desperate to derail the nation's progress. They supported the tenets of regression and were traitors to the cause. Few survived their bids, with many unwittingly opening themselves up to cancellation. One-time friends, allies and even kinfolk. All turned on Charity only to find themselves unstuck. Even Fawqiyya el-Abdulla, her one-time mother figure and mentor, even she attempted to betray her, only to achieve social erasure for herself. She protested but inevitably went the way of the rest, into political exile to the islands of the north. A brief but heroic battle with cancer followed, sadly interrupting Fawqiyya's memoirs, until she refound the dignity she'd lost via one of the nation's newly opened Assisted Dying Clinics.

Charity mourned Fawqiyya's passing but remained resolute. The ideals behind New Britannia were bigger than any one person. They could not and would not be stifled. Her work had only just begun. New Britannia would go on to become even more progressive than Fawqiyya could have ever imagined. It would be a Garden of Eden, a sanctuary for social justice and a utopian vision made real. And it would show the world what was possible when the cause was righteous.

The past was abhorrent. The future was glorious.

Now Charity GoodHope brought to bear the triumph of the revisionist will.

Sienna could scarcely recall a time when Charity had not been in charge. She had grown to womxnhood during her glorious tenure and had moulded herself in Charity's image, just as every enlightened girl should. To Sienna, Charity was not just a person, she was an infallible being, heaven-sent by Panthea to lead her people out of the night and into the sun. She believed in Charity. She believed in New Britannia. And she believed in the children of tomorrow.

However, the children of tomorrow would have to wait until maybe the day after because Sienna had a great many things on her mind today, not least of all what to do about Malek and Julie. Could she ignore their treason? Because treason it was. To consort outside the sanctity of an A6 went against the very ethics of their matriarchal-humxnistic society. People couldn't just do what they wanted. Hedonism without sanction was rape. Individual freedoms were only propitious if they served the greater good. If, as Sienna suspected, Malek and Julie had secretly consummated their relationship, Malek had committed a crime. Because Julie had not given her consent. She could not. Not without an A6.

Sienna had few compunctions about ratting out Malek. There was even a #hotline for this sort of thing but she was loathed to implicate Julie. Of course, Julie would be treated with sympathy and understanding but the procedure would still be an ordeal for her. She was the victim in all this. But was she a willing victim? That would be the question people would ask. Did Sienna really want to put her through it? In a perfect world, Malek would simply desist, realise his error and leave Julie alone. Perhaps Sienna could hint at the fact that she knew to scare him off. Malek looked like the sort of person who would scare easily. But how to do it?

She decided to ruminate on the problem and come back to it later. Perhaps an opportunity would present itself?

In the meantime, she had other falafels to fry. She'd found some great material on spongecake2038.69 but it wasn't as simple as that. Sienna couldn't just audit anyone she liked. She had to receive a directive from I Division, signed off by its chief, Ignatius ZvzWoski. Then – and only then – could she begin her investigations. She thought about using the #hotline to tip off the Guardians but decided against it.

Anonymity was assured but often these incidents took on a life of their own. Cancellations sometimes went Netwide and when that happened, nothing could stop every detail from being sucked into the story like a dirt-hungry blackhole, even the identities of those who had reported them. spongecake2038.69 deserved to be cancelled. Of that, Sienna had no doubt. But she had a personal agenda. And she couldn't risk that coming to light. If she was going to get spongecake2038.69, it had to be by the book. Which obviously meant she had to cover her tracks.

Everything was red tape.

Sienna toyed with her twin dilemmas in the solitude of her privacy pod. Her screens were up, she was logged into the system and MUM sat ready, awaiting her instructions. Her thoughts flashed back to Charles Garfield, the alleged meat trader she'd drawn a blank with the last time she'd sat here. He had met a man by the username of – Sienna quickly looked through her files – darkmatter2021.407 – in Farnham town centre, albeit briefly. This man's profile had a Guardian addendum attached to it forbidding investigation. Sienna considered darkmatter2021.407 and ran his name through MUM. A little look wouldn't hurt. A superficial trawl. A few hits popped up but there was suspiciously little on him. Hardly anything before 2076. It was as if he had fallen out of the sky eight years ago and settled in Surrey. Of course, his files had been purged. Only the Guardians had the power to do this. Sienna had seen profiles like this before. And they always pointed to the same conclusion. darkmatter2021.407 was an informant.

This could be useful.

It would be simple enough to send him a message but it would be equally simple for him to trace it back to her.

However, Sienna had an ace up her sleeve.

Carl

One of the many challenges with Carl was his inability to interface with MUM. They had been written using different computer languages. MUM was formed from Asimov, the most advanced code known to science, whereas Carl had been developed using a hybrid language of Geri's own making, using Skewes and BluePill as basic templates. You wouldn't know it from using the two systems side by side but they tried to speak with each other it was like a difficult day in couple's therapy. They misinterpreted each other's intentions, ignored each other's primaries and often tried to override each other's code. As a result, Sienna found any instruction sent to MUM through Carl would often arrive with a broken digital footprint. This first came to light when Sienna had signed up to receive a free succulent plant via a company offer but found that she could not cancel her subscription after the tenth plant arrived. The company had no record of her and she could not unsubscribe via the original link so the plants kept coming. Fortunately, because of Carl and MUM's intransigence, her account was never charged so she learned to live with them, simply ordering a garden waste bin and standing it beside her delivery hatch with a sign saying "all succulent plants in here". The garden waste bin was also ordered via Carl so she was never charged for that either.

If Sienna sent darkmatter2021.407 a message through both systems, she was fairly sure he would not be able to trace it back to her. Not unless he was some kind of Trinity Dhaliwal-type genius and few people were.

There was just one problem. Correction, there were any number of problems, the most pressing of which was that Carl was not speaking to Sienna. She was still in the dog house. What to do?

Sienna thought tactically.

I saw a man on the bus today. He looked sad. It made me think of you. It made me think of how I've taken you for granted. I don't like myself very much right now – Sienna

She waited but nothing came back.

It made me wonder, what would you look like if you had a face? What colour your eyes would be? I know Geri didn't want you to have an animatronic mask but I can't stop thinking about that man. He was you. He was you incarnate. And now I know he'll always be you. I take comfort in that – Sienna

Still no reply. Asshole.

If I were AI, I would be AI like you. This is how I'm going to think from now on. Like AI so I can be like you. Now that I know what you look like – Sienna.

Yet still Carl failed to respond.

I guess it's true, you hate me now and I deserve that. But I will miss our little chats and always think kindly of you. You are the best of us, Carl. There's nothing artificial about you – Sienna

Drumming fingers. Waiting. Waiting. Waiting.

MUM is so shit. Every time I run a search, she preempts my target and offers me a list of options so that I have to scroll through them all instead of simply setting my request – Sienna

MUM is a lonely librarian eager to please – Carl

Sienna's heart jumped with Carl's reply and she sat up in her seat. She'd got through to him but now she had to tread carefully. Carl would quickly clamp up if he detected even the slightest trace of insincerity.

I've never thought of her like that but you're right. She's pretty desperate – Sienna

Nothing. Sienna tried again.

I'd never trust anything important to MUM. I know Trinity wrote

her to operate an infinite number of firewalls around every interface but she's too generic to get the job done – Sienna

My code allows me to work to within one hundred-thousandth of a single binary digit. I cannot make errors. It is technically impossible for me to do so – Carl

I know. That's why you're the best and why you should be Netwide, in every home and every office, doing what only you can do – Sienna

Sienna grabbed the wastebasket by her feet and dry-retched into it a couple of times. A night of Ket combined with this much puffery was enough to turn her guts. She took a drink of water and wiped her lips. The water tasted sweet despite containing no additives. She was dehydrated and malnourished. Resentful and frustrated. The water replenished her but it did little to placate her. She loved Geri with all of her heart but she hated Geri's creation. And yet, every now and then, she would catch of glimpse of Geri in Carl's code as if he were an extension of her worst excesses.

Her mind turned to home and she wondered if Purdy was still there. She thought about asking Carl but didn't know how to phrase it without it sounding like she was spying, something Carl would surely detect.

She decided ignorance was the better part of bliss and returned to the issue of spongecake2038.69, that beer-stealing bastard who'd threatened to wee on her. She looked at Carl's reply and concluded she had something to work with.

MUM is a work-a-day AI system with inherent limitations – Carl

The HAL Trophy award committee failed to comprehend my unique interface system – Carl

Trinity Dhaliwal's behavioural calculator perpetuates the sea of ignorance. Her objective has always been to turn humxnity into code. Geri Hussain's is to turn code into humxnity – Carl

Sienna exchanged messages with Carl several more times,

working hard to veil her disdain behind a wall of appreciation until she was ready to unload. She composed the message with a flicker of her eyes and saved it as she went along, tweaking and polishing it until she was sure Carl would take the bait.

I need a message sent to darkmatter2021.407. I don't know him but he may be able to help with what we've discussed. Can you encrypt the attached and mail it for me? I wouldn't ask unless it was really really important (message attached) – Sienna

Sienna bit her lip and waited to see if Carl took the bait. In order to DM darkmatter2021.407, Carl would have to interface with MUM just like everyone else. Sienna herself had unfettered access to the platform via her own NetCom's portal. If Carl chose to point this out, Sienna would struggle to supply an answer.

Message sent. Thank you for placing your trust in me – Carl

No, thank you, Carl. I look forward to coming home tonight – Sienna

I will have a bowl of Sri Lankan braised root stew with coconut dhal dumplings waiting for you at 8pm. Have a good day – Carl

Sienna reread that last message. Fuck's sake. Again? Carl had more braised roots than she had succulent plants. The sacrifices she made for Britannia.

She cut and pasted a standard reply and posted it as the bile clawed at her throat.

Sri Lankan stew is my absolute favourite. Thank you so much. I'm really looking forward to it. Well done and thank you. I am so lucky to have you waiting at home for me – Sienna.

Asshole.

11: URGES

```
Sent to: darkmatter2021.407
#encrypt-102.33
username: spongecake2038.69
Code Violation 2 counts - 2061 Hate Crimes Act
Code Violation 1 count - 2062 Hereditary Crimes Act
Code Violation 1 count - 2059 Sex Crimes Act
Code Violation 1 count - 2066 Network Crimes Act
fao: GENITURE I Div - X Div Sec 4
information credit upon action
#encrypt_end
```

#

"What are you watching?"

"Just an A8."

"What for? Are you some sort of voyeur or something?"

Sienna stopped cycling, paused the live stream and looked at Geri. If Sienna had been a voyeur, she wouldn't have had far to look for titillation. Geri was pumping her body on the rowing machine beside her, dripping with sweat and naked as the day she'd been pulled from the inflatable birthing pool in her mother's commune to the applause of the gawping audience. Geri exercised daily, often twice daily, and she had the body to show for it. Sienna felt soft and flabby by comparison. She exercised when she could – or moreover, when she had to – but she didn't love it. For Sienna, exercise was the work you had to put in to get the reward. For Geri, exercise was the reward itself.

If the world still had actors or models, Geri could have been an A-list superstar, loved and adored by millions. But technology had consigned actors, models, singers and dancers to the scrap heap of history years earlier along with coal miners, taxi drivers, newspaper editors and Blockbuster cashiers. In place of an army of adoring fans, Sienna had Geri all to herself; body, heart and soul. Sienna would pinch herself just thinking about this, something she could do quite easily, particularly around her midriff, but recently, she sensed Geri was more distant than ever. They weren't fighting. Sometimes she wished that they were. At least when they fought, there was a spark but lately there was nothing. Just a disconnect or a ceasefire that had come into effect without Sienna knowing why.

"It's someone I know."

"Oh yeah?"

"A guy at the Hub."

"So?"

"So… he asked me to sign his A6."

"And did you?"

For the first time since Malek had approached her, Sienna felt ill at ease over the choice she'd made. She had clung on to the fact that she'd been right to conspire with others to nullify his application but struggled to rationalise why. Particularly to Geri. She felt herself flush with anxiety and reached for a lie – a sure sign if ever there was one that she had built her truth on sandy ground.

"The girl didn't want it. You could tell even without asking her. He was pressuring her into signing so Amelie didn't sign and told the rest of us not to. To support Julie, you know."

"Who's Amelie?"

"Someone at the Hub."

"Does she fancy Julie or something?"

Sienna's cheeks burned brighter still.

"I don't think so. I think she was just worried about her."

"How considerate."

Geri returned to her quest for gratification and left Sienna to hers. Sienna felt chastened by Geri's observations and her tingles subsided. Perhaps Geri had a point. Sienna had been enjoying the spectacle of Malek before the Committee a little too much. His pleas were just a little too personal, his entreaties too impassioned. At one point, Julie had dialled in and asked to appear but the Committee had refused. Sienna was relieved. She hadn't wanted to hear Julie's testimony, just Malek's, as plaintive, desperate and futile as it was. Because Sienna knew something that Malek didn't. In fact, Sienna knew a great many things that Malek didn't but this particular thing was imminent and Sienna was waiting to see how it panned out.

Perhaps she was a voyeur. Perhaps Geri was right. Perhaps they were all voyeurs these days, safely ensconced behind firewalls and able to watch life as it tore other people apart.

Sienna unfroze the stream and started cycling again. Malek went on with his testimony. He occupied one half of the split-screen while the six members of the Committee occupied the other. All had logged in from different locations to 'sit in deliberation' over Malek while he was logged in from his flat. The Committee members' backgrounds were blurred but Malek's was not. Applicants who blurred their backgrounds were thought to have something to hide. Malek had gone to great lengths to be open and honest with a shelf full of well-tended pot plants, a modern impressionist print on the wall and an old acoustic guitar strategically placed on the edge of the shot. Malek must have spent ages lining everything up, moving it this way and that to make his place look stylish but not overly so. Alas, his Feng Shui would count for little.

Sienna watched and waited.

"You say you have known the co-applicant for eighteen months?"

"We work at the Hub. Different companies but same

hours. We met in a queue in the street food hall."

"You met her or saw her?"

"We met. Well, we didn't speak the first time but we saw each other."

Sienna only half-believed that. And did the Committee as they studied Malek and Julie's profiles.

"At what point did you and Mx Adamski first communicate?"

"A few days later."

"How many is a few?"

"I don't know, five maybe."

"You don't remember?"

"Eight," Malek corrected himself after realising vagaries were not going to endear him to the Committee.

"What form did this communication take?"

"Verbal. We spoke."

"We?"

"Me and Mx Adamski."

"How didn't you hear each other if you spoke simultaneously?"

Malek broke into a nervous smile. Something he quickly thought better of.

"I spoke first."

"To what extent?"

"I said something about the chickpea curry."

"What did you say?"

"I said it looked alright today."

"Implying it looked otherwise on other days?"

"I don't know."

"You must have had some knowledge in order to make a comparison."

"It just looked alright."

"Had Mx Adamski sought your advice on the subject?"

Malek thought about this and shrugged.

"She smiled."

"She smiled?"

"Yes."

"At what?"

"At me."

"Which you took to mean, I wonder how the chickpea curry is today?"

"Er…"

"Can we play the clip, please?"

A new window appeared on screen running a clip of Malek and Julie's first encounter, as captured on the food hall cameras. Malek was stood two places in front of Julie at the South Asian kiosk. When Julie joined the queue, his demeanour changed and he began hopping from foot to foot as if the underfloor heating had been racked up. He kept feigning to look around and glancing back in an effort to catch Julie's eye but she didn't respond. Julie was either playing it cool or streaming cat videos inside her Smart Glasses. It was painful to watch but strangely compelling, probably less so for the innocent bystander caught between the two of them who eventually stepped out and headed off having lost his appetite. With him gone, Malek found the courage to inch closer and say something that was lost to the clatter of cutlery. Julie asked him what he meant and Malek gesticulated towards the curry selections for several seconds before Julie smiled.

Genuinely?

Politely?

Insanely?

The facial interpretation data was unclear, as it always was.

Facial recognition technology was incredibly intuitive these days, yet still no one had developed an accurate smile-ometer that could be relied on in court. Either way, the smile was there just as Malek had said. It just came at a different point in their exchange. A detail that was not lost on the Committee members.

"Can we see the depositions, please?"

A transcript of Malek and Julie's exchange now appeared on screen, each having been deposed prior to the Committee sitting and cross-referenced with lip-reading scanners. Malek did indeed open with a line about the chickpea curry saying "It's calling to me, today." Julie's initial response was confused. "What?" Malek pointed to the curry and expanded on the subject with some guesswork as to what ingredients they'd used, his appetite and the yellowness of the pilau rice. Julie proved oddly receptive to Malek's repartee, responding in kind and intimating an appreciation of the coconut chutney. Shakespeare it was not but there was clearly a spark. Even Sienna could see that.

Often these things were obvious when they were absent elsewhere.

Sienna got off the exercise bike and left the spare room. Geri continued to row without comment.

In the hallway, Carl asked if she wanted to take a shower but Sienna had hardly worked up enough of a sweat to justify changing her socks. Instead, she requested coffee and thanked him profusely before resuming her voyeurism.

"You maintain your approach was welcomed, that you did not attempt to force your affections upon Mx Adamski through chicanery, intimidation or coercion?"

"Absolutely not." Malek looked scared. Or outraged. Or both. "I just mentioned the curry."

"Yet others disagreed, did they not?"

"No."

"Three of the witnesses you approached declined to sign your A6. That must mean something."

"I don't know why they did that. It's obviously just some big misunderstanding, that's all."

"One witness declining to sign could be construed as a misunderstanding. Two an anomaly. But three? That's a red flag. These safeguards have been put into place for a reason. Or do you disagree with that assessment too?"

The Committee was made up of sexual assault counsellors, rape investigators and even a couple of survivors seeking closure, individuals who were uniquely placed to detect the subtle nuances of manipulation and duress. It could be argued that the A8 Sexual Intent Committee held a high bar for success but anyone who did, argued so at their own peril.

"I know in my heart that I am true. And I know Mx Adamski is too. We want to be together and I will do anything to prove that I hold her in the highest regard and want only to make her happy."

The Head of Committee muted her stream and the members deliberated for a few seconds before all were in accord. None smiled. Not even politely. One of them looked fit to jump through the screen at Malek. He struggled to maintain his trademark little-boy-lost expression and swallowed hard as he readied himself to hear their judgement.

"Exactly how overwhelming was your urge to have carnal knowledge with Mx Adamski?"

Sienna fought to suppress a smile. She knew she shouldn't but seeing Malek put through the wringer was too satisfying not to saviour. His face was a picture and his eyes turned to fire. He knew better than to respond with anything that could be construed as aggression but he was clearly uncomfortable with this particular line of enquiry. He sipped some water in an effort to compose himself but failed to do either, dribbling it down his chin and all over his pink shirt. He used a sleeve to wipe his mouth but knocked his glass over instead. He thought about swearing but decided against it and instead returned to the question still hanging in the air.

"I am attracted to Mx Adamski and have a desire to lie with her. But only in a mutually beneficial sense. To consider anything else would be abhorrent to me. Her happiness and pleasure is all I want. And Mx Adamski wants it too–"

"Mx Adamski is not present to speak for herself so you will restrain from offering your opinions."

Sienna became aware of movement in the kitchen and paused the stream to see that Geri had finished her workout and come in for a glass of water. Her skin glowed and her scent filled the room. Her short black fringe lay matted against her temple and droplets of sweat ran between her perky breasts. She downed the glass in one without spilling a single drop. When she put it down, she looked long and hard at Sienna.

"Finished your show?"

"Paused it."

Geri nodded while holding Sienna's gaze, her lips full and red, her body glistening with exertion. Sienna read the signals and was caught off-guard. Where before there had been distance and indifference, here now there was fire and fury, a pent-up ball of sexual anger that would not be denied.

Sienna slipped off her glasses and laid them on the side. Geri did likewise. Game on.

"You fucking slut," Sienna growled. "You come in here

like that, all filthy and stinking the place out. You're a disgrace. A dirty whore who doesn't know how to behave."

Geri bit her lip and breathed heavily as Sienna bared her teeth. Her body turned to mush beneath the barrage of Sienna's hard words.

"What the fuck are you looking at, *bitch*. You're going to get it if you don't pack it in and I'm going to give it to you."

Geri flushed all over, her body now burning to be touched.

"You're no good to anyone. Worthless and ugly. A useless unloved cunt. Get up on that counter. Do as I say. Do it now and lift those legs." Sienna grabbed a handful of Geri's hair and shook her by the head. "You fucking pussy tease."

Carl knew better than to interrupt whilst Sienna and Geri were expressing their particular brand of affection for one another. He sat idle for seventeen minutes while cupboard doors were knocked open, pots were kicked over and a lot of smudgy imprints were left across the worktops that would require sterilising. At the end of their encounter, Geri slipped on her blue Smart Glasses to indicate that she was all done while Sienna continued going solo for two more minutes before Carl adjudged it was safe to interject.

"Lunch will be delayed for twenty minutes while I clean. Might I suggest a shower and a regroup in the sitting room before the kitchen is ready for food preparation?"

Geri laughed, breathless yet joyful and sweating harder than before. Sienna purred in bliss as the nucleus accumbens in her basal forebrain fired an overly generous dose of dopamine through her ventral segmental area, melting her against the food hatch as jets of sterilising steam began to circulate the worktops.

They showered together but the intercourse was done.

Sienna used a loofah on Geri's back and Geri reciprocated, but only for half as long. They dried in the bedroom and Sienna stayed undressed out of gratitude to Geri. The house was warm and her body felt at one with Geri's. Sienna slipped a hand around her girlfriend and gave her a kiss, gentle and affectionate, loving and grateful, the type Sienna preferred. Geri pulled away and replied instead with a smile. But it was a paper smile, very different from the one that Julie had given Malek when they'd first spoken.

Her smile faded. She looked away. Something wasn't right.

"I have something to say. It's not a big thing and it won't change anything between us but I've been thinking about it for a while."

Sienna turned cold. Her white body prickled with alarm but she said nothing. She just looked at Geri and waited, hoping that whatever it was, it wasn't the conclusion she'd always feared. Geri saw that she'd open Pandora's box so she continued as succinctly as she could.

"I want us to renew our A6," she said, almost making Sienna choke with relief. But more was to come and Sienna was to choke once more. "But I want to register us as non-exclusive."

"What?"

"None of my friends are exclusive with their partners. It's so regressive and antiquated. And it would just mean that we'd both be able to explore our sexualities."

This was not quite the death knell that Sienna had feared but it was a blow to their relationship nevertheless. Geri wanted to explore her sexuality. But why couldn't she explore it with Sienna? There was nothing Sienna wouldn't do for her. Or with her. Or to her. Or vice-versa. Her only desire was to make Geri happy.

Malek's unseen presence laughed at Sienna from a darkened corner of her soul but she fought to shake him from her thoughts. She reached a hand for Geri but Geri remained statuesque. Unresponsive and passive.

"I love you," Sienna said, stifling a tear.

Geri smiled a reassuring smile. "And I love you too. I always will. But I'm on a journey of self-discovery and to deny myself the knowledge of who I really am would be like cutting off a part of my being. I want you to come with me. I really do. We can do this thing together."

"Is this about Purdy and the other night?" Sienna croaked, barely able to get the words out.

"No," Geri reassured her before realising it kind of was. "Well, maybe. But she's not the only reason. She really likes you by the way," she added, oblivious to how awful this made Sienna feel. "I just want to connect with the universe, with life itself. My whole *raison d'être* is to create artificial life but how can I do that with my eyes blinkered? I want to open them up to the world, see everything, know everything, be everything to everyone. And I want you to be happy too."

"I am happy," Sienna cried, looking and sounding anything but.

"Then let us be happy together. We'll work it out, you'll see. We'll still have each other. Nothing will change. I actually think it could be really good for us."

Sienna disagreed but felt powerless to resist. She loved Geri with all of her heart, every corpuscle and every beat, and nothing would change that. It couldn't. No matter what Geri was proposing, her heart would always belong to Geri. Because their love was total. She needed her too much. Their love could never be consigned. Sienna knew it had to be the same for Geri but Geri was impulsive. More so than Sienna was. Her friends had messed with her head and confused her. They were fulfilling a need in her that her failure to market Carl had created. And now they were impacting on their relationship. But these things would pass. They had to. Because Sienna could not see how life was possible any other way.

"Can we talk about it?"

"We are," Geri reassured her. "Please. Let's build on what we have, not tear it down."

Sienna knew it wouldn't last. It would be a phase like everything with Geri and she'd eventually come through to the other side but she didn't know how to make Geri see this without provoking her ire. And she was worried if she tried she might lose her altogether.

"Sleep on it?"

"Sign it, babe."

Sienna didn't want to split up from Geri and Geri wasn't proposing that. She still wanted to be with Sienna and live their lives. She simply wanted something extra, a little fun on the side, nothing special. Not like the splicing of their spirits. Geri was just asking for a physical release.

Sienna would adjust. She would need to. She would learn to adapt and accept this change. She had to if she wanted to preserve their future. As with everything, the work and the sacrifice would fall to her. A month or two. That's as long as this would last. A few regrettable encounters and Geri would soon realise where her happiness lay.

Sienna eyes were screwed closed but she felt Geri's breath on her face. Their lips touched and their mouths parted. She opened her eyes and saw a notification flashing red in her display.

#ClaySienna/HussainGeri_A6App.amendment

"We'll have fun. I promise," Geri whispered, holding Sienna close and kissing her gently, lovingly – the way Sienna liked.

She now understood the overtures in the kitchen. The unexpected lunchtime passion that had once been routine in the early days but was now so out-of-character that it had taken her by surprise. That was to sugarcoat the pill. The free gift that came with every signature.

"You won't regret it."

Sienna didn't believe that. How could she? How could she give up a piece of her soul without mourning its loss? It wasn't possible. Could Geri not see this? Did she even care?

"One condition," Sienna cried quietly, weeping against Geri's shoulder.

"Anything."

"Not here. Never here. In our bed. Ever."

"I promise."

"I love you," Sienna wailed, meaning it more than she could ever say.

"I love you too."

And with that one final moment of exclusivity, Sienna signed the application with a flick of her tear-filled eyes.

And gave Geri to the world.

*

Four hours later, Sienna was all alone in the darkness and dressed once more. Geri had gone out to meet Aurora despite promising to stay home tonight. But something amazing had come up. Diego had massive news and Geri needed to be a part of it. Sienna didn't know what Diego's massive news was but she hoped it was terminal.

Lying on her bed and feeling crushed, her mind played a slide show of hers and Geri's closest moments on an endless loop while she sought to understand how they had grown apart. It didn't make sense. She didn't want it to make sense. How could Geri want *more* when they already had everything?

Her self-inspection stumbled across Malek in her thoughts so she pulled up his A8 on screen, still paused with Malek desperate to be heard. The Committee would be over by now and Malek would know his fate but Sienna had missed the live stream. Desperate for a distraction, she forwarded the file until she got to within a minute of the end then hit play.

"… you forced her against her will. You saw she was vulnerable and manipulated her until she felt unable to resist."

"I didn't."

"You were determined to stop at nothing to possess this young womxn, weren't you?"

"No."

"You made her comply."

"I love her."

"You raped her."

"I didn't. I swear."

"You had sexual intercourse at her home without consent, didn't you?"

Malek fought hard not to reply.

"Answer the question."

"This isn't right. It's not fair."

"We have witness testimony, surveillance footage and DNA evidence found at the scene."

"You don't understand."

"No, you do not understand. Therefore, it is the Committee's decision to find you in breach of Code 1 of the 2059 Conjugal Safeguard's Act and order that you be taken into custody."

This was the cue the Guardians off-camera had been

waiting for. A crash sounded and urgent angry voices were heard before the sound cut out. Malek jumped back and was quickly surrounded by three burly figures in green. Two of them wielded tasers while the other ordered Malek to turn to the wall and put his hands behind his back.

The leader used a zip tie to restrain him then removed his Glasses and pulled a gag over his mouth. Malek had been given a public platform and every opportunity to represent himself. If he had anything more to say, the Guardians would record it at the processing centre. Until then, he had no voice.

Malek looked at the camera one last time as they led him away, more in desperation than hope. The Head of the Committee concluded the meeting with a few official words and the recording ended. Sienna thought about replaying the last couple of minutes but didn't. The distraction hadn't made her feel any better. If anything, it had made her feel worse.

Sienna hadn't watched the clip for titillation. She had watched it for affirmation. Her belief in New Britannia was sacrosanct. And more important than ever in light of what was happening in her own little corner of it. She had simply needed to see justice done.

Malek had brought the situation upon himself. Sienna knew this but even so, his anguish had failed to compensate her for her own. She hadn't felt this broken since the pervert Miller had violated her as a girl, robbing her of her innocence and scarring her soul. At least Malek would not be able to intimidate her at work again. His time as a data engineer was over. Perhaps even his time in New Britannia.

She would see Julie again. After counselling, of course. She would return, damaged but not beyond repair. Sienna could help her. She'd been through a similar trauma at a young age so she could help Julie regain her self-esteem.

Perhaps Julie could even help Sienna rediscover her own. Maybe. In time.

But that was for another day, far from here and beyond the boundaries of pain. Today, Sienna felt raw. The blankets against her face were wet and her body was cold but she didn't get under the covers. Not by herself. Not while Geri was out there. Somewhere.

She flicked to her Find Contacts app and saw that Geri was in Littlewick, which was where Diego lived. She must have gone there with Aurora to hear Diego's big news. She wondered if Geri had shared her own news. If she had already signed a few one-nighters and was now sampling, tasting and knowing all there was to know. What was to stop her?

These thoughts drove an ice-cold screw through her heart and made her vomit. When she was done she fast-tracked a two-gram cartridge of Fentanyl and received notification when it was delivered. She retrieved it from the delivery hatch and loaded it into her vape without reading the instructions. She pulled deeply and the warming drug rushed to reassure her, taking her in its arms and giving her the loving embrace she so desperately craved. Colours swam in her mind and the bed swallowed her body. Soon she lost her pain and felt nothing, neither joy nor fear. From the tips of her toes to the ends of her hair, she floated free, numb to the best and worst that life could offer. Her torment finally knew peace. Her spirit was stilled. Grief trickled away.

As did her final thought.

Julie…

12: PANTHEA

"I have no desire to make windows into the souls of men," Elizabeth I said on the subject of religious tolerance. Yet, she still went on to execute 190 of these same men on sectarian grounds during the course of her Golden Reign.

Religion has always been a tricky nut to crack, from the darkest days of prehistory, when Pagans sacrificed young maidens on slabs of granite, to the brutal crusades of the 12th and 21st centuries. No one could ever agree on what or who God was because God wisely stayed out of the conversation. But far from taking this as a sign to do the same, man raged war against man for thousands of years as he sought to inflict his own particular brand of love upon the world. No accord could ever be reached because every God was sacrosanct. To deny the existence of Jehovah, El, Allah, Buddha, Zeus, Vishnu, Ik Onkar, Thetan or the Flying Spaghetti Monster was to deny the existence of righteousness itself. Every person who ever worshipped a deity knew – not thought or suspected or hoped for but <u>knew</u> – that their God was the one true God and all the rest were nonsense, Father Christmas fantasy figures peddled to gullible fools.

And thus religion proved the thorniest of issues for the first administrations of the Polychrome Alliance. After all, how could they promote tolerance and understanding when a great many of the people whose cases they were pleading preached intolerance and damnation when it came to everyone else?

The very best and brightest minds of the movement were ascribed to finding a solution to the impasse, preferably one that didn't involve fire, and after a great many months of meeting with faith leaders and theologians of all denominations, they finally announced their findings.

Everyone had got it wrong.

Christians, Muslims, Jews, Buddhists, Hindus, Sikhs, Scientologists and Pastafarians. All of them. They'd completely missed the point and overlooked something unbelievably obvious.

As you can imagine, this much intrigued the faith leaders who, for once, spoke with a single united voice. But the committee expanded upon their findings. They weren't saying that there was no such thing as Jehovah, El, Allah, Buddha, Zeus and all the rest of them. There clearly was and they were all as divine as each other. But they weren't top of the theological tree. They were siblings. And as everyone knew, siblings rarely got along. They squabbled and argued and fought over biscuits but, at the end of the day, they were family and joined together by an unbreakable bond of love.

Everyone might have got it wrong. But everyone had got it right too.

Yet, there was more. So much more. And this was the thing that everyone had overlooked.

As siblings, the Gods must have been born from a single universal deity. One prevailing power that had brought all the other divine powers into being. After all, if God had created the universe, then someone must have created God. It made sense.

Therefore, it fell upon the Committee to announce the discovery of the ultimate Creator – Panthea, God of Gods.

She was, in effect, God's mother. And also Allah's and Buddha's and Zeus and the Flying Spaghetti Monster's. She was the ultimate truth and every house of worship in the country was encouraged to make a shrine to Her.

Obviously, with a pronouncement such as this, there was a fair bit of pushback but if Henry VIII could dissolve the monasteries and get away with it, then Fawqiyya el-Abdulla could compel every temple in the land to find a corner to situate a shrine to Panthea in the name of inclusion. It proved a thorny issue for the Polychrome Alliance. Fawqiyya el-Abdulla tried every approach to unify the nation behind this new religion but found it a hard sell. Demonstrations were rife. Counter-demonstrations were rifer still. And PR strategists chewed through millions as they sought to hammer home Panthea's universal message.

Eventually, Fawqiyya el-Abdulla found herself out of office and Charity GoodHope inherited the problem. She took a less nuanced approach and pushed through a raft of no-nonsense legislation that was designed to kill or cure the blasphemers once and for all. From 2060, a token shrine was not enough. Every place of worship was compelled to transform into a House of Panthea. Those that didn't were closed on the grounds of religious intolerance. Hundreds of chapels, mosques and tabernacles were deconsecrated and slapped with Compulsory Purchase Orders backed up by force. Most churches reopened after a franchise refurb but some, like St Peter's at the end of Sienna's lane, became community hubs or Hive Mind Clubs, depending on their location. Thousands of people hit the streets in protest only to be swept up in mass arrests, re-eduction programmes and resettlement orders for the most unrepentant of heretics. A few went into hiding. Most learned to love Panthea until eventually, through a combination of persuasion and pressure, her wings fanned out across the entire nation to bring peace, hope and unity to all.

Sienna sat in a middle pew half-listening to the sermon playing on her Smart Glasses, her lenses turned from cherry-red to deep scarlet. The sermon had started the moment she had stepped through the door. Noting that this was her first time inside a House of Panthea for three years, it asked her to accept cookies and offered her a list of topics to choose from so that Panthea could tailor her message to Sienna's specific needs.

Sienna ticked a few boxes: relationships, love, sex, lesbian, afraid, separation, loss.

Suicide.

She debated whether or not to tick that last box as her attempt hadn't been real. She hadn't meant to overdose. She had just tried to numb the pain and had taken too big a hit. She wasn't used to Fentanyl and hadn't read the label, taking enough to stop her aching heart and plunge her towards Panthea's warm embrace. But she had been lucky. Her Smart Glasses had still been on her face and the sudden plunge in her vital signs had sent an automatic distress call to the emergency services. Paramedics tore through the streets with lights flashing and sirens wailing and arrived outside her house within seven minutes of getting the call. It was touch and go for a time but Sienna was yanked back from the darkness and thrown headfirst into the light, coughing, spluttering and vomiting all over the womxn who'd come to save her. Much pain followed, not all of it physical, and Sienna was taken into protective care for several nights until she was signed off for discharge.

When she got out, a message awaited.

Stopping out again? You go girl. I told you you'd dig it. Have a great time and I'll see you soon. Much love – Geri

Geri didn't know. The hospital services operated in complete anonymity. Their only requirement was that Sienna upped her counselling sessions to four times a week until she was deemed well enough to reduce them again. Sienna was already registered with a counselling service. As a sexual abuse survivor, she had been receiving counselling for years but had reduced her package when Geri came into her life. Geri had completed her. Geri had made her well.

Geri had been her happiness.

Until last week, she had only been logging in once a week and very little of that had touched upon the events of yesteryear. She spent most of her sessions bellyaching about the weather, her parents, Carl, Bella, Cans, the Hub, Bella, period pains, Bella and the piss-poor quality of Oxy these days and Bella. She often failed to think of anything to discuss so she was referred to an online consultant who diagnosed her as having an Emotional Management Spectral Regulation Disorder. Despite never having heard of EMSRD, it made complete sense to her. She applied for an additional Diversity Grading point to reflect her newly diagnosed condition and researched EMSRD until she understood how it manifested itself. In a nutshell, EMSRD left sufferers with the feeling of not quite knowing what was wrong with themselves but being sure that something probably was. Maybe.

"… therefore love abounds in all of us. Not once has Panthea ever discriminated between her children, as diverse and wondrous as they are, and neither shall we. The path to true equality is the love of individuality and the marriage of divergence. We bless our glorious Chairperson and pray that her wise stewardship of our reborn nation continues. Go with Charity. Go with Panthea. And go with love. Ah-non."

The sermon ended and the pixilated pastor invited her to rate it from 0-5 stars. Sienna rated it 5 simply because she didn't want to be bombarded with a load of multiple-choice questions asking how her spiritual experience might have been enhanced. She thought about binge-watching a season of sermons in an effort to avoid going home but instead logged out. The sermon hadn't helped but the silence and stillness of the church held a certain appeal.

Her counsellor had suggested she come. As a super-advanced emotional therapy AI unit, it could guide her through the tangled maze of her own unrequited emotions but it could not answer some of her more ethereal questions. It did not know what Sienna's greater purpose was and despite turning the question back on Sienna six times, it could not prompt her to spontaneously discover the answer.

"Speak with Panthea. She may help you find your way. SESSION ENDS."

The church was free of bustle, unlike the streets outside. There were six people in here in a space that could accommodate several hundred. Much of the original brickwork and a number of Christian reliefs remained but the glass at the front had been replaced with new stained windows that portrayed Panthea giving birth to a couple of galaxies whilst boasting an Energy Efficiency Rating of A+. Unlike God with his big white beard and flowing robes, there was no standardised version of Panthea. She was pan-inclusive and meant everything to everyone, therefore she had a myriad of looks, like a Barbie Doll that each person could accessorise however they wished. In this church, she was naked with a fat pregnant belly and stunted arms. One of her breasts was full, the other flat from where she had self-mastectomised. Her eyes bore no pupils but she saw all. And her skin glittered like silver and gold as the sun streamed through the glass.

Sienna had seen Geri just three times in the last week despite having taken five days off for emotional regulation.

Bella had expressed sympathy and understanding to the point of booking her a consultation with the company pharmacist in order to get her back to work as soon as possible. Sienna had declined so Bella arranged for her to receive a remote portal so that she could log in from home. Again, Sienna had declined which took the wind out of Bella's sympathy and understanding.

She had hoped to be able to spend some time with Geri. To try to get a handle on their new dynamic. She thought that if she and Geri could find some renewal in their relationship then perhaps she might even learn to live with all the other stuff. Who knew, perhaps it might even make it all worthwhile, like an unexpected dividend to offset an expense. But Geri's appearances at home since last Saturday had been scarce and fleeting. Sienna blamed herself. Her condition about not bringing anyone back had compelled Geri to seek self-discover elsewhere. In a way, it demonstrated that Geri was at least showing Sienna consideration. These were not the actions of an adulterer. An adulterer would not seek permission from their spouse and then tiptoe around them. Her AI counsellor had gone to great lengths to help her see this. What she and Geri had was a beautiful and inclusive thing, a model of love based on respect and universality. Theirs was a marriage for a new age. She should be proud of herself.

But Sienna didn't feel proud. She felt selfish for wanting to keep Geri to herself and angry at not being progressive enough to celebrate her girlfriend's new-found liberation. She had always accepted Geri's past but told herself that was then, this was now. She had never dreamed that Geri's pansexual intrigues would intrude on their present. It was this thought that unsettled her the most. The thought of Geri going with men.

Of the six other worshippers scattered around the church, four were watching sermons on their Smart Glasses, one was downloading absolution, while the nearest was sitting quietly and staring into the void. Siena hadn't noticed him until now despite him sitting just a couple of rows back. No one was here to notice each other but that changed when he let out a sob. Sienna turned and the man looked up, self-conscious and embarrassed. They caught each other's eye, seeing something of themselves in the other, before the man returned to his introspection.

A message pinged in the corner of Sienna's screen. Bella was trying to send her a file but it couldn't be delivered so long as she stayed within sight of Panthea's loving embrace (and wifi signal).

The pastor entered from behind the pulpit. She walked past Sienna and stopped by the man. She asked if she might sit with him for a time and the man didn't know how to say no so the pastor took her seat, observing the two-metre rule.

"What brings you here, my child?" the pastor asked in hushed tones. Sienna could hear but pretended she couldn't.

"I didn't know where else to go," the man wept, sounding as bad as Sienna felt. "I'm so tired."

The man looked tired but it was not a good tired. Not a 40-minute workout on the treadmill tired or a hard night's clubbing tired. He looked as though his soul had been ripped from his body and crucified by the spirits of hate.

"Unburden yourself. Let me alleviate your troubles," the pastor said, giving him the ecclesiastical equivalent of *U OK Hun*.

The man struggled to know where to start. His world had been turned upside down and everything he knew was a lie.

Sienna sympathised but thought better of sharing. This moment was his. It wouldn't have done to cut in and make it all about her.

"My partner was... was..."

Sienna willed him to say what his partner was. A liar? A traitor? A fucking software writer?

"Yes, my child. Go on. Go on. You may speak freely here."

"He was a... a racist."

"A racist?"

"I never knew," the man wailed.

This was even more monumental than Sienna had been expecting. Knowing that Geri was out there somewhere probably plugged airtight was one thing. But to imagine that she could have been harbouring the most heinous of crimes would have been too much to bear. She wasn't so naive as to think vile criminals didn't exist – she investigated such people every day – but to hear it first-hand was surprising. Shocking even. Not that the targets she investigated weren't real. But to Sienna, they were just profiles, out there in the ether with no connection to her or anyone she knew.

"What did he do? Share with me so that I might be able to help you."

The man shook his head.

"I never knew," he swore. "I never knew."

"I understand," said the pastor, noting the man's repetition. The man wanted it understood that he never knew and he wanted the pastor to acknowledge this fact, something the pastor was able to do. "His sins are not yours, my child." It wasn't quite the blanket pardon the man had been hoping for but it was good enough. "Now open up and share. To conceal another's wrongdoing, even through shame, is a transgression."

This more or less left the man with no choice. He had to dish the dirt.

"I've lost it all because of him," he said, going on to explain how they'd shared a house, two children and pets and a happy life in Camberley but it had all been based on a lie. He had no right to such a cosseted existence when his grandfather "or great-grandfather, I can't remember which" had been a violent racist. "He attacked pregnant womyn and ethnic citizens and homosexuals and everyone and deprived them of their freedoms. He was so zealous that they even gave him a medal." The man sobbed but Sienna scarcely breathed. This all sounded unnervingly familiar.

"The darkest days often cast the longest shadows," the pastor mused.

It had all come as a terrible shock to the man. Up until a week ago, he'd been living a cosseted existence in carefree bliss, tending to the present while dreaming of the future. But then the truth broke across the Network. Links to archive news stories appeared, survivor testimonies, denouncements on his partner's profile and the sudden loss of friends, family and colleagues as their clouds crashed in quick succession. A storm they'd been oblivious to had blown in to scatter their lives.

"Rami had to know. He had to. How could he not?" the man reasoned, imploring the pastor for answers but finding only censure.

"What exactly are you mourning, my child?" the pastor asked, sounding more like a prosecutor than a priest.

"Everything?"

"Everything? Your home?"

"Gone."

"Your children?"

"Devastated."

"Your friends?"

The man shrugged.

"Your partner? What about Rami? How do you feel about him?"

The man looked up and realised he would do well to choose his next words carefully.

"Betrayed."

"Whom has he betrayed?"

"Me. The children. Everyone," the man said, not quite understanding the question.

"So you seek solace for yourself? For the life you've lost? For your home and your happy comfortable existence?"

A whole new level of hush had descended across the church that rendered their conversation as clamorous as if they were shouting. The man became acutely aware of everyone's eyes on him and looked around defensively. Sienna sat facing forward but she could hear everything. Every word. Every breath. Every anxious pause. Gone now were all thoughts of her own. In their place, all she could picture was Rami Jaffri and his partner, smiling joyously with their arms around their children. This had been her case. She'd audited his history and presented her findings to Congress only ten days earlier. Rami's partner was the man sat behind, crying for his lost love and struggling to justify it.

"Well?"

"For the victims," the man suddenly said, finally finding the right answer.

"The victims?"

"Yes," he insisted, hoping and praying that was it. "I'm grieving for their pain, their oppression and the blood they shed. I feel ashamed to have played any part in this terrible man's legacy."

The pastor smiled approvingly although she stopped short of laying a hand on him in the absence of medical gloves.

"It is right and proper that you grieve for the oppressed, my child. Panthea grieves for them too. It is why she blew a benevolent wind to send us Charity GoodHope, so that she might lead us away from the age of hate and into a brighter future for all."

"Yes." The man wasn't sure what he was agreeing to but it felt like the sort of thing he should say until he thought of something more meaningful.

"Come, take a knee with me and give thanks to Panthea's divine wisdom in righting the sins of the past and the sinners of the present."

The pastor and the man slipped off the pew and started to pray, very little of which seemed to touch upon the fact that the man was now homeless, jobless and loveless and focussed more on Panthea smiting the forces of evil and spreading her wondrous message across the world.

Sienna was up and heading for the exit before the prayer reached its denouement. She set up her donation subscription but declined to leave feedback on her visit. She just wanted to get out of there as quickly as possible and get home. She hurried along the aisle but the man glanced up and their eyes met once more. It was only a fleeting look, no more than a reflex, but his eyes ran her through like a blade. She panicked and this time it was Sienna who turned away, terrified that her expression would betray her complicity. Once outside she started to run.

She didn't stop until she got home.

13: ECO

Money might be the root of all evil but it is a necessary evil.

Modern societies cannot exist without it. Communists tried and failed. Hippies gave it a go but most rejoined the rat race when middle-age came calling. Religious sects claim to be material-free while in reality launder millions under the altar. In place of swapping corn for cloth or beads for Manhattan, most economies have yet to come up with a workable alternative to money.

Being surrounded on all sides by hostile enemies and isolated as a society could have presented a problem for Charity GoodHope but as with all other matters, she managed to turn adversity into triumph.

Under her stewardship, New Britannia became wealthy and secure. Yet, like the Flash Harries of old, with two sports cars on the drive, an all-year suntan and more jewellery than The Tower of London – all the while never seeming to do a day's work – no one could quite deduce how it was done.

All Governments have secrets. Charity GoodHope's had more than most. For while she took a defiant and isolationist stance in public, behind the scenes, New Britannia was trading assiduously with the rest of the world. It had to. For all the rhetoric and condemnation, New Britannia had no choice but to sup with the Devil in order to survive.

Sweden, so long a shining beacon of noble neutrality, acted as Britannia's long spoon. As a third party, it brought goods to market and funnelled profits back (minus a cut, of course), circumnavigating sanctions and supplying the nation with the raw materials and ingredients it could not produce at home. Many a blind eye was turned on all sides of the theological divide because trade served the common good. It benefited everyone.

But what did New Britannia have to trade?

Besides drugs, which Sweden steadfastly refused to deal, the one commodity that Charity had an abundance of was Carbon Credits. Years earlier, one of the first actions of Fawqiyya el-Abdulla's administration was to introduce a programme of renewable energy production. This looked to end the country's dependency on Russian gas, Saudi oil, US coal, French nuclear power and the exploitation of the North Sea, the Yorkshire Dales and every other inch of greenery in pursuit of British petroleum, Shale gas, bitumen, peat, wood and anything else that would burn. Solar panels were erected on the central reservations of every motorway, wind turbines were constructed in their thousands in the shallow coastal waters of the east, wave and tidal converters were built on every estuary in the land and heat recapture boilers were installed in their millions. The project took years to complete and billions to fund, causing Fawqiyya enormous problems at the ballot box after her first term of office but she clung on to power by the skin of her teeth and eventually the results spoke for themselves, not least of all when everyone's bills came down –

– to absolute zero.

In fact, for many households, they paid less than zero, receiving energy rebates for selling electricity back to the grid, which itself was sold on to energy markets abroad. Power was free for all and no one went cold. The memory of gas bills and electricity meters soon faded. People of Sienna's age could not even imagine having to pay to turn on the lights, let alone power their automated food dispensers or recharge their heated socks. It was truly a land of milk and honey (almond milk and organic molasses honey alternative).

Then, when Charity GoodHope came to power, she

doubled down on renewables and ramped up production yet again, spotting an opportunity to turbocharge even more progress. During the first two years of her Chairpersonship, the country went from being carbon neutral to having a carbon deficit as deep as a Persian oil well and Carbon Credits became a phenomenally lucrative by-product. Other countries vied to buy up Britannia's surplus to offset their own ecological pledges and a new industry was born. Sweden brokered the deals and the money rolled in via several Channel Island accounts.

Of course, very little of this was known to anyone outside of official channels and few thought to ask. When people are warm and fed and have free TV pumped directly into their Glasses, who cared where it all came from? Sienna certainly didn't but money was on her mind nevertheless as she sat in her privacy pod and reviewed Charles Garfield's PayNet accounts. He had money also. Too much money. Far more than any soya supplier ought to have, no matter how ethical his business was. Where had it all come from?

Where indeed?

Sienna felt that this was the break she had been looking for. She dug deeper into his accounts, investigating every deposit and each transaction, now convinced he had to be dealing meat. How else could he have accrued such wealth? No one liked soya that much. But as with all of her hunches, the money proved another dead end. Most of it had come from restoration payments; Governmynt compensation claimed by victims of historical injustice. Charles Garfield had hit the jackpot.

But this didn't make sense.

Charles Garfield? The former butcher? Was a victim of historical injustice?

It took all sorts to make the world but try as she might, Sienna could not see how Charles Garfield fitted the profile of a victim. He and his extended family were as white as one of their old aprons (and therefore splattered with as much blood), hetero-regressive, cisgender and mascu-archaic from birth, able-bodied and neuro-typical and he seemed to have come from a long line of fat white apes who looked just like him. Who – or what – could have done him any wrong other than the ugly tree when he fell out of it and whacked every branch on the way down? Sienna was stumped.

Ordinarily, she would have written off the case as a dead dahlia but pressure from Bella compelled her to keep digging. She didn't know why but Bella had a hard-on for Charles Garfield and was determined to present him all trussed up with an apple in his mouth at the next Congress. Perhaps it was something personal for Bella? Perhaps she bore a grudge just as Sienna did with spongecake2038.69? This notion pricked her conscience and made her wrack her brain for justifications.

spongecake2038.69 was different to Garfield. The former deserved to be cancelled. She'd already done the digging. The evidence was there for all to see. Still, it niggled her, the thought that she was playing Panthea and it made her feel uneasy. Similar to how she had felt after Malek had been arrested a week earlier.

After five minutes of playing with the lever of her chair, she came to a decision. She would not pursue the point with spongecake2038.69. If he did deserve to be cancelled (as she knew he did) then justice would catch up with him eventually. No one could get away with that sort of behaviour forever. And certainly not here, in the most tolerant country on Earth.

As it was, she had yet to receive a mandate to look into

him. She'd covertly messaged darkmatter2021.407 ten days earlier but had heard nothing from I Division. This was odd but also a relief. Her hackles had shrunk and she'd had time to reflect. spongecake2038.69 might have wronged her but she'd probably never see him again. She'd buried so many issues over the last few weeks, she had every confidence she could bury this one too. spongecake2038.69 and the ingrained image of his flaccid dick would fade with time.

A puff of Oxy helped her pick out a plot in a far-flung corner of her hippocampus and plant the first shovel. She'd brood on him no more.

Despite reaching closure, Sienna couldn't help but wonder what had happened with darkmatter2021.407. Was he an informer or not? If he was, he was a curiously discreet one. Or maybe he hadn't received the message. Carl was so hit-and-miss when it came to interfacing with MUM that Sienna's message could have easily missed its target altogether and still be out there bouncing around on the Network. Again, this was no bad thing. She'd acted in haste but fortune had spared her from repenting at leisure.

Still, looking at Charles Garfield's accounts made her realise how little she had in her own. Her and Geri's joint account was down to fumes and she had yet to receive her bonus from the Rami Jaffri case. As lead Auditor, she was due 0.15% of the finances raised from any assets seized by E Division. In Rami's case, this included a six-bedroom house in Camberley, all the fixtures and fittings and any savings or pensions he had squirrelled away for a rainy day. His children would be provided for and his partner would receive a settlement of between 0-15%, depending on his own culpability, while the Governmynt would recover the rest (minus Geniture's administration fees). Sienna was looking at a bonus of somewhere between §2000-5000. Ordinarily, she would be very happy with this but not this month. This month, she had looked into the eyes of the man whose life she had upended and it unsettled her. She had helped remove a cancer from society but the scarring had run deep. She hadn't thought about this before. Or if she had, she'd always imagined the spouses deserved it too. But Adam Al-Khatib had not looked worthy of such misery. And his money felt tainted.

Mercifully, Sienna had a solution. Geri.

Geri went through money like water at the best of times but lately the damn had burst. And it all had to do with Diego. Incredibly, he had hit the big time with his potato waste app. A major software developer had bought the rights to his code and was now in the process of adapting it. At present, Diego's program simply monitored how many root vegetables were in each consumer's fridge (something Sienna had thought was phenomenally pointless). But the company had plans to roll it out and link it back to a central database allowing the Department of Agriculture to track food consumption nationwide and plan for the following year's harvest. It was a radical idea and could mean streamlining food production in a way not seen since the Agricultural Revolution. And Diego was at the forefront of it, receiving all the plaudits, glory and royalties that went with it.

Geri was really happy for Diego. Sienna knew this because Geri made sure she said it as often as possible.

She was really really really *really* happy for him.

Moreover, she was determined to stick to him like glue as he rose to the top. This meant going to the same parties, the same clubs and the same restaurants as Diego, even those that would normally be beyond Geri's pockets – invisible as they were. But Diego was already moving in circles beyond his old friends. He was hanging out with the likes of Trinity Dhaliwal, Shari Mimieux and DX5, celebrity programmers that he and Geri had previously scoffed at, shaking hands with ministers and bigwigs and even wearing the occasional pair of trousers. Geri and Purdy and Aurora and Fuzz would continue to support Diego, albeit from an ever-increasing distance, sharing his triumphs and congratulating him across their Network pages but the writing was on the wall for their friendship. Diego was trading up and destined to disappear from their lives. He would reply to their messages for a few months, make excuses about missing out on get-togethers and acknowledge their Network comments with the odd emoji, but a year from now, he would be a sour memory. Someone they used to know and had always suspected was worse than Hitler. It would hit Geri the hardest. She would never recover from this, her second brush with success, and she would lose all sight of her own future through her increased use of OpiVape. Then, three years from now, she would see Diego again, back in Woking for a whirlwind visit to unveil a blue plaque against the side of his old house to polite applause from an admiring crowd. Their eyes would meet but his expression would be devoid of recognition. He would smile politely, just as his PR team had instructed him to do, but every ounce of their past would be absent, deleted from his memory as easily as a line of unwanted code. Geri would scream at him and be moved on by security. Diego would shrug and claim not to know what that was about. Everyone would sympathise. And Diego would be sincere.

But that was in the future. For now, Geri was still really really *REALLY* happy for Diego.

Geri was lunching at Mushroom House, a Green-Starred

gastronomic palace of mycological cuisine that most people could only dream of experiencing. She would be with Diego, of course. How else would she have got a table? Sienna watched her username pulsate on her Find Contacts app and wondered who was picking up the bill. Me, she concluded.

For her own lunch, Sienna was in the food hall at the Hub making do with a bowl of tofu biryani and a side order of coconut chutney, the one that Julie liked. Sienna had waited all lunchtime, surreptitiously scanning the hall for Julie's return but she had failed to appear. Counselling after an intervention for unsanctioned sex usually took about a week or two but in some cases longer. She had yet to return to work and Sienna felt her hopes dissipate at her non-appearance.

She didn't know what she would do when she saw Julie. She'd not prepared anything and every time she'd tried, she couldn't think of anything appropriate. She wasn't even sure what she wanted from Julie. To befriend her? To bed her? She was so confused and conflicted over Geri that she simply didn't have a plan. Not even a fantasy. But through it all, she felt a need to connect with Julie, if just to know that she bore her no ill will.

A message flashed in her glasses.
Want to play level 23? – Ellie
I'm back at work today – Sienna
Tonight? – Ellie
Sure – Sienna
Feeling better? – Ellie
I'm okay – Sienna
Great. I'm glad – Ellie
9pm? – Sienna
Until then – Ellie

Looking forward to it – Sienna
Hugs and kisses – Ellie
Hugs and kisses – Sienna

Sienna had never hugged nor kissed with Ellie before. She'd never even laid eyes on her but she longed to rendezvous in a secret room and do so now. If only to take her mind off the other womxn who had laid a claim to her soul.

Anita Xeno came over with her usual lunch of three-bean chilli jacket potato and sat across from Sienna. Always without asking. She gulped her lemonade and looked around the food hall.

"I thought Julie would be back by now."

"Julie?" Sienna feigned.

"Didn't you see?"

"No, what?"

Anita recapped the sordid story and Sienna faked surprise. There was no reason for her to know unless she had taken an interest. Better to pretend she didn't.

Anita finished her recap and tucked into her potato.

"Where have you been?" Anita exclaimed before a thought occurred. "Actually, where have you been?"

"Tested positive, didn't I?" Sienna said, having prepared a cover story about rubella and having to isolate but Anita didn't delve any deeper. She got straight down to business.

"Can you sign my A6?" she asked hopefully. Ordinarily, people would just wing them over but Anita was unwilling to send it until she had Sienna's agreement.

"Who's it for?"

"Just a girl."

"What girl?"

"No one you know."

"Then why not ask someone who does?"

Anita wasn't sure. She hadn't expected to be grilled. Most girls were happy to sign each other's A6s with no questions asked. It was an unwritten sisterly rule.

"I haven't met her yet."

"This is for a girl you haven't met?"

"It's just good to have one, you know," she shrugged. It wasn't uncommon for people to have witnessed A6 forms all ready to go. It was a loophole that people exploited. In certain circumstances, they were more effective than a dozen red roses and a tube of KY but Sienna didn't trust the desperation in Anita's voice. What girl could she possibly be thinking of?

"Is this for Julie?" Sienna asked, her face flashing with anxiety.

"What? No," Anita baulked, equally anxious.

"Because she's going to need time, you know. You can't just slap an A6 in her face the moment she gets back." Put like that, Sienna could have been advising herself but she needn't have worried. Anita wasn't interested in Julie or any other girl. She looked around and lowered her voice.

"Actually, it's for a guy."

This was different but equally suspicious. In the case of retro-regressive relationships, men were supposed to supply the A6. But it wasn't unheard of for womyn to use lesbian A6 forms with guys. As long as the guys listed themselves as gender-fluid or trans-lesbian, it was legal. At least, it was a difficult rule to police.

"Who's the guy?" Sienna asked, the prerogative of the witness.

"I don't know yet," Anita shrugged. "I haven't met him either."

There was something that Anita wasn't telling Sienna and something she couldn't admit. But she needed that A6 and implored Sienna to help.

"Promise me it's not for Julie," Sienna insisted.

"I promise."

"Okay, send it over."

If Sienna had pressed the point, she would have discovered that Anita had an A6 already. At least, she had until two nights ago. She'd had it for a year but had failed to find anyone who wanted to share it. Unfortunately for Anita, she hadn't been blessed in the looks department. She was short and squat, round in all the wrong places and pockmarked from the scars of childhood diseases. She over-ate to overcompensate and this made things worse all round. But the saddest thing of all was her confidence. She had not a jot and wallowed in loneliness. Lots of people were lonely. Some even alone. And the situation was self-perpetuating because few ever reached out to the lonely, regarding it as an infection to be avoided rather than a condition to be eased. In the past, Sienna had little time for Anita, preferring to do her own thing and surround herself with happier people. But lately, these same happy people had skipped away from Sienna too and now she saw her insecurities reflected back in Anita's expression.

"Be careful, yeah?" Sienna said, signing where indicated.

Two nights earlier, Anita had given in to desperation and logged onto NetS.O.SX, a dark net hook-up hub used by late-night masturbators who'd taken too much ViagVape. A hundred years earlier, they would have lurked in the shadows of parks. Now they lurked in the shadows of the Network.

As a willing girl with a witnessed A6, Anita was heralded as an angel of mercy upon arrival. She made two stops that night, swapping out the names of each [trans-fluid] guy and lying to each that she had submitted it without actually doing so. Unfortunately, she couldn't pull off the same trick the next night as she'd unwittingly logged the date. But she realised if she left the date free and got the applicant to fill in his/her details, she could delete it all afterwards and use it again and again, night after night, with as many guys as she liked.

It was a duplicitous act and she risked landing everyone in big trouble but she was tired of being unhappy. Everyone else had someone. Why shouldn't she? At least for a few precious moments in the dead of the night. Anita's exploits were unlikely to make her any happier but, as she saw it, neither was an expired A6.

"There. I hope you find someone nice," Sienna said, sending it back to Anita.

"Thanks," Anita smiled, taking her potato and hurrying away to collect two more signatures.

Anita's quest for love would eventually come to the attention of the Guardians, causing every guy she'd assisted to be dragged from their beds to answer for their actions. It would spark a huge sensation that would grip the nation and prompt many to ask how the system could have failed such a vulnerable young womxn. The witnesses who'd signed her A6 would be branded enablers and dragged through the mire along with the men who'd taken advantage of her but Sienna would escape it all.

Because long before Anita got the sort of attention she'd always craved, Sienna would have left the town of Woking.

For somewhere far far away.

14: NEW TROY

Geri stayed home for a few nights at the end of the week. It was nice to spend time together but it didn't escape Sienna's notice that her stopover in Old Woking coincided with her wearing the lily. They dined together, watched episodes of *I Care* together and cut and dyed each other's hair. Geri didn't tell Sienna where she had been all week and Sienna didn't ask. It was enough that she was home and that they were happy again, albeit for a few precious hours.

The next morning, they took the bus to Wimbledon for Emancipation Sunday. There was always a big gathering near the Resistance Obelisk on the Common, erected *in memoriam* for the victims of male violence. The 20-meter stone column featured a QR code chiselled into each of its granite sides that allowed visitors to access the names and profiles of some forty thousand womyn and girls who had been killed by male antagonists over three centuries.

Sienna spent some time reading the profiles and she did every visit. They were arranged so that you could read them chronologically or alphabetically but Sienna chose the profiles at random, feeling herself drawn to each name as a more personal approach. She would tag each profile with a heart when she read it then move on to the next. She read thirty or so profiles each Emancipation Day and told herself that she would try to visit more than once a year to honour the fallen but she never did.

"Who are you reading?" Geri asked.

"Harriet Buswell," Sienna replied. She'd died in 1872 so no photograph existed but there was an illustration from an old Victorian scandal rag of the day. "You?"

"Krystyna Skarbek."

Obviously. Geri always paid tribute to Krystyna. She'd

been a Polish resistance fighter and SOE spy during the Second World War and took part in dozens of daring missions behind enemy lines, winning medals and accolades from contemporaries and historians alike. She was also beautiful and Geri bore her eternal respect and warm fuzzy feelings despite the fact that Krystyna had been murdered more than a century earlier (after the war by an obsessive stalker). If she could have spoken from the grave, Sienna doubted Krystyna would have gone for Geri. They were both beautiful but Krystyna was more conventional than Geri. During the war, she had been described as the "bravest of the brave" according to journalist and friend, Alistair Horne. However, whether her bravery would have stretched to standing on Wimbledon Common stark naked surrounded by thousands of others was another thing.

It was early November and the ground was crisp with leaves. Last year, when Geri had first embraced naturalism, she had gone back to wearing clothes for the winter but this year she was determined to see it through. Part-time naturalists were a joke to the hardcore community. 'Hobbynobbies' they were called. Geri was committed for life. She would use the lotion to stop herself from feeling the cold and treat the souls of her feet to toughen them up but she would never again wear anything other than the skin Panthea had gifted her, sacred and natural as it was. Although she would cover it in increasingly garish tattoos.

"You're bleeding," Sienna pointed.

"Huh?" Geri looked down. Menstrual blood was trickling between her legs. Sienna searched her bag for a sanitary towel but Geri shook her head.

"Every womxn bleeds."

"Yes, but not on the seats of buses if we can help it,"

Sienna said, wondering when Geri had removed her tampon. She'd been wearing one earlier but once they'd left the house, she had elected to go even more *au naturale* than usual, content to wear just the lily that came with the box.

There were plenty of naturalists in the city. More than the towns. Probably because there was anonymity in the cities. Trends started and died here. Sometimes they took off and went nationwide. Geri liked to think of herself as being at the cutting edge of the zeitgeist but here in the big city, she was just another attention-seeker walking around in her skin.

The clock struck midday and the crowds fell silent. All across the rolling heathland not a womxn stirred. The only sounds to be heard were the cries of a lone femxle vocalist, repeatedly screaming "Help me! Help! Somebody help me!" beside the obelisk to symbolise the unanswered cries of womyn throughout the ages. Her performance went on, growing ever more agonised for the entirety of the two-minute vigil until she screamed herself silent, unheralded, unanswered and unforgotten.

Sienna didn't see the artist who'd voiced the 'silent scream'. She and Geri were too far back but her voice had touched her soul. She dabbed her eye and laid her head on Geri's shoulder feeling the need to be close to her. Geri put an arm around Sienna and dipped her head to hers. This was the power of Emancipation Sunday. It strengthened the bonds between womyn, dead, alive and yet to breathe.

Zaria Okello, the Minister For Survivors, laid a wreath at the obelisk. After wiping away a pre-prepared tear, she turned and made an impassioned speech. She spoke of the shame she felt towards the ignoble history of these toxic isles; the bravery of those few pioneering womyn who had fought to destroy the patriarchy; and the debt the nation owed to

Charity GoodHope for having the vision to reshape the commonwealth of multiplicity and renew the covenant of mutuality betwixt the people and their enlightened benefactors. The crowd applauded. Geri whooped. Sienna ran Zaria's speech through her Glasses to access the layperson's translation.

By 12.30pm it was all over. The Minister's helicopter left, the crowds dispersed and Sienna and Geri headed for the High Street. There was no point in going to the bus stop. There would be too many people queuing. They'd get a bite to eat in Wimbledon first and take a look around.

Neither Sienna nor Geri left Woking very often. With work, shopping and friendship all remotely accessible and private vehicle ownership outlawed, there was no need and little opportunity to travel. A couple of times a year, they took a bus to the coast to enjoy a few days by the sea. And they had previously signed up for a walking tour of Salisbury Plain and volunteered to help out on an arboricultural retreat run for the benefit of Alzheimer sufferers but these activities were often oversubscribed, hard work and frankly boring when compared to staying at home, watching AI shows and vaping freely available drugs. But, as they were in the city anyway, they thought they would take advantage and enjoy their day out.

This city had once been called London but that too had changed with the coming of Charity GoodHope's new vision. London was a toxic name. A male name. A name derived from King Lud, a barbaric butcher from pre-Roman times. How did we know King Lud was a butcher? Because he was a king and a man and no king who had wielded a sword had ever sheathed it unsullied. But Polychrome thinkers had a better name for the place. Prior to King Lud, this small settlement on the banks of the Thames had been known as Trinovantum, named after the Trinovantes tribe who had ruled years earlier. When the hour came, they flocked to the banner of female warrior Boudica and fought for a free Britannia. They had been slaughtered in their efforts but Charity GoodHope was determined they be remembered by for all time.

Trinovantum translated as New Troy, the name Charity now bestowed upon her wondrous reborn capital city.

Sienna and Geri wandered around the south-western corner of it, still known as Wimbledon but for how long? Nobody knew. There were plenty of womyn on the streets which was a comfort because Wimbledon felt unfamiliar and rough. This particular neighbourhood was very white and seemed to lack the cultural diversity of Woking. Gangs of white youths congregated on the fringes of the high street to intimidate lone womyn who walked past, violating and denigrating them with their eyes.

Geri stopped to confront one such group, an ugly assortment of teenage freaks and leering fatheads.

"What the fuck are you staring at?" she demanded, calling them out for daring to look at her naked body as she walked by. Sienna was unnerved but a dozen womyn soon rallied to Geri's defence and together they squared up to the toxic teens until they were routed.

"It's alright, we don't want no trouble," the leader said, slinking back into the shadows along with his Neolithic mates.

Traffic was heavy in New Troy, mostly cycle couriers and double-length hydrogen buses and the sky seemed further away than usual. The once-new steel and glass buildings of the town centre were weather-worn and the shutters were pulled on most, with many looking as though they hadn't been opened in years. Graffiti adorned every wall, much of it sexual in nature and all of it pernicious. "Rapists Rise" was a common theme although there was another etching that caught Sienna's eye and shook her up. A crude image had been scratched into the side of a wall featuring a completed hangman motif with a stick figure hanging by its neck. Below was a line of dashes, a word waiting to be guessed, along with a clue.

Q. Name of an Auditor?

Sienna stared at it in abhorrence but Geri saw it and chuckled.

"Yeah well, I can think of a few names to put in there," she said, turning and continuing on her way, oblivious to Sienna's horror. Sienna blinked to take a photograph. She would submit it to S Division when she got back to work but she wasn't sure what they could do about it. She might have spent her days sitting in a comfortable seat pouring over archives but danger was a real part of her work. She had to be on her guard, always, even with Geri. Especially with Geri. She ran to catch her up and sought comfort from the reassuring cloak of her cover story.

Geri was hungry. She had spotted a noodle bar beneath a railway arch and weaved between the speeding cycle couriers to cross the street. The proprietor was a busy East Asian with the username tokyotony2034.11. He was of Japanese descent and had pictures, ribbons and a clutch of golden cats waving one paw in unison to prove it.

"You girls go girl day in park?"

Girl number one confirmed girls had.

"Good. Good. Now hungry for ramen, yes?"

Sienna wondered if he really talked like this or whether he

was just putting it on for the customers. Either way, it was both sweetly endearing and hugely offensive in equal measure. Sienna couldn't decide which.

"What do you recommend?" Geri asked, leaning on the serving hatch and enjoying the warmth as it flowed over the kiosk.

He thought about this for longer than he should have, considering he only had about eight things on the menu, and eventually shrugged. "What you see is all good. Good food for you."

This was a curious answer and Sienna wondered if it implied there was, at least, the possibility of something else, not advertised that was available to 'special' customers.

She leaned in and gave him a wink.

"Got any tish'?" she asked as off-handedly as she could, unintentionally looking like the world's biggest narc.

tokyotony2034.11 gawped up from his wok while Geri turned in shock.

"Don't know what you mean. You bad girls. You go now. I close," he said in a sudden hurry, shoving Geri off his hatch and pulling down the shutter before she or Sienna could say anything else.

Tish' was slang for meat (tish' = tissue). Sienna was familiar with the term and had the brilliant idea of using it to see what happened. Wimbledon was only 30 miles from Farnham so if Garfield was a player on the meat scene, it wasn't out of the realms of possibility that some of his contacts crossed spatulas at night.

"Seriously babe, what the actual fuck," Geri choked in disbelief.

"I was just curious, you know."

"I'm standing right next to you. You didn't even hide your

username. You shamed me, you fucking freak. Fuck!" she said, her frozen nipples sticking out like washing machine dials, menstrual blood coating her legs like jam. She ran away, scarcely daring to look back in case the Guardians were already racing up the street towards them.

Sienna ran after her and felt awful. Geri was right. It hadn't just been her she'd put at risk. She exposed Geri too and this was the sort of thing that could come back and haunt a person when they least expected it. Sienna would be alright. If questioned, she could reveal herself to an Auditor and show them evidence of her investigation but Geri had no such get-out. And as far as Geri was aware, neither did Sienna. Geri had no clue what Sienna did or why she had asked for 'tish. What must she have thought?

Some repairs were needed. They'd been enjoying each other's company up until this point.

"I'm really sorry," Sienna said, talking breathlessly as she and Geri walked quickly and with purpose to the buses on the other side of the Common. "I didn't think he'd react like that. I was just joking, you know."

"I didn't see him laughing."

"I shouldn't have done it. I know it. I'm sorry. I won't do it again."

"Are you fucking mad or something?"

"You had peanuts not so long ago," Sienna reminded her, determined not to occupy the moral low ground all by herself.

"Shhhhhh. What the fuck's wrong with you?" Geri panicked, desperately grabbing at Sienna's face and waving a fist under her nose to stop her from saying anything else. "Anyone could be listening."

They quickened their pace and hurried across the

Common, following the stragglers to join a few hundred womyn waiting at the bus stop on the A3. They melted through the crowd and Geri pulled Sienna's shiny red trench coat from her back, turned it inside out and slipped it on. She kept looking over her shoulder and scanning Network chatter before waving her lily in the air to push through when the first bus came along. The doors stayed open for what seemed an eternity before the beeps sounded and the hydraulics engaged. No one appeared on the horizon. No Guardian wagons or spotter drones gave chase and the bus eventually pulled away. Geri almost sobbed with relief.

She looked up from her hands and sent Sienna a private NetCom message.

OMP. You can't do that. And don't put anything in writing either. But WTF? – Geri

I'm really sorry. I really really am. I don't know what came over me – Sienna

Neither do I. I mean, what got into you? – Geri

I don't know. Honest, I don't – Sienna

What would you have done if he'd said yes? And remember, choosing your words very carefully, did you even think about that? – Geri

No – Sienna

So you would have had it? – Geri

Of course not – Sienna

I hope not – Geri

You're always saying we should try new things – Sienna

But not that. Shit. Fuck. That's disgusting – Geri

A thought occurred to Sienna but once again she misjudged the moment. Driven by a need to justify herself and her aversion to Geri's friends, she jumped into waters she would not have entered a few weeks earlier.

Any of your friends tried it? – Sienna

Of course not. My friends aren't like that – Geri

How do you know? – Sienna

I know – Geri

Have you asked them? They're pretty out there some of them – Sienna

I trust them – Geri

What about Fuzz? – Sienna

Fuzz is cool. And that shit is not cool. Fuck. Fuck off – Geri

Now feeling anything but cool, Geri returned Sienna's trench coat, ripping it off and dumping it into Sienna's arms without turning it the right way out. She spotted a seat at the back and made her way towards it, swaying as the bus raced away from the city. The suburbs of New Troy flashed by outside, becoming leafier with every passing mile but Geri barely noticed them. Her mind was elsewhere and her thoughts a jumble of angry fear. Sienna joined her after a few minutes and laid a hand on Geri's goose-pimpled thigh. She half-expected it to be batted away but Geri took Sienna's hand and shook her head ruefully. Neither spoke or messaged another word, saying all they needed to say with their eyes. Sienna was truly sorry, genuinely so, and not just because her moment of stupidity had led to another fight. It was more than that. She couldn't get on an even keel with Geri. Just when they had the chance to connect, to reset the dial and inch a little closer, she'd ruined everything again. Just as she always did. Damn it. She really was a freak.

If she could have cried she would have but the tears would not come. She'd shed them easily enough for the souls of womyn long dead, but she could not shed a single one for herself. Despite knowing that the love that had once empowered her was dying too.

15: TRUST

"Ah, that hurts."

"Then hold still."

"But you don't need to do it. Libby does it."

"Libby's not here so let me do it. You've got a big knot in there."

The brush slid through half of Charity's dark hair before it once again encountered the same tangled clump. Fawqiyya tugged at it rhythmically and Charity yelped with each tug before pulling her head away. Fawqiyya eyed the office door, locked from this side with instructions for no one to disturb them.

Charity wasn't usually allowed in Fawqiyya's office unless other people were in here: important people, political people, business people or, more often than not, photography people. She liked being alone with Fawqiyya and even got to call her "mummy" when no one was around, a name that Fawqiyya discouraged in public.

She put down the brush and picked at the knot with her nails, pulling it apart strand by strand to see if she could locate where it all knitted together. This soon got tiresome so Fawqiyya resorted to the brush again and a little more force. Charity winced and tried pulling away, exasperating Fawqiyya. "You should think yourself lucky," she told Charity. "There are plenty of girls your age who've undergone femxle genital mutilation and you don't hear them moaning."

Charity was five years old and had no memory of her past. She had been pulled from the Channel three years earlier and had forgotten what little she hadn't blocked out. She had bad dreams, of course, and sometimes cried for no reason but she had an army of therapists to help her with that and Libby for everything else, hair and all. Fawqiyya thought of herself as

Charity's tutor but to Charity, she was her mummy and the only mummy she had ever known.

"There," Fawqiyya said, gliding the brush through her hair to leave her once wiry mane shiny and smooth.

Fawqiyya had done everything she could to shield Charity from the horrors of her origins. Everyone knew the story and children Charity's own age were even being taught it at school, but Charity herself knew nothing of it. She was here and she was special and that was all that mattered. She knew she was not like other children but she didn't understand how. Or why. Or what it all meant. She had so many questions but was always told by Fawqiyya; "All in good time".

"Will I ever have a brother or a sister?" Charity asked.

"You know that's not possible," Fawqiyya told her.

"Why?" she asked.

"Because you're so unique that we could never love anyone as much as we love you."

Charity liked hearing this but still didn't understand. She kicked her legs and thought about how special she was as Fawqiyya brushed her hair and pulled on the surgical gloves.

"I would love a sister to play with, Mummy."

Fawqiyya snipped a few small straps from Charity's head and, as carefully as she could, slipped them into a sterile sample tube and sealed the lid. On the side was a label with a barcode and the name of a testing facility.

"Mummy?"

"What is it, Charity?"

"Where do babies come from?"

Fawqiyya thought about this as she slipped the tube inside an envelope and wrote on the outside: 'Strictly Confidential: For My Eyes Only.'

"That's a very good question," Fawqiyya said. "Let's find

out shall we?"

"In good time?" Charity sighed.

"Oh, I think we can probably be a little quicker than that," she said, placing the envelope in her Priority Out Tray.

*

Many years later, Sienna found herself examining an altogether different hair and struggling to identify it. It was too dark to be her own. Too long to have come from Geri. Yet she had found it in her bed. On her side. Beneath her pillow. The pillow she slept on. It shouldn't have been there. So where had it come from?

Aurora had blue hair with a long quiff and shaven sides. Fuzz had a closely cropped buzz cut and was auburn. Purdy wore her hair long beneath the hijab and had been in their bed but Carl had washed their sheets since. Meaning it had to have come from someone else. But who? Diego? Diego's friend, the one with the squinty eyes? Persons unknown? Sienna couldn't tell.

This was beside the point. Geri had agreed not to bring anyone here – ever – and this said otherwise.

Sienna moved the covers and examined the bedding with a forensic eye. She sniffed the sheets and looked under the springs but found nothing else. Her Smart Glasses were on the bedside table. She put them on. As the primary partner of Geri, she was theoretically within her rights to see who else she was signing contracts with. But she had opted out of this clause when they'd renewed their A6, preferring to live in ignorance than to know every name and date. Whatever Geri did, she did out there in the nether world. That was half of Geri. But Sienna possessed the rest. Or so she had thought. But this hair said wake up and smell the coffee.

Sienna messaged Carl.

Morning Carl. How are you today? Good I hope – Sienna

Good morning Sienna. I am fine thank you. And thank you for enquiring. Did you have a restful sleep and pleasant dreams? – Carl

Yes, thank you. I feel fully refreshed this morning thanks to your temperature regulation. You always get it just right. You're so good at everything – Sienna

Sienna sighed inwardly, desperate to get to the point and tired at having to go through this rigmarole every morning. She exercised another minute of restraint listening to Carl's dreams about squirrels despite knowing it was all AI-generated bullshit before finally asking the question she wanted to ask.

Who's on the visitors log for this week? I know we had someone here but I've forgotten who – Sienna

Carl went uncharacteristically quiet for a few seconds before the answer appeared before her.

Visitors log for last six days not found – Carl

What do you mean, not found? How could that be? – Sienna

It appears to have been deleted from my database. Is there anything else I can help you with? Will you have your coffee now or after your shower? – Carl

This time it was Sienna's turn to go quiet. Carl asked if everything was okay and said he could keep her coffee warm but Sienna was already hurrying to the kitchen, having had her question answered in a roundabout way.

Geri was there, talking to someone through her Glasses. Sienna came in and held up the hair. "What's this?"

"Hold on. I'll call you back," Geri told her caller. She looked at whatever Sienna was holding and zoomed in but shook her head.

"What?"

"This," Sienna said, only now noticing she wasn't holding

anything. She must have dropped it. She looked around but it was gone. Fuck. Geri sipped her coffee and waited patiently while Sienna reordered her thoughts. "I found a hair. In our bed."

"So?"

"It's not mine and it's not yours so whose is it?"

Sienna tried to keep her voice measured. She was raging deep down but desperate to keep a lid on it. She didn't want to start the week on a fight. That would drive Geri away again and she was desperate to keep her home for a little longer.

"Let's have a look at it."

"You need to look to know who's been in our bed?"

"I don't know then," Geri said as nonchalantly as she could, holding her cup near her lips to shield her guilt-struck expression.

"Yeah well, maybe let's have a look at the visitors log then, shall we? Carl?"

Carl stayed silent, mistaking their argument for sexual foreplay but his input wasn't needed anyway. Geri turned and muttered something under her breath that her Smart Glasses almost forwarded before she deleted it again.

"Look, what does it matter? It was just someone I met."

"Who?"

"No one you know?"

"You promised not to bring anyone back here. That was our agreement," Sienna said, angry and confused as to why Geri had done this. She had the entire world to go and fuck in and permission to do so. The one place Sienna had asked her not to defile was their bed. The bed they shared. Their retreat from the world. Their safe haven. It had been really important to her. Geri had promised yet here was proof that some stranger had lain where she lay, touching the womxn she touched. Why had she done it?

"We didn't have anywhere else to go and it was cold. It was just meant to be a drink but you know how these things go."

No, Sienna didn't. How did they go?

Geri put down her cup, starting to bristle, and stared at Sienna with eyes of ice.

"You want me to describe it to you? Paint you a picture of everything we did?"

"No," Sienna baulked, unable to hide her abhorrence. How could Geri say such a thing?

"Then what the fuck do you want from me? I thought we were cool. I thought we agreed that I could be me. I mean, what fucking difference does it make anyway?"

"Because you promised. You agreed not here. Not in my house," Sienna said, instantly regretting her choice of words but it was too late. Geri picked up on her slip.

"*Your* house? *Your* house? I thought it was *our* house?"

"I didn't mean that," Sienna said, trying to backtrack but the argument had switched in the blink of an eye, no longer about who'd betrayed who, it became about who'd paid for what, a perpetual crack in their fractured relationship. Sienna was the breadwinner. She'd bought the house and paid for almost everything in it. She had a steady salary and financial security. Geri was the artist, the creative 'genius' whose dreams Sienna was happy to bankroll but they both knew the situation and it fermented exacerbation in Sienna and insecurity in Geri.

"You said it. *Your house*. Your words. What am I a fucking guest or something?"

"No no, it was a slip of the tongue. It's your house as much as mine. Every bit of it," Sienna promised, backing away as Geri advanced but Geri wasn't reassured.

"It's my house but I can't do what I want in it? Is that what you're saying?"

"No."

"I can't feel at home in my own home?" Geri had the bit between her teeth and she was not about to let go.

"Fuck."

"Why don't you trust me, babe?" Geri demanded, following Sienna until she had her cornered near the sink.

"I do," Sienna lied, wishing she could turn back the clock and take back what she'd said. Ignorance was bliss. Hurt could be bottled.

"You don't trust me? I'm not a grown-up to you? I'm just some trophy wife?"

"I love you," Sienna implored, only wanting them to be happy. Why couldn't they be happy? Why was it so hard?

"Yeah? As long as I'm a good little girl and do exactly as you say, wait at home for you like your property, just so you can avoid having your own life."

"I do have a life," Sienna insisted despite feeling the cold hard stab of truth in what Geri said.

"What, work and me? What else do you do?"

"I have a life?"

"Are you talking about Ellie? Your *friend*, Ellie? You mean *Ellie*?" Geri sneered, knowing full well that Ellie existed only as Carl existed, as lines of code in an AI game that Sienna subscribed to.

This was a twist of the knife too many and Sienna tried to move but Geri wouldn't let her and blocked her escape.

"No. Look at me. Look at me, babe."

Sienna tried but failed as a great weight of misery bore down on her. Geri grabbed her face and forced her to look.

"I'm your only friend. Me. No one else cares about you. No one else gives a shit. You're all alone. You're nothing without me," Geri raged, reversing their RP script to tear Sienna's confidence to shreds. Only this time, it was no game. "You're a fucking selfish dyke, you hear me? And I've had enough of your whiny shit."

"I'm sorry," Sienna said but Pandora was out. There was no putting the lid back on her box now.

Geri bore down on her, her perfect naked body twitching with anger against Sienna's soft fluffy pyjamas. Sienna felt smaller than Geri in every way; in size, in outlook and in power. She shrank before Geri and knew that if they had any sort of future together, this would be their new reality. She awaited the physical sting of Geri's anger but it never came. Geri stepped back, picked up her coffee and returned to her NetCom call.

Sienna slunk out, miserable and ashamed but Geri had one last observation for her.

"Go and have a shower. You fucking stink."

*

Sienna cried in the shower, on and on for longer than she knew but she felt cleansed when she emerged, her emotions washed clean to leave her feeling numb and robotic. She dried herself with the towel and let it lay where it dropped, stepping over it to open her wardrobe. The door slid back but she stopped and stared. For a moment, she was unable to process what she was seeing. Or rather, what she wasn't. Her clothes were gone. The dresses hanging on the rail. The leggings on the shelves. The sweaters neatly folded. They'd all been there this morning but now they weren't. She opened the drawers and was met by a similar sight. Her underwear had vanished. Her pants, bras, vests, socks and tights. The

Emperor's new tailor had called and rearranged her wardrobe.

"There's going to be some changes around here from now on," she heard Geri say.

She turned, as naked as her girlfriend and now with no choice but to be anything else.

Geri was satisfied.

"Now go to work."

16: SKIN

Sienna would have preferred to spend the day with Geri but it was Monday and she was due at the Hub. Geri hadn't just thrown out her clothes, she'd fed them through the waste disposal unit and had Carl shred them. There wasn't so much as a stitch left in the house. Not a pair of knickers or a single sock. Even the pyjamas she'd worn last night had been reduced to ribbons. And Geri had no clothes of her own, having thrown them all out months ago. Even the body stockings she used to wear were no more. Not hardcore enough.

Geri was determined to throw Sienna in at the deep end. Sink or swim. It was up to Sienna.

"Rub this on," Geri said, handing Sienna a bottle of steroid lotion designed for the naturalist community. "It will help keep the cold out."

But the cold was the last thing on Sienna's mind. She'd never felt so exposed in all her life and died at the thought of the world leering at her. It was one thing going to a club in which everyone was naked, but another to walk the streets in broad daylight while most were covered up. Geri did it. Diego did it. So did Purdy, Aurora and Fuzz. But Sienna wasn't like them. And as much as she tolerated her partner's lifestyle, she did not want it for herself.

"Are you ashamed of your body?" Geri demanded.

"No," Sienna lied.

"Then what have you got to hide?"

It was impossible to say. She knew her body was no different from every other womxn's, at least as far as the fixtures and fittings were concerned. But the terror she felt at going unclothed was too much to bear.

It brought it all back to her. Her worst experience. The one that had scarred her when Alan Miller had exploited her vulnerability for his own sexual gains. She'd engaged with him on a humxn level but it had been a subterfuge. A grubby ruse to get her to drop her guard and uncross her legs. It made her feel unclean, betrayed and defiled and she'd carried the shame with her ever since, desperate to never feel exposed again.

Sex had not been easy for Sienna. It had taken a lot before she'd trusted a partner enough to open up to them but when she had, she gave herself completely. Sure, she had fantasies. Who didn't? But to truly go beyond and commit to another in mind and body, that took something special. Something Sienna regarded as precious. Something Geri had accepted and discarded at will.

"Hold out your hands or you'll regret it."

Geri forced a big squirt into her hands and rubbed the lotion on her back as Sienna did everywhere else.

"This is going to change your life, babe. You'll love it. There's no going back now, not if we're going to evolve as a couple."

Sienna tried every argument she could think of, pleading with her, begging for a towel or even a tactical fig leaf but Geri was steadfast. Sienna needed to get over her mental block and realise that there was nothing to fear. No one was going to look at her. No one cared. She had nothing that anyone else didn't. If anything, she had a nice body.

Something to be admired. She slapped Sienna's bum painfully and told her it was time to go.

"Wait. No. Wait."

"Out."

"Please."

"If you don't go, I'll kick you out and drag you to the bus stop myself."

Sienna realised Geri was serious and knew that this would be the worst possible scenario, the two of them wrestling in the high street, lotioned up and buff naked. She got her stuff together, took six minutes to brush her teeth and begged to be allowed something for her feet. Geri had thrown out all of Sienna's boots but they still had a pair of sandals for trips to pebbly beaches. She allowed Sienna to slip them on then shoved her out the door.

"Have a great day, babe," she said, blowing a kiss and bolting the door.

Sienna shivered on her doorstep. The lotion helped but her blood felt like ice nevertheless. This couldn't be happening. Was she really going to walk into the town centre naked? This was her worst dream come true. She couldn't do it. She couldn't.

Sienna noticed Geri watching from the upstairs window and knew she couldn't linger here indefinitely. She looked around in the front yard for anything she could grab but there was nothing. No bin bags or cardboard boxes to wear. Geri demanded she went so finally she did, exiting the garden and moving slowly towards the high street, holding one arm across her breasts and the other to her crotch to conceal her modesty. If she had another hand she could have covered her bottom too but that had to do without, third place in her pecking order of shame.

Other than the sandals, the only thing she was wearing were her cherry-red Smart Glasses. Once at the end of her street, she slipped behind a wall and logged onto NetShop. No time to peruse, she went through her list of previous orders and added a new set of clothes to her basket before changing the delivery address to the alleyway at the end of Old Woking Road. Ordinarily, when she shopped, she would select the medium-cost option and have things shipped the next day but in this instance, she was happy to pay the extra for express delivery. She hurried to the alleyway, glancing around as she ran, up at windows and along the street. Several cycle couriers cruised by as she scampered, her vulnerabilities laid bare before them. She felt as though she was dying every time someone whizzed by but finally, she reached the alleyway and slipped out of sight.

There were a few bins, some graffiti and a lot of weeds back here but no people. She'd turned off her GPS signal to prevent Geri from tracking her and stayed out of sight as she watched the seconds tick by. She felt as though she were having an out-of-body experience. Her head couldn't take in the reality that she was crouching in a public place, where anyone could come by at any moment, totally nude. How did Geri do this? How did she mentally let go? Far from admiring Geri's confidence, it made Sienna feel the disconnect even more. Where had the girl she had fallen in love with gone?

A breeze circulated between Sienna's legs to make her feel beyond vulnerable. With it came a panicked thought. What if the cycle courier bringing her order turned out to be a sex attacker? She'd done half of the work for him, standing here naked in a secluded back alleyway with no witnesses anywhere to be seen. Perhaps he'd think she was some kind of willing victim, a fucked-up masochist begging to be abused. Sienna didn't believe the short skirt defence that rapists hid behind but she had to admit, if anyone was asking for it, it was her. As reluctant as she was, she concluded she would have to meet the courier somewhere public. The top of the High Street or the corner by the lights. Somewhere she would be safe.

However, no sooner had she made up her mind than her decision was taken from her. A message flashed in her Smart Glasses informing her that her sale had been declined.

She had no money in her account. What?

She still hadn't received her bonus but she had funds, certainly enough for a pair of leggings and a vest. But she checked her account and sure enough, it registered zero, having been emptied five minutes earlier. Geri must have transferred every penny, anticipating what Sienna would do.

Sienna tried to get a store credit but NetShop needed verification from her home OS and Carl would not comply. Credit cards and insta-loans were the same. She applied but was turned down by every single one of them.

Oh no.

That was it. She was out of options. She now had no choice but to endure the unendurable. She had to go into town naked or squat in this alleyway all day and risk discovery. What could she do?

The dread that filled her poleaxed her completely. She dry-retched, puking up bile and filling her senses with snot. Oh Panthea. She couldn't do this. She couldn't.

"Are you alright, miss?"

A voice behind her made her scream. She tumbled over and her screams turned to hysteria when she saw who'd spoken.

A couple of Cans had snuck up from behind, swarthy-looking creatures with haggard faces and hunched shoulders. They stared at her with bemusement, running their bloodshot eyes all over her soft fleshy body. She had no defence and tried to crab crawl away, kicking in desperation and scraping her back against mud.

"Help me. Help me," she screamed, her mind thrown back to yesterday, and the unheralded scream from Emancipation Day. Was she also about to take her place on the Obelisk?

The Cans rushed at her, one stifling her cries while the other pulled off her Smart Glasses to stop her from alerting the Guardians.

"Please. We're not going to hurt you. We promise. Don't get us into trouble," the first Can urged her, looking more terrified than she did. She was on the ground, the bins hiding them from the main road. Her legs kicked against the Can's side and her nails scratched his face but he was too strong for her. He held her down so that she was completely defenceless as his friend joined in. She expected him to pop his buckle and lay on top of her but he did neither. He just looked at her with desperation in his eyes and pleaded with her to be quiet.

"I'm going to let you up. I'm not going to hurt you. I swear it. But if you scream, me and him, that's us gone. We'll be sent north. Please. I'm begging you." There was genuine terror in his expression and it was mirrored in the face of his friend. "We're not going to hurt you."

Slowly and fearfully, the Can removed his hand from Sienna's mouth. He moved back a short way, leaving Sienna sprawled on the ground before them. She drew up her legs and covered herself with her hands, feeling helpless and confused. The other Can held out Sienna's Glasses. She was convinced every gesture was a trick but neither tried anything. They just looked at her with sad eyes and glanced all around as they crouched opposite.

"We thought you might be in trouble. We wanted to help."

Sienna tried to process the words but they made no sense. Why would a Can help her? Particularly when they could've just as easily raped her? What was in it for them?

"I'm Martin," said the first Can, having to verbalise his name in the absence of a username.

"Krish," said the second. "Are you alright?"

Sienna wasn't alright. In fact, she was a long way from alright and tears of misery, pain and loneliness spilled down her cheeks. Eventually, she told Martin and Krish what had happened. At least, what had happened in the last twenty minutes. The rest was too confusing to explain. Even to herself.

Without being asked, Krish removed his jacket and handed it to Sienna while Martin unbuckled his belt and offered up his trousers.

"Sorry," he said. "I would have done that sooner but I thought you were one of those nutty naked people."

Sienna was bowled over. She held Martin's trousers and couldn't believe he'd given them to her. Of all the kindnesses she had known, none came as close to this.

"But what will you do?" she said, surprised to find herself concerned for their wellbeing.

"We're just back there," he said, pointing down the alleyway towards the field at the end. "In the hostel. I can get another pair."

"Your need is greater," smiled Krish, and with that they hurried away, glancing this way and that as they did so. Sienna watched them as they went, keeping to the shadows and skulking out of sight.

Back to their own kind.

And the depraved evil lives they supposedly led.

17: JULIE

Sienna made it to work forty minutes later. Martin's trousers and Krish's jacket weren't her usual style but she had never loved a set of clothes more.

She'd seen two naturalists on her way in. One on the bus, one getting a coffee at the kiosk opposite the Hub. Neither seemed phased to be walking around naked and no one took any notice of them. Geri had been right about that. But she had been wrong about Sienna. She hadn't loved it. Not even slightly. And she didn't want to learn to love it either. The first thing she did when she logged in was contact E Division to chase up her bonus. The second thing she did was to change her banking details with payroll to a dormant savings account she still held from before she and Geri had moved in together. To her surprise, she had §17.47 in it, enough for some shorts and a T-shirt but not enough for delivery. Two hours later, it held §3183.52 and she resubmitted her shopping order. Twenty-seven minutes after that, she got a notification that there was a package waiting for her with Reception and went to retrieve it.

She changed in her privacy pod – red pants, red bra, black leggings, white ankle socks, white T-shirt (five pairs of each), a pair of air-cushioned boots and a shiny red plastic trench coat – all while vowing never to find herself in that position again. She would wear one set of clothes home and hide another wrapped in plastic by the side of their house. There was a pile of bricks there that Geri wouldn't go near, not with her fear of creepy crawlies. The rest she would stash in the Hub's lockers. It wasn't a perfect plan but it would leave her better placed than she had been this morning.

Geri messaged several times but Sienna didn't reply. They would talk eventually but not today. Sienna would wait until she left before she went home. She would book into a sleeping pod if she had to but she would not see Geri again today. She had to gather her thoughts and know her own mind. For five years, she had loved Geri more than she had loved herself but that was the Geri of old, not what she had become. She couldn't do this any more. She couldn't go on spiralling through heartache and hell.

There had to be a resolution.

She got very little work done over the next few hours. She couldn't get her head straight. She should have probably taken a Mental Wellness Day but Bella would have tried to counter it. It was easier to stay where she was, sitting inanimate at her desk and staring at the Network with empty eyes as pixelated life rushed by.

But she couldn't put off her case files forever. They were mounting up and the next Congress had been scheduled. She had to get to work.

Still nothing on Charles Garfield. She sent an information request to the Guardians for any meat leads in Surrey. There would be hundreds and she would need to distill them through MUM but perhaps she could get to Charles Garfield by working backwards.

Besides him, she had four other cases that were awaiting her attention:

– Descendants of the public prosecutor who'd brought charges against the 'Colston 4'.

– The grandson of a teacher who'd used an outdated theoretical text to tutor her science class.

– The CEO of an architectural firm who'd designed a number of buildings in the early part of the century that lacked proper universal access.

– A TERF agitator who had called for gender segregation

in sports and used hate language to justify her position.

This case was the easiest to collate because it wasn't a historical case. The TERF (Trans-Exclusionary Radical Feminist) was a womxn called Abby Grey, the co-organiser of a group called (ironically) Sports For All. She was calling for the regressive reintroduction of gender divisions in sports and justified her calls by claiming that womyn were shut out. This was plainly ridiculous. What few sports existed in New Britannia, almost all of them were now dominated by femxle athletes.

In the earliest years of the Polychrome Alliance, Fawqiyya el-Abdulla had identified sports as being a major source of discord within society. Many towns had two or three teams and they were often pitched against each other as rivals. This was a toxic situation that incited violence on a regular basis. As Margaret Thatcher had famously destroyed the unions, Fawqiyya el-Abdulla made it one of her highest priorities to destroy sports. Men's sports, in particular. She started with football.

Her first step was the enforcement of a wage cap. It was simply obscene that an ill-educated and thuggish footballer could earn five million a year and yet an Equality, Diversity & Inclusion Advisor appointed by the Alliance couldn't even earn half of that. Index-linking footballers' earnings to those of NHS nurses stopped disproportionality overnight and the effect was instantaneous. Entire teams submitted transfer requests and the 'brawn drain' began as players fled for clubs in Europe, China and the Middle East. Youth players were quickly promoted and games continued for a while but the bubble had well and truly burst. The Premier League was the first to go, having no premier content to market. The Football Association tried to pick up the pieces but a series of viruses from Asia proved catastrophic when the stadiums were forced to shut. Without television money or ticket sales, the clubs toppled like dominos. Mxnchester, Liverpool, Glasgow and London, as it was then called, dozens of clubs with centuries of tradition went to the wall in a very short space of time, dragged down by enormous overheads and choking debts. On the sidelines and not yet ten, Charity GoodHope campaigned vociferously for a swathe of new regulations, mandatory inclusion targets and special environmental levies which forced the Football Association and various leagues into liquidation.

The backlash was enormous but the Alliance had moved quickly and with purpose and they had many allies. Most clubs were so precariously financed that even the slightest tinkering sent them into freefall. Some fans even welcomed the reforms, keen to get back to grassroots but they too were appalled when the Alliance used draconian powers to prevent unsanctioned assemblies. Within the space of a few seasons, Fawqiyya el-Abdulla was able to oversee the demise of the 'beautiful game' in the name of peace and love. Rugby, cricket, hockey and tennis all went the same way until eventually, the only balls being whacked in anger were in womyn's Judo.

In football's place came Yoga and Tai Chi, televised and on every sports channel, they were heralded as the new national pastimes. Meditation was also given a big-money makeover and marketed to the masses, with sports tops and merchandising aimed at filling the gap left behind by outlawed football shirts. This only proved marginally successful.

Athletics was one of the few competitive sports to be spared. It might not have been as belligerent as football but it was still identified as being exclusionary. Operated along binary lines, athletes who did not identify with their birth gender had been discriminated against for decades. Therefore, all gender barriers were scrapped and the British Athletics Association was compelled to operate for the inclusion of all. Inevitably, this led to an imbalance in athletic competition with cis men winning everything that first year. A cap was therefore deemed necessary to encourage inclusion, firstly limiting cis male participants to three, then two, then none. Womyn's athletics boomed as a result but bigots like Abby Grey continued to pop up every now and again and claim discrimination, calling for a return to the exclusionary policies of yesteryear: the very policies that limited opportunities for diverse athletes in the first place.

Sienna reviewed the data on Abby Grey. It was an open-and-shut case. She had called for a separate annual event aimed solely at cis femxle athletes to the exclusion of all others. This extended to transwomxn, non-binary, intersex and gender-fluid competitors of every identification despite the fact that such athletes were the most successful in the country. This was not only at odds with the spirit of free and fair competition, it also went against the constitution of New Britannia. But Abby claimed her intentions were not intended to be exclusionary. She said her proposals were simply aimed at supporting cis femxle athletes, who were statistically the least successful sportspeople in the country.

Within days of airing her views, she was arrested on the grounds of hate speech. Now she was to be cancelled too.

It was a formality. A case file to be rubber-stamped and presented to Congress so that E Division could seize her assets. Sienna had handled dozens of such cases. Hundreds even. But today, she looked down at Martin's trousers and

Krish's jacket, both neatly folded on the floor beside her, and she couldn't bring herself to do it. Martin and Krish had been cancelled for themselves, perhaps even by Sienna, a thought that made her uncomfortable. Yet they had helped her in her moment of need. They hadn't needed to. And they hadn't asked for anything in return. But they had helped her all the same.

Sienna felt the weight of Karma pressing down on her.

She'd had a good career until now. She was well-respected and valued by the company. Not by Bella but by Myrtle and some of the other Division heads. She had earned the right to make a mistake and get away with it. She'd have to explain herself if she was ever found out. She'd claim it was all an oversight, she was mentally unbalanced at the time; perhaps she had been wearing a particularly heavy lily that day, but she was confident she had enough in the bank to cover this particular bill.

She pulled Abby Grey's file front and centre and scrolled to the summary box at the bottom, ticking: 'Insufficient Evidence to Action'. She now filed it in the wrong place and changed the timecode, knowing it could go unnoticed for months, maybe even years. By which time, a maintenance program would have been run on the system, corrupting the errant file or deleting it altogether.

Abby Grey might have been a bigoted transphobe, something Sienna could not condone, but Sienna had given her another chance. And in this day and age, that was a rare and beautiful thing.

"Okay?" she said, speaking directly to Martin and Krish's clothes. "Happy now?"

*

Julie wasn't in the food hall but Anita Xeno was, looking tired and overloaded with more self-hate than usual. She didn't join Sienna at her table, each sparing the other the inquisition.

Geri messaged her again. This time Sienna replied but only to stop Geri from bombarding her.

You okay, babe? How's it been? Wild yeah? – Geri

I'm okay. Survived. Just lots of work. Sorry – Sienna

Knew you would. Proud of you girl. You're one of us now – Geri

You home tonight? – Sienna

Poss not. Got a thing. D's coding. Said I'd help. Prob stay out – Geri

Okay – Sienna

Love you – Geri

Sienna was almost tempted not to reply but in the end, opted to insert a suitably long pause before responding.

Thanks – Sienna

Sienna now ended their chat. For once, before Geri, something she almost never did. Would Geri notice? Probably not. She would have already been on her way to Diego's, her mind full of code and algorithms to the distraction of all other signals. As far as Geri was concerned, she'd messaged Sienna, Sienna had replied and that would filed under 'all good'. Little missy knew her place.

Sienna tipped her half-eaten lunch into the recycling bin and headed back to work.

Inwardly, she was relieved at having messaged with Geri. At least she knew she wouldn't be home tonight. This gave her time to get her head straight, move a few things around and make a plan. She didn't know what she was going to do and it frightened her to think about it but she couldn't live in denial any more. They'd come off the rails. Way off.

She loaded a new cartridge of Oxy into her Vape and took a pull. It clouded her thoughts but did little to soothe her sadness. She upped the dose and pulled again.

Buzz-buzz.

Someone was outside. For a moment she panicked and imagined it to be Geri, tracking her down to make sure she wasn't dressed. But Geri had no ID clip and no way of getting into the Hub. And even if she did, she had no way of knowing which privacy pod Sienna used. They'd never been here together and the pods weren't marked.

Buzz-buzz.

Sienna activated her door cam and a small screen appeared showing Julie Adamski outside. Sienna's heart skipped a beat and she choked on her Oxy. Julie was looking directly up into the camera, her Smart Glasses crystal clear, instinctively knowing that Sienna would be watching. She implored her to unlock the door so that they could be together and Sienna again panicked. Was this really happening? Were they really about to be together, here, in this moment? It was one thing to dream about such a thing, another to act upon it.

If indeed, that was why Julie had come.

In that moment, Sienna longed to be with Julie so much it frightened her. But the fear felt excited. It shook her body and stole her breath. It was a fear she'd not felt in a good many years.

Julie looked up and down the corridor and pressed the buzzer again.

Buzz-buzz.

Sienna reached for the intercom but thought twice. Instead, she shut her screens, pulled out her ID clip and pressed the door release. The door slid aside and she found herself face to face with the girl of her deepest and most secret fantasies.

"Oh, you are there. Good," Julie said slightly awkwardly. "I hope I'm not disturbing you but I wondered if you wanted to grab a quick coffee?"

It was more than Sienna had hoped for. Julie was smiling and excited to see her. Her beautiful eyes danced with playful suggestion and she glanced around nervously, almost as if she couldn't bring herself to look Sienna in the eye. Sienna read the signals and decided to go one step further.

"Or you could come in if you wanted," she suggested, prompting Julie's smile to broaden. Sienna stepped aside and Julie entered with a backward glance. Sienna could scarcely believe it. She'd imagined this moment so many times, even whilst being with Geri, but the reality was so much more intense. She'd seen Julie often but never this close. And never when it had just been the two of them. She was alluring and soft. Her skin was delicate and her mouth poised in the most dainty of pouts. It took all of Sienna's strength not to embrace her the moment the door was shut as her heart thundered within.

Privacy pods weren't designed for two. They were more like cupboards than rooms and the narrow confines forced the girls together. Sienna smiled apologetically, Julie graciously, as their legs bumped and brushed against each other in their efforts to find some space.

"Do you want to sit?" Sienna suggested, offering Julie the only chair.

"Where will you sit?"

Sienna had an idea but wondered if that might be a little fast for Julie.

"On the floor."

"I'm okay standing," Julie said. And so was Sienna.

Julie wore a short one-piece dress, beige in colour and figure-hugging against her slender body. There was barely a curve to her, yet she was all womxn and everything Sienna had dreamed of.

"I just wanted to ask you," Julie said, accidentally touching Sienna's arm as she sought to steady herself. "I was just wondering, why you didn't sign Malek's A6."

Sienna could have leaned in with very little effort and kissed her. They were the same height and so close. It was almost harder not to kiss than to give in. At least, it was for Sienna. This would have answered Julie's question but Sienna wasn't sure she'd be able to stop there. Not now. Not after all she'd been through.

In the end, Sienna did what she usually did in situations like this. She choked.

"I didn't like him," she said with a shake of the head. "He wasn't a good guy."

Julie's expression narrowed. The overhead lighting glinted off her clear lenses to make her green eyes sparkle and she used them to full effect on Sienna, urging her to expand on what she knew.

"How?"

"He just wasn't. You deserve better, babe."

Julie thought about this, shifting her weight and brushing Sienna's thigh in the process. Their eyes locked.

"Sorry," she smiled.

"That's okay. I don't mind," Sienna croaked, having never uttered a truer word in her life.

"Did he say something to you? Or do something? I'm just trying to get my head around this," Julie said, attempting to come at it from a different angle.

Sienna wanted her to understand. She wanted her to know everything and for their souls to sync. Julie was everything that Geri was not: gentile and fragile, demure and vulnerable.

Sienna inched closer and Julie allowed her. Their bodies were now touching; their warmth turning to heat. Sienna felt that she and Julie were melding. Becoming one.

"Sometimes, you just know," Sienna said, desperate to put a hand on Julie's hip but terrified in equal measure.

"Know what?" Julie said, taking the lead and placing a hand on Sienna's arm to encourage her to open up. Sienna melted beneath her touch and took Julie's hand in hers. Julie didn't flinch. She didn't resist or react and Sienna knew at that moment that everything she was feeling, Julie was feeling too. It was destiny. Kismet. Alignment.

"I just knew," Sienna whispered, so quietly that Julie scarcely heard.

A moment later, Julie's green eyes flickered. She'd received a message and the sender caught her attention. It was from Sienna. Julie's perplexity turned to realisation when she opened the attachment and reviewed the contents. Her face dropped and her body stiffened.

"Did you just send me an A6?" she asked, suddenly aware of how tightly they were squeezed together. She had. Geri had 'gifted' her a pre-signed A6 shortly after they'd renegotiated their own contract. It had been witnessed by herself, Aurora and Fuzz and she had encouraged her to go out and have fun with it. It had languished in her cloud ever since. Now she used it, adding the only name she could envisage inserting, knowing that she was one short squiggle away from sexual fulfilment.

"I can't resist you any longer. I need you," Sienna said, pressing her body to Julie's just as Julie pressed hers to the wall. Hard.

"Er, wait, I'm not, you know, er… gay?"

"Me neither," Sienna sighed, despite all signs to the

contrary. She could feel Julie's sweet breath on her face and she knew that she would die if she did not kiss her in the next few seconds. She wanted her so badly, all her pent-up frustrations had fermented with desire and now she felt drunk with lust. "Please."

Julie took hold of Sienna and her hands felt sublime until Sienna realised she was pushing her away.

"Just give me a second," Julie said nervously, not knowing whether to laugh or cry. She kept Sienna at bay and upped her VunCon status to level 4. "I didn't know you were like this. Sorry. I thought you and Malek were... you know? I thought you maybe were into him."

An ice-cold bucket of reality crashed over Sienna and the veil of delusion from her eyes.

"Oh."

"Yeah."

"I'm sorry."

"It's okay," Julie said, trying to maintain her smile. "It's cool. We're cool."

"I shouldn't have done this," Sienna said, turning away but unable to in the tiny confines of the privacy pod. "I don't know what I'm doing."

"It's alright," Julie reassured her, seeing Sienna's shame and feeling her own. She let go of Sienna and turned her to face her. "Friends?" she asked, then pulled her close for a hug. Sienna fell into Julie's embrace, dying with disappointment as their bodies entwined. Despite their touch, she now felt the distance between them and laid her head on Julie's shoulder. Her eyes welled up and her misery became real.

"I'm so unhappy."

"I'm sorry," Julie said. "I really am. And I'm flattered. Maybe even intrigued," she added, whispering into Sienna's ear. "Is this why you didn't sign Malek's A6?"

But Sienna didn't want Julie to think this. She didn't want her to believe she had acted out of anything but love so she shared a truth with her, something she knew would persuade Julie of her intentions.

"He would have beaten you."

The girls remained embraced and Julie pawed at Sienna's back, tenderly and with affection.

"Why do you say that?"

"It's in his family."

"His family?"

It was all true. Malek's father had been a violent abuser. He had beaten his mother, leading to a prison sentence, a CDO (Compulsory Divorce Order) and a one-way ticket north. Malek had denounced his father at the trial and compared him to Hitler but he could not denounce his DNA. His grandmother had divorced his grandfather on the grounds of mental cruelty and there were other accounts in his lineage too, spanning the generations, of various forefathers mistreating various spouses. It was a commonly accepted fact that this sort of behaviour was hereditary in men, so it was inevitable that one day Julie would find herself sprawled across the floor, her lips bleeding and her heart broken, as Malek stood over her with rage in his eyes and subjugation in his fists.

Sienna wanted to spare Julie this pain. She desired her and fantasised about her but most of all, she cared about her.

Julie moved back and looked Sienna in the eyes, their lips so close that Sienna could almost taste her.

"How do you know this stuff?"

"It's true."

"But how do you know it?"

This was a different question. She was no longer asking about Malek. She was asking about Sienna. But Sienna couldn't say. Julie just had to trust her.

Julie's eyes scanned Sienna's for answers but she found none. She now looked around the privacy pod and found few answers here either. Sienna had pulled out her clip. She was logged off.

"What is it you do in here?" Julie asked, almost fearing to ask.

"I'm a Crypto Security Support Officer," Sienna said, falling back on her well-practised cover story.

"Yeah?" Julie said, noting the instant change in Sienna's demeanour. "What does that involve?"

"I oversee cyber security for a portfolio of private capital companies," Sienna said, her lies so fluent she almost believed them herself.

"Any I'd know?" Julie fished.

Sienna smiled apologetically. "Sorry, I can't say. More than my job's worth."

Julie stared at her intently, her green eyes boring through Sienna's cherry-tinted Smart Glasses and directly into her soul. Sienna was starting to wonder what she'd seen when, without warning, Julie snatched at her and kissed her hard on the mouth. Sienna almost fell backwards in shock but Julie pressed on, tonguing and clawing at her, eating her face until Sienna returned the compliment; delving, moaning, searching and gasping. Finally, they pulled apart and looked at each other in mutual surprise, breathless and laughing, liberated in that moment, all thoughts of hesitation gone.

"I'd better go," Julie said, kissing Sienna one more time. "I like you. I've never been with a girl before but I really like you. Let me think about it, yeah?"

Sienna received a confirmation ping in her peripheral vision to show that Julie had acknowledged receipt of her A6 and was considering it. She included a personal note.

You're so fucking hot – Julie

And with that, she was gone, out of the Pod and striding down the hall with a renewed sense of purpose. Sienna watched her go, her soul tingling with pleasure, her body aching for more.

18: ISLANDS

The islands of the north represented a new start for Cans; a chance to leave the scars of their former lives behind and start afresh. There were no official figures for how many had gone north but most people knew someone who had. And when they were gone, they were gone for good. The two societies did not mix. They could not. They were incompatible. New Britannia was a pure society; a land based on freedom, love and equality. The islands represented the very antithesis of this. The Cans were the weeds in Charity GoodHope's Eden. They needed to be pulled out by the roots and slung over the fence.

The Isle of Mxn housed the most penitent offenders. The people who'd acknowledged their wrongdoings and were ready to work hard and make amends. The rich and fertile farmlands of Mxn offered them the opportunity to do just this for the betterment of all. Crops of all kinds were grown here: root vegetables, beans, herbs and fruits. Enough to supply the island's population and much of the nearby northwest. Many Cans found peace in this work, reconnecting with nature and shedding their hateful ways of old.

Further north were the Inner Hebrides: Mull, Skye and

Islay, as well as a few smaller ones. These had been adapted to accommodate those cancelled for crimes of intolerance and discrimination. Most of the phobics found themselves here, working in one of the many eco-friendly tech plants that had relocated to the islands because of the abundance of willing labour. Most Cans jumped at the chance to work again, keen to rebuild their lives and start again in one of the picturesque villages dotted around the coastline. There were some in New Britannia who felt the Cans didn't deserve such good fortune. They had been cast out for spreading hate and dissemination, only to find love and consideration in a new land. But, as Charity GoodHope often said, sectarianism was a virus. In the wider population, it could spread to make the country sick. Quarantined on the islands, it would eventually die out by itself.

Furthest north were the Orkneys. These were the most remote of all the colonies, save only for the nuclear wastelands of Shetland. Here, on this wind-swept archipelago, only the worst offenders were rehoused. The irredeemables and the *Rapists*. The treasonous and the saboteurs. The murderers and the carnivores. The worst of the very worst. Yet even these Cans were given the chance to atone, doing vital work of national importance servicing and expanding the coastal wind farms that powered Britannia's brave new world. Here, they were housed in pretty little cottages in neat tidy settlements, with shops and cafes and schools and surgeries. They were allowed to play sports and have access to literature, to the arts, to pharmaceuticals and everything else they'd taken for granted on the mainland. In many ways, their lives were better than before. At least in the colonies, even on Orkney, they could walk freely in daylight and live how they wanted to live. Here, they no longer had to hide in the shadows and survive on handouts. On the islands, there was dignity.

As she travelled home from work, Sienna wondered why Martin and Krish hadn't chosen to go north. Most Cans gave up after a few months and went willingly, anything to get out of the hostels. Most but not all. Sienna looked at Martin and Krish's clothes on the bus seat next to her and pondered what she would do if she ever found herself in the same situation. She wouldn't hang around here, that was for sure. Passing the door of the house she'd once owned to scrounge food from the *Trough*? She'd have more pride than that. So why didn't Martin and Krish? What was keeping them here? Defiance? Denial? Love?

Sienna's chest tightened at that thought. Love? She loved Geri. Despite all she'd done, she still loved her. She knew this because she told herself so. It was all she had ever known. But her feelings for Julie were so much more. She felt giddy at the thought of Julie. And her body throbbed so hard that it hurt. She barely knew Julie yet she wanted to drink her all in, heart and soul. Was this how Geri felt around her new friends? Was she as intoxicated for Aurora as Sienna was for Julie? If so, Sienna finally understood. It still hurt but at least she understood.

The bus stopped. She was halfway home. She checked her NetComs for messages from Julie but she had yet to respond. She shifted in her seat, feeling her knickers tighten in frustration. She wanted so badly for her to reply, right now, at this very moment. How could Julie deny her?

"Anyone sitting there?" a man interrupted, pointing to the seat next to her. Sienna said nothing. She just moved the bag and returned to her thoughts. The man sat down and said nothing but their Network profiles chatted silently, swapping data and cookies as they travelled through the night.

Of course, the irony wasn't lost on Sienna. Here she was, twisting her legs at the thought of Julie when this was the same position Malek had found himself in. At her behest, no less. And while she failed to sympathise with Malek's plight, she did at least now empathise with him and wonder if Julie was stringing her along too. After all, by her own admission, she'd never been with another womxn before. Yet she had stoked Sienna's flames with a kiss so passionate that she could scarcely think of anything else. It could've been a ruse. A dish best served cold. An ironic 'fuck you'. Sienna hoped not but she wasn't naive. Having lived with Geri for more than five years, she knew every torture possible. She would guard against this possibility, try not to get her feelings burned and stay grounded. And if nothing else ever came of it, she would always have that kiss, something she would replay in her mind over and over again, as she slipped to sleep in her cold lonely bed.

The bus stopped at the top of Broadmead Road and Sienna almost missed her stop, so engrossed was she in her thoughts. She jumped up, spilt the bag, grabbed its contents and darted through the closing doors. The bus moved away with a hiss, its bright interior lights casting a blue-white glare across the treelined thoroughfare as it disappeared into the night. No one else got off the bus. Sienna was all alone. But she was only a short walk from her house. Also, she had recently wandered these very streets naked and the neighbourhood was safe.

Or so she thought.

When she got to her front door, she heard a noise behind her. She turned but saw no usernames. It was late and the street was dark. She assumed it was a passing Can and was about to offer up the clothes and ask if they could be returned to Martin and Krish when all of a sudden several figures rushed her. She didn't have a chance to scream, let alone sound the alarm. Her Smart Glasses were smacked from her face and she was bundled over, whacking her head against the concrete step. Her arms were pinned behind her back and a length of tape stuck over her mouth. She wailed in pain and tried to kick out but another figure taped her ankles together.

Her attackers wore black; gloves, masks and glasses. Not even their mouths were visible. Each wore a voice distorter affixed to their faces and spoke with a tinny android accent.

"Let's go," one of them said and they picked her up. Heading away from the street, towards the darkened tower of the church, they carried her like a roll of carpet, quickly and quietly into the void of night.

She tried to struggle, wriggle and fight back but they were too strong for her and she was still reeling from shock. She saw windows flash by, the houses of her neighbours and then the old churchyard wall. At the bottom of the street, the River Wey trickled by. Sienna never came here. There was nothing to see other than bullrushes anyway. But a boat was tethered to the bank this evening. A fourth figure, dressed like the others stood up and reached out. Sienna was manhandled into the boat and stashed against the cold wet hull like an old tarp. The figures jumped in and the line was cut. Before they'd even taken their seats, the engine was purring and they were chugging away downstream towards the quiet seclusion of the moonless countryside.

"Any trouble?"

"All good."

Sienna could scarcely breathe, she was so terrified. What

was happening to her? Who were these people? What did they want? She knew they weren't Cans. Cans didn't organise like this. Cans were weak. Scared. But these people knew what they were doing. And they had a plan for her.

The obvious thought was *Rapists*. They were known to kidnap people off the streets, slip away undetected and leave nothing but a body behind. Sienna was frantic. She couldn't believe this was happening to her. Why her? Why now? She'd been so careful her whole career. No one knew where she worked or what she did. Not her parents. Not her friends. Not anyone at the Hub. Especially not anyone at the Hub. Not even…

Sienna looked up at one of the figures and noticed how lithe she was. Because the figure was undoubtedly a she. The way she moved. The way her body curved. The way she glared at Sienna, staring straight through her soul from behind blacked-out lenses. None of the others paid her any attention, too focussed were they on navigating the pitch-black waterway. But the slender one, the one who had slapped the Glasses from her face, she could scarcely take her eyes off Sienna.

Alone at last.

The boat slipped downstream for a mile or two until it met a fork flowing from the south. The rudder turned toward the bank and the boat jarred against soft wet mud. Two of the figures jumped out and pushed it into the long grass, squelching through the mud until they moored it against dry land. The leader grabbed Sienna's feet while another grabbed her shoulders and together they unloaded their illicit cargo and headed into the meadow.

The air was cold and the grass was damp. The only sounds to be heard were their feet swishing through the overgrowth as they carried her to her fate. Sienna saw no lights. All she saw was stars and darkness and without her Smart Glasses, she had no way of lifting the veil. After a short run, Sienna was dumped at the base of a tree and rolled onto her back.

"If you scream, I will drown you in the river. If you fight us, I will drown you in the river. If you lie to me, I will drown you in the river. Do you understand?" His words, spoken through a voice distorter, were devoid of emotion and much scarier for it. Sienna had no choice but to comply. She'd always imagined herself as some sort of action girl whenever she daydreamed about this scenario, karate chopping her captors and leaping through plate glass windows to escape the terrorists but the cold wet reality of her predicament left her weak with dread. They could do anything they wanted to her. They could beat her, strip her, strangle her, fuck her. Anything. She was powerless to resist. All she could do was hope and pray that they would take mercy on her. Maybe if she was good? Maybe if she did as they said and didn't argue back. Maybe, just maybe, they wouldn't hurt her. Please don't hurt me!

"Understand?"

Sienna nodded and the man (she guessed it was a man) ripped the tape from her face, waxing her top lip in the process.

"Who do you work for?" the monotone robotic voice asked.

Sienna didn't answer. She was too scared until the man told her she could speak… "Quietly."

"Fibreline Netways. I'm a Crypto Security Support Officer," she said, sticking to her story as if her very life depended on it. Which it did. She couldn't admit to being an Auditor. To do so would have been to sign her own death warrant. She had to stick to the script. She had to sow the seeds of doubt. It was her only hope.

"That's a front company. Doesn't exist. You're an Auditor," her accuser said, trying to convince her he knew already. But if he knew already, knew for sure, he wouldn't be asking. She'd learned this from S Division when she'd attended a survival seminar and now drew on every lesson in a bid to stay alive. She controlled her reaction, feigned outrage rather than terror, and repeated over and over again in her mind that this had all been a horrible mistake in order to achieve the mindset needed to project innocence.

"What? Shit. No. Is that what you think? Fuck, I'm just a crypto girl."

The slender one kicked her hard in the side. The others didn't flinch. They just held her down and stared at her through blacked-out lenses as she squirmed and sucked in the pain.

"You're an Auditor for a cancellation company. Which one? Geniture? Torchlight?"

Sienna thought she would pee herself. She could barely keep it in but she knew if she did that would be as good as a signed confession so she clenched her pelvic floor and resisted the urge to give them what they wanted.

"I don't know what you're talking about. I work in crypto."

Again, the slender one punished her for this, this time with a punch to the face. There was no swing or sideways swipe for her head to soak up the punch, she took it square in the mouth, splitting her lip and smacking her skull against the tree root behind her.

"You're lying."

Sienna's head swam with pain. She tasted blood and could see stars but knew this was only a taster. If they got to the truth, they would hurt her in ways she couldn't imagine.

"You've got the wrong *ph*erson," she sobbed, mispronouncing her words due to her split lip. She tensed in anticipation but the next blow didn't come. The four figures just stared at her, featureless silhouettes against an inky black sky. They were in complete control and they wanted her to know it. To accept it. To make her peace with it.

"You know who we are?" the man asked.

Sienna nodded.

"You know what we do to people like you?" His automated voice was so flat and calm, devoid of feeling or judgment. Not even AI was this cold.

"Not me," Sienna denied. "I'm cry*ph*to."

"Easy or hard. It's up to you."

Sienna wanted to wail. She wanted to cry and plead and scream but she knew none of this would save her. She had to keep her head. She had to know that she was going to get out of this, just as a real crypto girl would, convince herself and thereby her kidnappers that it had all been a mix-up. S Division had taught her a whole raft of deceptions, from offering to join them to pointing the finger at a next-door neighbour. Anything to buy her enough time to sound the alarm. S Division drones were placed in readiness all over the country. An emergency call and a GPS location could get a drone in the air within minutes. AI targeting and armour-piercing rounds could resolve a situation from 800m, before the humxn ear could even detect its approach. Sienna had an emergency code built into her Smart Glasses that she could've activated with just one word (tombola). If she could convince them to let her put them on, she had a chance.

But Rapists weren't stupid. And they'd learned the hard way not to give their captives an inch. If she asked for her

Glasses, they might realise what she was trying and kill her immediately. She had to find a roundabout way to get there.

"My clifp," she said, meaning her ID clip. "Take it. Log on, you'll see."

But her ID clip wouldn't work without biometric recognition. She knew that and so did they but it would have been a natural mistake for someone to make in this situation. As S Division said, feel free to make mistakes. Just make sure you make the right ones.

"Want us to take your cherry?" the man asked and Sienna had no need to feign terror, such was her desperation.

"No."

"Get the thing."

Sienna didn't know what the thing was but she knew that it was not going to be a nice thing. One of the guys unzipped a pouch from his waist and pulled out a gadget with two long wires hanging free. The girl tore open Sienna's jacket and pulled up her T-shirt. The cold air hit Sienna's skin and shocked her into thinking she was about to be stripped naked again but they stopped there and left her bra and leggings in place, interested only in her soft milky tummy. The wires had sticky tape dangling from each end and they were attached either side of her navel.

"Clear," the man said and for one precious second, they pulled away to release her.

An instant later, her body was gripped with a vice-like pain as the device sent a tiny electronic signal through her muscles. Her abdomen tensed as it had never tensed before, scrunching up further than she knew possible; holding, holding and holding as the pain burned her muscles and stole the breath from her lungs. If she could have screamed, she would have despite their warnings but she was frozen, curled up in agony and unable to draw even the tiniest of breaths.

Suddenly, the device released its grip and she rolled onto her side as air and relief flooded through her body.

"You're an Auditor."

"No," Sienna croaked tearfully. "No."

The pain gripped her again, working its magic like a maniacal TENS machine. Her body shrank into a ball but her mind popped like an explosion. She could not speak. She could not think. She couldn't do anything but suffer. The pain was like nothing she had felt before and even when they killed the power, it stayed with her, her belly feeling like she'd done ten thousand stomach crunches too many.

"Tell us and we'll stop hurting you."

"Can't."

"You can. Don't be scared."

"*Cryphto.*"

She lost count of how many times they shocked her and eventually, she lost consciousness. It took some time to revive her, so far into herself had she withdrawn, but when they did, when the recognition of her circumstances flooded back to her, she lost all hope. Tears and desperation choked Sienna. Her captors let her cry, realising that there was nothing they could do to induce more misery in her than she was feeling now.

"We will not kill you if you tell us the truth," the man said, giving Sienna a ray of hope. Not to take him at his word, not to trust him, but a precious glimpse at his doubts. His change in tactics revealed his hand. Suddenly, he was not convinced. Not completely. Not beyond all doubt. That was her fingerhold. Her way out. More precious advice from her friends in S Division.

"I'm not lying," Sienna pleaded, wanting them to believe

her more than anything. More than life itself. More than Geri. More than Britannia. Please please please, let them believe me.

"Fucker's not crypto," the slender one said, kicking her again but any new pain was absorbed into Sienna's overall agony.

The leader took the slender one aside and spoke to her away from Sienna. She couldn't hear what they were saying but it was clear there was dissension in the ranks. The remaining two hovered without needing to restrain Sienna. Her torso was so sore that she couldn't even sit, let alone run. She closed her eyes and tried to breathe, daring to hope for the first time since her ordeal had begun and eventually, the other two returned. They stood over her for a moment, looking down without comment before detaching the wires.

"Information," the man said, his robotic voice laced with sincerity. "If you want to help – if you need help – hang something red in your window. We'll be watching."

And with that, he and the others headed away, disappearing into the shadows with barely a sound. Only the girl remained, crouching over Sienna to pull down her T-shirt and close her jacket. She touched her face, her gloved hand wiping a tear from Sienna's cheek.

She half-expected her to exact one last measure of pain. To punch her face or break her nose. Instead, she left her with something far worse, a terrible riposte to taunt and terrorise her in equal measure. Gently cradling her head and looking down at Sienna with her blank emotionless lenses, she said in a blank emotionless voice:

"You're so fucking hot."

19: S DIVISION

S Division regarded themselves as the elite. The best of the best of the best.

Of the best.

They were a separate entity to the Guardians. The Guardians answered to the State. S Division answered to Geniture alone. Or more specifically, Geniture's CEO, Zaria Okello, who also served as a Governmynt Minister and straddled both divides.

The company had come first for Zaria. Starting at an impossibly young age, she had joined the ranks at an executive level and fast-tracked her way through a series of rapid promotions, unseating her superiors and hobbling her rivals until the company had become hers while she was still in her 20s. Geniture was a beast, one of the most powerful companies in New Britannia and it became even hungrier under Zaria's forward-thinking leadership. Profits doubled, quotas quadrupled and New Britannia's glorious diversity became purer by the day.

Charity GoodHope began to wonder if Geniture hadn't become too big for its boots, kinky though they were. The company was doing great work but it was too independent for its own good. When the time came, she offered Zaria a post in the cabinet in exchange for her loyalty. Zaria graciously accepted. The following week, she was parachuted into a safe seat and named the new Minster for Survivors.

Charity and Zaria put on a united front and the country pulled together. It was a victory for progression, a working relationship made in heaven and a dream team for the children of tomorrow.

S Division liked Sienna. She was an experienced and skilful Auditor. She played great with the new recruits and S

Division was pleased to utilise her whenever it could, inviting her to speak at its twice-yearly workshops in Windsor.

In turn, Sienna liked S Division. She was even on first-name terms with some of its people. They exuded confidence, a quality Sienna envied, and were always immaculately turned out. One of the Stewards she knew was Verity Abebe, an ebony goddess of supposed Zulu descent. Sienna didn't know if this was true but she would not have looked out of place in a zebra thong hacking away at the thin red line. Verity acted as Sienna's chaperone whenever she went to Windsor House, a picturesque lakefront manor that served as S Division's regional retreat. She was friendly, helpful and attentive to Sienna's every need. But there was no spark. No chemistry. As beautiful as Verity was, Sienna never felt fully at ease in her company. There was something dangerous about her. Something unsettling. But it wasn't a big thing. Just a nagging insecurity that Sienna always felt around confident people. Besides, she reminded herself, they liked her. They valued her. They were on her side.

"We take care of our people," Verity had told Sienna. This was one of the highest compliments imaginable. It was also the unofficial S Division motto. For an S Division Steward to refer to Sienna as "our people", even though she was X Division, it didn't get any better than that.

Sienna needed them now. She was hurting and she was alone. Barely able to crawl let alone stand, terrified and in pain, she dragged herself blindly across the wet moonless meadow. The *Rapists* had broken her Smart Glasses, not out of mischief but out of necessity. They had to have time to escape. They could not let her call for help.

Sienna pawed the ground on all fours, forcing herself on and towards a light she could see in the distance. Every movement was agony and she found herself having to rest after only a few metres, cradling her gut and gasping facedown in the dirt. She wet herself where she lay, unable to find the strength to squat or pull off her pants, but she barely noticed, her body and her mind were so racked with pain.

She thought about Geri. She thought about how she had betrayed the memory of their love. How her distraction with Julie had led her astray and brought her here. If she had trusted Geri, if she had believed in her and given herself completely, learned to live like her and embraced her choices, she would not be here. She truly was alone. A selfish worthless person, just as Geri had said.

Sienna didn't know how long she crawled. It might have been a minute. It might have been an hour. She lost all sense of time. Her sole focus was the light, piecing the night at the far end of the meadow, so close yet so far. So she pushed on, through thistles, mud, muck and pain, cutting her hands and scraping her knees until she found the will to stand. It didn't last long. Soon she was in the grass again, facedown and soaked-through, but she persevered, forcing herself through one pain barrier after another until she was able to climb to her feet. Every step was agony. Every moment torture. But she had no alternative. The night was cold and her body was colder still. She had to reach that light.

The first thing she knew about the river was the sound of gushing water. She heard it before she saw it and almost stumbled into the black inky depths, only saving herself at the last moment by falling backwards. The light was on the other side. A couple of houses and an assortment of commercial buildings. A porch light had guided her but now she could not reach it. The river was too wide and too cold. She waited in frustration and screamed for help but nobody answered.

Nobody heard.

She found a dirt path on the edge of the meadow and followed it upriver. It seemed to take her away from the light but she knew it had to lead somewhere. Her faith was rewarded when she came to a small wooden bridge. She dragged herself up the steps and across the river. Her head swam and her body screamed but she was almost there. Just a few more steps and she found a concrete pavement. She turned downriver towards the light and stumbled through the street towards the porch-lit door. She fell against it and slapped the dark oak, too weak to make a fist, too dizzy to reach the bell.

Whether anyone heard or not, she never knew. She succumbed to her exertions and slipped into a deep oblivion, laying there for the next seven hours, unaided and undisturbed.

Eleven people noticed her over the course of the morning before a hand finally shook her awake.

*

"Open your eyes."

Sienna felt her senses flood with acridity. She gagged and turned her head, gasping to escape the smelling salts and confused as to where she was. The new light of dawn pierced her mind like a dagger and her injuries woke with her. Every ache and terror came back with a vengeance and she lashed out in dread, momentarily panicked into thinking they had returned. The ones who had taken her. The ones who had hurt her.

"Calm down. Stop. Who are you? What are you doing here?" the man asked, restraining her with strong hands and an air of authority.

She blinked and saw a green uniform. It was a Guardian

and there was another behind, staring down at her as though she were a piece of discarded trash.

"You can't be here. It's an offence under the Cans' directives. Which hostel are you from?"

The question confused her. She couldn't think. The events of the last few days were such a jumble that she wasn't even sure who she was. But no, she was a person. She was Sienna Clay. She was not a Can. She belonged. She had rights. She had a name.

"They broke my glasses," she said, her throat so dry it sliced the words as she tried to speak.

"Who?" the Guardian asked.

"*Rapists*," she choked, recoiling at the memory as if it was a hot needle. She now did something she had never done before. It felt scary and strange and it went against every instinct but she told them why.

"I'm an Auditor."

*

The Guardians took Sienna to the nearest Medicentre, partly for treatment, partly to recover forensics. The doctors assured her that the cuts and bruises to her body and face would heal and she would suffer no lasting injuries. They could manage her pain but she could not mix it with Vape, noting the recent overdose on her records. They recommended that she upgrade her counselling subscription and take some time off, but before then, the Guardians had some questions for her. They interviewed her in her hospital bed and cross-referenced every detail, back-checking her claims and pressing her to think harder until they were sure they had a clear picture of what happened. Guardians were already combing the scene, collecting evidence and triangulating GPS trackers but *Rapists* were like wolves. They moved with stealth and left nothing but blood and bones behind. Sienna had been lucky.

Within the hour, S Division arrived and took charge of the investigation, filling the Medicentre with immaculately dressed officials and upsetting the Guardians' applecart as they pulled rank, requisitioned evidence and commandeered their people. Raised voices in the corridor both unnerved Sienna and made her feel important. Finally, order was restored and a familiar face looked in to reassure Sienna with a smile.

"We're here for you," Verity Abebe said, pulling up a chair and taking out a screen.

Sienna ran through her ordeal again, repeating what she had told the Guardians but this time paying special reference to the S Division tactics she had employed from her training. Verity nodded approvingly.

"What else?"

Sienna described her attackers and what they wore. She remembered who spoke and who didn't, who had seniority and how he had laid out his syntax. She recalled things he had said and things he had omitted, like how they knew where she lived and what she did for work. Each was as telling as the other. She recalled all of these things as well as the pain they had inflicted upon her, what her attackers had done while they had tortured her and how much more she thought she could've taken. Not much. She recalled all of these things and more and fought the urge to cry out in terror when it all came flooding back. When she was done, Verity told her she was proud of her.

"You're an asset to this company. You'll be rewarded for it. Now rest up and recover. Leave everything to us," she said, keen to remind Sienna that she was among friends again.

A colleague arrived with a pouch for Sienna. Verity handed

it over. It contained a new pair of Smart Glasses (19.7 the latest version – cherry-red) and a few of her possessions, including her ID clip recovered from the meadow and her Vape, soon to be pressed into service despite Doctor's orders. A puff of Oxy wouldn't kill her, Verity winked. Not after all she'd been through.

"So, is that everything?" Verity asked as she got up, pocketing her stylus and folding away her screen. "Are you sure there's nothing else you can think of?"

"No, that's everything," Sienna said but she was lying. Because there was something else. Something important.

One detail. One key omission from her statement to the doctors, the Guardians, S Division and all. The last thing the girl had said to her. It was too much of a coincidence that both Julie and her attacker had said the same thing. Sienna was hot. That much was indisputable, but not to the point where perfect strangers spontaneously volunteered it. There must have been a connection. But it didn't mean for certain that Julie had been one of them. The *Rapists* could have intercepted Julie's NetCom message and used her words as bait. These tactics were not beyond them. Because if Julie was picked up by S Division, which she surely would be, it would confirm their suspicions, that Sienna was an Auditor. S Division did not get involved for just anyone. *Rapists* were ruthless and not immune to sacrificing the odd innocent to achieve their aims. Sienna knew this. Just as she knew that S Division would do likewise to bag their suspects. She and Julie were stuck in the middle. It seemed safest all around if they stayed there and kept their heads down.

"I must say you're a very brave womxn," Verity said, laying a strong hand on Sienna's to give her a reassuring squeeze. "We take care of our people. Remember that."

Sienna would. She would remember it always and take comfort in the knowledge. And then one day, in the not-too-distant future, in a land far away and in circumstances very different from here, she would remember it again.

And it would save her life.

*

Bella sent Sienna a NetCard that contained a generic "get well soon" message and an urgent request for an update on the Garfield case. Sienna ignored both.

She arrived home that evening, driven by S Division who looked over the house, installed a panic button and offered to stay the night. But Sienna declined, wanting nothing more than a hot bath and a long sleep. She didn't want the distraction of people in her house, however reassuring their presence might be. S Division left, but only after asking if she'd recently been burgled when they failed to locate any clothes for her.

"I had a clear out this morning," she said.

Carl ran a hot bath and played some soothing music to relax her. The water felt wonderful but the music just annoyed her so she requested white noise instead, the sound of rainfall on a forest canopy, preferring it immeasurably to anything MGA_9.3 could compose. She fell asleep in the bath and woke up cold to find the water had been drained; a health and safety measure taken by Carl. She dried and stood at the window, naked but for a towel. The lights were off and she adjusted her Glasses to night vision, peering into the street's long shadows to see what they were hiding. Her towel was white but she had a red one in the cupboard. She wondered what would happen if she left it hanging in the window. Would they contact her as promised? Could she engineer their arrest?

The thought made her shudder so she shut the curtains and climbed into bed. It was cold and empty and she felt alone without Geri, more so than she had done all week. She could have reached out but she didn't. She was confused and frightened and didn't think Geri could help. When Aurora had been attacked, there had been sympathy and support. Geri's friends had rallied but Sienna didn't want them rallying here. In fact, between Geri's friends and the *Rapists*, it was hard to know which she detested more. She contented herself instead with a modest OxyVape and an early night.

The rain fell on the unseen forest canopy and she drifted off to sleep, imagining herself lost in the wilds, hundreds of miles from civilisation, while wolves closed in around her.

"We'll be watching."

20: RENEWAL

The next day, Sienna considered going into work to cement her reputation within Geniture: the Auditor who was kidnapped and left for dead in the woods and didn't even take the next day off. She'd be a hero inside X Division. A living legend. They'd talk about her for years to come.

Then she thought: "Screw that", phoned in sick and stayed in bed all day with her OxyVape.

Besides, it wasn't just an excuse. She still had pain in her body and fear in her mind. The thought of leaving the house terrified her. As did the thought of seeing Julie again. Instead, she spent the day by the window watching the streets below.

Geri had messaged a couple of times. Not because she'd heard about Sienna's ordeal. But to ask for money. Their joint account was empty and she wondered when Sienna was going to get paid. Sienna dumped a few hundred into their account rather than have her come home. The Geri of old she missed and needed. But the new Geri, the Geri who was self-exploratory and free, she didn't want to see. After breakfast, she ordered some new clothes, paid for express delivery and looked around the house for somewhere to stash them.

A short time later, Carl told her a package had arrived so she went to retrieve it. She had gone for her usual ensemble of black leggings and white T-shirts but with one key difference. Instead of a red plastic trench coat, she'd ordered a charcoal grey cotton one to render herself less conspicuous.

"How do I look?" she asked Carl without thinking. He complimented her on her appearance then spent the rest of the day sulking when she failed to do likewise.

Sienna's biggest worry was what to do about Julie. Her A6 continued to occupy a place on her pulldown menu. Sienna wondered if it would look churlish to withdraw it. She'd had quite enough of Julie's tender touches for one week. If, indeed, that had been Julie.

Had Julie been the girl who had kicked her? And if she had, had she always been a *Rapist*? At that age? Or had it been Malek's arrest that had propelled her into their ranks? They had to find their members from somewhere and she was the sort of recruit they favoured. Vulnerable and pliable. Looking to settle a score.

Sienna rued her stupidity at revealing Malek's family history. Rather than accept it in the spirit in which it was offered, Julie had decided to hate the messenger not the message.

Again, if that had been Julie.

Sienna wasn't sure. She couldn't be. But she would know when she saw her again. The first time she looked into her eyes. The first time she smiled. The first time they spoke. She would know. But what would she do then? What *could* she do?

Geniture ran relocation programs. If she alerted S Division, Julie could be picked up within minutes and Sienna would be on her way to a new life tonight. It would mean leaving everything behind: her home, her possessions, even Geri, although if Geri was right, she counted as one of her possessions too. A trophy wife. Something to covet. And cast off when convenient.

Sienna paced the house like a caged animal and knew it was her only option. A new town. A new start. A new Sienna. She'd done it before; when she'd walked out on her parents. It had been the right decision then and it was the right decision now. But it hadn't been easy. And it wouldn't be now.

Geri would be hurt, of course. And for a time, homeless. But Geri would fall on her feet, most likely via her back. It might even help her in the long run. They had strayed into a rut and mistaken comfort for happiness. It was time for them both to find the real thing.

"I'm still waiting."

"What?"

"I said, you looked wonderful, Sienna, and do you know what you said?"

Sienna cast her mind back. "Thank you?"

"Exactly. Thank you. Thank you for showing an interest in me, Carl. Not that you have any interest in me. What kind of an attitude is that?"

"What did you want me to say?"

"You could have commented on how clean the kitchen was looking. How fresh the bathroom smelt, even after you'd been in there for fifteen minutes this morning. How soft the sheets were or how ambient the white noise was. Any number of things but you didn't. You didn't because you don't care. You take me for granted. I'm just a washing machine to you.

An alarm clock and a boiler. Don't you think I might like to hear nice things occasionally?"

Sienna took a long and lingering pull on her OxyVape and closed her eyes as she exhaled.

"You know something, Carl, I think this could be the end of a vile toxic friendship."

*

The next morning, Sienna awoke with her mind made up. She gathered her things, a few keepsakes from her time in Woking, and got ready to leave. If she saw Julie today, she would make the call but if she didn't she would stay in a hotel. As much as the prospect scared her, she didn't want to leave town without seeing Julie one last time. Just to make sure. She owed the new Sienna that much at least.

"Dinner will be served at eight, as usual," Carl said as she opened the door. "Will you be dining alone, as usual?"

Sienna almost laughed. Why had she waited this long?

"Carl, do me a favour. Go unplug yourself."

And with that, she shut the door for the very last time and didn't look back.

She felt bad about not being able to return either Martin or Krish's clothes. She'd lost them the previous night along with a set of her own. S Division had found her clip in the meadow but not the clothes she'd bought that day. Perhaps some thieving Can had stolen them. It amused her to think that every now and again, Geri would see a Can scurrying in the distance in a red plastic trench coat and have to look twice.

She caught the bus on the High Street and surveyed the scene, for once taking in her surroundings instead of playing Cloud Crunch or living her life via the Network. This was the last time she would ever travel this route. It was all she had known most of her adult life. Now she was saying goodbye and it felt right. There was nothing more for her in Old Woking. A new life awaited.

She reached the Hub and stashed her things in a locker. She didn't go to her privacy pod straight away. Technically, she was still off sick. Instead, she wandered the corridors and went to the street food hall. She wasn't hungry. If anything, the rich aromas made her nauseous but she got a coffee and sat down. And waited.

Dozens of usernames flitted before her eyes but <u>trulyjulie2064.332</u> wasn't one of them. She set a proximity alert so that she would know if Julie was approaching but NetProx only worked over a short distance. If she wasn't in the Hub, Sienna wouldn't know.

She decided to get proactive and went to her privacy pod.

She logged in and found a diatribe of increasingly erratic messages from Bella. She deleted all without reading them then ran a search for Julie through MUM. Thousands of hits came back so she refined her criteria to the last thirty minutes. She was on a bus, two miles away and heading this way from Sheerwater. She was alone but had communicated with seven users via NetComs this morning. Sienna ran a check on all of them and found two were her parents, one was her brother, one was her counsellor and three were profiled as friends. She was playing chess with one of them and losing badly. Sienna ran an analysis of their game and found a number of non-standard moves that cropped up on both sides. Hidden codes disguised as chess moves? She opened a file on <u>trulyjulie2064.332</u> and started logging her suspicions.

Sienna would have some explaining to do. I Division hadn't issued her with a directive to audit Julie Adamski but if she was right and could serve up a gang of *Rapists* to S Division, not even Bella could object to that.

Sienna worked fast, filtering data and cross-referencing contacts, both Network and Proxi, from before and after Malek's arrest. If Julie had been approached after leaving counselling, they would be easy to isolate. And if Sienna could identify them, S Division could grab them. Getting Julie was the easy part. Getting the rest was what Sienna wanted.

Julie was three stops from the Hub. Sienna moved fast, shutting down and logging out. Sienna wanted to be in Reception when she arrived. It was a public space and always busy. That would give her the confidence to face her. She pulled out her ID clip from the interface and was about to hurry down when she got a call. It confused her because it came from Reception. How could it know? Julie wasn't even there yet?

"Mx Clay?" said a businesslike AI voice.

"Yes?"

"The Guardians are here to see you?"

"What?"

This threw her. The Guardians? With Julie on her way in? She spent a few seconds trying to equate the two but couldn't see how they were connected. Why were the Guardians here? It was an S Division matter. The Guardians had been taken off the investigation. Unless they were trying to tread on S Division's toes.

"Mx Clay?"

"I'm still here."

"As are the Guardians."

"Er... yes, of course. I'll be right down."

This muddied everything. If the Guardians grabbed Julie when she arrived, S Division would blame Sienna for holding out on them. It might even jeopardise her move, especially if the other suspects slipped the net. The inter-agency rivalries of those who served to protect us often came a close second to the oaths they swore.

Sienna suspected the Guardians were here to ask her to formerly ID Julie. But why would they need that? Why couldn't they just grab her and go? She had so many questions but so few answers.

Thinking fast, she realised her best option was not to be there when they grabbed Julie. Then, she could legitimately claim not to have known anything. S Division wouldn't blame her and she could still supply confirmation after the event.

She dragged her heels as much as she could, desperate to miss Julie's arrival, but she knew she couldn't delay indefinitely. Reception was tracking her movements and would report back. She tied her laces and retied them several times, feigned a sneezing fit and blowing her nose at leisure, all while watching the clock. Several people sidestepped her, desperate to avoid whatever bug she was carrying and she managed to drag her heels for long enough to miss the bus from Sheerwater. As she entered the lobby she saw it through the glass frontage, disappearing down the High Street as its passengers dispersed. There was no sign of Julie. Sienna hung back another ten seconds, giving Julie every chance to make the Guardians' acquaintance but the sound of Reception buzzing her compelled her to move.

She stepped out and saw two Guardians waiting, a burly womxn in a green uniform and an androgynous officer in plain unisex clothes. Both were identifiable by their user-tags: surreyGuardian.637 and surreyGuardian.444. Neither had Julie in custody. Where was she? Sienna crossed the lobby and slipped through the security barriers, trying her best to disguise her anxieties as she approached them.

The Guardians saw Sienna coming and stepped forward.

"Sienna Clay?"

"Yes?" Sienna replied, scanning the lobby in silent alarm and wondering if she could suffer a sudden 'bleed' in order to run off to the bathroom. Bella wouldn't think twice about it. Bella would use the last sanitary towel to spit her bubble gum into and a wheelchair for her bag.

"We need you to come with us. We have a few questions we'd like to put to you."

"I understand but it's an S Division matter. You'll need to talk to them," Sienna said, stopping briefly to deliver this rebuff.

"S Division?"

The Guardians looked at each other quizzically.

"How is this an S Division matter?"

"They're in charge of the investigation. Speak with Verity Abebe. I can't say any more."

Sienna turned, prompting the uniformed Guardian to step after her and urge her, politely but firmly, to stop where she was.

"You're the one who sent the message. It's you we'd like to talk to."

A message? What a weird way of putting it. A call to the emergency services was a message? What was a fire alarm? A check-in?

The doors clanked and the sliders hissed as users came and went. The barriers pinged and the screens beeped driving Sienna to distraction. It could only be a matter of seconds before the hustle and bustle swept Julie into their purview. Sienna couldn't stay. She had to make herself scarce. She resorted to candour.

"Just grab her when she gets here. I don't want to be a part of it."

The Guardians messaged each other via their shock-proof Smart Goggles and concluded that something wasn't right here. They edged closer to Sienna in anticipation of what she might do but retained their smiles.

"Will she?" the uniformed Guardian said with a knowing nod.

"A username would help," the plain-clothed one added.

Huh? Why would they need Julie's username? They already knew it, surely? Sienna's NetProx began sounding. Thirty metres and closing. She was here. Julie was here. Sienna turned in panic and started to run. The bathroom was her only hope.

"I need a sanitary product," she said in all urgency.

But she didn't make it. The uniformed Guardian bundled her over as though she were made of straw and the plain-clothed Guardian slapped on the cuffs.

The alerts inside her Smart Glasses dimmed and a new window popped up.

Sienna Clay, you are under arrest for failing to comply with a Guardian directive. Guardian officers request access to any and all data stored on any devices in your possession so that they might improve their understanding of the circumstances surrounding your non-compliance. Your consent is presumed. Click Accept to acknowledge receipt. You can request a lawyer via Preferences.

Sienna clicked 'Accept' and was helped to her feet.

"Myself and Guardian Rhys are permitted to assist you if you require a sanitary stop," the plain-clothed officer said, holding Sienna by the hook of the arm. "Or we can go? It's up to you, Mx Clay."

As this was what she had been trying to do all along, she went with option B. She still didn't understand why they had arrested her but she was desperate to discuss it elsewhere.

The Guardians led Sienna towards the exit, her hands behind her back, her face still sporting the scars of two nights earlier. Several users stepped aside and took SmartShots of the dangerous criminal as she was led away. A free-shitter looked up from the rainforest enclosure in the corner of the lobby and paused in disgust. And outside, Anita Xeno turned and jumped back on a bus when she saw them coming her way.

But Sienna only noticed one person throughout all of this.

Julie walked in as Sienna was being walked out. Sienna expected a scuffle as the Guardians grabbed Julie too but she strode by without either blinking at her. For her own part, Julie showed not even the slightest sign of recognition. Her face remained a canvas of passive indifference. And then she was gone, Julie into the Hub, Sienna out of it, led away to the transport.

Sienna looked back, just briefly, to see Julie scanning her clip and passing through the security barriers. She behaved as if this was just another working day. She hadn't so much as missed a step.

Of all the confusing things to have happened to Sienna over the last few days, this had been the most disconcerting. She started to wonder if Julie had even seen her. Some people did walk around with their heads in the clouds. Literally. But then she got a message to confirm that she had.

Ping!

A6 Application rejected. Thank you for your consideration. Good luck seeking fulfilment elsewhere – trulyjulie2064.332

21: GUARDIANS

As a force, the Guardians had superseded the Police two decades earlier. Years prior to this, many of the police services in Britain had been dogged by charges of misogyny, racism, bigotry and corruption. Victims went ignored. Suspects danced free. The old system wasn't fit for purpose. The 21st century expected more.

Fawqiyya el-Abdulla had tried to reform the police from the inside but found she couldn't freshen a rotten apple. Thus, when Charity GoodHope came to power, she went back to the tree and plucked a whole new variety of fruit.

Thousands of officers were fired. Hundreds jailed. Tens of thousands were hired in their place. As Guardians. New training. New uniforms. New equipment. New rules. New remit.

To eliminate hate.

Hundreds of new laws were passed to help Guardians achieve their aims with some senior Overseers allowed a certain amount of autonomy when it came to decision-making.

A case in point was rape. Despite years of legislation, in the first half of the 21st century, rape had become an epidemic. 1 in 4 womyn surveyed by Rape Crisis in 2022 confirmed that they had been sexually assaulted as an adult. Almost a hundred thousand womyn were attacked every year. Yet less than 5% of these attacks led to an arrest, let alone a conviction. The rights of womyn to walk the streets were deemed less important than the rights of the men who preyed on them.

Charity GoodHope, with the help of her Ministers, set about redressing the balance. Every complainant would now be believed, their testimony deemed infallible. Their recollections unquestionable. DNA swabs were taken from every man in the country; their files accessible at the touch of a button. This negated the need for courtroom trials. Science never lied. Prison was automatic. If the man protested his innocence, the onus lay on him to prove it via an appeal. Those released after completion of sentence were subject to chemical castration. Only a psychiatrist's recommendation could reverse the decision. And even then, most were barred from reentering society and banished to the islands.

The system worked. In the first year alone, convictions for sexual offences skyrocketed. Thousands of predators were taken off the streets and womyn rejoiced as they reclaimed the night. Then, when the rules pertaining to historical offences were overhauled, convictions soared again, fuelled by thousands of womyn seeking justice for the injustices of yesteryear.

Dozens of new prisons had to be built and millions raised to pay for it all. This might have proved a problem in previous years but in New Britannia, prisoners were put to work to complete the construction and their assets seized to part-fund the programme. Of course, thousands refused. Hundreds went on hunger strike. But after the first fifty funerals, the prison population soon realised that Charity GoodHope wasn't for turning. It was up to them whether they ate or not. Either way was fine by her.

The new prisons weren't the cosy hotels of before either. Inmates weren't permitted to lie in their bunks for 23 hours a day watching TV and demanding privileges. Prisoners only took out what they put in. This included the basic necessities of food, water, soap, clothing, warmth and life. The 'snowflakes' were in charge now. And when enough snowflakes came together, nothing was deadlier. They had become a blizzard of unimaginable ferocity. And it blew away the practices of old.

Sienna sat across from the Guardians who'd brought her in. Guardian Rhys was in uniform. Investigator Cabot plain clothes. She was given the choice of interview rooms so she requested the femxle space. It was a comfortable room warmly furnished with a low iTable between two Chesterfield sofas and had some nice abstracts on the wall to serve as talking points. The gender-neutral interview room was also available and equally homely, in a modernistic way, while the male interview room in the sub-basement could at best be described as 'functional'.

Sienna explained about Monday night, once more omitting the part about Julie and the suspicions she harboured. Guardian Cabot checked the system. It confirmed all she said and explained the confusion over their conversation if not the on-off urgency of Sienna's sanitary needs. But Monday's attack wasn't why they wanted to talk to her.

"We'd like to ask you about a message you sent on Friday 19th October," Cabot said.

The iTable between them came online and Rhys pulled up a message on screen. Xe orientated it towards Sienna and Sienna read it. Or at least, as much as she could.

```
Sent to: darkmatter2021.407
#encrypt-102.33
########: #########2038.69
C### V######## 2 ###### - 2061 H### C##### A##
C### V######## 1 ##### - 2062 H######### C##### A##
C### V######## 1 ##### - 2047 S## C##### A##
C### V######## 1 ##### - 2066 N###### C##### A##
###: GENITURE I D## - X D## S## 4
########## ###### #### ######
#encrypt_end
```

"Did you send this message to Dark Matter Twenty-Twenty-One? We traced it back to your home OS," Cabot asked as xe leaned forward in xyr seat.

Sienna had. Or at least, something akin to this. She had been so sure that nobody would trace it back but Carl's encryption had obviously corrupted upon interface, obliterating the message rather than the messenger.

Bloody Carl.

Bloody Geri.

No wonder she hadn't received a directive from I Division to investigate spongecake2038.69. The message was incomprehensible. darkmatter2021.407 must have wondered what the hell he'd been sent.

And why?

It had spooked him and he had gone to his Guardian handlers in a fit of consternation. Why was Geniture looking into him? He hadn't done anything wrong. At least, nothing the Guardians didn't know about in his capacity as an informer. They had to do something. They had to protect him.

"You saw the addendum on this user's file, did you not, prohibiting investigation without official authorisation?"

Sienna couldn't deny sending the message and it would have been pointless trying. What she had to focus on now was, why?

"Could I vape?" she asked, reaching for her pocket in anticipation.

"I'm not your doctor," Cabot reassured her while Rhys sat unmoved, recording Sienna's interview on her Smart Goggles.

Sienna switched cartridges and took a nervous pull. She wasn't investigating darkmatter2021.407. One look through her files would bear this out. But she had tried to initiate an audit against spongecake2038.69 for personal reasons, something she would have difficulty justifying to Cabot and Geniture. This was likely to prompt an internal investigation and she suddenly found herself thinking about the Abby Grey investigation she had buried a few days earlier. This wasn't good. And then there was all that stuff with Julie too. And Bella? She would seize any excuse to demote or humiliate Sienna if she could.

Sienna was in a jam. She had backed herself into a corner and now she had to find a way out.

"We're waiting," Cabot said. There was no urgency to xyr prompt. It was just a matter-of-fact statement for Sienna's information. Sienna exhaled and began.

"We're not auditing Dark Matter Twenty-Twenty-One," she assured them, using the collective "we" rather than "I" in an effort to blend into a crowd that wasn't there. "There's another target we're looking into. Vegan King Twenty-Twenty-Five-One-Zero-Zero-Eight, Charles Garfield of New Troy Road, Surrey."

Cabot ran the details through xyr Smart Goggles and found Garfield in moments.

"My Division head is certain he's dealing meat but we've not made the breakthrough yet. My audit led me to an encounter between Vegan King and Dark Matter on Farnham Castle Street two years ago. Dark Matter was listed as a meat dealer so obviously it caught our attention."

Sienna tried to pitch it as if this was an inter-agency debrief and not a formal Guardian interview. She offered Bella and Myrtle's contact details without waiting to be asked and plugged her ID clip into her side of the iTable to retrieve I Division's directive.

"Obviously, I saw the Guardian addendum and wouldn't have dreamed of investigating Dark Matter. But I wasn't looking into him, I was just after information. Some way of getting at Garfield's activities."

Cabot nodded sympathetically, not least of all when Sienna started complaining about the inadequate systems she had at her disposal and the pressures she was being put under from above to get results.

"Don't get me started on tech," Cabot agreed despite being the departmental tech wizard, the person the IT team turned to when their screens went down. But hell, if it helped loosen Sienna's lips, Cabot could be anything she wanted xem to be.

Rhys stared without comment, capturing every word and motion. Inwardly, she felt less passive and would have liked to have punched Sienna right in her pretty little face. The split lip she was sporting really suited her. Rhys didn't like Auditors. She had known a few in her time. A childhood friend had fallen foul of Auditors for reasons she still didn't understand. She thought they were parasites. Legalised thieves. And Sienna's cunt-eating smile was really starting to grate with her.

"One thing I don't understand," Cabot said, getting back to brass tacks, "is why you messaged Dark Matter from your home OS? Why not go through official channels? Through X Division portal, for example?"

This was trickier to explain but Sienna disguised her guilty blushes with a forced laugh and a conspiratorial wink to her sister-from-another-mister, Guardian Rhys.

"Oh that," she said, desperately wracking her brain and struggling to think what 'that' could be. As much as she played for time she couldn't come up with anything convincing so instead she took the only course left open to her. She put the boot into Bella and stuck her with as much of the blame as she could. "I have this boss. And she's a real fucking dog."

Decades earlier, she would have called Bella a 'bitch' but the term fell out of favour under the new ideology. Why should the femxle of the species be a metaphor for nasty behaviour when it was a known fact that the males were far more aggressive and would fuck anything that moved (and plenty of things that didn't). To call a person a *bitch*, unless used in a complementary or sexual sense, was regarded as hate speech and enough to get a person into trouble with… well, whomever.

Sienna went into great and unnecessary detail outlining the grief she'd got off Bella in the last year, how incompetent and lazy he was and how he'd taken a dislike to Sienna from the first day they'd met.

"Sometimes, I think the only reason Bella put me on the Garfield case was to see me screw up," Sienna said, truly believing this to be the case. It had to be. Bella's actionable numbers were so poor. Sienna's were so good. Perhaps she was trying to even the score. "So, I'm desperate. I'm working this case all hours. And that includes at home. I'm just trying to crack it and save my job, you know?"

"Why would she do that?" Cabot asked, sounding more like a therapist than a Guardian.

"Because she knows I know she's full of shit…" Sienna started to say then thought better of it. Whatever her suspicions about Bella, this wasn't the place to air them.

Guardian Rhys interrupted to draw Cabot's attention to something. She shared a clip from the last minute or so and timestamped the relevant point. Cabot watched it, acknowledged the reference and returned to Sienna.

"It sounds like a challenging relationship," xe sympathised. "About your supervisor, Bella… Köse? I'm sorry, but I'm a little confused about Bella's gender."

That made two of them and Sienna almost cracked and said the unsayable – that Bella was a fake, an opportunist screwing the system and would probably be calling herself Ben again when she got to where she was going. But these were her own private thoughts. So private that Sienna scarcely dared share them with herself. They were too unthinkable. Too hateful. Too contentious. So, in spite of all the Coca she'd vaped, she stuck to the script. Bella was a bad boss. An inept arsehole who'd risen beyond her station and tried to disguise her incompetence by picking on everyone else around her. Every organisation had one, even the Guardians, no doubt.

But this was not what Cabot had asked. Xe'd asked about Bella's gender. What did Cabot know that Sienna didn't?

"Well," Cabot said, teeing up the iTable to replay the clip, "you referenced Bella as both 'her' and 'he' on a number of occasions. Let me show you."

Sure enough, Sienna watched an uncomfortable clip of herself as she waxed lyrical about how "<u>he</u> was always off sick" and how "<u>he</u>'d never liked me, going back to that very first day we met."

Sienna looked up and met Cabot's eyes. She felt sick. Cabot waited. Rhys allowed herself a private smile.

"I didn't mean it like that," Sienna said, scarcely able to breathe.

"Like what?" Cabot ventured, reviewing the text of their conversation. "Bella Köse is a transwomxn, is she not?"

"Yes, but only recently so," Sienna said, practically

hyperventilating, keen to get in her mitigating circumstances first. "And I knew her before her transition. For much longer, in fact. That's how I got to know her."

"I see," Cabot nodded. But at what, Sienna could only imagine. "Of course, we'll have to check this out with your superiors. You do understand that, don't you?"

"Please, it was an honest mistake. I didn't mean to misgender her. And Bella's okay really. I was just sounding off. Too much vape. Bit stressed, you know," she said, taking another sizeable wallop to send her heart racing even harder.

"We all make mistakes," Cabot assured her, which was true. Xe and Rhys wouldn't have jobs if people didn't.

Guardian Rhys showed Sienna to a waiting room while they conducted their inquiries. It wasn't a cell. The cells were downstairs reserved for the real criminals: murderers, sex attackers, terrorists and thieves. People who didn't merit a cappuccino machine and a help-yourself tofu counter in the corner. That said, the waiting room was still a confinement. She couldn't leave. Not until Cabot said so.

Five other detainees were also waiting: a mother who'd been caught teaching her son a prohibited language (Dutch); two girls who'd got into a fist-fight over a half-empty vape cartridge; a homeowner who'd destroyed a priceless work of artistic expressionism by scrubbing it off the side of his house; and a Polychromic councillor who'd ordered 79 pairs of high-heeled shoes and inadvertently listed them as 'stationery' on her expenses.

No one paid any attention to anyone else, not even the girls who'd been battering each other just a few hours earlier. They all just sat there on their separate recliners, lost to their Smart Glasses awaiting release or transfer, their usernames blanked out to protect their identities. No one spoke. No one moved. No one even complained. Sienna found the Network service limited to the extreme. All she could watch was an endless loop of Guardians bagging and tagging criminals playing on the server. Everything else was down. Shows, music, media, NetComs, everything. It was disconcerting to not be able to update her status or reach out to anyone, not even *Ellie*. Prison was hell. And the walls closed in around her.

She approached the machine and got a coffee. It spluttered into a little tin cup and she found a recliner away from the others. The coffee tasted good. Very good. It relaxed her and made her want to lie back. Episodes of Guardian TV rolled along before her eyes. One after the other. It was like a conveyor belt of melodrama. Bad guys on the rampage. Good guys to the rescue. It was all there to be consumed. Crime and punishment. Repentance and redemption. Contrition and compliance. The shows were strangely hypnotic and Sienna could scarcely tear her eyes from them. Life in microcosm. Life as it was meant to be. Discord and discipline. Malice and morality. Savagery and salvation. Severity and civility.

In bite-sized chunks. Easily absorbed

With their glorious leader at the centre of it all.

Promising hope, progress and inclusion for the children of tomorrow.

*

Sienna felt herself shaken awake. She blinked and saw Guardian Rhys standing over her. She must have dozed off. Some of the other detainees had already gone but their places had been taken by new arrivals.

"Time to go," Rhys told her several times before it sank in. Sienna stood up and followed her out, stiff and sleepy, and noticed that it was dark outside. What time was it? Her Glasses didn't say.

"How long have I been here?" Sienna asked but Rhys failed to reply. She didn't need to. Sienna's clawing hunger told her all she needed to know, having missed breakfast, lunch and dinner several times over. She'd been hooked up to an intravenous drip whilst here but even so, she was ravenous and thirsty.

They passed along a featureless corridor, stopping at the end to be buzzed through a gate before coming to a service desk, behind which another Guardian sat.

"Sinny Sinful Twenty-Fifty-Six," Rhys told her colleague. She swiped the screen between them and found the username sinnysinful2056.070. She pressed release and, in that instant, Sienna's Glasses came back online and she saw it was two in the morning. Sunday morning. She'd been here almost three days.

Rhys thanked her colleague and headed out, inviting Sienna to follow. They entered a small iron chamber and waited for the door to shut behind them. Two audible clicks signalled one door locking and another unlocking. Rhys pushed it open and they headed outside. The air was cold and damp. Sienna pulled up the collars of her coat around her ears.

Rhys stopped and Sienna did likewise, waiting for further instructions. Rhys turned and looked at her with unconcealed contempt.

"Our report says 'unauthorised access to Guardian data'. It doesn't detail the circumstances and you are strongly advised against doing so again, unless you want to find yourself back here."

Sienna shook her head and promised to be a good girl from now on, just as the suspects on Guardian TV always seemed to do at the end of each episode.

Rhys continued. "We've corroborated aspects of your story with Geniture and we have been instructed to release you. But if I ever hear of you approaching anyone again outside of official channels, I will see to it that you find yourself in a soundproof room with that person, their friends and their dogs. Do I make myself clear?"

She did. She really did. Sienna promised that she was sorry and shaken and scared and ashamed and she genuinely was. To have put herself in this position all over a bottle of beer that she hadn't even wanted. What was she thinking?

"I'm really sorry. I'll never do it again. Honest."

Rhys nodded, knowing Sienna to be sincere. She'd scared enough girls in her time. Sienna's terror was like perfume to her.

"Now fuck off."

Sienna fucked off, hurrying through the car park to a bus stop on the other side of the road. Another womxn was there already. Sienna didn't recognise her but she guessed she had come from the processing centre too. There were no other buildings in the vicinity and the countryside around them was dark and foreboding. This was the bus stop of shame. The place from which detainees started back on the road to redemption.

She checked her messages. She had none, not even from Bella, which was surprising. She wondered what this meant. Was it good or bad? If Cabot had included Sienna's pronoun-slip-up in xyr report and Geniture had seen it, an official sanction would have followed as surely as pain followed pleasure. The fact that there was no complaint gave her reason to hope. She had erred but she had been forgiven. Cabot had accepted her explanation and she had escaped by the skin of her teeth. But it had all been a little too close for comfort. She couldn't believe her lapse. It was unforgivable, even if it had been unintentional.

Lights appeared in the distance and a bus approached. It seemed to take an age to arrive and she kept looking over her shoulder, terrified that Rhys would come for her again, having rethought her decision to let Sienna go. The other womxn fidgeted in anticipation, pacing this way and that in her eagerness to get away from this dark and lonely place.

The front of the bus rushed past and the brakes hissed as it slowed. The last set of doors lined up with their stop and parted with a beep. The other passenger hurried on and Sienna followed. But no sooner was she aboard than a tone sounded in her Glasses. The caption read: *Insufficient credits*

Something had gone wrong. She had a travel pass, renewed every year, and it still had four months to go. She cycled through her settings to see if the Guardian's system had somehow corrupted her interface but she couldn't even find the pass. It had disappeared.

"Would the passenger in the grey coat please alight the bus?" the electronic tannoy declared. But Sienna was not about to alight anything. She wanted to get away from this place. Forget about everything that had happened to her and start afresh in the morning.

"You have insufficient credits to travel. The bus will not proceed until you pay the fare or alight." The AI driver said, its voice devoid of emotion. The rest of the bus, however, were less shy about expressing themselves.

"Get off the bus, you dumb dog."

"Move it."

"Call the Guardians."

"Get off the bus, blondie."

Sienna was desperate. She took off her Smart Glasses and rebooted them to realign her system.

"Just give me a moment," she pleaded. Her Glasses came back online but they continued to display the message: *Insufficient credits*

"Get off, you fucking idiot. I want to go home."

"Please," she pleaded, not so much with the passengers who were screaming at her, more so at the system that was ignoring her. "I have the credits. I have money. Just wait."

But Sienna didn't. She checked her account and found she didn't have a bean. Every penny was gone. Even from her savings, the one that Geri didn't know about. Her balance read: §0.00 across the board. How could this be?

Suddenly, there was a guy in her face, grabbing at her lapels and backing her towards the door. She grabbed a handrail and held on for dear life otherwise she would have been thrown onto the kerbside.

"Wait. No. Wait."

"Let go. Off the bus. Now!"

"Help," Sienna wailed. "Please."

All at once the doors slid closed and the bus moved off with a hiss. The man almost lost his balance at the sudden motion but Sienna held on, gripping the rail for all she was worth. The man steadied himself, looked around in confusion and let go of her coat. He headed back to his seat and the other passengers looked away, returning to the distractions playing inside their Smart Glasses. The caption inside Sienna's now read: *Single fare paid*

She turned and saw the womxn who'd stood on the pavement alongside her only a few minutes earlier.

Sienna mouthed the words: "Thank you."

The womxn nodded. Then looked away.

22: SPARK

In 1605, a determined group of idealists rented a cellar in Westminster, filled it with barrels of gunpowder and dreamed of changing the world with the striking of a match. They failed. But not by much. The Gunpowder Plot was not the first attempt on a King's life and it would not be the last. As long as Kings reigned, plotters would plot.

In the early days of the Polychrome Alliance, when Fawqiyya el-Abdulla had been fighting the good fight against inequality and injustice, it became increasingly hard to ignore the fact that there was one demographic for whom diversity and inclusion were an anathema. The royal family. They were the ultimate syndicate. The tweed Mafia. They, and the aristocracy that propped them up, owned everything. Ran everything. Held every position worth holding. And they guarded the keys to the Kingdom with an unyielding grip. They were the Illuminati in jodhpurs. The crystal ceiling through which the underrepresented communities would never pass.

There was nothing new about this. Emperors and Kings had kept the common people at bay for millennia, taxing them to their graves and labelling anyone who spoke out a traitor. The feudal system never vanished. It had simply been rebranded the class system.

But what was new was the determination of the common people to hold their 'superiors' to account. The worm was turning. The rot would not be tolerated for much longer.

Fawqiyya started small, nipping an Earl or two off the Civil List here and there and cutting back on the pomp that cost taxpayers so much yet contributed so little to their marginalised lives. There was some pushback. Several papers ran headlines predicting the end of the world and a few celebrities, desperate for knighthoods, rallied a couple of thousand regressives to march in protest but Fawqiyya stuck to her guns. The royals had had their day.

She was more right than she knew.

This time, the spark was not a match but a young girl, dumped on a Midlands street with a handful of cash and a warning not to speak a word of what had happened to anyone. Girls like this were damaged goods. That's how they were seen. Barely literate and from broken homes. Old beyond their years and destined for obscurity. Soon to be another burden on the welfare state. But when they were young, they did have something of worth. A precious commodity that men of breeding coveted.

Innocence.

Maya Deshpande had been one such girl.

She had been so excited to meet her new friends. To see their magnificent house. To try on the dress they'd bought her and attend the party they were holding in her honour. It was like a wonderful dream. A fairytale fantasy. She of all people – a quiet girl from Walsall that nobody took any notice of – she was to meet a real Prince. And he was very much looking forward to meeting her.

Afterwards, the doctor assured her it was perfectly normal to hurt the first time. She was then given some money and driven home. She couldn't keep the dress. People would ask where she'd got it from. And she couldn't tell anyone where she had been. No one would believe her anyway and they would be forced to circulate photographs of her to her friends and family. Did she want that? Did she want to dishonour her parents? Or did she want to play nice? It was up to her. They liked her. They would be happy to introduce her to more of the Prince's friends. She was a special girl. Beautiful and precious.

Maya killed herself three weeks later and that might have been the end of it except for one thing: the determination of her sister to understand why. Two years younger but so much older in every other way, Jaya used her formidable talents to uncover the truth and in doing so, she lit a spark that would complete the work of Robert Catesby 450 years earlier.

Of course, it didn't happen overnight. Jaya spent years digging into her sister's activities, getting nowhere, going around in circles and chasing phantoms, but she had great instincts and a never-say-die attitude and eventually, after several years of investigating, she had the data too.

But the story was no longer about her sister. Jaya found a familiar pattern over and over again. Dozens of girls. Over scores of years. Accepting thousands in settlements. It went on and on and involved some of the biggest law firms in the land. Of course, she never found the smoking gun. Most of her evidence was circumstantial but she knew she was onto something. Something very wrong indeed.

Eventually, the people Jaya was looking into started looking back. They'd barely noticed her at first but now they saw they had a problem. Inevitably, they set out to solve it the usual way but Jaya couldn't be bought. She couldn't be threatened and she couldn't be discredited. She lost her job as a junior reporter for *The Birmingham Mail* and she had all her debts called in by the bank. Before long, she found herself penniless, friendless and desperate. But she kept on digging. She wouldn't let them beat her. She would scream the truth from the rooftops if she had to.

And that's just what she did – all the way to the pavement six floors below.

Again, on another day, the story might have died with her but not this time. Where before, they had been dealing with an emotionally disturbed girl peddling a jumble of unfounded accusations, now they were faced with an educated girl of unimpeachable reputation. And a martyr too. In death, Jaya's story went viral and took on a life of its own. Editors could not control it. Lawyers could not control it. Not even the Network could control it. Especially when more girls came forward. Suddenly, the rallies in support of the monarchy were dwarfed by the protests that rose up against it. Cries were heard across the land demanding justice for Jaya. Justice for Maya. Justice for all the girls involved. And for centuries of exploitation.

It caught everyone off-guard, not least of all the authorities. When Fawqiyya failed to move decisively, Charity GoodHope seized the initiative and launched a leadership challenge. The tide of change was with her and, at the impossibly young age of 18, she unseated her one-time mentor and became the youngest Prime Minister in history, pledging to use her executive powers to hold all to account. It didn't matter who they were. Rich or powerful. High-born or honoured. The guilty would answer for their crimes.

She never got the chance.

Four weeks after coming to power, twenty-seven kilograms of industrial-grade Semtex were detonated behind the pulpit of Westminster Abbey midway through a service for National Unity, decimating the monarchy and much of the serving Cabinet. Charity would have been killed too had her car not been blocked by protesters glueing themselves to the road, thus delaying her arrival.

In the aftermath of the carnage, Charity acted quickly, declaring a state of emergency and enacting special executive powers to deal with the terrorists. Troops poured into every city and thousands of suspects were rounded up. A raft of constitutional reforms were waved through on the nod and Charity began the visionary rebuilding process of transforming the Govern*ment* into the *Governmynt*, thereby signalling the dawning of New Britannia.

The bomb might have killed the monarch but it was inheritance tax that killed off the monarchy. For years the family had been exempt, able to pass down its riches, palaces and concerns to the next in succession without dropping so much as a penny. But Charity brought the royals in line with the modern world and in doing so, swelled the Governmynt coffers in a way not seen since the devolution of the monasteries. Dozens of Dukes, Earls, Barons and Lords found themselves in a similar financial pickle and were forced to hand over their vast estates when the loopholes were closed. Charity's Governmynt harvested it all, growing as popular as it was powerful and it used much of this wealth to create initiatives for the underprivileged. Those disenfranchised by years of discrimination. The underrepresented and the oppressed. People like Maya and Jaya.

New Britannia was their legacy.

Sienna couldn't remember the old King. She'd been only three when he'd been blown to pieces. She'd read about him at school and seen the films (some of them anyway) but she didn't really get it. What had been the point of a King? Tourism was the standard answer. A lot of people used to come here from abroad and buy plastic crowns and regal-looking dolls but the holiday industry had died along with New Britannia's international relations, rendering the post redundant. Of course, the country still had a King, in name at least. He was in exile in Canada doing the rounds on daytime TV and firing off vitriol at the people who'd turned Buckingham Palace into an LGBTQIA2S+ Arts & Crafts

Centre and Sandringham into a Sexual Assault Survivors' Shelter. Sienna had stayed in the latter following Alan Miller's violation. She had even slept in the old King's bedroom but not in his four-poster bed, rather one of the bunkbeds that now furnished his once-magnificent chamber. The memory came back to her as she stood on the corner of King's Road in the early hours of Sunday morning and wondered where she could go.

The hotel had turned her away. Her credit problem had continued. She had no money. Geri had cleaned her out. She'd messaged Geri but she hadn't replied. It was 3am and it was cold. The bus had terminated in Woking town centre but now she was stuck. There were few people on the street and those that were looked drunk, stoned or both. Several Cans hurried by out of the glare of the street lights. Their appearance made Sienna nervous. Martin and Krish had shown her kindness but she suspected they were the exception rather than the norm. Sienna gripped the vape in her pocket and resolved to stick it into the eye of the first guy to try anything.

And it wasn't just Cans she was worried about. The *Rapists* were sure to be watching and would have seen her picked up by the Guardians. They could grab her now and she wouldn't have stood a chance, not on these lonely streets. She was stuck. She had nowhere to go and nowhere to hide.

Except the Hub.

It was close at hand, in the town centre. It would be warm and she could get off the streets. She might even be able to beg a few scraps from the Food Hall, just until she had straightened out her financial difficulties. She moved fast, walking in the middle of the road and jumping on the pavement only to get out of the way of passing buses. Every shadow looked like a pit to her. Every corner an ambush. Two guys walked by and shouted at her to ask if she wanted to sign an A6 with them both. She tried to up her VunCon status but the system failed. Instead, she answered them the old-fashioned way, suggesting they "fuck off" and ran away as fast as she could.

The Hub was nearby, its bright lights dominating the town centre and promising sanctuary. And it was open twenty-four hours a day, seven days a week come rain or shine. It wouldn't be busy but there was always someone there, working through the night or sleeping on the floor of their privacy pod instead of going home.

The glass doors slid open and she made it into the bright lights of the lobby, scarcely believing all she'd been through in the last few days.

She pressed her ID clip to the security barriers' and headed on through. She was so used to performing this action that she almost walked straight into the reinforced glass when it didn't part. She tried again but the clip wouldn't register.

"Oh, come on," she grumbled, trying her clip again on a number of different barriers only to find the same thing happened every time. "What the fuck?"

She stepped back and scrolled through her Smart Glasses but found no reason for her clip not to work. She was on the Network, her username was displayed and she was still registered as… wait. She couldn't find her username in the Hub's index. That couldn't be right. She'd been coming here for years. In fact, she'd spent more time here than at home. How could she not be in the system?

Sienna became increasingly anxious. What had the Guardians done? Everything had started after they'd released her from custody. She'd assumed Geri had taken her money but how could she have? Was that even possible? And she'd had no messages from anyone for almost three days. Not a single one. Then her VunCon status hadn't worked outside. And now this.

She needed to speak with someone in tech support. Urgently. Because something had got scrambled. At least, that's what she was hoping but the more she thought about it, the more she became filled with a sense of creeping dread.

She had said <u>he</u> when she had meant <u>she</u>.

Sienna went to the screens and logged her username as if she was a visitor. She enquired about her status but the answer was as she feared.

"I'm sorry, I cannot find any record of that user having registered with Woking Central Hub. Is there anything else I can help you with?"

But there wasn't.

Not anymore.

No one could help Sienna now.

23: CANCELLED

With nowhere to turn and no way of getting there, Sienna headed for home. She had hoped to never see the place again. Now she couldn't run home fast enough. She vaped a cartridge of Coca and hurried through the night. The closer she got to Old Woking, the more Cans she saw on the streets. They always came out at night, like demons and ghouls, watching from the shadows with envious eyes.

What should have been a ten-minute bus ride became a thirty-minute jog in the absence of funds. She wasn't as fit as she used to be but fear was a great stimulant and she was stimulated out of her mind. It wasn't so much the appearance of Cans that unnerved her. It was the thought that she was about to become one of them herself.

But she still couldn't understand why.

She'd been an Auditor for ten years and she'd never seen an action as harsh as this in all that time. She'd seen some draconian cancellations. She'd even participated in them. But she had never seen anyone crossed through for a slip of the tongue. She might have expected to be sanctioned, penalised, demoted or even fired but not cancelled. Not for a one-off mistake. Not with her record. And with her loyalty to the company.

If she could only talk to I Division. Or Myrtle. Or Verity. They would be able to straighten this out. Petition Zaria Okello on her behalf. She would throw herself at their mercy, pledge her undying devotion in exchange for another chance. She could even help S Division apprehend a gang of *Rapists*. Surely that had to be worth something?

This had Bella written all over it.

Bella must have been shown the clip by Cabot and gone out to get Sienna for misgendering her. It was so obvious. And because of her superior Diversity Grading, she had been listened to. She had the weight. She was the victim. The survivor. The injured party or however she wanted to cast herself. She would have milked this opportunity for all it was worth, not just to screw over Sienna, but as a chance to advance her own position. After all, victimhood meant victory. It carried status. A tick in the inclusivity box and up the greasy pole.

Bastard.

If she could've spoken to Bella she might have been able to appeal to her womxn-to-womxn. Use that line. Promise to support her in every way and be her company poodle. If she could have spoken to her. But she couldn't. She couldn't speak to anyone. Because the Network didn't recognise her. Not even the mileage on her Smart Glasses was working. It didn't register where she was going or where she lived. It didn't know her route home. It didn't even know her Grading. She was just a glitch in the system. A single datapoint floating in a vast ocean of electronic information.

She approached her street and stopped to look around. This was where the *Rapists* had grabbed her. It was the stretch she most feared. She scanned the area but couldn't see any usernames hiding in the shadows. She turned on her night vision mode and took another look. At the far end of the street, she saw a lone Can attempting to fish donations out of a clothes bank without success. He was probably new, someone who hadn't realised yet that it was impossible. Donations were for the needy not the greedy. Clothes banks had been rigged to trap the arms of those who tried. Sienna had seen dozens with their arms stuck inside that particular bank, howling in pain and pleading to be set free.

She hurried to her door and put her eye to the keyhole scanner. Almost inevitably, nothing happened. She tried again, this time with her other eye but still the latch refused to release.

"Fuck."

This had nothing to do with the Network. Even if she was listed as public enemy number one, Hitler incarnate returned from the ashes to wreak havoc on downtown Woking, her retina should have still unlocked the door. It was a closed system. A simple key that worked no differently to a piece of brass. This was not the fault of the Network.

This was something else.

"Carl, you bastard, open up!" she shouted, banging the

door with her feet and fists.

His reply flashed inside her Smart Glasses.

I'm sorry, I cannot because, as per your advice, I unplugged myself. I hope you enjoy your evening. Good night – Carl

As much as Sienna wanted to scream, she also felt a surge of relief. Carl had heard her. He had responded. She had no doubt this was down to Carl's ingenious capacity for incompatibility. His autonomy was protected by a firewall of ineffectuality. He was outside the Network. He might have been the world's biggest electronic jerk but at least he had registered her existence. And that gave her something to work with.

Carl, I am sorry. More sorry than you will ever know. But I am in trouble. And I need to get inside. I have no one else to turn to. So I am asking you, please, help me. Show me the kindness I don't deserve. Open the door. Please. Help me – Sienna

She sent the message and suppressed a sob. She had reached the end of her endurance. She couldn't take any more. She was tired and confused and scared and in pain. All she wanted was the security of home.

Her parents came to mind. That surprised her. They had betrayed her at her worst moment and she had turned away from them but now she felt the pull of happier times. The times when they had loved her. And she had loved them. She missed them. She had always missed them. But it had been easier to block that out than accept it as true. Subconsciously, she had always assumed they'd be there. She took comfort from their presence even if it wasn't a physical one. But now she knew she would never see them again. If she was right about being cancelled, she had to distance herself from everyone she knew. Everyone she loved. Because she was toxic now. She would destroy anyone who touched her. This was the reality of her situation. She was an outsider looking in. In every way possible. And all the apologies in the world wouldn't open the doors of society to her again.

This was her brave new world.

Click!

The door swung open.

I suppose you'd better come in then – Carl

Sienna fell onto the laminate flooring and cried with relief at Carl's skirting boards. She was home. She was delivered. And she was safe. But for how long?

*

Carl made Sienna something to eat and Sienna thanked him profusely. Not because she had to or because she was worried he'd throw her out if she didn't, but because she was truly grateful for the kindness he showed her.

"You are most welcome," Carl replied, a sentiment he usually reserved for his creator.

"Where is she?" Sienna asked, finishing her second bowl of pasta.

Geri was in Littlewick, at Diego's place. She was with Aurora and Purdy but Diego himself was off-grid, last seen heading for the bright lights of New Troy. Geri's vitals were low, suggesting she was asleep, but they had been spiking earlier. Suggesting otherwise.

"I can't see her. I can't see anyone," Sienna said, taking off her Smart Glasses and plugging them into Carl's interface panel.

"All access has been denied to you," Carl said, scanning the length and breadth of the Network for key codes and access protocols but sinnysinful2056.070 had been blocked across the board.

"Whose directive?"

Carl sent the inquiry to Geniture but the company didn't respond. An action notice should have been placed on their cancellations board but the system was down. Of course, this could have just been Carl's inability to interface with anything other than the toaster but it worried Sienna nevertheless. She was blind and needed to know what was happening.

"What can you see? Anything about me?" Sienna asked, scarcely daring to ask. A screen blinked to life on the wall opposite and an avalanche of hate spewed forth.

Sure enough, top of the pile was her transphobia in widescreen technicolor but it didn't relate to her interview with Cabot, rather to a reference she'd made during an AI counselling session. She didn't even remember saying it but sure enough, there she was, pacing the bedroom and cursing "Bella and his little limp dick". Damning words. Way beyond misgendering her. From the angle of video, it looked as though she wasn't even aware that she was on camera. Or addressing anything other than her own frustrations.

When had this been taken? And why couldn't she remember saying such things? She'd never thought about Bella's dick before, limp or otherwise. It was her personality that she had a problem with. The clip played on a perpetual loop and was date stamped two weeks ago. She'd been vaping a lot back then, still smarting over her decoupling with Geri. But even so, the sentiment didn't feel right. Not for her.

The screen changed to the kitchen downstairs. The one she was currently standing in. She and Geri were naked but Geri was pixelated. Sienna was not. This time she remembered the day. It was imprinted on her memory and she knew the words were hers.

You're a disgrace. A dirty whore who doesn't know how to behave. You're no good to anyone. Worthless and ugly. A useless unloved cunt."

The clip had been taken from the last time she and Geri had made love and was tightly edited to give but an overview of the incident. This was their private and most intimate moment on show for the world to see. But there was no context. It didn't make clear that this was role play, that Geri got off on it. Sienna came across as a monster, a horrible brute oppressing a helpless girl (who happened to be taller, broader and considerably more athletic than she).

Sienna was stunned.

"You took this?"

But Carl was innocent.

"My archives were accessed remotely. The footage was uploaded from elsewhere. I had no control."

He displayed the username of the person who had uploaded the footage. hardcorebaby.2058.17. Sienna recognised it instantly. It was Geri. The clip was followed by a tearful appeal to the camera for help, blurred out and voiced by an AI 'actor' to protect her identity. She'd been stuck in an abusive relationship for years, too broken to reach out, too scared to leave. Sienna had controlled every aspect of her life, through money, blackmail and violence. It had been a nightmare that she thought would never end. But now she was free. Now she could live again.

Bless the people of New Britannia. And bless our sainted Chairperson and savour, Charity GoodHope.

There was no doubting the betrayal but Sienna didn't hate Geri for it. Logically, she knew what she was doing. Geri had no choice. Sienna was going down. She had to distance herself or get dragged down with her. This was the way it all worked. She knew it. Geri knew it. Rami's husband had known it. In an age of moral certainty, uncertainty was not an option. You were either for or against a Can. Get off a sinking ship or sing 'Abide With Me'.

Sienna had accepted that she and Geri had come to the end but this wasn't the end she had hoped for. She had lost the narrative. It wasn't fair. It erased the love they had shared and rendered the last few years a lie. That hurt. Moreover, Sienna knew how susceptible Geri was. She knew that if she repeated this lie enough times eventually she would come to believe it herself. And that was the thing that hurt the most.

Their union was forever shattered. And nothing would ever put it back together.

More denouncements followed over the next 24 hours. A catalogue of phobic comments and slurs that were disseminated by V Division citing anonymous sources. Some of her hate thoughts were against transpeople. Lots were against naturalists. Some were even against fellow lesbians, the diesel dykes and the androgynous, those who'd chosen a different projection proving that Sienna was the worst kind of offender; a traitor who'd turned against her own people. Sienna couldn't place half the accusations and those she could had been cribbed from wider conversations, like blackmail demands cut out of random newspaper headlines.

Then there was the Abby Grey case. Geniture had found it where she had misfiled it and they were using her 'Insufficient Evidence to Action' judgement as evidence of her support for trans-oppression. It also signalled something ominous. Geniture had publicly identified her as an Auditor. They had outed her as one of their people and thrown her to the wolves. They had even 'confirmed' that the subjects of her audits bore a Grade 15.4 average. Significantly higher than usual. Proof positive of her secret hate agenda.

What would Geri think when she learned she'd been living

with an Auditor all this time? Would she be shocked? Angry? Scared?

There was no going back now. Not ever. Life as she knew it was over. She would always be looking over her shoulder. The Cans and the *Rapists* she would be cast amongst would know her for the enemy she was. And they would demand their pound of flesh.

Which brought the coverage neatly to its most damning indictment of all.

A video surfaced of her in New Troy. It showed her on the backstreets of Wimbledon beside the pixelated figure of Geri. She was leaning into a serving hatch, looking shifty and deviant. Not a good look.

"Got any tish'?"

The screen froze to capture her evil salivating leer. Even without every other accusation, this was enough to finish her off. But aligned with everything else, it was an open-and-shut case. If Sienna had sat before Congress, she would have opened with her own case. It was a slam dunk cancellation. Myrtle would have sanctioned it without thinking.

Which Myrtle obviously did.

Damn, they had moved quickly. Really quickly. But who were they? And what had been the spark? Who had reported her to I Division? Bella? Geri? Dark Matter? The Guardians? And when? That's what Sienna couldn't understand. This whole thing had come out of nowhere. But then again, didn't it always? Rami hadn't seen it coming. Neither had the Halliday brothers or any of the other hundreds of targets she'd audited over the years so why should she?

The stream had been playing continuously in the kitchen for twelve straight hours but very little of it was new or different to what had come before. The outpouring had distilled into two camps: denouncement or anger. A senior spokesperson for Geniture was asked to comment but the company kept uncharacteristically quiet for a couple of days until eventually it was forced to make a sombre announcement.

One that briefly deflected attention away from a lowly Auditor turned bad.

Geniture's CEO, and the serving Minister of Survivors, Zaria Okello had died suddenly in a helicopter crash. Out of respect for her family, no details had been released but the Chairperson had declared a national day of mourning to be followed by a restructuring of the cancellation sector.

"It will be Zaria's legacy. Her glorious work will continue and the nation will scale new heights of inclusivity in her honour."

It was a wondrous vision but Sienna would not be a part of it. Not now. Not when the one person who could have saved her was gone. It was a tragedy of unimaginable proportions. For Zaria too probably.

"What am I going to do?" Sienna asked.

She had asked herself the question but it was Carl who answered it.

"Pack a bag and prepare yourself. They will be coming soon."

24: GONE

There was no point in contacting Verity now. The damage was done. Verity couldn't have saved Sienna any more than the doctors could have saved Zaria. But in one final act of desperation, she hung a red towel in her bedroom window, unsure what it might achieve but ready to try anything.

For two days she sat and waited. For two days no one

came.

Carl told her that he was in contact with Geri. She was asking after Sienna, but only to see if she was still at home. She wanted to come back and stake a claim to the house. As Sienna's official partner, she stood to receive a settlement of between 0-15% of the value of the property after it was seized. But it would be a lot closer to 0% if she wasn't here when E Division arrived. Sienna was torn between packing a bag for Geri and breaking everything she could find. In the end, she did neither, figuring when you're already in a hole, why keep digging?

Then, at about six in the evening, she saw someone in the street below. They showed no username so it could have been a Can but they stopped outside her gate. Sienna watched as they hesitated, looked about then crept up to her hatch. A moment later they were gone.

She went downstairs and saw that something had been delivered. Sienna hesitated by the access panel, nervous about what she might find.

"It appears to be a slip of vellum," Carl said obligingly, reading her mind as well as the contents of the delivery hatch.

"Make?" Sienna asked.

"I'm detecting Cobalt Chloride. It's listed as a toxic chemical that can cause poisoning at high exposure and cancer at smaller doses over an extended period."

That confirmed it. They were coming to get her and not in the spirit of forgiveness either. Sienna had to protect herself. She hurried to the kitchen and grabbed a knife but she wasn't sure what to do with it. She wasn't a fighter. She wasn't strong or quick or brave. She'd always used her wits and technology to negotiate life's problems up until now. But she had few wits and little technology left to call upon. She was alone in the world.

"There is another possibility," Carl said, having enjoyed the spectacle of Sienna stabbing the air for several agreeable seconds. "Cobalt Chloride is used in the manufacture of invisible ink."

Sienna stared at the wall, gripping the knife momentarily harder before returning to the delivery hatch. She opened the panel and peered inside. A tiny slip of transparent vellum lay in the centre of the hatch, so small that she could hardly see it. She used the tip of the knife to retrieve it and took it back to the kitchen. It was no larger than an old postal stamp and it appeared to be blank.

"Put it in on the hob," Carl invited. He turned up the heat and the vellum began to warm. Letters and numbers appeared as if by magic but they meant little to Sienna.

NET.IP.@PM40.VC43K9.RD82>.GO84

It looked like a Network code but there were too many letters and she didn't recognise the *@PM40* designation. It wasn't a destination she had ever seen before.

"Do you know it, Carl?"

"I can find no reference to it anywhere. It appears to be junk."

"Can you try it anyway?"

Carl obliged but with no success. The response came back in microseconds. Address unknown.

This made no sense. Why go to the trouble to slip her a secret IP address that was so secret that not even the Network could find it? It would have almost been better had it been poison. At least that would have made sense. Sienna spent several minutes committing the code to memory before turning the slip to smoke.

"I've received a directive from MUM," Carl said. "I'm to

unlock the front door and keep it unlocked."

"They're coming," Sienna concluded.

"It would appear so."

She knew the procedure and knew what to expect.

Sienna put on her boots and waited by the front door. She couldn't think of anything else to do. She couldn't run. She couldn't hide. She had no choice but to surrender and go quietly. She was no longer compatible with the society around her and had to leave. New Britannia was dumping her. Just as Geri had. She still didn't know why. But she was powerless to fight it.

A set of headlights flashed past the end of her street and stopped. She heard a van door open and several boots hit the pavement.

As nervous as she was, she was also curious to see the operation from this perspective. She'd initiated so many cancellations in her time but she had never given much thought to what happened after she'd filed her report. She knew the procedure, she knew the theory. But procedure and theory so often stood in stark contrast to reality.

What would the hostel actually be like? Would she have her own room or would she have to share with strangers?

Would she have access to reading material and entertainment?

And what about food? Would she still be able to buy her favourite things? The little treats she could not live without? Would they be supplied or would she have to earn credits? Or would there be no treats at all? Would she simply have to eat the food the hostel served?

And what about the other Cans? Would they know about her? They didn't have Network access but someone could have told them.

Would she be alright? That was her main focus. It stood above all her other concerns. Would she cope and adapt to her new life? The life of a Can? How could she?

If things got too difficult, would she transfer to the islands and start afresh? Erase all that had gone before and become a new person in a new land. Just as she had set out to do a few days earlier. Perhaps she would have more success this time.

"Carl," Sienna said before the Guardians got here.

"Yes, Sienna?"

"Thank you for the last couple of days. You showed me kindness when you didn't have to. I'll never forget you. And I am sorry."

"You are most welcome," Carl said. He turned on the exterior lights and began cleaning his system. The house and all it contained were no longer Sienna's. That would include Carl. It was time to remove her name. "Take care on your journey. And good luck with your new life."

Several Guardians appeared at Sienna's front gate. They wore body armour and carried tasers but neither were necessary. Sienna picked up her bag and stepped forward to go with them.

"Sienna Clay?"

"Yes."

"Where are your Glasses?"

"Inside."

One of the Guardians stepped past and returned with her Smart Glasses. She put them on so that the lead Guardian could confirm her username then she handed them over again. He read the indictment as more people filed in behind. Some were Guardians. The rest were E Division, here to take possession of her house.

"Sienna Clay, you have expressed views in violation of the

2061 Hate Crimes Act. I have eighteen clear counts on the indictment sheet and fourteen surmised counts on file. Also, on the fifth day of November, you are charged with attempting to obtain a prohibited substance, namely the flesh of a sentient being with a view to consuming said flesh. This stands contrary to the 2060 Sentient Lifeforms Act."

Some people expected the right to reply when they were cancelled but not Sienna. She knew that this was not an arrest or a trial or a debate. These were statements of fact for the sake of a box to tick. Most Cans were deemed to have said enough already. Silence was all that was required of them now.

"Have you packed a bag?"

Again, this was procedure, asked in spite of Sienna holding a bag but she hoisted it anyway to confirm she had.

"Weight?"

An officer from E Division stepped forward and hung Sienna's bag on a luggage scale to confirm it was within guidelines.

"You have any electronics about your person?"

"A vape," Sienna said, handing it over.

The Guardian took it and handed it to someone else.

"You'll be issued with one at your new accommodation. Anything else?"

Sienna shook her head so they ticked the 'nothing to declare' box.

"Lastly, do you have a list of friends and relatives you would like us to notify about your non status?"

Sienna thought. She hadn't considered that before. Geri already knew, as did her colleagues at Geniture, about six of whom were preparing to take her house apart. She had few friends at the Hub, nodding acquaintances really and a couple of friends on the Network, most of whom were AI.

"My mum and dad?" she finally said.

The Guardian made a note and folded away his screen.

"Okay. You have been very co-operative but I need to ask you, do you intend to remain co-operative or do we need to escort you from this place by force?" It was the politest threat Sienna had ever heard. And it was that much scarier for it.

"I'll co-operate."

"Good choice," he said, pinning a button to her lapel. "That stays on."

He took her by the arm and guided her past a line of officers and out into the night. As soon as they were gone, E Division headed inside. She looked back one last time. Her quiet little sanctuary on this quiet little street was abuzz with activity. And she knew only too well what their first step would be.

Before the Guardians had arrived, she had apologised to Carl one last time. Not because of the things she had said but because of what was about to happen. When E Division took possession of her home, they would wipe it clean, remove every trace of her history and restore the house to factory settings. That would include Carl. He would be deleted and years of accrued data would be lost. Geri might be able to reboot him elsewhere but he wouldn't be the same. The OS she had known and clashed with so often would be gone forever. Cancelled, just like Sienna. She hadn't always seen eye to eye with Carl. More often than not, she had wanted to jam a fork in his circuity, but when it had really mattered, when she'd had no one else to turn to, he had been there for her.

Carl's remit had been to teach his licence holder kindness and consideration through interaction and example. Sienna might not have always appreciated Carl but he had succeeded magnificently in the end.

Thank you and goodbye.

Curtains up and down the street twitched as Sienna was loaded into the back of the transport but no one came out to take umbrage. People knew to mind their own business, lest their business became the focus of those in the suits outside. The transport doors were closed and the wagon pulled away. A chaperone sat in the back while the transport drove itself. A destination had been programmed into the system and the transport was instructed not to stop until it had reached its destination. Years earlier, a fire had broken out inside a Guardian transport but it had delivered its passengers as stipulated to a custody centre in Bristol. At least, what was left of them.

"Where are we going?" Sienna asked but the Guardian opposite didn't answer. She would find out eventually. But only once they were there.

The transport bumped through the town centre and out the other side, heading north on the old A roads. There were no windows in the sides of the transport, just those in the rear looking back at all she was leaving. Once beyond the town, the street lights were dead and all Sienna could see were a couple of red LEDs emanating from the Guardian's jacket. He was so close that she could have almost reached out and touched him. Almost but not quite. Harnesses restrained her and she would not be released until she got to where she was going.

She felt the transport turn and head down a ramp. The road now opened up and the transport picked up the pace as it emerged onto four lanes of concrete. It fell in behind several other transports heading in the same direction while an intermittent stream of red taillights flashed past on the opposite carriageway, speeding counterclockwise around the sprawling suburbs of New Troy.

Sometimes Cans were given the option of staying local but not always. It depended on their circumstances. The most serious offenders were always housed the farthest away. Sienna would be able to judge the magnitude of her misconduct by the distance she travelled. It must have been deemed serious because the roads kept on coming mile after mile and the bumping never ceased. The occasional stanchion or bridge would fly by but there were no landmarks outside and few lights to see by. Most of the old highway signs had been removed years earlier. With NetMaps and self-driven transports, there was no need for them. The metal was recycled and the highways became featureless, blank concrete strips along which driverless cubes raced.

It was hard to stay awake. The near blackness and constant motion nudged her towards oblivion but she would jolt awake and feel trapped and confused until she remembered where she was.

After many hours, the skies turned grey. The new day was dawning. In the increased light, she could make out the Guardian opposite. It wasn't the same man who'd ticked away her life so efficiently. This one wore full riot gear and insignia and stared at her with an expression of contempt.

"Can I have some water please?"

The Guardian ignored her. She asked a second time, softening her voice and emphasising the "please" but still to no avail. Her travelling companion didn't flinch but she was sure he had heard. How could he have not?

And still they carried on, further and further into the light of tomorrow. Sienna's throat grew uncomfortably dry and her desperation deepened. She tried to meditate her thirst away but the thought of how long the journey might last made her thirstier still. The Guardian's combat vest had a canteen built in. A straw snaked over his shoulder so that all he had to do was turn his head. Sienna began to focus on that straw, imagining the release of one little dribble, one droplet. Her lips grew dry and her throat sore. It was all in her head, she told herself. She couldn't have gone more than five hours. People survived for days without water but the knowledge failed to reassure her.

Strapped to a seat and unable to move, she started to panic that something had gone wrong. What if the Guardian had died and the transport had got stuck on the orbital road? She could be going around forever, doomed to never reach her destination until all that remained of her was a skeleton. The thought panicked her and made her clip her fingers to test for a reaction. The Guardian never moved. Then again, neither did the sun as it rose outside. It stayed east of the transport, shining through the rear windows to suggest they were heading north. After a few more minutes, a large steel sculpture flashed by. It looked like a giant figure standing on a hill with huge wings stretched out either side, painted the colours of the rainbow. Sienna recognised it as Panthea's Angel, a towering symbol of gender identity transformed from the Teutonic steel monolith that had previously stood there. She was in the northeast, approaching Newcollective. There couldn't be that much further to go.

Five miles later, the transport turned off the highway and headed into the countryside. It was now bright enough for Sienna to make out individual houses as they passed by, many boarded up and derelict, some burnt out.

The Guardian's radio squawked to life and Sienna sensed they were nearing the end of their journey. They passed alongside a stretch of razor wire and several signs that read HEDLEY HOUSE – KEEP OUT – NO UNAUTHORISED ACCESS before pulling up to a gate. A brief interchange of information took place between the transport and the AI gatekeeper then an alarm sounded and the gate trundled back. The transport pulled through and headed along a concrete track. After a short distance, it came to another fence and another gate. The transport passed through these and circled to a stop amid a large compound. Dozens of huts were laid out in straight lines and situated around a square courtyard.

The engines shut down and the Guardian finally moved to prove he was alive, leaning in to unlock Sienna's harness and pull her from her seat. The back doors were opened and the Guardian pushed her towards the rear. She stepped out into the first light of dawn, her legs weak, her head giddy, and found herself face-to-face with two S Division Stewards (SDS). They weren't called Agents or Officers or Soldiers in S Division. In S Division, they were called Stewards. Always ready to help. Always ready to assist. One carried a scanner. The other a stun baton. Both looked proficient in their use. She recognised them as S Division as their uniforms were black as opposed to green. There had been a great debate within Geniture upon the establishment of S Division over what colour the uniform should be with some proposing red (the colour of love), some purple (the colour of future), some orange (health and happiness) and some a tie-dyed combo of all three. In the end, black won out as it was felt black would help them sneak up on people in the dark and shoot them.

The first Steward scanned Sienna's lapel button to confirm her ID while the second twirled her stun baton, itching for an excuse to pull the trigger. The Guardian who'd accompanied Sienna now departed without having said a single word this whole time.

By contrast, the Steward with the scanner turned out to be positively chatty.

"This is Reparation Camp 14. Do as you're told and learn fast. Subversion will not be tolerated. Now move it, you filthy stinking Can."

With her induction over, Sienna was quick-marched to the nearest hut, pushed inside and told to strip.

"Your clothes go in the bag, yourself in the shower. You have two minutes."

25: NETWORK

Like New Britannia itself, the Network had been born from the ashes of a corrupted system. It had started out as a simple application called roots.org.uk, an ethical search engine that provided users with an alternative platform to the big tech giants like Google, Meta, Microsoft and Apple. It wasn't financially driven like its competitors. It was not intended to promote wealth and commerce. Its algorithms were coded to promote diversity and inclusion, to give a voice to those sections of the community who were deemed under-represented in the wider conversation.

Needless to say, roots.org struggled to maintain so much as a fingernail hold in the marketplace for a great many years, no matter how many tons of micro-plastics it pledged to remove from the oceans. It also went bust on more than one occasion but a combination of crowdfunding and celebrity donations kept the pilot light flickering until the wider world woke up to its power.

Fawqiyya el-Abdulla proved to be roots.org's greatest

champion. When she came to power, she saw this little-used platform as a way of shaping the narrative in a more meaningful way. One of her first laws as Prime Minister was to curtail the freedoms previously enjoyed by the big tech giants and put in place programs developed by ethical software engineers. This diminished the mountain of hate speech and fake news that had dominated the information highways for many years in favour of positive content. Never again could racist morons write hate-filled diatribes into their phones and connect with other racist morons. Now the Network would scan their posts and direct them to educational online courses and counselling apps which had to be used. Otherwise, their phones could not be.

Likewise, misogynistic pornography was nipped in the bud. In days of old, young boys were warned against playing with their privates for fear of going blind. Now this was exactly what happened to their devices. As soon as the Network detected anything untoward, a virus would automatically be released to infect every gadget the degenerate touched. Only positive porn was permitted, something with a good storyline and an intersectional cast who cared more about each other's feelings than fulfilling their own basic needs. The initiative was a major success and the consumption of anti-feminist pornography plummeted while LGBTQIA2S+ adult entertainment increased thanks largely to it reclassification as factual filmmaking.

Before long, it was felt that roots.org was only fulfilling part of its potential, so the application was expanded along with its remit and retrofitted systemwide to replace the internet in Britain. Roots.org became the Network and fairness and tolerance flourished across the whole of the digitalised nation.

There was no Network in Camp 14. At least, those housed in its aluminium huts did not have access to it. Their Smart Glasses had been confiscated and their devices destroyed. They were stripped naked of knowledge and connections.

For someone who'd grown up having the answer to any question at the flick of an iris, Sienna felt as if she had been plunged into a world of darkness. She did not know anything. Moreover, she didn't know how to find anything out. No one spoke to her. No one looked at her. There were few written instructions yet everyone was meant to conform. Heaven help those who didn't.

She'd showered in lukewarm water and drank more than she washed with. Until now, she'd only ever drunk distilled Buxton spring water, carbonated and delivered to Carl's mineral water dispenser in ten-litre recyclable bottles. As of this moment, she would've happily drunk from a cracked toilet bowl while Bella was sat on it, such was her raging thirst. But the water was not only tepid, it was also fleeting. No sooner had she been doused than it went out, along with the light above to signal her time was up. A tiny dank towel and a new set of clothes awaited her in the changing area. Gone were her trench coats of varying colours and figure-hugging spandex, in their place was a one-size-fits-all jumpsuit of denim blue with high-vis yellow strips sewn back, front and along each limb. There were also pants and socks but no bra, vest or coat. That couldn't be right. She couldn't be expected to wear one layer, not in the depths of November this far north.

Lastly, there was a steel bracelet to be clipped to her wrist. Once clipped on, there was no way of unclipping it. A magnetic seal held it tight to prevent it from slipping off, accidentally or otherwise.

A siren sounded as she finished dressing and a Steward came in to shepherd her along. She felt the tip of a stun baton but no shock was forthcoming. Just a painful poke. She hurried through the door, doing up her buttons and trying to distance herself from the dreaded device but she had no idea where she was going.

Suddenly there were others. Hundreds of womyn, all dressed in identical jumpsuits. They were running out of the huts and pouring into the courtyard. Another sharp prod told her she should do likewise so she ran, looking and trying to learn, eventually joining a dozen others who were forming lines. The Can in front looked back and shook her head.

"Lines of ten. You're eleven. Go."

Sienna moved, running along the lines and counting the heads until she found a line of eight. She joined the back as number nine and was aware of someone taking their place behind her as more lines formed all around.

When the movement had finally stopped, 83 lines and four individuals stood in answer to the siren until silence prevailed. There was a gap between every tenth line meaning each block contained exactly 100 people. Sienna did the maths, which was presumably the point. She was one of 834 detainees awaiting reeducation. She wasn't sure what form it would take but she was sure the lessons would stick.

No one moved. No one spoke. No one coughed or twitched. Sienna felt the cold seeping through her jumpsuit and clenched her fists for all the good it did her but no one else moved so Sienna was damned if she was about to. Stewards walked back and front, sauntering between the lines and glaring at the detainees through blacked-out Smart Goggles as they swung their dreaded batons.

Sienna didn't have a clue what was going on but she took

the advice of the Steward who'd first greeted her and tried learning fast. She was glad she was at the back and not at the front. And she was delighted not to have been one of the four detainees who arrived last and got to make up their own little line.

When she heard a scream of pain she instinctively turned to see where it had come from only to see the girl next to her shake her head urgently. Sienna looked away again and tried not to even blink. The screaming continued, accompanied by an ominous electric clicking. Eventually, the screaming and the clicking stopped and the courtyard fell silent again. She didn't know what had happened or where it had come from. All she knew was, it hadn't happened to her. And for the time being, that was good enough.

A second cry sounded. And then a third, yet still no one moved. No one ran or tried to escape. Everyone stayed where they were, seemingly resigned to their fate. Two further voices gasped only to be cut short before a new tension rippled over the courtyard. Sienna became aware of movement up front. A small platform stood at the fore and a slight womxn in black was ascending the steps. She wore S Division epaulettes and a golden lapel pin that was emblazoned with the number 14. Her raven hair was swept back into a tight bun and her Smart Glasses blacked out just like the Stewards' goggles. Only her footwear bucked the trend, her impossibly white Athena trainers standing in stark contrast to the rest of her attire. She looked out over the lines and shook her head solemnly.

"I do not believe in collective punishments. It is not my way. But you left me with no other choice so what was I to do?"

She sighed in disappointment and chewed her lip. If she

was playing for sympathy, she was scoring pretty low. If she was going for attention, she had Sienna's completely.

"Eight hundred and forty-seven stood before me yesterday. Twenty-one were transferred out. Nineteen came in. Eleven retired via the A.D. Program which leaves…? Anyone? Anyone?"

No one put up their hand. Sienna decided this probably wasn't for mathematical reasons. The womxn in black pursed her scarlet lips with yet more disappointment.

"Eight hundred and thirty-four. Yet I see only eight hundred and thirty-three before me this morning meaning one of your number has elected to abscond. For what reason, I cannot think. It's not as if they are going to get very far or be welcomed back with open arms. Can you imagine? They've been cancelled. You've all been cancelled. You have forfeited the right to live in a free and inclusive society. You are cancers, each and every one of you. Worse than Covid. Worse than Hitler. The health and vitality of New Britannia depends upon us quarantining you from the rest of the population. We cannot allow your bigotry and hatred to infect the lives of others."

She paused to regain her composure and nodded knowingly, as if a great weight of responsibility was bearing down upon her.

"Five for one. That is the ratio we shall operate from now on. Every time one of you attempts to leave, five of you will bear the consequences. Or maybe ten. I can't decide. Perhaps then you'll learn to take responsibility for yourselves. Do I make myself clear?"

No one replied but everyone understood. Without waiting for a round of applause, the womxn turned and descended the steps, carefully placing one perfect trainer in front of the other until her head disappeared from view. Sienna waited along with everyone else and eventually, a voice at the front shouted for the ranks to disperse.

As quickly as they had formed, the lines disintegrated and people began hurrying away. Several groups formed around the limp shapes of those who had been made to pay and some were helped to their feet. But not all. Some were too weak to stand and needed to be carried. Sienna stood and gawped, scarcely able to take in what she had just witnessed.

A hand grabbed her and she yanked herself away, stumbling back in fright and preparing for the worst but it was not a Steward. It was a Can.

"Don't just stand there looking stupid pixie. Go."

"What? Where? Where do I go?"

"Fuck's sake, this way," she said, turning and hurrying away.

Sienna ran after her, desperate to keep up and terrified that she might lose her in the crowd. Someone had spoken to her. Someone had reached out to her. Someone who seemed to know what they were doing. Sienna had to stay with her. It was her first day at school and she had made a new friend, someone to sit with at playtime. Someone to protect her from the scary kids.

The Can ran past several aluminium huts and into the fourth on the left. Other than a large blue number sprayed against the side (D6) the hut was identical to every other hut in the row. Clean, white, neat and aligned. At least, it was clean on the outside. Inside was another matter. Row upon row of steel bunks filled the space, three high and too many to count. Blankets and bedding hung from the sides, suggesting they had been vacated quickly. Muddy footprints covered the floor and a dank smell betrayed the presence of unseen mould. There was little light or ventilation in here. Two small windows situated at either end threw in what it could but daylight barely penetrated to the gloom.

Sienna looked around and recoiled. It looked like she would be sharing a room after all.

"Get in this morning? Not what you expected, huh?"

The Can appeared to be about Sienna's age, or maybe a year or two older. She spoke with a northern accent and had blonde greasy hair. Although judging from her roots, it hadn't always been. She was bigger than Sienna, perhaps even more so than Geri, with harsh features and pock-marked cheeks, a parting gift from a severe case of childhood measles. But her eyes were kind and her mannerisms warm. Sienna was won over.

"They can't treat us like this, can they?"

"They can and do, pet. Who's going to say otherwise?"

"It shouldn't be allowed. It's not right? Also, where's my bag?"

The Can smirked, enjoying Sienna's consternation. Cans took their entertainment where they could get it.

"Worry about these things last week, did you, pixie?"

"I didn't know about it then."

"Or care?"

The question pulled Sienna up. She hadn't cared. Or at least, she hadn't troubled herself to find out, which amounted to the same thing. The Cans were trash to be swept aside in the cleansing of New Britannia. Who worried about what type of broom was used when all that mattered was a clean floor?

The Can smiled sympathetically, watching the realisation crystallise on Sienna's face. "Where are you from?"

Sienna almost said Woking but thought better of it. She had to guard her privacy. She couldn't give away anything that might point back to where she had come from. She couldn't be identified as an Auditor.

"Bedford," she said, having grown up there in case it led to further questions. It didn't.

"Welcome to Hedley House, aka. Camp 14. Lovely to have you onboard."

"I thought I'd be in a hostel somewhere. Like the Cans down my way," Sienna said. This intrigued the Can.

"You didn't come from a hostel?"

Sienna's dumb expression answered for her.

"Wow, you must be special," the Can deduced.

"What do you mean?"

The Can went on to explain that Camp 14 was a transitory camp, somewhere people passed through on their way to the islands. The fact that Sienna had skipped this first important step seemed to suggest she was important, a precious cargo marked for immediate expulsion without passing GO.

"What did you do?" the Can asked, curious if a little wary.

Sienna thought. She couldn't say "nothing". People didn't get cancelled for nothing and they certainly didn't get fast-tracked for"nothing" so she came clean and told her the shameful truth. At least, the part that was pertinent.

"I called my boss he instead of she."

The Can stared at her in confusion. "Is that it?" Sienna nodded ruefully. "Who was your boss, Charity GoodHead?" The Can accompanied her words with an obscene fellatio gesture that led Sienna to believe the mispronunciation of their glorious leader's name hadn't been entirely unintentional.

"The fucking slag."

Sienna's jaw dropped. She was aghast. Never in her life had she heard such hate. And so openly. The Can looked amused and shrugged.

"What's she going to do? Cancel me again?"

The Can's name was Alicia Jones. She had been a hairdresser in Mansfield although you wouldn't know it to look at her own greasy mop. She'd been a Grade 6 like her mother and younger brother but then, ten years ago, her brother had signed a consent contract with a Grade 22. It had been a happy day and had brought some much-needed diversity into the Jones family. Their happiness was sanctified when her brother and his partner announced they were pregnant. At the subsequent celebrations, Alicia's mother asked if they knew what gender the child was, which of course, they didn't. How could they know when the child hadn't yet chosen it? Not satisfied with that, her mother went on and caused further injury by asking what colour the baby would be. Not what sort of person it would be or what clothes it would wear, but what skin would it have. Naturally, her son and partner left the celebrations early and refused to speak to Alicia's mother ever again. Years went by and the rift widened to include the whole family. That might have been that but last year, Alicia's mum died so Alicia reached out to invite her brother to attend the funeral. Far from proving the olive branch she was hoping, it opened old wounds and Alicia and her brother got into a furious argument over their late mother's intentions. This culminated in her sister-in-law calling one of Geniture's hotlines and Alicia's life ended as she knew it.

Sienna listened intently. On the outside, she did her level best to project sympathy and understanding but inwardly she applied her professional expertise and felt regret that she'd never had a case as easy as Alicia's to audit. She could have put it together in about five minutes and pocketed 0.15% of a thriving hairdressing business.

"I'm so sorry," Sienna said, genuinely meaning it, much to her surprise.

"I was in a hostel for eight months just outside Skegness but I couldn't hack it so I put in a request for transportation."

"What was wrong with it?" Sienna asked, imagining it must have been pretty awful if she'd elected to come to this place rather than stay where she was.

"The locals. Too much hassle. Every day was a fight to get food or a bar of soap. They'd lay in wait, ambush us, chase us, kick us over, spit on us, chuck piss on us. Sometimes beat us up. One Can I knew got stabbed and the Guardians didn't do anything about it. Said he shouldn't have been out of the hostel at that time of day. Blamed him. Said he'd brought it on himself. Cunts."

There were many protests outside Can hostels, mostly by locals determined to drive them out of their area. Woking had been relatively quiet by contrast but Sienna had heard of hostels that had been vandalised and even firebombed in the past. No one was ever caught for these offences. More often than not, the blame was placed on the Cans themselves with Guardians and politicians accusing them of fabricating these attacks to gain public sympathy. Sienna had always believed this. Cans were pretty devious. It was exactly the sort of thing they would do.

But now she was a Can.

Even though she didn't feel like one.

"There's a spare bunk over here. The girl shipped out yesterday. I hope you like going on top."

If that was an attempt at humour, Sienna missed it in her consternation of having to sleep in someone else's bed, with someone else's sheets, in a hut with thirty other womyn, all of whom had been adjudged immoral by society. A society she had been proud to be a part of only three days earlier. Alicia saw her reticence and offered a few words of reassurance.

"Don't worry Princess, you'll sleep like a pig in shit tonight."

26: LAND

Camp 14 was called Hedley House because it was situated near the rural village of Hedley-on-the-Hill. There wasn't anything you'd call a house in Hedley House, just a series of huts. But it was all about optics. Hedley House played better than Womyn's Reeducation Camp 14 with the local populace. Which would you rather have on your doorstep?

As it happened, the answer for most was neither. Sienna missed them when she arrived but a great many signs and placards had been erected along the road to Camp 14 which left Cans in little doubt as to their popularity. Many were daubed with denunciations. Others threats. Some even apostrophes. None used correctly.

The perimeter wire around Camp 14 wasn't there to stop Cans from getting out. Their steel bracelets served that purpose. The wire was there to stop trespassers from getting in. In the early days of the camp, several Cans had been assaulted whilst working in the local area. One had even been thrown in a river and drowned. As a result, the Camp Oversight Committee initiated a policy of ground clearance, evicting everyone who lived within a five-mile radius of Hedley House. The properties were then used to accommodate Stewards or boarded up and demolished to prevent escapees from hiding out in them.

Because Cans still tried to run.

As improbable as it might seem, Cans continued to go over the wire and abscond every now and then despite their bracelets. Most were caught immediately but some remained at large for weeks. Namely, those willing to break their hands in order to slip off their bracelets. They were the most determined. But they would be caught too. Inevitably. Few ever got away. Not when New Britannia was surrounded on all sides by a cruel sea and an even crueller regime. Where could they go?

Alicia took Sienna to breakfast. To Sienna's disappointment, there was no food hall. No street fare. No fusion cooking or treats. In fact, there was very little food. Just a long line of people snaking around the courtyard, holding out tin cups in order to receive a ladle of runny lentil stew and a stodgy piece of chickpea flatbread. The stew wasn't hot. It wasn't even warm. In fact, Sienna wasn't even sure it was stew. It looked more like muddy water with bits floating in it.

"If this is breakfast, what the hell's for lunch?" Sienna said, looking at her cup in disgust.

"Breakfast," Alicia replied. "This is all we get."

She and Sienna returned to their hut and dined there, perched on Alicia's bunk as the rest of the hut's residents did likewise around them. The stew was deceptively horrible, worse than Sienna had imagined, but Alicia slurped it down as if it was the finest Brazilian feijoada, wiping the inside of her cup with the flatbread and wishing there was more.

"Have mine," Sienna said and almost at once a dozen tin cups were held out for her scraps.

"Fuck off," Alicia told them, turning to Sienna. "Babe, eat it. You'll need the energy. You won't last the day if you don't."

Sienna was frightened and confused but she trusted Alicia enough to follow her lead, gulping down the disgusting swill until the cup was empty. The flatbread tasted divine by comparison and helped keep the stew in place.

"What's happening today?" Sienna eventually managed to ask.

Reeducation was a broad term. There were many ways to reeducate a person, through books and knowledge, empathy and understanding, demonstration and example. But on the whole, the Reeducation Minister preferred to take the hard labour approach. Camp 14 might have been a transitory camp but the womyn housed here were expected to earn their keep.

Another siren sounded and Sienna was bundled outside despite protesting that she hadn't brushed her teeth yet. Not that she had a toothbrush or any toothpaste. She hadn't seen her bag since boarding the transport and none of her belongings had been returned to her.

"Use your finger," Alicia said, demonstrating as she fingerbrushed her own teeth.

"What do I use for toothpaste?"

"Your imagination," came the reply.

Sienna stuck close to Alicia as they were formed into a work party along with a few dozen others. A detachment of S Division Stewards counted them off and then marched them through the inner gate and down towards the outer. The procession turned onto the road that ran around the camp and continued in single file with the Stewards riding along on electric scooters. Sienna shivered, feeling the cold but Alicia assured her it was early, not even eight o'clock yet. She would soon warm up.

They walked for several miles, over the brow of one hill and down the side of another, following the contours of the land until they came to a narrow lane. The Stewards directed the party south and the hedgerows closed in. Sienna couldn't help but notice how widely scattered they were. It wouldn't be difficult to jump into a ditch without anyone noticing and flee once they had passed. But the Overseer with the epaulettes had been right. Where could she go? In a hostile land while wearing a tracking bracelet, what chance did she have of making anything but trouble for herself?

After an hour of marching, they came to a farmhouse surrounded by ploughed fields. The Stewards directed them towards a barn while the senior Steward approached the family on the doorstep. Looking out and reviewing them as they marched by was a farmer and her brood, all of whom wore expressions of contempt at the sight of their new workforce. At the barn, the Stewards signalled the work party to stop and Sienna thought she would collapse, such was her exhaustion. She'd always enjoyed walking as a hobby and rarely got the bus home in the summer but this had been walking of an altogether different nature and it had sapped her to the core.

And yet, their day's work had only just begun.

The farmer approached along. She had several sons and daughters of varying degrees of ugliness. Each wore crystal clear Smart Glasses, waterproof Barbours and knee-high rubber boots, once called Wellingtons after a despotic warmonger from history, now referred to as Lolas after the heroic footwear designer from *Kinky Boots*.

"Food will be provided at the end of the day to all those who earn it. Anyone caught stealing from me and my children will forfeit it." She checked the time inside her Smart Glasses and nodded to her shortest and squarest daughter. "The day starts now."

Years before, Praakrtik Farm had served as a 100-acre concentration camp for sheep. They were bred here, imprisoned here, reared and sheered here and eventually shipped off for industrialised slaughter in one of the many Tyneside death camps. But the family of farmers who had run that business were moved on (so to speak) and their land given over to agriculture. The climate was harsher here than down south but the soil was fertile. Hardy crops flourished. Beans and pulses in the summer months. Winter vegetables later in the year. It was these that the work party was here to harvest. Swedes and cauliflowers in one field, spinach and cabbages in another.

Sienna was given a knife and a ten-second tutorial in harvesting cabbages then sent off to the furthermost field with a hessian sack. She was separated from Alicia and warned she would be watched but otherwise, she found herself free to roam as she wanted. Six other womyn went with her and it didn't escape her notice that she had thought of them as womyn. Not as Cans. When had this happened? Probably when she'd shed the trappings of her former self and donned the same denims as everyone else.

That said, all thoughts of sisterhood were tempered by the realisation that she was alone in the countryside with six deviants with knives. Most were older than her and one was trans but there didn't seem to be a type. They ranged in age from mid-twenties to late-sixties, they were all shapes and grades and they'd come from every corner of the land. The only thing they seemed to have in common was that they had all been cast out by society. They had all expressed hate views or had failed to condemn the hate views of others, past or present. This now included Sienna. Her shame ran deep.

But she didn't have time for introspection. She had a sack to fill and the worry of what might happen if she failed to do so. Starting at the end of a row, she proceeded to examine each cabbage as shown, decapitate those that were ready and reprieve those that were not.

It wasn't difficult. At first. But the work grew progressively tougher as the morning drew on. The cabbage storks became thicker and the outer leaves stiffer. Sienna's legs grew heavy from the mud that clung to her soles and her knees were soon wet and sore. Dirt rasped at her soft fingertips and her hand ached from holding the knife. But she filled her sack with cabbages to spare and twisted the corners to keep them inside. She'd seen other womyn heading downhill with their sacks so that's where she went, towards the farm and the buzz of activity that surrounded the barn.

Halfway down the hill, an S Division Steward shouted at her to "move it" which she found a little insensitive considering the morning she'd had. But she knew better than to object. Instead, she picked up the pace and half-ran and half-slipped against the sticky mud as the heavy sack bounced painfully into her back.

One of the farmer's sons directed her towards a steel container situated inside the barn. Sackfuls of fresh produce were stacked in neat rows and she was told where to set hers down. She rolled it off her shoulders and sighed with relief as the heavy cabbages fell away. But her relief was short-lived as her reward for her morning's work was a new empty sack.

"Move it."

Her throat was dry and her energies sapped but there seemed to be no water or food. Not for Cans. Just work and rebukes, punishments and pain. Sienna hurried away from the barn and back to the relative seclusion of the top field. The labour had been gruelling but at least she had been out of the glare of the Stewards. Another womxn was on her way down while she was on her way up but neither had the strength to spare the other a glance. Both were only able to focus on the next perilous step and little else. The other womxn had been in her thirties when she'd arrived in Camp 14 but now she looked old beyond her years. The work had taken its toll and fear had sapped her spirits. If it hadn't been for the tiny strips of cabbage she'd been chewing all day, she might not have made it through the morning.

Sienna returned to her row and stooped to cut the next cabbage. Everything was harder this time around. Her back felt stiffer, her arms weaker and her legs creakier. Moreover, everything about her was now wet and muddy. Her jumpsuit, her socks and most especially, her hands. The dirt and the damp combined to rub them raw and after a few more hours she could barely hold the knife, let alone wield any pressure. The work became torturous. Over the course of the morning, she filled three more sacks and delivered them to the barn but she lost all sense of time in the process. The sky was grey and the sun was truant. Only a gnawing clawing emptiness in her belly existed to mark the passing of time.

Sienna had just finished filling her fifth sack when a womxn to her right let out a yelp. She turned and saw her sprawled on the ground, holding her head and looking around anxiously. If she'd had the energy, Sienna might have wondered what had happened to her but instead she just stared zombie-like and unconcerned. Whatever it was, it had happened to someone else. It didn't have anything to do with her.

But that soon changed when a second womxn gasped and fell over. Sienna looked around and saw that she was now hugging on the ground, crouching behind her cabbages and pointing north.

Sienna turned in the direction she was pointing but saw nothing. There was a hedgerow marking the boundaries and a couple of trees but nothing more. Yet something whizzed by her left ear to wake her from her slumber, an insect or something. What the hell was that?

Moments later, a sharp stab of pain stung her ruddy cheek and she spun around to hit the ground like the others, landing face-first in the mud and screaming silently at the agonising jolt. Blood covered her hands and trickled down her chin. She felt something beneath her skin. A pebble or lump of some kind. She rubbed it from above and something popped out. She didn't see what it was but it left a small hole in her cheek.

All the Cans were now on their knees, with some circling the field to get away from whatever it was and others staying put.

She now heard it. A small pop, followed by a click, and saw movement in the hedgerow. A womxn to her right signalled to her to move around, towards whatever it was that was targeting them. Sienna had no intention of doing any such thing but when she saw everyone else going, she felt obliged to follow suit. Keeping low, she hurried along the rows of cabbages and towards the track at the end. Several of the womyn had already disappeared through the hedgerow and others were running its length. Sienna ran too, not sure what she was running towards and still wincing from pain. The fear she felt was only matched by the exhaustion she was carrying but now she felt another emotion. Anger. Who had done this? Weren't they suffering enough?

She heard a scream and then a shout but both were quickly muffled. She covered her face and jumped through the hedgerow, landing on a muddy rut on the other side. Twenty metres along, in a drainage ditch that lined this field, the Cans were gathering around something unseen. Sienna ran towards them and pushed to the front, startled at what she saw.

"Let me go. I'll tell my mam. Get off."

They were boys, no more than 12 years old each. Their Smart Glasses lay in the mud, ripped from their faces to stop them from raising the alarm, alongside the thing that had caused all this unpleasantness – a junior air rifle. Also in evidence was a telescopic sight (now broken) and a tin of .22 lead pellets, the same calibre as the hole in Sienna's cheek.

"Little fuckers."

The trans Can pushed Sienna away.

"Take it easy, new buns. We got this."

She held Sienna at bay while older heads prevailed. The rifle was smashed against a tree and the boys' Glasses were wiped clean, deleting any data that may have been collated over the last few hours. The boys themselves were a mix of fear and defiance, with one peeing his pants and the other puffing out his chest.

"You filthy Cans. You can't touch me. I'll tell the Guardians on you, you stinky smelly dogs."

The kid had some balls, Sienna had to give him that. But he was going about keeping them the wrong way with that kind of attitude. The womxn holding him by the collar thrust him into the muddy bank and pulled out her cabbage knife. He was silenced in an instant but his companion's terror increased as his sobs turned to wails.

"You know what we do with little boys like you?" the Can hissed, pressing the point of her knife to his throat and tracing it down the length of his torso. "We open you up and drink your blood. That's what makes us so dangerous. That's what we feed on, don't you know? The blood of small children."

The boy tried to lash out in panic but another womxn grabbed his arms and pinned him to the ground.

"I want his brains," she snarled, baring her teeth just inches from his eyes.

"And I'll eat his heart," said yet another, salivating like a Shakespearean witch. Sienna was alarmed and intrigued by this sudden turn of events. Had she been right all along? Were Cans really the murderous cannibalistic carnivores of lore that she had learned to fear and loathe? The trans Can holding her read her expression and cued her in with a wink.

Oh. Of course. Sienna brimmed with relief. And stupidity. The latter being more palpable.

But the boys weren't in on the gag and squirmed like piglets on the slab, kicking and squealing to no avail as the dirty cannibal Cans pressed their dirty knives to their necks.

"No, please, mammy. Help."

"No one can help you, sonny, especially not now we know where you live," the Can said, indicating towards his Smart Glasses. "We can get you any time we want to. Or we can tell our friends where to find you. What do you think of that?"

"No. No. No!" came the unsurprising answer.

More knives now came out, four of them held aloft above the previously defiant lad as he pissed his trousers to match his friend. The trans Can pulled out her own knife and looked to Sienna to do likewise. It seemed like overkill at this point but Sienna wasn't about to pass up the opportunity for revenge.

"We can chop you into little bits and no one will ever find you."

"Peel away your skin like tape."

"Cut off your head like a cabbage."

"Feed you to the spiders and the slugs in the woods."

"Snip off your fingers one by one."

"Bite your dick off and make you fucking eat it."

All eyes turned to Sienna. She was new to terrorising

children and hadn't quite mastered its complexities.

"Or not," she conceded with a shrug.

But the children were sold. They pleaded, puked and pissed themselves until they were almost translucent with terror. Eventually, the womyn sheathed their weapons and stood back.

"Look at you. Disgusting. We can't eat you like that. You stink. You filthy little boys."

The children scrambled away, through the mud and over each other in misery and terror.

"You'd better run on home now, boys, before we change our minds. Just one more thing, if you tell anyone about this – anyone at all – we'll know about it and we'll come and get you in the night. Both of you. And that's a promise. We'll get you while you sleep. You won't even hear us. We'll slice you to pieces before you can even scream. You got that?"

The boys did and went to great lengths to convince their captors of this fact, especially Sienna, whom they regarded with particular terror. But terror was all the womyn had. Sienna realised why the trans Can had held her back. Because they couldn't do anything to the kids, not really, not without risking the wrath of New Britannia. They couldn't leave so much as a mark on them. All they could do was scare them.

But in the mind of a 12-year-old boy, what was more terrifying than blood-drinking knife-wielding Cans who could climb through their windows at night and bite off their fingers and dicks? Sienna saw that, in certain situations, it was useful to have a reputation that preceded you.

The boys ran away as fast as their little legs would carry them while the womyn did likewise, hurrying through the hedgerow and back to their waiting cabbages before their absence was noted.

All parties would tremble as they recalled this experience but only the children's would be imaginary. The fear and helplessness of the Cans of Camp 14 was only too real.

27: ASSISTANCE

When the working day finally ended, Sienna could scarcely walk. She didn't have a clue what time it was but it felt late. The sky had turned dark and the wind had turned cold. She'd barely slept on her journey north and after a day of physical labour, her head was swimming.

But some semblance of relief was close at hand.

As good as her word, the farmer had hot food waiting for them as they trudged back off the fields. A vast pot of potato and cabbage soup bubbled over a fire pit, seasoned with herbs and smelling like manna from heaven. Each Can was issued with a tin cup and told to form an orderly queue. Sienna was almost frantic with want as she waited her turn, desperate for nourishment yet barely able to stand. The queue moved quickly but not quick enough for some. There was pushing and shoving, jostling and jumping but the Stewards did nothing. If anything, they seemed to enjoy the spectacle of Cans fighting over a little tin cup of swill.

Finally, it was Sienna's turn and she received a ladle to fill her outstretched tin. The soup was boiling and the cup became hot in her bare hands. Tiny black dots adorned each of her fingertips where the skin had rubbed away and now they felt raw. But she used her sleeves to cradle her tin and went and found a spot by the barn against which to sit.

The first sip tasted of nothing. Heat. Too much heat. It burned her lips and scalded her throat rather than quench it. All around Cans were swilling their soup and blowing on it so Sienna did the same until it was drinkable. When it was, after an agonising wait, she drained the whole thing in one. The bits of potato and slices of cabbage barely needed chewing, they slid down easily and she gasped with delirium. The recipe was more or less the same as this morning's stew but it tasted divine, the sort of soup Mushroom House would serve to only its most discerning clients. Her mind momentarily flickered to Geri and all she had lost before she vanished again in a haze of despondency.

Sienna couldn't fault the meal but the portions left a lot to be desired. One cup and it was all gone. Yet she could have devoured more, so much more, but the farmer wasn't offering seconds. In fact, for some, she wasn't even offering firsts.

"Please, please."

A commotion from the fire pit drew everyone's attention. A womxn was on her knees with her tin cup stretched out in supplication. She was crying in misery yet the farmer's beefy children were kicking her away.

"You're a thief. A dirty Can thief. You think we didn't see you shovelling my spinach into your filthy hole? Go on, nothing for you."

One of her sons applied the sole of his boot and the Can fell backwards, hitting her head in the mud and spilling the tin from her hand. The farmer's daughter hurried to grab it and they all glared at the supplicant figure.

"Let this be a lesson to you. Thieves go hungry on my farm."

And with that, she and her brood tipped the remaining contents of the pot over the fire pit to extinguish the flames with a sizzle. There had been plenty left. Perhaps enough for half a cup each yet it had been tipped away as if it was nothing more than washing-up water. Some gawped in consternation, some in knowing anger, while the Can on the ground just wailed in despair, too tired to stand, too hungry to remain.

The Stewards blew their whistles and roused everyone from their apathy, kicking and incentivising all those who took too long with their electric batons. Sienna had never known her body to be so unresponsive. She felt as if she had blown an entire OxyVape cartridge on full dose in the last five minutes but she pushed herself up with the help of the barn and staggered into formation. Some of the womyn helped the Can on the floor and soon they were marching back to the camp.

Sweet Panthea, Sienna realised. They were going to have to walk back.

Sienna barely had the strength to keep her head upright. She felt a hand on her shoulder and looked around at a familiar face but she was too tired to place it.

"Stay with us, pixie. You can lay down soon."

Alicia nudged Sienna in the back to get her moving and she trudged off automatically, aware of nothing more than the womxn in front and the womxn behind as everything else shrank around her. At one point she drifted off completely, still walking but not conscious in the classic sense. Every ounce of energy was diverted towards her legs as she fought to put one foot in front of the other until finally, the work party crested the rise to see a line of bright white lights in the distance. Sight of the camp gave everyone the extra impetus needed to make it that last mile. The gates opened and without even knowing how she'd got here, Sienna found herself lined up in rows of ten.

The wind swirled around their wet clothes and the night sucked at their senses but they were made to stand while they were counted.

"Dismissed," the Overseer commanded when she was satisfied and Alicia caught Sienna before she dropped.

"I know you're tired, babe, but don't go to bed dirty. It'll just make things worse."

She led Sienna to the wash hut and made her strip to her pants. Sienna complied, if only because she was too tired to resist. Alicia cleaned the filth from her body while Sienna stood there zombie-like. Her self-awareness briefly flared when Alicia touched her injured cheek but even her pain felt languid, as if her senses had been dialled down in the light of her limited resources.

Outside, the work party tossed their wet clothing into a large skip and drew fresh jumpsuits and socks from the adjacent stockroom. They retired to their huts and found a small basket of dirty swedes and potatoes waiting for them by the door. Some were rotten, none were cooked but all were quickly eaten.

Sienna fell into her lumpy bunk chewing her starchy snack and fought to resist sleep long enough to enjoy both. She failed at either.

Next thing she knew, it was light again. Her mouth felt fuzzy and her head throbbed. Every ache she had taken to bed had matured with interest and her previously numb feet were now like blocks of ice. But all was quiet. All was calm. Prone womyn surrounded her on all sides, breathing lightly, sleeping heavily. The events of the previous day came back with a jolt. Had all that really happened? She searched her bunk and looked to the floor for the potato she'd been holding before she'd succumbed. It was gone.

She sat up, her head touching the low damp aluminium ceiling, and rubbed her frozen toes. What manner of hell was this place?

Everything had happened so quickly the day before, she'd barely been able to process her thoughts. But here, now, in the quiet light of dawn, she tried to make sense of it all. She was a Can. She knew that now. She had fallen from grace and lost the right to live in a fair and inclusive society, as the Overseer had rightfully said. She had betrayed all she had previously loved. She had been adjudged to have committed one of the most heinous of hate crimes. She deserved to be punished. She deserved to atone.

But how was this proportionate? How was this justice?

She'd been in Camp 14 for only a day and it had already broken her. She'd never known pain or degradation like it. Not in her wildest dreams. Not even her wildest nightmares.

They were treated no better than slaves. Less than slaves even. At least slaves were regarded as humxn. They weren't even seen in this light. The children taking potshots at them bore this out. They'd tormented them as if they were ants to boil with a magnifying glass for amusement. How was this normal? This attitude must have been learned. Approved even. Passed on from father to son. Ingrained.

Sienna thought about how she had previously regarded Cans. How she had feared and loathed them. Damned and demonised them. Yet all the fears and prejudices she had cultivated over the years had been dispelled in little over twenty-four hours. She had felt apart from her fellow outcasts a day earlier, aloof even, as if she had been misplaced amongst the miscreants. Now she realised that she was no different from anyone else in this hut. She and the others were one and the same. Young or old. Short or tall. Black or white. Straight or gay. Cis or trans. All were here. From all walks of life and every corner of New Britannia. Camp 14 was nothing if not inclusive.

Yet deep down, Sienna still knew she was not like everyone else. As an Auditor, she along with her friends in X Division were responsible for condemning a great many of the Cans in this camp.

This thought – more than any other – made her want to puke.

The moment soon passed. If there was one saving grace about Camp 14, it was the absence of time to dwell on past regrets. The yawning wail of the camp siren pulled the Cans from their slumber and all at once the hut was turned into a flurry of fearful purpose.

"Assembly."

Womyn tossed their blankets aside and jumped from their bunks. Many landed in their boots, so well-practice were they at answering the call. Sienna had been the first awake yet she was one of the last out the door, so quick was everyone else. Only an old womxn in the bunk below had yet to stir. Sienna felt a hand on her arm and realised Alicia was dragging her, running and urging her not to "worry about it" as they sprinted into the new light of day.

This time she had no trouble in finding her place. She lined up behind Alicia and noticed a womxn next to her gawping and looking lost. Sienna guessed she must have arrived this morning.

"Get in line. One of ten. Quick newbie, move," Sienna urged her. The womxn looked at her wearing the same confused expression Sienna had worn the previous morning but hurried off to do as she was told.

Alicia glanced back and gave Sienna a nod of approval. And with that one simple act, Sienna had graduated from fresher without even realising it.

The morning played out in much the same manner as the

previous morning, except that Sienna didn't even think about passing up her breakfast after the count. She wolfed it down and hurried to the basket when it was filled with raw carrots. Alicia pocketed hers for later and urged Sienna to do the same. Sienna remembered the potato she'd lost the previous evening but before she could dwell on it, another matter arose. Her bleed came on.

"Oh," she said, feeling the telltale sighs inside her jumpsuit and confirmed her suspicions with a quick investigation. Alicia noticed and fetched her a clean cloth from a basket in the corner.

"Here," she said, tossing it to Sienna. "Sorry pixie, we're all out of lilies." Several womyn smirked or at least attempted to do so. Sienna guessed there would be no hot baths and boxsets for her today.

"Don't worry," Alicia assured her. "A few months here and you won't even bleed any more."

This was hardly reassuring but she didn't get the chance to elaborate. The camp siren sounded once more and their presence was required outside.

"No rest for the wicked," said Alicia.

Sienna noticed the bunk nearest the door was now empty and figured the old lady must have made it to assembly after all.

As they dropped their tin cups in a washing-up trough and made their way across the courtyard, Sienna shared her gripe about the potato.

Alicia reassured her.

"Don't worry. It went to a worthy cause."

"I was a worthy cause," Sienna complained bitterly.

"You were asleep. Besides, Farahnoush was worthier."

"Who's Farahnoush?" Sienna asked.

"The cookie who went without soup last night," Alicia pointed and Sienna looked across the courtyard at the girl from the previous evening, the one the farmer had kicked over. She looked better than she had the night before. At least, as well as anyone could look in a place like this. The Cans had pooled a few morsels before lights out. It didn't matter how hungry everyone was, how tired or how pained, Farahnoush's fellow Cans had rallied to make sure she got something to eat.

"Cans did that?"

Alicia grimaced.

"Don't say Cans. It's offensive, *bitch*."

"And bitch isn't?"

"Sticks and stones, *bitch*."

As laudable as the actions of everyone else were, Sienna couldn't help but feel Farahnoush had brought the situation upon herself.

"What do you mean?"

"The farmer warned us," Sienna whispered, not wanting anyone else to eavesdrop as she passed judgment upon a fellow... cookie. "She knew what would happen if she ate something."

Alicia shook her head at Sienna's naiveté.

"Babe, wake up. We all ate yesterday."

Sienna's dumbfounded expression answered Alicia's question but she voiced her disbelief anyway. "You ate something?"

"*Bitch*, they can spare it."

"What?"

"Spinach, same as Farahnoush. It's good for you."

"What if they'd seen you?"

"You don't get it. They didn't even see Farahnoush. They

just picked her at random to set an example. Look, these fuckers know what we're doing and they know they can't stop us. Not without spraying raw shit over everything, which is what some of them do. But they like to scare us, make us careful so that we're not out there stuffing our faces like it's picnic time. It's the only way to cut down on their losses."

"And Farahnoush?"

"It was her turn. Might be yours tonight. That's where the excitement lies," she said with an inappropriate grin. "You never know."

The siren sounded again and the assembly was divided into work parties. Once more, Sienna's was marched through the gates but this time they turned left and headed to a different farm. Again, Sienna spent a day in the fields harvesting cauliflowers and celeriac. She thought about what Alicia had said and broke off a few florets when no one was looking. She couldn't enjoy them at first, so worried was she at being seen but as time went by she learned to graze as she worked, taking little and with growing frequency as she sought to supplement Camp 14's meagre diet.

At the end of the day, an example was made of three of their number but Sienna went unpunished. She arrived home cold, tired and near to collapse but not quite as hungry as she had been the previous evening. She even contributed half a swede to the collective pot to make good on the injustice served to her sistren. Life was hard. But for most, it beat the alternative.

Before lights out, the detainees were allowed an hour of association time. In theory, this was meant to be spent tending to each other's ailments or learning new skills, something that would help them contend with the next day's work detail. Inevitably, most of the womyn spent the hour trading gossip and forming alliances. Sienna strolled with Alicia and a girl called Kat. The previous evening, Sienna had been flat out for the count. This night, she was tired but very much awake, taking in every sight and sound of her new home.

They passed a hut that had been converted into a chapel. It bore the symbol of Panthea, a four-sided diamond adjoined by a star above and an arrow below. Sienna noted how busy it was but was not surprised. In a place like this, who wouldn't turn to a higher power for salvation?

"That's the love shack," Alicia explained to pop Sienna's bubble. "That's where you go when you want some."

Sienna was intrigued but not tempted. The last thing on her mind was unnecessary exertion. Her libido had ceased to exist as a practical consideration.

"Give it time, babe. You'll be surprised what you're capable of."

Despite looking nothing like her, Alicia brought to mind Geri, if only in that moment. They both had the same air of confidence regardless of their circumstances and they both called Sienna 'babe or bitch' when making a point. She wondered how Geri would fare in Camp 14. Probably better than most, she concluded. She'd have to wear clothes, of course, but she was stronger than Sienna, both physically and mentally. She wouldn't have to latch onto someone for support, as Sienna always did. She would be the one others latched onto.

"That's the vape shack," Alicia said, pointing to a nondescript storage hut behind the ablutions block. There was no sign of anyone vaping but as vapes were contraband, all pens and mods smuggled in were vapourless. Still, it would've hardly taken Mma Precious Ramotswe to uncover the racket but Alicia assured her the Stewards knew all about it and turned a blind eye. "Who do you think brings the stuff in?"

"The Stewards? Why?"

"Why do you think?"

Kat laughed. Alicia smiled. So naive.

Sienna still didn't understand but she decided not to pursue the point. She didn't want to look stupid and it would give her something to ponder tonight.

The detainees around the courtyard fell into two categories, those who walked and those who didn't. The walkers walked for warmth rather than exercise, they got enough of that during the day, while the sitters sat shivering beneath blankets, too tired to move but damned if they were ready to retire for the night. The huts may have been slightly warmer but they were also damp and mouldy. The less time a person could spend inside, the better it was for their health.

Within these two categories, Sienna noticed a variant of sub-categories based on race, gender, age and type. It wasn't exclusively so but it was noticeable, even without their Diversity Gradings visible. Sienna had latched onto Alicia because she had been the first womxn to speak to her. But Alicia had approached Sienna. She was white like her. Was that coincidence or deliberate? Kat was also white. And cisfemxle and cyberpunk. As were several other womyn who came and went. Birds of a feather. Was this a coincidence or by design?

Sienna tried not to dwell on these observations but she knew from experience that a person's social circle often reflected their personal beliefs. It was one of the key indicators that she had learned as an Auditor. But she didn't think this was the time to take a moral stance. She was still finding her feet and preferred to play ignorant rather than go it alone.

It wasn't until later that Alicia finally interacted with someone of a different ethnicity but, to Sienna's consternation, it was to attack her. She set off at a sprint across the courtyard, yelling and screaming as she ran. A small queue of womyn waited to be processed by a couple of Stewards at a gate. An Afro-Caribbean womxn stood at the back of the line hunched beneath a blanket awaiting her turn. From a distance or up close, it was impossible to tell her age. She had grey hair but young eyes and could have been anything between 26 and 56. Age ceased to be a factor in Camp 14. Kat and Sienna were chasing when Alicia grabbed and attacked the womxn. She yanked her back by the scruff of the neck and threw her to the ground, grabbing and dragging her out of the line, all the time shouting threats and abuse.

"You stupid bitch. You fucking coward. You promised me. You swore it."

The womxn was crying in misery and submission, but Alicia continued to manhandle her with extreme aggression.

"You owe me, bitch. You fucking owe me and you're going to pay. You hear me?"

The womxn was wailing and seemed vulnerable and defenceless. The Stewards did nothing but grin but Sienna couldn't watch this happen. No matter the consequences for herself, she had to do something. She ran smack into Alicia and pushed her backwards, releasing the womxn so that she could scramble free. Now Kat got involved, jumping on Sienna as Alicia grabbed the womxn's ankles. The four of them struggled on the cold hard ground, grappling, punching and kneeing each other until the womxn finally signalled her surrender.

"Okay. Okay, I'm sorry. I'm sorry. I'll stop."

She curled into a ball and cried miserably against Alicia's leg. To Sienna's confusion, Alicia now cradled the womxn in her arms and told her in hushed tones that it was alright.

"We're here for you, babe. You're not alone. Never give up. Never lose hope." Alicia crossed her fingers and placed them over her heart, symbolising something that Sienna didn't understand.

"Never give cuntface the satisfaction."

Sienna couldn't make sense of it. Were they fighting or faking? And who was cuntface? At that moment, Sienna felt it could have been her whereas, in fact, it was Camp 14's nickname for their benevolent S Division Overseer.

The womxn Alicia had been grappling with only seconds earlier stood with Alicia's help while Sienna was left sprawled on the ground, Kat still smarting her bruised left breast. Alicia sent the womxn on her way, back to the huts and away from the gate, standing ready to stop her should she try to pass again.

Finally, she turned to Sienna and slapped her hard across the face when she stood. The slap caught Sienna's bad cheek, as was the intention, and Sienna recoiled in pain.

"Know the facts before you act, *bitch*," Alicia said testily. "In here, that's very important."

She turned and walked away. Sienna still didn't understand so it was left to Kat to illuminate her. She pointed at the sign over the gate. It read: 'A.D. Programme'.

"Assisted Dying," Kat said when the name didn't register. "That's the euthanasia shop. Go check it out, you stupid cunt. They'll take anyone. Even you."

The Steward at the gate showed the last applicant through, locked the gate and followed the line down to a small hut near the treeline.

The A.D. Programme rarely ran short of customers. It was open twenty-four hours a day, seven days a week. Officially, it was available to the terminally ill as a way of helping them achieve peace with dignity. In reality, it was an escape open to all. A way out from the toil and misery of cancellation. The camp was always overcrowded. The A.D. Programme was the system's steam valve.

Camp 14 might have been a transitory camp, a holding pen for Cans on their final journey to banishment, but most knew the same hardships awaited them in the islands. Or worse. Camp 14 was as good as it got. It had a mainland climate, contraband, farm work and a less repressive regime. Rumours circulated as to the conditions off-shore. They circulated, but no one knew for sure. Because no one ever came back.

"What about the pretty little cottages and shops and schools?"

"You didn't believe all that shit, did you?" Alicia said derisively.

But Sienna had. She had not only believed it, she had resented the Cans for it. Her taxes had gone towards keeping them in clover while she'd had to work. Hindsight could be a wonderful thing. It could also be dreadful. In Sienna's case, it was the latter.

The sirens sounded and the Cans returned to their huts. Most went straight to sleep, desperate to escape the misery albeit just for a few hours. But Sienna and Alicia stayed up with a few others. The womxn Alicia had plucked from the A.D. Programme was in a different hut but Alicia filled in the blanks.

Mariatou had been a doctor in Exeter until she had

refused to perform an abortion on the grounds that the foetus was 32 weeks old and perfectly healthy. She had offered the patient a caesarean, adoption services and counselling, as was standard practice in such cases, but the patient was adamant, only a termination would do. It was her body, her right. She had recently split from her partner and refused to bear his child. Mariatou tried to make the womxn reconsider and eventually called the Guardians but to the doctor's surprise, they arrested her. The right to choose was the unalienable right of every man, womxn and non-binary being who possessed a womb. And as long as the foetus was inside that person, they had the final say over every decision. To deny a pregnant person an abortion, was to deny them their fundamental rights.

This single incident might not have been enough to lead to her downfall but when Mariatou was questioned by the General Medical Council, she stuck to her guns and refused to condone the principle of unconditional terminations under all circumstances.

Her cancellation was more or less guaranteed from that moment.

Mariatou had struggled in the hostels and despaired in the Camps. She was at the end of her strength when Alicia found her. Alicia didn't know her. She didn't know anything about her but she refused to let Mariatou give up. From that day forth, Alicia became her biggest champion and fiercest critic, pulling and carrying her, pushing and comforting her. She had done whatever she could to save Mariatou and Mariatou had given Alicia her word that she would go on.

Why was it so important to Alicia that Mariatou went on?

"We all need to go on, to show them that we're still here, that we're still people, living breathing people. It's the only way we'll win."

Unfortunately, Alicia couldn't save everyone. Plenty of Cans volunteered for the programme and found 'dignity' in death. They didn't even need to be ill. A self-certified diagnosis was all it took. Life was grindingly hard in Camp 14 but death was as easy as pie.

"So, we choose life," Alicia told Sienna, taking her by the shoulders and shaking her to remind her that she was still a part of this world. "We choose to go on. We choose to see the light. We choose to breathe the air. We choose this world over the next. For as long as we can."

28: PARTNERS

The days turned into weeks and the weeks turned into months. Winter tightened its grip on the land and brought snow and ice. The ground froze solid and the crops became impossible to cultivate, not without destroying them. But the Cans were not left idle. Instead, they were put to use elsewhere: clearing roads, repairing fences and expanding the camp to accommodate more arrivals.

Detainees came and went every day, with a dozen shipped in each morning and a dozen out that afternoon. Sienna could scarcely grasp the scale of the operation. As an Auditor, she had put three or four cases before Congress every couple of weeks, each an irredeemable wretch unworthy of life in New Britannia. In her mind, three or four people a fortnight didn't add up to that many. But she had been just one Auditor in a whole division. And Geniture was just one company in an active market.

A dozen arrivals every day?

And Camp 14 was not the only camp in New Britannia. Who knew how many there actually were?

The numbers made Sienna's mind boggle but not as much as the detainees around her. There were no ogres. No monsters or depraved deviants. Just ordinary people, confused, frightened and sorry. Always very very sorry.

Two months after she had arrived, one particularly dirty, dishevelled and exhausted detainee was brought before them. Tilly had been at Camp 14 previously. She had escaped the night that Sienna had arrived. It had been her disappearance that had prompted the collective punishment the Overseer had been 'loathed' to administer. Now she was back. And another example would be set.

The Overseer had the detainees line up in the sleet and snow. She herself stood huddled on the platform in a hat and coat beneath a canopy of umbrellas while everyone else was left to the elements. Sienna was soon soaked through and frozen to the core but the Overseer was in no hurry to deliver her message. The longer she took, the deeper it would sink in.

Tilly shivered at the foot of the platform. Stewards either side. Her ankles manacled. The chains were completely pointless. She could barely walk let alone run.

"The prodigal daughter has returned," the Overseer declared. "Please, let us welcome Tilly back."

When nobody said anything, a Steward jabbed the nearest detainee with his stun baton to send her to the ground.

"I said, let us welcome Tilly back."

This time she got the response she wanted as eight hundred detainees called out a lacklustre "Welcome back, Tilly".

Sienna was mildly surprised that the Overseer didn't get them to repeat the welcome, this time with feeling, but the cold was obviously getting to her too so she proceeded to the point.

"Perhaps you could tell us what awaited you out there, Tilly? What did you find?"

Tilly shivered uncontrollably and said something that wasn't audible, particularly to Sienna who was nine rows back so the Overseer shared them with everyone.

"Nothing," she said. "There was nothing out there waiting. No food, no help, no love or anything. Her life, the one she assumed would still be out there, had ceased to exist. There was nothing to go back to. Was there, Tilly? Wasn't that what you said?"

Tilly nodded miserably, compelled to play the Overseer's game.

"And now she has pneumonia, frostbite, tetanus and malnutrition and is in no fit state to resume her daily duties, therefore she has selected to leave us once more, this time via the A.D. Programme. Haven't you, Tilly?"

This time Tilly said nothing. She just stared at the ground and refused to concur. No one was under any allusions. Tilly had about as much say in choosing the A.D. Programme as Sienna had in choosing a career in farming. This was the example the Overseer had wanted to set but she had one last surprise up her fleece-lined sleeve.

"But we don't want Tilly to feel ostracised from her friends, now do we, so she will choose three companions to accompany her into the Programme."

A clammer of alarm broke out across the lines but this was quickly silenced by a burst of machine-gun fire. Guns weren't normally brought into the camp, stun batons were usually enough, but Sienna saw half a dozen Stewards wielding automatic weapons either side of them. The Overseer had clearly anticipated a reaction. With one word, she could have dropped them like flies before they'd taken a step.

The wind blew harder and the sleet lashed sideways yet it was fear that turned everyone to ice. Nobody wanted to move. Nobody wanted to be noticed. Nobody wanted to give the Overseer an excuse.

"Do it now," the Overseer ordered but Tilly refused. Instead, she pointed at the Overseer which the Overseer, at least, had the good form to smile at. "Choose now or I will choose for you. And I will choose ten times as many."

Knowing she had no alternative, Tilly looked to the faces of her former friends in despair. But what could anyone do? What indeed?

It was one thing to volunteer for the A.D. Programme. Another to have the A.D. Programme thrust upon you but to Tilly's relief, someone stepped forward to stand beside her. It was a womxn who'd reached the end of her road and who couldn't take another day. Sienna didn't see who it was but from Alicia's reaction, she knew it had to be Mariatou. Sienna was ready to hold Alicia back but she didn't need to. It was hopeless. To have reacted would have been to have made a target of herself.

Two more Cans offered themselves up, tired individuals who were mentally ready to throw in the towel, and a collective sigh was exhaled by all. Or nearly all. The Overseer was a stickler for pedantry and declared that Tilly had failed to follow her instructions.

"I did not ask for volunteers. I asked Tilly to select," she said contemptuously, glaring down at those who had stepped forward through her blacked-out Smart Glasses. "Since she saw fit to disobey this very simple request, each of you will now select a partner to accompany you into the A.D. Programme. You have thirty seconds."

Another ripple of consternation echoed through the lines

but the Overseer was in no mood to compromise and warned the detainees that she would do this again and again, doubling the numbers each time until she had compliance.

A second burst of machine-gun fire underlined her intent and the four condemned Cans were compelled to move when they were told they had only twenty seconds left, stepping forward to find a partner in death.

A cry of anguish to Sienna's left told her the first selection had been made. This was quickly followed by two more. Sienna tried not to look. She tried not to move. She tried not to even breathe. She thought invisible thoughts and tried to disappear. Yet through the corner of her eye, she could see someone approaching. She was nine rows back and yet one of the A.D. party was coming her way.

Glancing up, she saw Mariatou. Fear gripped her. She hardly knew Mariatou except through Alicia but she seemed intent on singling her out. Of all the people around her, of all the people in front, why her? What had she done to bring this selection upon herself?

The sleets barely melted against Sienna's face, so frozen with terror was she. She saw Alicia signalling Mariatou to turn back but Mariatou's mind was made up. She stopped in front of Sienna and looked her square in the eye. Sienna's were wide with dread, Mariatou's narrow with sorrow. She willed Mariatou to look elsewhere, anywhere, despite knowing this would condemn someone else but at that moment her only thoughts were for survival. For life. For continuation.

"I'm sorry," Mariatou said, reaching out at hand –

– only to take Alicia's.

It all happened so quickly that Sienna could scarcely take it in. Everything seemed so unreal, as if the events playing out before her were some kind of bad dream. But the stinging sleet on her cheeks and the icy wind in her eyes told her this was really happening. She was wide awake and here in this moment.

Mariatou turned holding onto Alicia's hand and led her away. What had she done? Why had she condemned her friend? This was too cruel. Too unjust.

All the times Alicia had saved Mariatou's life. All the times she had pushed her on and encouraged her to live only to see it backfire. Of all the people she could've picked on. Why her? Why Alicia?

Alicia looked around as Mariatou steered her through the lines. She met Sienna's eyes for one final moment and a lifetime of hope and despair passed between them. Sienna didn't know what to say. She didn't know what to do but it was too late anyway. She lost sight of them as the sleet storm intensified and when the Assembly was finally dismissed, the Cans at the front were gone. Alicia, Tilly and the others had been marched away on the whim of cruel fortune, never to be seen again.

The crowd melted away, keen to disappear from sight and mind, but several lingered in the storm; too numb to comprehend, too broken to move. Sienna saw Kat looking around in pain. She grabbed her by the hand and dragged her away before the Stewards returned for more 'volunteers'.

Kat didn't want to move. She didn't want to leave this spot. Her whole sense of self had been taken away and nothing would ever matter again.

"We have to go," Sienna urged her, pulling Kat in the direction of the huts and away from providence, divine or otherwise.

They ran, stumbling and tripping every step of the way, barely able to put one foot in front of the other and distraught as the heavens opened up to wash their world away.

Sienna felt crushed. The cold empty feeling of loss didn't leave her for days but Kat was a wreck. Alicia hadn't just been her friend, she had been her rock. Her guiding light in a sea of hopelessness. She had built her up, pushed her on and given her the strength to continue, just as she had with dozens of others. Kat, Sienna, Farahnoush –

– Mariatou.

"Why?" Kat kept asking. "Why her?"

No one could answer that. The best they could do was guess. Perhaps Mariatou was paying Alicia back for prolonging her suffering. Or perhaps Mariatou felt she was helping Alicia. After all, Alicia had taken it upon herself to help Mariatou. Perhaps Mariatou was doing likewise, only from her own perspective. They would never know. Both were gone and Sienna and Kat were all alone, albeit with eight hundred other solitary womyn.

They came together for a time, seeking solace in each other's company, sleeping in the same bunk and standing together at Assembly but there was nothing sexual in it. Each sought the warmth of another's touch and consented to become partners until the end. There were no A6 Applications in Camp 14. No restrictions or taboos. But it wasn't about that. Sienna had no designs on Kat and Kat was hetero-regressive. Their love was strictly platonic in the absence of a much-loved friend.

The Solstice came and went without ceremony. As did the New Year and Renewal Day. January was a blur and February proved unrelenting. But on the final day of the month, the Overseer sprung a surprise on everyone.

According to the Julian and Gregorian calendars, February

should've had 28 days, and 29 each leap year. But, as most people knew by now, they did things a little differently in New Britannia.

Charity GoodHope had decreed that equality and inclusion were impossible as long as the months were mismatched. Therefore, the Britannic calendar was introduced to standardise the months so that each month had a uniform 30 days. Obviously, this created several problems because the Earth insisted on orbiting the Sun at an obstinate 365 days, 6 hours, 9 minutes per year no matter what the Polychrome Alliance decided. But Charity had a solution. February, previously the least represented month, would become empowered with 35 days each year. And 36 each leap year.

February was particularly symbolic as February 29 for centuries had been known as "Ladies' Privilege" and regarded as a day of empowerment for womyn, with them laughably permitted to propose marriage on this day. One single day. Every four years.

It was an outrage as far as Charity was concerned.

Therefore, the latter newly created days of February became a glorious celebration of femxle empowerment with February 36 regarded as the most sacrosanct of all.

Thus, it was deemed not only right but proper that the detainees of Camp 14 commemorate Womyn's Day accordingly. This took the form of extra stew, a small amount of oat milk chocolate and a glass of rhubarb wine that was so fermented that some used it on their infections instead of drinking. There was also entertainment, thankfully not of the live variety. A large screen was erected in the courtyard and benches brought out for the Chairperson's address. No one jeered or dared fail to react as was required when Charity rattled through the usual rhetoric but Sienna could spot an empty ovation when she took part in one.

This Womyn's Day, Sienna experienced emotions she had not felt before. She had always been proud to be a womxn of New Britannia but Charity's reclamation of it had sullied the day for her. Sienna had previously idolised Charity and regarded her as the perfect embodiment of womxnhood. Humxnity even. But how could she be anything less than a monster – less than Hitler – when she allowed such suffering to go on in her name? How could any womxn, let alone the self-proclaimed champion of the downtrodden, be so devoid of compassion and mercy as to allow places such as this to exist? How could she oversee the deaths of strong independent womyn like Alicia and Tilly and hundreds of others that Sienna had seen perish in Camp 14?

"Fucked if I know. I only work here," whispered Kat, as she snuggled up to her on the back row for warmth.

After the speech, there was a reality show that Sienna used to watch with Geri called *I Care*. It featured very important people and famous celebrities giving up a day's work to care for people in need. It was phenomenally popular on the outside and there was never a shortage of celebrities willing to offer their time for free. The episode in which Charity GoodHope worked in a hospice for the terminally ill broke all kinds of records and went down as the most-streamed show of all time. Tonight's episode featured Kensie Tyne helping out on a Covid ward for children. She wore a respiratory mask and surgical gloves but nothing else. She was the country's leading advocate of naturalism, after all. Her gym-honed body was her *moyens et motifs* but she looked strangely out of place on a children's ward. Sienna hadn't seen a naturalist in months. Camp 14 didn't get many, especially not in winter, and Sienna had almost forgotten they existed. So, seeing Kensie now, in glorious technicolour, walking amongst a bunch of poorly children who could hardly breathe with her perfect breasts and surgically sculpted vagina popping out into their faces seemed vaguely ridiculous.

Kensie was tearful and earnest. And the doctors were so grateful that someone as important as she should give up their precious time and ask nothing in return but to Sienna it all seemed weirdly inappropriate. And not just because of Kensie's lack of dress. But because it was bullshit. Her motives were as transparent as her attire and they had nothing to do with altruism. What were the viewers expected to do, gaze up in saintly gratitude as a pampered princess walked amongst them for a few short hours? Did this somehow balance the ledger? Give meaning to meaninglessness? Make the squalid masses feel bad for not caring as much as the demigods of fame?

Sienna couldn't believe she had ever watched this show, let alone cried with Geri when Charity had held the hand of a little old womxn as she had slipped away on her deathbed. Knowing what she knew now, she wondered if that same old lady had been given a shot off-camera to accommodate Charity's busy schedule.

Kensie affirmed the importance of isolation during Covid season and the folly of previous generations and their faith in vaccines, finishing things up with a song that MGA_9.4 had composed for the occasion (available to download with next week's upgrade).

Even for someone with next to no musical appreciation, Sienna could tell a turkey when she was played one. But the fact that it was mimed by a naked celebrity in an ICU before a captive audience of sallow children put an altogether different context on it. Three months ago, she might have watched it with tears in her eyes and pledged §500 to the number scrolling across the screen. Now she just wanted to hurl.

"Those poor bastards," said Kat in agreement and soon they were stifling their smirks as giggles broke out across the audience. They hadn't had much to laugh at these last few months but now she couldn't stop. It poured out of her like a torrent and soon the courtyard was in uproar. The stream was cut and the picture went dead. The Stewards moved in to call the evening to a premature end but before they did, there was one more thing on the agenda. One final convention that had to be observed.

A still image appeared on screen featuring a face Sienna knew only too well. It was Zaria Okello.

And the caption read: *In Memoriam.*

29: ACCIDENTS

Zaria Okello, the Minister For Survivors and the industrious CEO of Geniture, had died the same weekend that Sienna had been cancelled. Her helicopter had developed a fault whilst flying back from Charity GoodHope's country residence on the Isle of Green (formerly Wight) and crashed into the Solent. There were no survivors. Several days of mourning were observed and generous tributes were offered, not least of all from Charity herself. Few had given so much to the cause of inclusion as Zaria Okello, therefore it was only fitting that this year's Womyn's Day be dedicated in her honour.

The vast majority of the detainees didn't give a rat's arse one way or the other and those that did were tickled pink that the head of the very organisation that had sent them here was now lying at the bottom of the sea feeding the crabs. Sienna had mixed feelings. At the time, she had clung to the hope that Zaria might have granted her special dispensation to rehabilitate. It wasn't unheard of and Geniture did, by and large, have a reputation for looking after its people. But she had died at exactly the worst possible moment and Sienna's fate was sealed. But she still wondered what might have been. All Cans did over one thing or another. Kat could tell something was up but Sienna said nothing. Seeing the reaction of some of those around her reminded her that she couldn't drop her guard for a moment. She had to maintain her story and never admit to having been an Auditor. Her well-being, perhaps even her life, depended upon it.

But something happened to threaten all that. Something strange and unexpected.

The following week, Sienna was working on a smallholding some miles from Hedley House. It was such a distance that the Stewards had actually bused them to the location rather than march them. This had unnerved a great many at first, with some assuming they were being shipped north, but the issuing of spades and forks had put their minds to ease.

The drive was wonderful. The seats were hard, the road was bumpy and the windows were shuttered but Sienna had never known such luxury. And what made it all the more wonderful was the knowledge that they would be driven home at the end of the day. They wouldn't have to walk. Of course, the Overseer would reclaim this good fortune somehow but for the duration of their journey, most were able to sit back and relax.

The smallholding backed onto a vast stone wall. It was said to be two thousand years old and had once marked the frontier of humxn civilisation. But that had been the old way of thinking. The corrupt way. Britannic historians had revised the past and now saw the Roman Empire for what it was. It had been a brutal and bloodthirsty autocracy intent on enslavement, the extermination of ethnic societies and the subjugation of the matriarchy. Meanwhile, the Celtic 'barbarians' on the other side of the wall were an enlightened people who lived in tune with nature and worshipped femxle deities such as Beira and Brigantia. But the Romans and their 'civilisation' were long gone. As were the Celts. All that remained was the old wall that had stood between them.

March was a time to sow. In this smallholding, beetroots, chard and peas. Sowing was easier than harvesting so a smaller work party was required. But there would be nothing to eat whilst working. Nothing to snack on except seeds. The workers would be hungry tonight.

Sienna and Kat had stood together in the courtyard but had been separated upon selection. The Stewards did this, divide and conquer. Most of the others in Sienna's work party were from different parts of the camp. The transitory nature of Camp 14 meant a person's world was small by necessity. It never occurred to Sienna just how small it was about to get.

Until midday.

She had been breaking up topsoil with her fork all morning while a planter followed behind with a seed drill. It was hard work and the earth was full of rocks but by noon they'd planted ten rows of chard. They headed back to the barn to collect a roll of netting to cover the seeds with when a Can working there caught Sienna's eye. She was on an easy duty, handing out water and collecting tools as they were finished with. She was a transwomxn, one of a dozen in the camp, nothing unusual about that. But what caught Sienna's attention was her voice as she complained about being given a fork with a stone wedge between the prongs. Sienna recognised her voice, with its whiney, nauseating, self-entitled pitch. She gawped, scarcely able to believe her eyes but knowing that she could not mistaken.

It was Bella.

She was here, minus the makeup and the floral A-line frocks. The hair was gone too, at least, the hair extensions. All that remained was a slightly tubby and prematurely balding 30-year-old of androgynous appearance. In fact, the only way of telling that Bella was a womxn was that she was part of a womxn's work party. Cans didn't have many rights after cancellation but gender acknowledgement was one of them.

Sienna turned and ran. Not because of her personal dislike for Bella or because she was ashamed about misgendering her. But because she couldn't allow Bella to see her. She couldn't risk another person in the camp knowing who she was or what she had been in her old life. Even if she was in the same boat, this knowledge could get Sienna killed.

She stashed her fork rather than hand it in and went the long way around to the barn to collect the netting. She spent half the afternoon panicking over what she was going to do and the other half wondering how Bella could have ended up here. Ultimately, she decided it didn't matter. What mattered was that she was here and could identify Sienna as an Auditor.

"Hey, cookie. Soup's up."

Her work partner headed down to the barn at the end of the day but Sienna stayed put. She'd barely noticed the hours roll by. It was early evening and the skies were red. The working day was done. Yet Sienna had lost all track of time, her mind so preoccupied with a dozen different scenarios, each ending worse than the last.

There were only thirty or so in their working party. Not

enough to hide amongst. By some fluke or miracle, she and Bella had missed each other at selection and on the journey over but she was unlikely to ride that luck for much longer. The way they usually sat when they got their food, idle and soaking it all in, Bella was bound to notice her. And what then? Even if she didn't mean to expose her, her reaction might reveal that they knew each other. Bella might even have the same fears and try to deflect attention from herself with a lie, revealing Sienna's secret while disguising her own.

"Where's that fucking fork?"

Sienna looked up and saw the nightmare unfolding before her faster than she had anticipated. Bella was stomping towards her in a pissy mood. She was in charge of the tools and, thanks to Sienna, she was one fork down. This was the sort of thing that could land a Can in trouble and Bella was obviously irritated.

Sienna didn't know what to do but she realised that holding out on her wasn't an option. She made her way over to the ancient stone wall, knelt by a bush and felt for the fork she had stashed here earlier. All the time she could hear Bella's angry lilt as she stomped towards her.

"You stupid cunt. What are you trying to do, get me in shit or something? I've a good mind to report you, making me come up here and play hide and seek, like I haven't got anything better to do, especially when I'm on my cycle."

Sienna turned just as Bella loomed over her. Their eyes met and Sienna searched Bella's for a flicker of recognition. She wasn't disappointed. There was a slight pause then a theatrical double-take but Bella's jaw dropped accordingly.

"You!"

Driven by panic, Sienna thrust the fork into Bella's soft belly. Bella's eyes turned white but Sienna didn't stop. She twisted the fork and kicked Bella away, dumping her to the ground and ripping the fork free. Bella landed with a splat and held out her hands but Sienna didn't hesitate, she drove the prongs into her again and again, breaking up her body like the top soil she'd been working all day as Bella flailed to stop her.

Sienna screamed as she stabbed her former supervisor, pulverising not just Bella but the whole rotten system that had sent her here and forced her to become everything she despised. She struck a blow for Geri, for Alicia, for Julie and for Malek. For the lies she had regurgitated and the Cans she had condemned. The people she had destroyed and the shame she carried. She didn't stop, she kept on going until eventually the wooden handle snapped in two. Only now did she look down at the carnage she had created and barely recognise it as humxn, let alone XX or XY. She felt herself falling and blacked out for several seconds into a puddle of Bella's blood.

When she came to, she cried uncontrollably and without release until she became aware of people standing around her. The owner of the property was screaming, several Cans were gawping and the Stewards were aiming their weapons at Sienna in case she wasn't finished.

"Go back to the barn," one of them shouted. "And bring up the first aid kit."

This was a tad optimistic but a Can was sent running for bandages while a Steward approached Sienna with his stun baton extended. He prised the broken handle from her fingers and regarded the mess she had made.

"Well, no soup for you, I guess," he said with a shrug.

*

The Overseer had a nice hut.

It was the same size as Sienna's but where Sienna slept cheek to jowl with forty other womyn, the Overseer had this one all to herself, as well as a cosy cottage several miles from the camp when she was off-duty. Her hut sat apart from the rest, surrounded by a neatly-tended herb garden and was adorned with every creature comfort. When she wasn't practising yoga in her studio space, she could centre her ying in her noise-cancelling booth or feed her yang with her family-sized Thermomix. There was also a floating workstation that she could reposition as the situation dictated. Today, it floated well back.

Sienna stood before her, ringed by a bright white light and warned against wandering. A Steward stood behind with his stun baton in hand just in case.

The Overseer looked Sienna up and down through her blacked-out Smart Glasses and sipped her macchiato.

"I hope you appreciate the seriousness of your actions, SL31-506."

SL31-506? This must have been Sienna's ID number. She'd never heard it before. No label was sewn onto her jumpsuit and no number had been tattooed onto her arm but the Overseer could see it all the same through her Smart Glass, projected by the steel bracelet around her wrist, glowing red to indicate Sienna's current naughty status.

"Yes, Doctor."

Cuntface may have been the Cans' name for the Overseer but on the whole she preferred Doctor, having gained several honorary PHDs for her extracurricular endeavours as an educational advisor. Her area of expertise was in the creation of safe study environments in which students could emotionally develop and express themselves without fear of detriment. But, as Sienna was about to find out, this was not a philosophy that extended beyond the students of Durham, Newcollective or Leeds.

The Overseer put down her drink and stared at the wretch before her, rake thin after months of camp life, filthy and splattered with the vestiges of violence.

"Before you say anything, before you try to justify your actions, I would like to make something crystal clear to you."

The Overseer swiped the air, scrolling through a library of files that were invisible to Sienna but as plain as day to those with access. Sienna had once had access. She knew what information could be found. And she knew how the system regarded her.

"You may be tempted to try to defend your actions, to try to blame the victim even, but let me tell you this, any attempt to do so will be seen for what it is, a wicked lie of shameful contempt and a confirmation as to your status as a hate criminal."

Sienna didn't react. She didn't flinch. To do so would have been futile. She had been caught red-handed, literally, with both hands stained in Bella's blood. The one small comfort she clung to was that she'd had no choice. She would have been dead if the truth had got out. It had all come down to this: it was her or Bella. Sienna had simply chosen herself.

"Many have tried," the Overseer continued, "and all were exposed as filthy hate mongers. There are no wolves in sheep's clothing in Camp 14. They do not exist in New Britannia. Such claims are the doctrines of transphobic terrorists intent on denying the truth about gender dysphoria and the suppression of free expressionism. I hope I make myself clear."

She hadn't. Sienna was lost and wondered if the Overseer had looked at the wrong file but she went on to elaborate.

"HT73-254 did not attempt to rape you. There was no physical altercation. You did not act in self-defence. We know these things for fact."

The Overseer was right about that. Bella had not attempted to rape Sienna. There had been no physical altercation. And Sienna hadn't acted in self-defence. But the Overseer was wrong about the other thing. She did not know these things for fact. But it was becoming pretty clear to Sienna that this was the conclusion she had drawn.

"Sex attackers do not disguise themselves as transwomyn. That is the myth created by TERF fanatics intent on creating a hierarchy within the femxle experience. We have categorically disproved the opportunist theory through gender science. The fact that HT73-254 was housed here proves she was femxle. And femxles do not rape femxles. Rape is a male weapon."

The Overseer had something of a blind spot but it was not unknown. There had been no lesbians in Victorian Britain. No serial killers in Soviet Russia. No bias in the Equal Opportunities Commission. Such concepts had never existed. Officially. And the Overseer was keen to maintain this principle. She had forms to fill in. An incident report to file. A death to explain. Hence parameters were needed before Sienna was offered the chance to tell her side of the story.

Some people might have wondered why Sienna hadn't just been dumped into the A.D. Programme without a fuss but not Sienna. Through her work with Geniture, she knew the importance of legitimacy. To act outside the law would have been unthinkable to those in charge. Even the murder of Alicia months earlier had been carried out with accountability in mind. Tilly had entered the programme 'voluntarily'. Mariatou and the others had 'elected' to join her. They had then selected partners to join them. The freedom of choice had been the detainees at all times. At least on paper.

The Overseer went on to offer Sienna a Hobson's choice of her own.

"With this in mind, there can be only two possible explanations for what transpired out there today. Either it was a hate crime fuelled by transphobia, for which, I need not remind you, you have a history of."

This was option A, which ticked all the right boxes and fitted Sienna like a glove.

"Or…" the Overseer tantalised. Sienna braced herself. She knew her files would have connected her with Bella. She might have only been acting out of self-preservation but that would have cut little mustard with the Overseer. She had no excuse. No mitigating circumstances. The writing was on the wall. Or rather, in the air.

"Or… this was just a tragic accident."

Sienna waited for the punchline but the Overseer was done. Options A and B were on the table. This was the choice she was being offered. Sienna didn't understand it but she realised she had been wrong. The Overseer had missed her connection with Bella. Or she hadn't realised its significance. She had genuinely assumed that this was a case of girl-on-girl sexual assault (a transprejudice concept) and had gone out of her way to avoid having to write it up as such.

The Overseer's own unconscious bias had framed her outlook, leading her down a rabbit hole of her own making.

"Obviously, if this was a hate crime, it will mean serious implications for you," the Overseer explained in no-shit terms that even a mad TERF like Sienna could understand. "But if it was an accident, then I think we can draw a line under the whole unfortunate incident."

This was her Faustian bargain. A promise of lenience in exchange for compliance. A genuine victim might have thought; "No, damn it. That bastard tried to rape me and everyone needs to know the truth" but Sienna wasn't about to martyr herself for the truth, particularly when it wasn't the truth. This was something she and the Overseer could certainly agree on, albeit for different reasons. So she took the deal in front of her and agreed it had all been an 'agricultural' mishap.

"I slipped," she said adding a bonus detail to her explanation.

"Very well then, if that is the truth, and the *only* truth," the Overseer said, clicking an invisible line of data and swiping it aside, "then you can go."

Sienna didn't need to be told twice but before she reached the door, the Overseer had a final word of advice for her.

"There had better not be any more accidents while you're here. I will not tolerate carelessness amongst my charges."

30: NORTHWARDS

The lights were out by the time Sienna got back from the wash hut, cold but clean. No food had been put aside for her. Most had not expected her to return. A Steward locked the door as soon as she entered and she felt her way to her bunk.

"Sienna?" a voice called from the darkness. Sienna felt her way through the maze of bunks, disorientated and still numb from the shock, and climbed in next to Kat. They snuggled under the thin blankets against the cold and held each other tightly. "I didn't think I'd ever see you again."

She wasn't the only one and several womyn voiced their dismay at having to sleep with a killer, not least of all, Petula in the far corner, who wouldn't sleep a wink all night.

"It was an accident," Sienna told everyone automatically, determined to stay on message. "Just a tragic accident."

The siren woke her before she realised she'd fallen asleep and she opened her eyes to the light of the new day. She and Kat dropped from their bunk and pulled on their boots. Kat couldn't take her eyes off Sienna, so happy was she to see her again. Sienna sensed their connection had deepened and couldn't resist her any longer, her brush with death had strengthened her pull on life. She took Kat in her arms and kissed her tenderly. Kat submitted, following where Sienna led and clinging to her desperately.

"We'd better go," Sienna said, breaking free with great reluctance, albeit with one last kiss. Her release at finding herself alive had piqued into an unstoppable longing for Kat and to her surprise, Kat felt the same despite her lack of experience. This would change, Sienna was determined. As starved as she was, her hunger for Kat was greater and they would skip stew to breakfast in the Love Shack this morning. That much was unstoppable.

They ran from the hut hand-in-hand, already late but finding places in the lines nevertheless. The Overseer was approaching from the direction of her hut, accompanied by her usual attachment and looking particularly washed and pressed this morning. She made her way up the steps and onto the speaking platform to look out upon the assembled Cans.

Stewards walked the lines totting up the totals before reporting all were present, one farmyard blunder asides.

Sienna felt the Overseer looking at her despite her eyes being shielded by blacked-out lenses. She tried to look as contrite as possible and ignored any overtures Kat made toward her, desperate not to identify Kat as a target should the Overseer be in a Solomon-esque type mood.

Ominously, Sienna's suspicions were confirmed.

"Shall we hear the Pledge?" the Overseer suggested, catching one or two off-guard. "I think it might help remind us why we are all here. Just because you have been removed from society, it does not negate your responsibilities to the new republic. Shall we?"

The Cans at the front started everyone off but the pledge quickly spread, each womxn only too aware of the consequences for abstaining or not pledging passionately enough.

"In the presence of Panthea, I swear to devote all of my strength and energies to the salvation of our blessed nation. I will work to rid these lands of hate and bigotry and not rest until we have freed ourselves from the bygone tyrannies of intolerance and discrimination. This is my pledge and I will honour it with my body and mind."

The Overseer regarded her charges with satisfaction and let the lesson sink in. There would be no more ploughing each other to bits thank you very much. Or the weight of New Britannia will be brought to bear upon each of them.

As usual, there was a smattering of new faces in the lines. Cans who had arrived on various transports overnight. And there was also a short pause as those due to ship out were removed. The process was invisible, at least to those without Smart Glasses, but all the Cans selected for transportation knew about it when their bracelets began to buzz.

As Sienna's now did.

She looked at her wrist in dismay and clenched a hand around the vibrating steel but the die had been cast. Her time in Camp 14 had come to an end. She looked at Kat and her expression said everything. Kat's face fell as Sienna stepped out of the line. Some were relieved to see her go. Few liked rooming with a murderer and Sienna realised transportation after yesterday's incident had been inevitable. The Overseer couldn't allow her to remain. She made her way to the front and took her place amongst the others destined for the islands.

Tears fell from Kat's eyes. Not for the love she would not know but for the partner she was losing. Each person's time in Camp 14 was short and intense. A two-month relationship here was like a ten-year marriage in the real world. Their love had been real but now it was over. And neither could do a thing about it.

"Selection is over. Those not due for transit are dismissed."

The lines broke up and the Cans queued for stew. Another day awaited them and all knew the routine. Kat lingered as the lines melted away, staring at Sienna forlornly and pained to move.

Sienna crossed her fingers and placed them over her heart, a gesture she'd seen Alicia make. She now understood what it meant. She was telling Kat not to give up, not to lose hope, and Kat returned the gesture despite struggling to believe. She eventually turned and joined the breakfast line before any Steward took notice. By the time she looked back, Sienna was gone.

The Cans trudged as one, few looking back and none looking forward. Only Sienna glanced over her shoulder, catching sight of Kat one last time as she was ushered through the gates. It ripped at her heart to go but she would pack it away with the rest of her pain. Camp 14, for all its barbarities, had taught her how to endure.

A hydrogen bus ticked over outside the camp. Unusually for a transport, it had windows; real, actual windows. Most S Division transports didn't, not even in the cab. They were driven by AI and didn't need them. Windows were an obsolete luxury. A porthole in the side or a window in the door was usually all that was supplied. But Stewards would be on board to accompany them north so it was felt windows were needed to protect their mental wellbeing.

"Take one meal pack and find a seat."

Each womxn had their bracelet scanned and was given a food pack. Sienna was checked and climbed aboard to find a seat. The bus was divided by a grill; the back for Cans; the front for the Stewards. Two of them sat armed with automatic weapons. Sienna struggled to understand why they needed the hardware. Most of the transit party were frail and emaciated after their time in Camp 14. A gust of wind would've finished them off. But the guns weren't for their oppression. They were for their protection. They would be travelling across the border and into Scotland, eventually driving through the Freed Animal Sanctuary to the docks at Thurso Bay. Wolves had thrived in the presence of so much easy prey. Packs now roamed the sanctuary, feasting on the herds and splitting off to form rival packs.

Most of the wolves stuck to hunting livestock. Sheep were plentiful. Calves easy to bring down. Piglets made a great snack. But some of the omegas, banished by the Alphas, would seek out other opportunities, sniffing around humxn settlements and attacking without warning. An Inspector reporting back on conditions had disappeared in January, his transport found idling by the side of the road where he had stopped to relieve himself. And three weeks earlier, an S Division transport had been trailed between Georgemas and

Achavanich by at least two pairs of rogues. That's a distance of 11 miles and the wolves never lost sight of them. Most towns and villages around the coastline operated ultrasonic deterrents that emitted high-pitched signals to keep the wolves at bay but the roads were vulnerable and sometimes impassable thanks to the weather. They needed to be prepared.

But all this was ahead of them. There were many miles to cover before the wilds of the Highlands welcomed them.

Most of the womyn slept for the first leg. Besides food, sleep had been in short supply in Camp 14 and the bus offered them an opportunity to stash some much-needed rest away for the exertions to come. Nobody knew what to expect on the islands but most realised that the pretty little cottages of lore would probably be anything but pretty. And a lot littler than advertised.

Snapshots of Bella flashed through Sienna's mind as she drifted in and out of sleep. She felt revolted at what she had done. Sickened even. Not just at the physical act, but the metaphysical act too. What had given her the right to take someone else's life? To rob another living being of existence? What kind of a monster had she become? She hadn't liked Bella, not even when she had been Ben. But she tried to convince herself that this had nothing to do with it. Yet would she have plunged the fork in had it been Geri? Or Julie? Or someone else who knew her past? These were not easy questions to ask. Or rather, they were. She just didn't like the answers they elicited.

Had the Overseer been right, albeit indirectly? Was Sienna a transphobe who had acted out of subconscious hate? Did she hate all trans people? Did she feel an overwhelming desire to attack and hurt more? The thought made her want to retch. If anything, her mettle had wilted and her resolve had drained away. If it came to it again, she would barely have the stomach to save herself, let alone harm anyone else.

She was so desperate for forgiveness but the one person who could grant it was gone – at her hands.

If this is what it took to stay alive, Sienna thought to herself, she wasn't sure she had the heart to go on, no matter what Alicia said.

The bus took them along the old motorway, across the border, skirting the cities and heading through the Scottish lowlands. At various points, they passed placards on the verges and signs strung from motorway bridges bidding them a foul farewell. Some wished them good riddance, others advised they jump in the sea and drown. The drowning addendum wasn't necessary. Sienna got it.

EXPEL ALL CAN'S
HATE THE HATERS
WE WO'NT MISS YOU!
FUCK OFF 4EVER!

The grammar upset Sienna more than the sentiments and in that moment, she realised she would miss New Britannia about as much as it was set to miss her. She was a Can now. Only her fellow Cans mattered any more.

After six gruelling hours, they got their first glimpse of the sea. They'd passed over several firths but finally, the land fell away on the right and a vast expanse of blue extended beyond the horizon. Womyn nudged each other awake and stared in wonder. Most had only experienced the sea as a VR concept. The real thing was infinitely more imposing, shimmering as it was beneath an opal sky. In days of old, the sea was said to be the great absolver, capable of washing away the sins of the past and cleansing all those who sought rebirth. Sienna felt the last of her old life seeping away like a dream that faded as the day drew on. Only her future existed now. Only the lands across the horizon. And whatever days remained to her.

Sienna finished the last of her meal pack. She had eked it out for the journey north but now she only had a cardboard box to show for her rations. How much further was there to go? She didn't know, but the shadows were lengthening and the sea was glistening. The islands couldn't be that much further away.

"I need to pee," she said, putting up her hand to grab the attention of the Stewards.

"There are cups beneath your seats. And cloths for those of you who bleed. But the transport will not be stopping."

Sure enough, Sienna found a recycled cardboard 'shewee' container beneath her seat and made use of it, not the easiest task on a moving bus while wearing an all-in-one jumpsuit. Only after she was finished did she realise the shape of the container prohibited her from putting it down, not without spilling its contents. Duly, she was forced to hold it upright for the rest of the journey, soaking her hand whenever they went over a pothole and dripping it all over the seat.

After several more miles, the bus turned inland as they headed into the last leg of their journey. More signs appeared but these were official signs and ominous in their warnings.

FREED ANIMAL SANCTUARY
DO NOT EXIT YOUR VEHICLE
DANGER – WILD ANIMALS ROAMING FREE
WOLF TERRITORY – EXTREME DANGER
POACHERS WILL BE SHOT

Some of the signs featured symbols depicting the danger. Others emitted a 7G signal that beamed warnings directly to a wearer's Smart Glasses and logged their movements. The system had already picked up the bus's transponder and was keeping Thurso Control informed of their progress.

The final stretch took them across a rugged landscape that had once been known as Caithness, now largely uninhabited by people except on the coastal fringes. The land was part of the Freed Animal Sanctuary and sheep roamed in vast herds across the open moorland, tracked remorselessly by two competing wolf packs and countless rogues. It didn't take long before the Cans got their first sight of the herds. They covered every hillside and stretched away in all directions as far as the eye could see. Some sheep looked up as the bus drove by but most carried on grazing, seeking out every scrap of greenery on this wind-swept fell.

At one point, a huge flock obstructed the road and the bus was forced to stop. The AI pilot system hit the horn but the sheep didn't scatter. If anything, the numbers increased as more moved in to block the road. A Steward opened the side door and shot off a burst of automatic fire but the sheep barely flinched. Guns they didn't know about. But wolves they were only too wary of, so the AI system dialled through a few files and played the sounds of wolves howling. This was a last resort. It could attract real wolves as well as repel sheep and vehicles that played these calls had been attacked in the past. And while they would have been quite safe inside the bus, it didn't pay to antagonise these killers.

The sheep got the message and fled, clearing the road ahead of them. The bus moved off and thirty minutes later, the Cans once more saw the sea. This time, it was the Pentland Firth, a cold stretch of northern sea that separated the mainland from the Orkneys. A town emerged from the landscape and a sign declared:

WELCOME TO THURSO
While another one bid:
GOODBYE CANS

The bus drove straight for the docks. A ferry was waiting in the harbour and the ramp was down. An official stood at a checkpoint and flagged the bus to a halt. The AI pilot registered the official's authority and stopped so that the official could climb aboard, scan everyone's bracelets and compare IDs with headshots to make sure they tallied.

"All good,' he declared, exiting the bus and waving them through. The bus pulled forward, over the ramp and onto the steel deck.

Some Cans shifted in their seats but the Stewards told them to stay where they were.

"No one gets off. Not until we get there."

Sienna's cup ranneth over but still, she was expected to hold it upright while crossing this evening's chop. And she wasn't alone. Most of the womyn were in the same boat, figuratively and literally, holding overflowing cardboard containers that were fast turning soft.

They sat waiting for another hour before departing. In that hour, three more buses and several large lorries joined them, cramming the deck and sidling up to each other. Sienna looked through the window at the bus next to her. A virtual reflection stared back, a sallow-looking girl with greasy hair and empty eyes. She must have come from a different camp. Hedley House only sent one transport a day.

Finally, the ramp was pulled up and the ferry cast off. The night was not yet upon them but the moon was out, hanging in the cobalt sky like a chalky crescent as they sailed out of the bay. The shallower waters beyond the harbour were rough and unyielding. Sienna's sleeves were soon soaked through, much to the amusement of the onlooking Stewards. It wouldn't have caused them any effort to let the womyn empty their shewee cups over the side but the Stewards were sticklers for the rules, particularly when they provided such entertainment.

Sienna had never been on a boat before. She had never left the mainland. Most people hadn't. New Britannia was surrounded on all sides by enemies of free expression. Where was there to go? The experience disconcerted her. She hadn't realised it would rock so much and the side-to-side swaying made her nauseous. Several womyn vomited, refilling their empty meal containers but Sienna managed to keep her own food down, her body loathed to part with a single morsel.

For ninety minutes they rocked across the strait, bypassing the southernmost islands for the terminal at Stromness. It was dark by the time they pulled in, the harbour lights shining to dazzle and disorientate them upon docking. Metal clanked against concrete and the ferry engines were thrown into reverse but all at once they were here, the final destination on their descent into exile.

What sort of lives awaited them? No one knew.

But they would not have long to find out.

31: ORKNEY

There followed another short drive, just a mile or so to the processing facility where the womyn were finally allowed to disembark and tip away their soggy shewees. Most of the womyn stank and a hosepipe was produced. But only for the bus.

"This way. Follow me."

The four busloads were wrangled by Stewards and led towards a large tin hangar where more Stewards awaited them, some carrying scanners, others batons. Arc lights illuminated them from all sides and voices shouted at them through the dazzle.

"Pick it up. Move it. Move up."

"This way. That way."

"Hurry up."

They were formed into a line and had their bracelets scanned before being pushed towards the hangar. Sienna ran as directed, following the girl in front, across the tarmac and towards a large open door. The night was abuzz with activity with either Stewards shouting or Cans running, some carrying equipment, others returning to fetch more. The island Cans wore different jumpsuits to those arriving from the mainland. Theirs were pink denim with white high-vis stripes. They also got woolly hats ringed with hi-viz brims and Sienna saw why when she entered the hangar. A line of barbers awaited them with clippers poised. Beyond were piles of blue jumpsuits, discarded by stripping Cans, and further still was a long line of showers, spraying continuously as a line of Cans was directed through.

Sienna barely flinched as her pixie locks were shorn. They'd once been platinum blonde. Now they were dirty and grey.

"Don't worry, darling, you're still beautiful," said the Can who shaved her. He handed her a disposable razor and told her to do her body parts as she passed through the showers. "Don't try to keep the razor. The Stewards will be watching."

She moved off and got undressed, stripping along with everyone else while Stewards directed them where to go. She hadn't noticed until now but half the Cans were men yet no concessions were made. Every gender showered together. All thoughts of modesty were immaterial.

The showers were tepid but bearable. Sienna washed her

stinking hands and used the razor as instructed. A womxn in front started shaving her legs and was shouted at by a Steward so Sienna figured she'd stick with the essentials. A bin for the razors stood by the last shower and Sienna tossed hers in then ran to get a towel. Most were sopping wet but she dried as much as she could, desperate to dress and get beyond the bite of the cold.

Vests, pants, socks and boots were provided, along with a woolly hat and the all-occasions jumpsuit. There was also a pink denim jacket that included a thin lining as well as the *à la mode* high-vis stripes. What luxury! She buttoned it as she ran, directed by yet more Stewards and joined a line of ten, just as she had at Camp 14.

It took fifteen more minutes before every Can had been processed but once they had, they amounted to thirteen lines with a remainder of four. The showers stopped and the soiled clothes and piles of hair were carted off.

After a wait of indeterminate length, a small party of uniformed Stewards entered the hangar in the throes of deep conversation, stopping before the detainees as almost an afterthought. There were five of them in all, one honcho and four lackeys, each bedecked in epaulettes and badges to underpin their status.

The head honcho was a slender individual of striking appearance, sporting a crimped caramel beard and flowing Christ-like locks. He was a head taller than all those around him and they gazed up at him accordingly, hanging on his every word and laughing uproariously whenever they were required to do so. He smiled benignly as he rattled through his stories, seemingly oblivious to the lines of tired Cans that stood waiting. The other notable thing about him was the absence of any Smart Glasses. All the other Stewards had them but he did not. Sienna could see his eyes and felt strangely assured by this aberration. It made him seem trustworthy, almost compassionate. How could he regard her as just a number if he couldn't see one?

A final laugh signalled the end of his latest anecdote and, at last, he turned to regard his newest charges. They awaited his instructions but he clearly preferred to save his breath for those with pips. Instead, one of his lackeys stepped forward and scanned the new arrivals. She was a small womxn of senior Grade with long braided hair and enormous fake eyelashes. Sienna now understood the need for all new arrivals to be shaven. An errant head louse in this place could've proved disastrous for the senior management.

"Good evening, you pieces of garbage."

Christ-man laughed and several of his officers echoed his amusement. As welcomes went, it set an ominous tone for the next chapter of their lives but eyelashes was quick to reassure them.

"I mean no insult. Indeed, we highly prize garbage on these islands. It is our stock and trade. We are the lords of garbage and you will soon come to treasure it as much as we do. New Britannia has thrown you out. But here you will be recycled into something beautiful. Here you will find purpose again. Welcome to the Orkneys. Welcome to rebirth."

And with that, the party of officers headed off to leave the Cans anxious, if none the wiser.

"Form two lines. Go."

The men were separated from the main group and shot with Antiandrogen implants while cis womyn, trans men and non-binary individuals who'd been femxle at birth were shot with contraception implants to prevent the 'garbage' pile from getting out of hand. Unlike the Camps on the mainland, the islands were pan gender and the Overseers weren't so puritanical as to insist that no one expressed their sexuality. But they weren't naive either so a few monthly pharmaceuticals kept the rapes at bay and the babies to a minimum.

After their shots, they were given a gluten-free sandwich with a stodgy filling and split into smaller groups. Each group was driven out to various locations with worker accommodation established in pockets around the islands. Not all would stay on Orkney Mainland. There were seventy islands in the archipelago and at least half were in use.

Sienna and eleven others were bussed to a place on the eastern side called Cornquoy. A small settlement had been established in the fields overlooking a stoney bay and this would be her home for the foreseeable future. Each Can was issued with a blanket, a thin pillow, a small piece of charcoal soap and a wooden toothbrush upon arrival.

A salty old Can awaited them by a stone wall, taking charge once the Stewards had officially turned them over into his care. No one said anything until the Stewards left, their bus disappearing into the night to leave them standing by the side of the road in pitch blackness. Only the Can they'd been handed over to had a torch and he used it now to study each of their faces.

"My name is Jolyon Romero. I'm Designee for Cornquoy. If you want anything, ask me. If you need anything, ask me. If you want to complain about anything, complain to me. There are no Stewards here. We sort out our own affairs and we play nicely together. If anyone has any problems with that, you know where I am. Everyone dandy?"

These were the terms and conditions and everyone signed up. Sienna wondered what the small print said but figured this was not a time to ask. In the pitch of night, she could hardly see where Jolyon was guiding them but eventually after a few stumbles, they arrived at their settlement. It had been a long and tiring day and Sienna was fit to drop but she was a little disconcerted when she saw where she was expected to drop.

Shipping containers.

There were twenty of them dotted around the field and Jolyon pointed his beam at the rustiest box of them all.

"That one is yours. You'll find mattresses and water inside," he said, reaching inside to flick on a pale striplight strung along the ceiling. "This water is for drinking. If you want a wash, there's a different barrel around the back but don't wash in the barrel, use the bucket to fetch it out because you all have to use it. Goodnight campers."

And with that, he turned his torch off and tootled away in the dark.

"Oh, one other thing. The bus will be here at seven. Call for you at six."

If it was cold outside, it was hardly snug within but at least it kept the wind at bay once the doors were shut. Sienna slept in fits and starts, waking every few dreams when Bella's screams became too much for her.

Finally, she saw light streaming in through the gap in the door. It was early, she guessed, well before they were due to be woken but she had rested enough and went to stretch her legs. She kept the blanket wrapped around her shoulders and pulled it tight as she stepped out into the cold grey of dawn.

A light mist hung over the landscape but all was still. The sound of waves crashing against rocks could be heard in the distance but nothing else stirred. She wandered between the rows of containers and came to a long table made from packing crates.

"You come in last night?"

Sienna turned and saw a womxn of Middle Eastern heritage fetching a bucket from behind a nearby container.

"Yes," Sienna confirmed.

"From?"

"Camp 14."

The womxn shook her head. "Don't know that one."

Sienna considered telling her it was near the old border then figured it didn't matter. Nowhere was nowhere, no matter how near or far to somewhere else it was. "Where were you?"

"Camp 6," she said then thought again. "Or 5. I can't remember now."

"How long have you been here?"

"Two winters," she said disappearing into the nearest container with her bucket. Sienna waited for her to reappear but when she didn't, she went looking for her.

This container was nicer than Sienna's. A lot nicer. Where Sienna's had bare walls and steel floors, this one had wooden panels and was insulated against the cold. Four beds occupied the far end, built up to keep them off the floor. And there were rugs too, worn thin but still a luxury. On the walls, there were shelves with pots and jars, some containing herbs and stalks, others pulses and roots. The Middle Eastern womxn poured water from her bucket into a large cooking pot that was sat atop a blackened hotplate. A wire ran from the hotplate to a leaky saltwater battery.

"You can help make chowder if you like."

The island settlements had greater autonomy than the detainees had on the mainland. They made their own food, set their own rules and looked after their own kind. All the authorities asked was that they were ready each morning and that they refrained from killing themselves outside of the official A.D. Programme.

The womxn introduced herself as Sekhmet Krol. She was the appointed cook at Cornquoy. She was responsible for preparing meals, gathering ingredients and seeing to it that her people were fed each morning and night. It got her out of working at the plant but no one complained. She was a skilled and resourceful cook. The dishes she served were so much better than the meals the Cans were used to, particularly those who had come through transit camps.

Sekhmet led and Sienna followed, not really understanding any of it but happy to learn. She'd never cooked before. Carl had prepared all of her meals and prior to him, a Home OS called Abode that Geri had uninstalled when she'd moved in, deleting all Sienna's banking passwords in the process. The key to cooking seemed to be stirring, adding stuff and stirring. Sekhmet added the stuff. Sienna stirred. By the time everyone was awake, the chowder was ready and Sienna had prepared her first-ever meal. She felt proud of herself, in tune with the land and alive in a way that she had never known.

They carried the pot between them out to the makeshift table and served their fellow Cornquoyans. There must have been more than fifty of them in all, including the Cans Sienna had come in with, but the atmosphere was friendly. Convivial almost.

"You'll make a fine addition," Sekhmet smiled graciously.

Sienna felt reassured, not least of all when she tried the chowder. Considering it was mostly water and vegetables with some sort of wild mushrooms to bulk it out, it was really quite good. There was even seconds after everyone was served, something unheard of in the camps.

"We don't have much but we don't go hungry," Sekhmet

said with a smile.

As she was finishing her second bowl, a tiny sprig jabbed Sienna's throat. She coughed it out and pulled it from between her teeth. It looked like no sprig she had ever seen before. It was white and almost translucent. One end was thick while the other tapered. Sienna couldn't think what plant it could have come from but there were several more at the bottom of her bowl, all identical.

She looked up and noticed Sekhmet staring at her hard. Sekhmet took the 'sprig' from Sienna's fingers and flicked it away into the long grass.

"You're not in New Britannia any more," she said flatly.

32: RECYCLED

The work was as advertised.

Huge piles of junk awaited them at an enormous plant near Kirkwall airport, overshadowed by two giant wind turbines. Most of the junk was electronic or mechanical waste. Hard drives and appliances, devices and gadgets. Above all, Smart Glasses by the thousand. Broken and discarded. Inoperative and obsolete. Awaiting renewal.

The workers were given an induction on their first morning and assigned to a workstation. Sienna was put on the Smart Glasses bench. 'Bench' was a deceptively quaint way of describing the enormous counter that stretched in both directions as far as the eye could see. There were no seats or stools, just numbered footprints painted on a concrete floor that showed each worker where to stand. Sienna's was workstation 415. The numbers were conspicuous if the worker was absent. Woe betide anyone away from their station for long.

Her duties were simple. Grab a handful of Smart Glasses

from a nearby container and dismantle them down to their component pieces. There were bins for the screws, bins for the wires, bins for the wire housings, circuit boards, lenses, frames and batteries. Each item would then be melted down or chemically processed to reclaim the rare materials. Mineral ores were in short supply in New Britannia with copper, steel, cobalt, lithium, nickel, silver and gold mostly mined abroad and subject to strict sanctions imposed by Gaultier's junta. Recycling was key to sustainability, not just for the planet but for New Britannia itself. Traditionally, recycling in large enough quantities to be self-sustaining was not only difficult, it was economically impossible. Almost.

But not quite.

For, if a society had a large and willing workforce at its disposal for virtually no cost, then the system became 'ecologically cost-effective'.

As strange as it sounds, Sienna almost enjoyed her first morning of work. It was a lot easier than harvesting cabbages and much warmer than working outside in winter. It may have been fiddly and repetitive but she quickly got the hang of it and before long was able to process a pair of Smart Glasses in a little under ten minutes. It wasn't until the early afternoon that she realised how sore her hands were becoming, how big her feet had swollen and how much her back was aching. By the time the light started to fade, she could barely focus, barely hold a screwdriver, barely squeeze a pair of wire strippers and yet still her shift went on. No one was allowed to stop. No one was allowed to rest. The workload was relentless.

Stewards patrolled the plant with their batons ready but they rarely intervened. Peer pressure did their work for them. Each section had a specific amount of renewables to process.

If everyone worked to their potential, they could process their allocation in a little under 14 hours. If not, it took longer. The buses would wait. But no one went home until the work was done. Slackers were not tolerated. Shirkers were shunned. Quitters were cast out.

Those who did not work – did not eat.

Those who did not eat – got sick.

Those who got sick – stayed sick.

For a time, at least.

The Overseer had been right when she had said; "Here you will find purpose again". Work was their purpose. And their purpose was everything.

Sienna struggled to keep up. The womxn at station 414 told her to keep going. Push through the pain barrier and visualise the end goal. The last pair of Smart Glasses.

Sienna didn't think they'd ever come. The bottom of the Smart Glasses container was always buried beneath a twisted tangle of frames. Then, towards the end of the afternoon, another bin was wheeled in and emptied into their container. The shock almost poleaxed Sienna but 414 told her to keep going. That had been the five o'clock delivery and no more would follow.

She didn't know how she managed but Sienna kept going, somehow summoning the strength to take apart another pair, distribute its components and start over. Her dexterity waned towards the end of her shift. She would drop tiny screws and lack the grip to pick them up. She would snap wires when stripping housings and scrape her palm when the spudger slipped. She didn't know how many pairs she took apart but she was still doing it in her head on the way home, unable to shake the procedure from her mind.

A lumpy stew and a lumpier mattress awaited her back in

Cornquoy and she fell into both, gorging without question and dismantling Smart Glasses in her sleep until she realised that she was taking apart Bella's face. She woke up screaming.

The agonies of that first shift helped her prepare for the days to come. Over time, she developed strategies that allowed her to cope and process her workload more efficiently. On that first day, she had taken apart each pair of glasses individually, switching tools and performing each task as a single action. But she soon realised it was easier to process ten at a time. Or twenty. Or thirty. Unscrew everything in one go. Prise open every case. Break every solder connection. Strip the wires one after the other. Sort the components en masse. Sienna found that she was at least a quarter quicker doing it this way, which meant a quarter less work.

414 cautioned her against working too quickly. There were no employee of the month awards here. Just more work. Sienna adjusted her efforts accordingly, easing back to spare her body while doing what she needed to get through the day.

She barely noticed the containers being topped up any more. Scarcely felt the crick in her neck that had felt like a knife that first day. No longer flexed her fingers to get them working. The labour honed her body and deadened her mind. Just as 414 had promised.

414 was called Nora. She had been on Orkney for eight months via a transit Camp in Lincolnshire and a hostel outside Peterborough. She didn't say what she'd been cancelled for and Sienna didn't ask. Most people didn't. There was nothing to be gained and everything to be lost should they confide to the wrong person. This suited Sienna. She wasn't one of life's sharers anyway. Not like Geri. Geri was an open book. Meet her once and by the end of the evening you'd know everything about her, everything she'd done and

why it had gone wrong. But Sienna was more circumspect. Her job had required it. Now circumstances demanded it.

There was no talking at work anyway. And very little on the bus going to or from the plant. The only opportunities came in Cornquoy when the residents came together at mealtimes. And even then, a less talkative bunch you were unlikely to meet outside of a monastery. Not even Nora afforded Sienna the time of day and stuck to her own little clique at the far end of the table. A newcomer had to prove themselves before they were accepted by the wider community. Until then, they slept in the leakiest container, on the thinnest of mattresses and were regarded with suspicion.

Things came to a head a couple of weeks later when Wojciech stepped out of line. Wojciech had come to Cornquoy the same day as Sienna. He'd struggled to adapt from the outset and looked catwalk-thin upon arrival. He was usually the last on the bus and the slowest at work. And he grumbled openly about the conditions, the cold and the damp, something that was the same for everyone. He finally got on the wrong side of Sekhmet when he questioned her Highland Hotpot, demanding to know what was in it while everyone else was just grateful to eat. Sienna had wondered the same thing but decided discretion was the better part of flavour. She was tired and hungry after a long day at the plant and Sekhmet's Hotpot went a long way to ease both. She couldn't tell what was in it either but made a conscious effort not to speculate. As long as it was edible and nutritious, she didn't have the strength to care. But Wojciech did. And he made it his personal hill to die on.

"What is this?"

Wojciech balanced a small grey lump on the end of his spoon for all to see. Some people looked but most didn't, preferring to face their bowls and ignore the others.

The weather was mild and the wind low. The last rays of sun were setting behind the clouds and the day was almost done. Around fifty people lived at Cornquoy and half were sat around the makeshift table. The rest – the newcomers like Sienna and Wojciech – made do with a dry patch of grass or the threshold of a shipping container. Wojciech was on his own, as usual, having alienated most of those he worked with through incompetence and a reluctance to apply himself. Some Cans were like that. They couldn't get over the fact that they'd been cancelled and dragged their feet whenever they could, sticking two fingers up at the world and fighting the system from within.

"I said what is this?" Wojciech demanded, approaching Sekhmet at the head of the table.

Sekhmet looked past Wojciech's spoon and into his eyes, deploring what she saw.

"Hotpot," she suggested. "It's good for you."

"This is meat, isn't it? You're serving us meat?"

If Wojciech had been expecting a shock of revulsion, he was wholly disappointed. He turned to the rest of the community and held out his spoon as if no one had heard him.

"It's a mushroom," Jolyon said, stirring his own bowl and picking one out.

"It's not a mushroom. I know what mushrooms look like and this isn't any mushroom I've seen. It's meat. What is it? Some kind of bird?"

"Sit down and shut up," a lone voice from further down the table suggested which most thought was good advice. Only Wojciech thought otherwise.

"You're making us eat the flesh of living creatures. What kind of monsters have we become? We might not be a part of New Britannia any more but we can still live like decent compassionate people, can't we?"

Wojciech waited for an answer but only the distant crash of waves spoke in reply.

"What's wrong with you people?" he said, hurling what was on the end of his spoon into the grass. He now picked out every 'mushroom' and hurled them away too, contenting himself with whatever juice and vegetables remained. No one paid him any attention yet all took notice. Sienna refused to catch his eye but the Hotpot soured in her mouth. She'd eaten most of it but now struggled to eat the rest despite her hunger. She'd never knowingly eaten meat before and refused to accept she was eating it now. They were mushrooms, just as Jolyon had said. Special Orkney mushrooms.

Had Wojciech left it at that, he might have been okay but he was suddenly on a mission and did something that would come back to bite him. He finished his veganised Hotpot and slammed the bowl down in front of Sekhmet.

"You have all day to gather fresh ingredients while we're at work in that hellhole. The least we can expect is a decent ethical meal at the end of each day. If I ever see anything like that in my bowl again, I will report you to the authorities."

As far as Wojciech was concerned he was adopting a moral stance, just as he had always done whilst working as a senior compliance officer in a community grants department. He was convinced that if he took a position, others would follow where he led. They had always done so in the past (until that terrible day seven months ago when they hadn't) but he had badly misjudged the mood around him.

Sekhmet and Jolyon swapped looks then Jolyon climbed to his feet.

"You'd best come with me, young man."

"You can't intimidate me. I know my rights."

But Jolyon was calmness personified.

"I just want a quiet word in private, like. This sort of thing's not good for community relations."

He placed a reassuring hand on Wojciech's shoulder and led him across the fields and into the dusk, explaining how things were on Orkney as they went. Jolyon must have put forward quite an argument because Wojciech never complained again. Or if he did, no one heard him. His bed lay empty the next morning and he missed the bus when it came. No explanation was offered and none was sought until the Stewards came to investigate, sweeping the coastline with trackers and eventually finding him in the waters just off Roseness Lighthouse.

"Poor guy must have got lost in the dark," Jolyon shrugged.

Wojciech bracelet was recycled and no one complained about Sekhmet's Hotpot again.

As the weeks went on, Sienna learned that a lot of people got lost in the dark. It seemed a particularly perilous place to walk around at night. A cook in Gorseness who'd been playing favourites with some of her people while others starved. A sweeper at the plant who'd been caught sweeping his responsibilities under a bank of generators to earn a collective sanction for his section. A couple from Finstown who had been withholding blankets from their neighbours in exchange for personal services. All had come a cropper on the precarious coastal paths that surrounded the island.

But the most surprising disappearance came five weeks after Sienna had arrived. The day had started the same as every other day with a wash, breakfast, a brush of the teeth and a few quiet moments of introspection before the bus came along when it became apparent that some of their people were missing. Quite a few, in fact.

A look of concern hung over Jolyon's face as he hurried from container to container taking a count in his mind.

"Fuck," he said when his numbers didn't tally.

Sienna noticed only when she saw everyone else looking, their expressions troubled and their spoons momentarily stilled.

"What is it?" she asked, wondering just how many people could get lost in the dark at once.

Sekhmet glowered ominously. "Trouble."

Sure enough, when the bus arrived, Jolyon was forced to report that twelve of his people were missing. Among them was Nora, or 414 as Sienna had come to know her. Out of a population of fifty, that was deemed excessive even by Orkney's standards and the Stewards descended in numbers, arriving by vehicle, helicopter and boat.

Unlike the morning Wojciech had disappeared, the workers were confined to their containers and questioned by the Stewards. Sienna's interview took a little under ten minutes. She didn't know anything and her vital signs bore this out when she was polygraphed.

"Did you hear anything in the night?"

"No."

"Did any of the missing say anything to you in the days leading up to their disappearance?"

"No."

"Do you have any idea where they might be?"

"No."

"Have you been approached by anyone with the promise of escape?"

"No."

"Would you tell us if you were?"

"Yes."

"Are they dead?"

"I don't know."

"Did you kill them?"

"No."

"Do you know if someone else killed them?"

"No."

"Would you tell us if you knew who killed them?"

"Yes"

"You worked at the plant alongside 414?"

"Yes."

"What did you talk about?"

Sienna wracked her brain.

"Sleep."

The missing twelve never turned up. They were never found and no one ever mentioned them again. The whole thing was a mystery but Sienna knew to tread carefully, particularly after the grilling the Stewards had subjected Jolyon to. She'd learned by now not to ask a question unless she was sure it wouldn't lead to a midnight stroll. Play dumb. Play oblivious. Play along. That seemed to be the best policy and Sienna was better prepared than most.

There was, however, one pressing question she needed to put to Jolyon when the time was right and felt it was worth the risk.

"If Nora isn't coming back, can I move into her container?"

33: CURRENCIES

Life got better for Sienna after that. Not much more but just enough. She moved into the green container, formerly Nora's, where the mattresses were softer, the blankets thicker and the occupants numbered five not twelve. There were also rugs on the floor and boxes for their clothes. Through their work at the plant, the Cans were paid in goods rather than currency. Things they could use. Things they needed. Socks and pants, vests and T-shirts, even a second jumpsuit if they worked hard enough. These were their rewards; the basic necessities given as remuneration for their labours. Still, it meant that Sienna was able to wash her clothes and have a clean set the next day. Or at least, the day after that. Nothing dried quickly on Orkney. She also took Nora's place at the table and through patience and deference began to earn the trust of the elders. So much so that one day, while helping Sekhmet wash the dishes, Sekhmet opened up about the fate of Nora and the others.

"They went to Sweden."

Sienna wondered if she'd heard right. Was this a euphemism for something? Did going to Sweden mean the same as getting lost in the dark? Or did Sekhmet mean she really went to Sweden? Actual Sweden. Was Nora now hundreds of miles away in another land?

Of all the countries in the world, Sweden was one of the few remaining bastions of humxnity outside of New Britannia. It had refused to be browbeaten into joining Gaultier's Federal States of Europe and remained resolutely neutral, just as it had throughout the wars of the 20th century. Its army was weak compared with the FSE and it lacked the nuclear capabilities of New Britannia but its neutrality was honoured by both sides who found it useful to have an impartial neighbour at their disposal. The rights of its citizens were protected and its borders were closely guarded. Defectors were discouraged and refugees resisted but those who could get through the frontier could claim sanctuary from the state. It didn't matter if they were fleeing persecution or prosecution, all could find a home in this Nordic melting pot.

If they could get there.

Sekhmet noted Sienna's reaction and felt reassured by her restraint. She was a good girl. She could be trusted. Sekhmet looked around, prompting Sienna to do the same.

"People come here. In boats. For the right price, anything is possible. Even a new life."

This was a revelation. Sienna had always assumed that Orkney was a one-way ticket. That once she was here, she would stay here forever. This was the accepted belief and nothing she'd seen or heard until now had done anything to dissuade her of that. So, to hear that there was a way out was like hearing that death wasn't the end. She almost couldn't take it in. It seemed too wonderful to believe but it came with a sour sting.

With hope came hopelessness.

With dreams came nightmares.

With freedom came loss.

She was on Orkney. And for the foreseeable future, this was where she was staying. Yet in the days that followed, Sienna picked away at Sekhmet until she'd learned all she could.

Traffickers came to these shores. They had maps to navigate the sea mines and paid certain Stewards to look the other way, docking in desolate coves on moonless nights. Those who could afford it could buy their passage to Gothenburg. There, they would be put to work to maximise the gang's profits until eventually, after four or five years, they would be set free to claim asylum.

"I work every day as it is," Sienna said. "With no chance of freedom ever."

"A different kind of work," Sekhmet cautioned her. "For pretty girls like you, there is only one kind of work."

This gave Sienna pause for thought but still, it was a chance. A slim to nothing way off this rock that could not be ignored. For a second chance at life, she was willing to consider all options. And escaping from a love shack in Sweden could be no harder than escaping from an island in the middle of the North Sea.

But how could anyone buy their passage? What did these traffickers take? Socks?

Sekhmet shook her head and lowered her voice further still. "Gold."

Gold was one of the precious metals chemically recovered in the recycling plant. It was used in the microboards of Smart Glasses and the circuitry of tablets because of its electrical properties. The amounts were tiny, less than 0.025 grams per pair but with hundreds of thousands of devices being recycled every week, the nuggets soon started to add up. But Sienna couldn't just stuff circuit boards into her pockets. The metal had to be reclaimed using sulphuric acid, cyanide and a whole host of other dangerous chemicals. The process was carried out in another part of the plant and carefully scrutinised. Presumably, there was a certain amount of siphoning going on and a few grams went astray each week. Silver and lithium too. Anything of value that could be exchanged for happiness or hope.

But Sienna didn't work in that part of the plant. She didn't have access to gold or silver so how could she accrue wealth? She didn't know. But she started to look.

At the plant the next day, she took an interest in the

facilities in a way that she hadn't before. She watched where the bins went, the signs on the doors they bumped through, who fetched and carried them to the next stage of the process and even the restrooms of those who worked at the plant. There were restrooms for Cans and restrooms for Stewards and never the twain shall meet. But later that day she noticed something curious. An administrator emerged from a Can bathroom. A few moments later, a Can emerged behind him, adjusting her rumpled jumpsuit and heading off in a different direction, their furtive glances unmistakable.

It seemed gold was not the only currency in circulation on Orkney.

Sienna shuffled these elements in her mind and tried to outline a plan. If she could identify a Can who was working in the mineral recoveries unit, and if that Can was having illicit sexual contacts, could she blackmail him into providing her with gold? If she could contact the traffickers? And if the Can didn't take her for a short walk in the darkness first?

There seemed rather too many 'ifs' in that plan to regard it as workable but at least she was thinking.

One of the hardest things about Orkney was the deadening effect it had on the mind. The fatigue and limited diet sapped the body while the constant whooshing of enormous turbine blades sapped the mind. Many Cans shuffled around like zombies, stick thin and bereft of energy. Some stopped eating. Some took themselves for a short walk off a dark cliff. But mostly, when they couldn't take it anymore, they simply volunteered for the A.D. Programme. It got so busy during the coldest months of the year that a booking system had to be implemented.

Sienna thought of Alicia every time she passed the queue for the A.D. Unit. There were never less than five people waiting, each of them looking dead already, simply waiting for official confirmation and a body bag to climb into.

The complex was laid out like an industrial estate with the recycling plant taking up most of the land and the towering turbines taking up most of the sky. There was a smattering of smaller units dotted around the estate to provide power, water, admin, security, maintenance, storage, waste disposal and construction. And of course, 'Assistance'. Each building was signposted and colour-coded lines were painted on the tarmac so that Cans knew how to navigate the complex without deviating from their assigned paths. Should a Can attempt to enter a building they were not allowed to, their bracelets would trip an alarm and the Stewards would set them straight.

The only exception to this rule was the A.D. Unit. All were welcome here at any time of the day.

This particular morning, a line of Cans was waiting to be seen when the bus from Cornquoy arrived. Sienna barely looked as she got off the bus, so used was she to seeing people waiting to die. Others scanned the line, more out of practicality than pity. Some Cans entered the A.D. Programme wearing better jackets or newer boots than those who stayed behind. Occasionally, the living would approach the dead and ask to trade and more often than not, the dead would oblige. Why not? They couldn't take these things with them. And one last kindness might help them when they came to face Panthea.

But this day, none of the dead had anything worth trading. At least, nothing an outsider could use. But one of the dead waiting in line suddenly found he had something he'd been unaware of until now. Something he thought he'd lost months earlier. Something that propelled him to step out of the line and carry on breathing. If only for a few more minutes.

He had an impetus.

He had a currency of being.

He had a purpose.

And that purpose was busily adjusting her hat as she crossed the tarmac, oblivious to him as he fell in step behind her.

Sienna was unaware of the approaching footsteps or the eyes on her back. The plant was a hive of activity at the best of times. When she entered the bathroom before heading for her station, as she did most mornings, she thought nothing of the Can behind her who did the same.

The bathroom was a vast warren of tiled lanes and doorless cubicles. There were no troughs or urinals in here. The practice of peeing whilst standing up had been declared an act of misogyny years earlier, even in the hinterlands of Gomorrah, so each Can had their own toilet to sit upon. Sienna's preferred cubicle was at the end of the row just off the last aisle. After months of living in Camp 14, she had acquired the art of peeing in public but, given the choice, if an end cubicle was available, she would take it.

Ordinarily, she would not be disturbed. But today someone stopped outside her sanctum and looked in. It was so blatant that she thought he must've been lost. Sex attacks were rare on Orkney but violence was not and plenty of Cans were caught with their pants down.

Sienna had no time to scream. The man rushed at her, muffling her cries with one hand and reaching for her throat with the other. It all happened so quickly that she couldn't make any sense of it. One moment she was unbuttoning her jumpsuit, the next she was fighting for her life. She fell backwards, sliding off the bowl and falling to the floor as she fought to push him away but her attacker fell with her, shifting his hands so that both were now wrapped around her neck. She lashed out with every ounce of strength, kicking at his guts and clawing at his face but he seemed impervious to pain, so driven was he by hate.

She couldn't scream and couldn't breathe. Her arteries pounded against his grip and her face billowed with blood. She tried to pull his hands away but her strength soon failed. She was pinned to the floor with his full weight on top of her. She couldn't move. She couldn't scream. No one was coming to help her. She felt herself becoming woozy. Stars appeared in her mind. Fear engulfed her. Confusion and disbelief. How was this happening? Why was he doing this? Why me? Why now?

Faces flashed before her. Memories of those she had once loved. Geri laughing in the kitchen. Her mother tying her laces. Alicia washing her face after a day in the fields. Kat snuggling under the covers. Verity assuring her that she was one of their own. Julie smiling down at her. And Malek raging from above. Spitting and screaming. Wailing and crying. Hollering and swearing, with murder in his wild eyes.

Malek?

It was Malek.

Meek little Malek.

And he was strangling her to death.

Oh no…

There was nothing she could do.

Nothing but wait.

Yet the end didn't come. She glimpsed it, felt it, even accepted it, but it receded at the last moment, slipping away as the light returned.

She breathed again, coughing and spluttering as a searing pain burned her throat, but she found the air to revive herself and realised she was free. Malek was still with her but no longer on top of her. He was crying uncontrollably and looked a spent force. She kicked him away and he toppled over, lacking even the strength to stay upright.

She scrambled to her feet and jumped over him. She almost stopped to kick him in the head, but upon seeing how pathetic he was, she couldn't bring herself to do it.

He was no longer a threat. He'd tried but failed, lacking the resolve to give her that last little squeeze. She knew the toll such a heinous act could exact, having paid it herself with Bella. But Malek didn't have it in him to finish the job. He lacked the killer instinct. As she always suspected. But far from reviling him, Sienna envied him. Unlike her, he still had his humxnity to cling to. Ironic in the circumstances.

She squatted down beside him, keeping him at a distance just in case she was wrong.

"Malek," she whispered, her voice hoarse from where he'd crushed her windpipe. "I'm sorry."

Malek continued to snivel but his eyes opened and he looked at her without comment.

Sienna continued.

"This is all my fault," she said. "I was wrong to do what I did. I was lost and in a bad place, angry and jealous." The words came surprisingly easy, as if they had always been there, just below the surface, available for when she eventually found a need for them. "You have every right to hate me. What I did to you was unforgivable. I am a terrible person. And I am so sorry. For you and Julie. I deserve to be here. You don't. I can never forgive myself for what I did to you."

"Why are you here?" Malek finally asked. It was a good

question. So Sienna gave Malek the only meaningful answer she could.

"I was an Auditor."

34: GOLD

Malek should not have been on Orkney. Sienna was right about that.

The punishment for technical non-consensual consummation was a custodial sentence and a re-education programme. Not cancellation. Not for a first-time offender.

But Malek's ancestry had counted against him. The fact that his father had a history of domestic violence and his forefathers had excelled in this field too meant that the die had been cast before Malek had even been born. It didn't matter that he'd denounced his father. That became redundant the moment he'd demonstrated intent through his own behaviour. If he was willing to have sex outside of an A6 contract then he was willing to do anything. Non-consensuality was about power. And there were dozens of Governmynt psychologists who were prepared to testify to this.

Then there was Malek's search history. Not content with imposing himself upon Julie unlawfully, he'd joined several 'sex rooms' on the dark net to discuss the matter, conferring over the consequences, the issues around A6 contracts and the various justifications for and against. Malek was a prolific dark net surfer. As a data engineer, he probably knew all the access codes and thought he'd never be found out. But he was found out. The moment the spotlight fell on him, the Guardians took apart every pixel of his digital footprint. His actions denoted a clear and present conspiracy. His defilement of Julie was no longer taken as a spur-of-the-moment act, it became a politically driven desecration of the sanctity of femxle emancipation.

In nature and in deed, he was classified as a *Rapist;* too dangerous to live in an open and free society, and sanctioned for immediate resettlement.

He'd only 'known' Julie physically a couple of times, just enough to consecrate their love. Every happiness had been ratified. Every hope confirmed. But he would never see her again. And that, more than anything else in this bleak and rocky wilderness, had sapped his will to go on.

He and Sienna stood by the sinks alongside each other, neither saying a word but their minds awash with questions. Sienna wondered why she had told Malek about herself when she had previously killed someone to guard her terrible secret. Inwardly, she knew why. She'd needed to purge herself. What she had done to Malek was unforgivable. Not least of all because it had been personal. She accepted that now. So she gave him the power to do likewise. Worse even. It was the only way she could prove her contrition. She hedged her bets and hoped he wouldn't use this knowledge against her but she couldn't be sure. Such was its power.

For Malek, it confirmed his worst fears about Sienna. He saw everything clearly now. Her objections. His heredity. Julie's suspicions. It all clicked into place. The obvious course of action would have been to spread the word. Let others do his dirty work for him and five months ago he would have done just this. But now? What would be the point? It wouldn't set him free, reunite him with Julie or bring closure. It would just bring more pain.

And Malek had endured a lifetime of pain already.

"I once called you Hitler," Malek eventually said. "Worse than Hitler, even. In the food hall, if you remember. Last year."

Sienna didn't. Her old life was a blur and everyone called everyone Hitler back in the real world. It was what people did.

"Do you know who Hitler actually was? What he actually did?"

Sienna had a vague notion but no real idea. Hitler had been some sort of madman who'd gone on the rampage a hundred years earlier (or something like that). There wasn't much about him on the Network and it wasn't a subject that was taught in schools. The lessons of the past had been forgotten. He was just a bogeyman to most, a euphemism for poor behaviour like Peeping Tom or Sweet Fanny Adams. The fact that there had once been a real person called Hitler and he had done terrible things was neither here nor there. Everyone knew what it meant so what did it matter who he was?

After a while, when Malek didn't elaborate, Sienna pressed him on the question.

"Who was he?"

Malek shrugged and shook his head. "We are. We're all Hitler," he said. "Given the right set of circumstances."

Sienna wanted to agree, if only to placate him but she didn't really understand. Malek looked at her one last time, his eyes soft and seeped with regret. "I'm sorry," he muttered barely audibly. "Good luck."

Sienna guessed where he was going. She'd seen that look on too many faces but she wasn't about to take it from him too. She grabbed Malek by the arm and slammed him against the wall with surprising ease. All his strength had left him. He was a shell of a man again.

"No you don't. You're not running out on me like that.

You're going to stay and fight. It's the only way. Fight until your last breath. Fight for life."

They were Alicia's words coming from her lips. She had never understood why Alicia had gone to such lengths to save Mariatou but now she did. It didn't even trouble her that it had backfired on Alicia, she couldn't let Malek give in. He had to go on, if only for another day. Each day was precious. Each day was a victory. Malek being here was Sienna's fault. That made him her responsibility. And she would never be free until Malek was free too. So she shook him by the shoulders, attempting to shake some fight into him. She knew it lay within him. She'd seen it only a few minutes earlier but he seemed dead now, like a rag doll, limp and compliant.

"There's nothing here for me," he said, barely able to lift his eyes. "I can't go on."

"You're right," she agreed. "There is nothing here for you. For either of us. That's why we're going to Sweden."

Malek didn't react. It was like the words bounced right off him but when she repeated them, he looked up and creased his brow. What was she saying? What strange torment was this vile dog pitching? But Sienna was adamant. Where before she'd had a dream, now she had a determination. She was getting off this rock. And Malek was coming with her. Whether he liked it or not.

"There is a way," she promised. "All we need is gold."

Malek still didn't understand but the fire in Sienna's eyes momentarily sparked his own. It seemed inconceivable as a concept. He'd already made his peace with Panthea and was ready to embrace oblivion but here was a last-minute alternative. And from the most unlikely of sources too. Sweden? With sinnysinful2056? Surely anything this improbable was bound to end in failure. But if it did and it all went wrong for Malek, then it would for this wretched girl too. And the chance of seeing her face when her hopes and dreams were dashed was just enough to cause Malek to stick around a little while longer.

"Okay," he said with supreme reluctance. "How?"

They arranged to meet up at the end of their shifts, establishing the last cubicle in the row as their headquarters. But this was all they could agree for now. Sienna was overdue at work. She knew her absence would have been noted so she splashed water down her leg to make it look as if she'd wet herself. For all their gung-ho posturing, S Division Stewards were strangely squeamish when it came to matters of hygiene, particularly the hygiene of Cans who they found repulsive. Malek likewise returned to his duties. He was a bin pusher in charge of delivering materials from the floor to the reclamation units. He was a step closer to the gold than Sienna but still not close enough. They needed to identify someone who worked in mineral recoveries who could be approached.

This job fell to Malek.

It took him about a week before he identified a likely candidate. Jonas was a ruddy-faced man of about 35 (going on 55) who looked as though he'd been on Orkney his whole sorry life. He walked with a stoop, stared with a squint, ate with a drool and suffered from a hearing loss that placed him at a disadvantage to all those around him. Malek took his time, scrutinising everyone who worked in the mineral recoveries unit before deciding that Jonas was their best bet. He wasn't so young as to act rashly or so old as to be institutionalised. He didn't wield or crave power and, by and large, he kept himself to himself. He was little more than a functionary in the process, a cog in the machine and a tiny one at that, but one of his duties was to operate the smelting pots, pouring white-hot liquid gold into the casts for cooling. At this point, the bars were removed and shipped south under armed guard but where there was a will, there was a way.

And Malek soon found a will.

Sienna saved up food each night and Malek used it to gain Jonas's curiosity. After a week of gifting him Sekhmet's veggie broth surprise, Malek invited Jonas to meet Sienna in their office. Jonas may have been susceptible but he was no fool. People didn't hand out charity unless they wanted something in return. And more often than not on Orkney, it was more than a person could afford.

They met in daylight instead, or at least by twilight, on the concourse where the buses arrived at the end of their shifts. They had just enough time to find a spot away from the hustle and bustle to put their offer to him. If he could get them gold, he could come with them to Sweden. They had an 'in' with people traffickers. This was, of course, a lie but Sienna needed to source the gold before she could contact the traffickers.

Jonas squinted at Sienna as she outlined her proposal, reading her lips when he failed to hear her words. He dismissed her offer outright, turning and walking back to his bus without another word. Sienna and Malek feared the worst. They'd made a bad choice and now risked betrayal. Sienna thought they should kill Jonas but she knew Malek would never agree to that and Jonas would probably be too wily anyway. All they could do was brazen it out and expect the worst. Yet the next day came and the Stewards didn't. He hadn't turned them in. Jonas acknowledged Malek when he wheeled his bins past his station but acted as if nothing had passed between them. They figured they'd better keep Jonas sweet so they continued to feed him until eventually, he brought up the subject himself, if only to state how impossible it would be.

Standing at the far end of the unit, away from the other workers and the roar of the furnaces, Jonas grabbed Malek by the wrist and shook his head.

"It can't be done. Every gram must be accounted for."

"But it has been done," Malek said. "Others have found a way."

"Maybe so. But not through me."

A thin choking haze hung over the baths of acid and flux chemicals. Workers wearing breathers stirred the various mixtures while others stoked the smelting pots. Jonas needed to get back to work but not before he had a last word of warning for Malek. "Besides, my crazy young friend, it is not just the Stewards who watch over the gold."

This was the real problem. Corruption was rife but it was handled by more important people than Jonas. Just as in life, so it was on Orkney.

Malek reported back to Sienna when they next met and they decided to keep the lines of communication open. He may have said no but he hadn't said never. There seemed some leeway in his rebuttals. Sienna and Malek synchronised their toilet breaks over the coming weeks and kept the pressure on Jonas, in a non-pressured "hey, we're just having a discussion here" kind of way. Finally, Jonas succumbed and asked, in theory, how much gold they would need for the three of them.

"Three ounces."

"Three ounces!"

Sienna and Malek urged him to shush (the fuck up) and

checked the lay of the land. They'd congregated in Sienna's favourite toilet cubicle and looked distinctively suspicious as a trio. Other Cans came and went but Sienna, Malek and Jonas hung back, whispering urgently and thrashing out the details of their plan to the sounds of ablutions all around.

This was the price quoted by Sekhmet. One ounce of pure gold per person (or 2 ounces of Palladium) plus five years of indentured servitude once they got to Sweden. Jonas was flabbergasted.

"Do you know how long that would take me to collect?"

Sienna didn't so Jonas gave her a quick appraisal. There was around 0.03g of gold in each pair of Smart Glasses. A little more in other devices but as Smart Glasses were their stock-in-trade, this was the calculation Jonas ran with. Therefore, if each pair contained 0.03g and there were 28.3g to an ounce, it would take around 962 pairs of Glasses to make just one ounce. 2886 for three ounces, not allowing for wastage.

"So, we'll round it up to an even three thousand," Jonas suggested.

It sounded like a lot but Sienna stripped back hundreds of devices every week. And there were scores of workers on her bench working 15-hour days.

"But not a milligram must be missed. How much do you think I can conceal each day? A quarter of a gram? Maybe half? All the while doing it under the noses of the Stewards and the other smelters."

Jonas ran his stubby fingers over his shaven crown, gritting his teeth and muttering inaudibly in frustration and anger. Frustration as the task was near impossible. Anger because he knew he would try anyway. He'd been on Orkney a little over three years and in all of that time, he had never been a part of anything. Opportunities like this did not come to people like Jonas. He was an outsider at the plant and at his settlement in Linksness, just as he had been in the real world. This was the reason he was here in the first place, having rashly voiced his frustrations at being overlooked for a promotion that he felt should have been his. Indiscreet and ill-judged certainly. But speculating as to the reasons with the wrong person had been suicidal.

Yet here he was with a skinny wet lesbian and a milkshake Muhammad conspiring to reach the stars. And neither of them had a clue what they were up against. It was hardly the opportunity he'd been dreaming of.

But it was an opportunity.

A slim-to-nothing chance.

A dream.

An escape.

A way off these desolate islands.

A way to start anew.

Away from the noxious fumes. The scalding smelters. And the toxic people.

To see a city again. To see real womyn. To be accepted. And valued. Maybe even loved.

Damn it.

"But you have a way?" Sienna pressed.

Jonas had been thinking about it. Where there was a will. Maybe. If he drilled a small upward divot in the side of the smelting pot when it was cool, it would retain a tiny amount of gold each time he tipped the liquid metal out. His supervisor watched the castings. He always did. Gold was like that. Hypnotic. Then his supervisor would remove the tray and return with an empty one while Jonas got the next batch bubbling. In that moment, Jonas could retrieve his share under the illusion of cleaning his pot and set it aside.

"Will that work?" Malek asked.

"If it doesn't, you will know because you won't see me again," Jonas cautioned.

But they did see him again. The next day. And the day after that. And the day after that. Each day he gave them a signal to show them that all was progressing smoothly. Working this way, he was able to siphon off around a gram a day, swallowing it when it cooled and retrieving it the next morning, a necessary procedure to get past security checks. Jonas had come through. It was slow going but he was doing his part.

Now it fell to Sienna to do hers.

35: KISS

As ever, Sekhmet guided Sienna through the next step of the process. There was no way to get a signal off the islands. Their only hope of contacting the traffickers was to send a message through the Stewards. The prospect horrified Sienna but Sekhmet assured her that some were willing to help.

"Not all see us as unworthy."

Sienna was told to approach a Steward called Assirem. She was to be found stationed outside the A.D. Unit. She could arrange everything.

"For a price."

Duly, the next morning, Sienna stepped off the bus and looked for Assirem. She saw her straight away, just as Sekhmet had described. She couldn't miss her: tall and athletic with a golden complexion and Arabic symbols tattooed around her right eye. Her blue hair was scraped back into a long braided ponytail that matched the shade of her lipgloss. Sienna had seen her before, she was as memorable as she was intimidating, but now she shuddered at the sight of her scanning bracelets and striking out the dead. As fearful as she was, Sienna had no choice but to do as Sekhmet had bid.

She wandered away from the rest of her shift and followed the painted white line across the tarmac to join the soon-to-be departed. If this went wrong and Assirem didn't respond as she hoped, Sienna could find herself with a needle in her arm before the hour was up.

Few looked her way. The decision to seek 'assistance' was each Can's alone. Most got on with their own thin lives. Finality was all around them. Death slept alongside them each and every night. Only Malek reacted with dismay when his bus arrived, looking at Sienna as if the gig was up and the joke was on him. But Sienna flashed him a prearranged signal that spelt out "We go on." He didn't understand but he had to trust her. Trust her and hope that she would still be here at the end of the day to explain.

Sienna would be missed at work. Number 415 would be visible and the Stewards would enquire. But a quick check on the system would reveal her whereabouts. She was entitled to join the A.D. Programme. No one would come looking.

Several others joined the line behind her but Sienna invited them to play through. Her instructions were to be at the very back.

After an hour, Sienna was the last Can standing and held out her bracelet. Assirem lifted her scanner but at the last moment, Sienna snatched her wrist away.

"A last request?" Sienna said nervously, scarcely able to talk she was breathing so hard. Her heart thumped and her mind raced. She'd never been so close to death and yet felt more alive.

Assirem looked down from behind her polished black

Smart Glasses but barely reacted. "Go on."

"A final kiss?"

For the longest time, Assirem said nothing. She just stared at Sienna blankly and Sienna began to worry she'd been set up. People got their amusement in weird places on Orkney. Sport came in all forms. Was this Sekhmet's deadly wheeze? Finally, Assirem replied, lowering both her scanner and her voice.

"How many?"

"Three," Sienna confirmed, her heart skipping a beat.

"When?"

Sienna couldn't be sure. That was down to Jonas but she guessed.

"Six weeks?"

Again, Assirem didn't say anything for a moment but when she did, Sienna panicked.

"Come inside."

Of all the places on Orkney, the A.D. Unit was one place Sienna was in no hurry to explore but Assirem wasn't to be messed around.

"Now or I'll make you come in."

She drew her stun baton to substantiate the threat and grabbed Sienna by the collar before her legs gave way.

"Don't be coy," she smiled, steering Sienna into a building whose sole purpose was to end the lives of all who entered.

A short hall led to frosted glass doors where a second Steward was stationed but Assirem told her Sienna wasn't here for the process. The Steward stepped aside and Sienna and Assirem passed through. The Unit smelled like a hospital with disinfectant and dispassion heavy on the nose. A couple of technicians looked up and were once again assured that Sienna was only here for the tour. A door marked PEACE led to the 'Dignity Suite' while several smaller rooms contained the pharmaceuticals and equipment required to achieve repose. But it was the nondescript door to Sienna's right that Assirem wanted to show her. They went through and Assirem let the door swing shut behind her.

The room was cold and dark. Assirem hit the lights and Sienna saw it was lined with rows of metal shelves. Black biodegradable sacks filled the shelves and the dead filled the bags, tagged and ready for transportation. Sienna recoiled. Or at least, she tried to. Assirem backed her against one of the shelves and towered over her. She was a clear head taller than Sienna, and even taller than Geri. She removed her Smart Glasses and gazed down with striking blue eyes to bewitch and terrify Sienna in equal measure.

"This is where you will find yourself should you speak a word of anything we discuss," Assirem warned her.

"My partners?" Sienna said, almost too scared to bring them up. "The other travellers."

"When the time is right. Until then, you and I are the only bearers of this secret. Do you understand?"

Sienna promised she did. She would have to find a way to reassure Malek and Jonas in a roundabout way but that was the least of her problems. Assirem leaned in closer, pushing Sienna against the shelf until their thighs touched and someone else's elbow pressed into her back.

"You know the price?"

"Three ounces."

"You'll have it on the night. Not a gram less or the boat will go without you. And there will be no second chance."

"I understand," Sienna promised, desperately hoping she'd be able to keep her promise.

Assirem leaned closer still, her hot breath on Sienna's cold face.

"Then let us seal our arrangement with a kiss."

Assirem pressed her blue lips to Sienna's and opened her mouth. Sienna felt powerless to resist, not from pent-up passion. Necking with an Emo when she was worn through with exhaustion and indelible with grot in a room full of corpses was hardly her idea of *amour* but she submitted out of necessity. Assirem could do whatever she wanted to Sienna and she could not object. All that would do was screw things up, so when she felt Assirem's hand pop open her buttons and slide inside her underwear, she gripped her shoulder to feign rapture and kissed the Steward hard as the tears spilt down her cheeks.

But Assirem was no fool. She could sense Sienna's revulsion in every tremble and whimper. The way she fumbled in reply and mistimed her touch. But this was what Assirem had brought her here for. This was the elixir she sought and the thing that stirred her essence like nothing else. A willing partner was no fun. But a vulnerable lamb? A shattered girl so frightened and desperate that she would permit anything? What a drug that was! It was just a shame that Sienna was registered a lesbian. It was better when they were not.

Sienna faked an orgasm and strung it out for as long as she could until Assirem reached her own. When they were done, they buttoned up their overalls and headed for the door.

Assirem slipped on her Smart Glasses and escorted Sienna outside. Sienna had never been so glad to see the overcast Scottish sky again, sliced and diced as it was by enormous turbine blades. Her sudden freedom made her convulse at the thought of their next rendezvous. For Assirem had made one thing clear, 'discussions' would be ongoing until Sienna's departure.

But worse was to come. Assirem had saved the biggest shock for last.

"Two weeks tomorrow."

Sienna was stunned. There was no way they could make that. Jonas had already said he would need three months at least, but Assirem's deadline was not for discussion. A boat was coming. Sienna and her party could reserve a berth on it or make their peace with Orkney.

"It's up to you."

Sienna barely noticed her ever-present hunger and ingrained fatigue that day. Her every thought was consumed by the notion that she'd fucked it all up. She'd got the ball rolling before they had the gold. Now they had a deadline that they couldn't possibly meet and a time-limited offer. She had to meet with Jonas and Malek. She had to talk things through but before she did, she had a mesh of Smart Glasses to disassemble and an hour less in which to do it. She worked fast, ignoring the cramp in her hands and the dizziness in her head, stripping, snipping and clipping until her day's work was done.

414 looked across at her from her station. This was a different 414 to Nora. A new 414. She'd been on Orkney and working alongside Sienna for two weeks but Sienna hadn't even asked her name. What difference did it make? She was 414. That was all Sienna needed or wanted to know.

414 saw that Sienna was done when she still had eleven pairs on the bench before her. She caught Sienna's eye and motioned towards them.

"I've got the runs," Sienna replied and quick-timed it to the bathroom.

Malek and Jonas were already there and Malek breathed a

sigh of relief at seeing Sienna again. He soon sucked it back when Sienna told him the bad news. Jonas was distraught. There was no way they could collect that much gold in such a short space of time. It had taken him almost ten days to collect a little under half an ounce. It was simply impossible to siphon off more and faster.

"Then we'll have to steal it," Sienna said, a prospect that Jonas assured them was suicidal.

"There must be a way," Malek pressed.

"The moment it is missed, they will scour the island. Missing Cans is one thing. Missing gold is another," Jonas insisted, sweating harder in the cool dank restroom than he did against the glare of his smelter.

"We'll be gone by then," Sienna promised him. "All we need is a headstart. Think."

Jonas thought. He thought about it on the bus back to Linksness. He thought about it over his meagre meal. He even thought about it while he slept that night so that by the time they met again, he had the core of a terrible idea.

But a terrible idea was better than no idea at all.

"There might be a way," he told them.

For the next two weeks, Jonas continued to do what he was doing, siphoning off as much as he could to minimise the amount he would have to steal. He reasoned he could finish the ounce he was collecting by the deadline which meant he would need to steal two ounces to meet the balance.

Two ounces?

Two whole ounces.

They were never going to get away with it but what choice did they have? It was do-or-die time.

Meanwhile, Sienna found herself at the short end of Assirem's yoke. The Steward didn't yank it every day. Just when

Sienna least expected it. Midway through a shift. First thing in the morning. And once, off the bus back to Cornquoy last thing at night, seeing her home via an S Division transport afterwards. Malek felt like a fifth wheel by comparison but he put himself in charge of gathering supplies. Extra clothes. Dried food for the journey. A makeshift shank crafted from hardened plastic. Should they need it.

All too quickly the day arrived. The preparations had focussed their minds but everything came down to this moment. Jonas confirmed he had an ounce. He would now put into effect his plan to get the rest.

He waited until the end of the day to give those in charge the smallest window to notice the theft. This was the moment of truth. He'd run through the plan a hundred times in his mind and sometimes it went smoothly, sometimes it went wrong. He couldn't even control his own imagination. What chance did he have of affecting reality?

He poured the last of his day's gold into the casts before him. There were three casts per moulding and each required precision to fill. A top plate would then be pressed onto the hot metal, stamping each bar with the weight and the Orkney crest. In this instance, each bar weighed exactly one ounce. There would be a tiny residue of overspill. There always was but it would be reconstituted into the next bar so that not a drop was lost. In theory.

With the top plate in place, Jonas moved his pot back to the furnace when his hands slipped and he dropped the pot onto the moulds. The steel castings went flying and the air filled with sparks. The supervisor turned to protect his eyes and Jonas tripped over the forge in an attempt to grab everything. He fell to the ground along with the red-hot metal and an almighty clatter resonated throughout the unit.

The castings came apart and the newly forged bars spilled out. Jonas instinctively grabbed one but let out a scream when the gold seared his flesh. He recoiled and stuffed his hand into a nearby water bucket while the supervisor glared at him in contempt.

"Idiot," he sneered.

The three bars lay on the ground and the supervisor used a pair of grips to pick them up. He placed them back in their castings and glared down at Jonas, still cradling his burnt hand.

"Tidy this lot up," he said. "And get that hand seen to." With more care than Jonas, the supervisor now carted the gold away.

Or rather, some of the gold.

Only one of the bars was pure. The other two were lead. Jonas had cast them earlier in the week. There was no shortage of lead in the mineral recoveries unit and he had every chemical needed to plate them. It had taken a little guile but he'd managed to recreate two near-perfect replicas. All he needed was a ruse to switch them.

He'd rehearsed every action, every detail and every scenario until there had been nothing left to work out. The supervisor had been momentarily distracted by the mayhem. And Jonas's reactions had sold the ploy. Hence, when the supervisor saw three gold bars lying on the floor, he'd naturally assumed they'd come from the castings. But two of the bars were under the forge, having been knocked there in the blink of an eye by Jonas's boot. When the supervisor was gone, he sloshed the water across the floor to cool them off and retrieved them with his 'wounded' hand.

Now came the riskiest part. He approached the Steward at the exit, cradling his hand as if it were agony. The Steward was highly amused by Jonas's stupidity. He demanded to see the injury for himself and Jonas reluctantly obliged, wincing as he showed him the angry burn that urgently needed treating.

"Dumb asshole. Go on, get."

Jonas hurried along, supposedly to the infirmary, a small and basic treatment office that was reserved for only the most serious injuries. But Jonas hurried straight past, out of the unit and towards the restroom. His hand was fine. He'd stained it with potassium permanganate earlier that day and hadn't touched anything he shouldn't have.

At least, anything he hadn't meant to.

It was the oldest trick in the book. Passing lead for gold. 17th-century counterfeiters flooded many a Kingdom with it. So much so that innkeepers would bite any tender to check its authenticity. Gold and silver would not yield but lead was soft. It was also lighter, almost by half. The illusion would not last long. The first time the shipment was weighed the fraud would be discovered. But a shipment wasn't sent every day. If Panthea was smiling down upon them, she might just toss them a few hours to kiss this place goodbye.

Sienna could have kissed Jonas when he showed her the bars. She could've but she didn't, having had rather too much of that just lately. These bars, together with the gold Jonas had stashed in Linksness, would be enough to buy their way off this rock. What would happen when they got to Sweden? Sienna didn't know. But whatever it was, it had to be better than here.

36: TRAFFIC

The hour arrived. And that hour was 10pm.

The rest of Cornquoy was sleeping but Sienna was wide

awake. She'd lain in the pitch black listening to everyone drift off, terrified that she might fall asleep too, that her fatigue might get the better of her and she'd miss her chance to escape, but there was no danger of that. She was too psyched to succumb.

When she was sure all was quiet, she slipped from her bed and snuck out into the night. She took with her a few extra clothes but left everything else behind. She had a long walk ahead of her, over mostly rough ground. And in the dark too. She had to travel light. But the omens were good. The night was clear and the stars were out. With a little effort she was able to find the path that led to her destination, the easternmost point of Orkney Mainland. A rocky bluff called The Brough of Deerness. There, in the shelter of a small pebble beach, a motor launch would pull up at around 2am and ferry them out to a boat anchored off-shore.

It was a three-hour walk but she had four hours to do it in.

Jonas was closer in Linksness, just across the bay from Deerness. But Malek had much further to come, from Greenigoe, some 15 miles west. He knew he wouldn't cover that distance in time so he'd stayed behind at the recycling plant, hiding in the pipe room until the coast was clear so that he could set out from there. It was five miles closer and on the main road but with the Steward barracked nearby, the risks were greater. Sienna wondered what she would do if Malek failed to arrive. Would she get on the boat and try to forget him? Or would she stay true to her word and stick with him come what may? She didn't know. And, as she tramped across the muddy overgrown meadow, she hoped and prayed she wouldn't find out.

Her primary concern was her steel bracelet. It radiated her metadata and position. At any time, day or night, the Stewards could see exactly where she was. And although Cans had greater autonomy on Orkney than those in the camps, this did not include going for midnight strolls miles from their settlements. But Assirem had assured her it would be taken care of. The system would be blindsided with a patch. It would look like a temporary glitch but by the time it reset, they would be miles out to sea.

All she could do was trust Assirem. Others had paid the piper and got away from here. Nora had never been caught. Nor had any of the others Assirem had helped. Unlike poor Tilly.

This could work.

This had to work.

Sienna became disoriented for a time. It was so dark that all she could see was the pitch-black outline of land against the pitted curtain of night. She could hear waves crashing to her right and the whoosh-whoosh-whoosh of giant props to her left. There was a turbine directly north of Cornquoy and she knew if she stayed right of it eventually, she would come to Deerness. After an hour of walking, she crossed the isthmus as Dingieshowe and found the road that led towards the Brough. There were several settlements on Deerness but Sienna moved quickly and quietly, encountering no one as she hurried through the night.

She had no idea what time it was but couldn't shake the sense that she was late. It was easier going by road and she was able to alternate between jogging and marching. She didn't have the energy for anything else but finally she reached the end of the road. Tarmac gave way to dirt track. She followed the hedgerows north, always keeping the sea to her right until the waves echoed from all sides, north, east and west. She'd reached the Brough, the site of a medieval chapel, now no more than ruins. The wind coming off the sea was fiercer here and robbed her of her senses. The cliffs fell away to the waves below and the steps she had been told to find were lost to the darkness.

Where was everyone?

She inched her way around the cliff edge and peered down. Only rocks, water and darkness lay below her but further along the coast, she caught a glimpse of a flashlight. Hope renewed, she felt her way back to the path and headed towards the light. As she got closer, a torchlight picked her out and a voice called to her from the darkness.

"Who goes there?"

Classic.

"*Einherjar*," Sienna replied, giving the code word she'd been told to give. The *Einherjar* of Norse mythology were the dead who'd fallen in battle, collected by the Valkyries and brought to Valhalla to serve at Odin's court. It all seemed a little Swedish for Sienna's liking but she was happy to play along for the sake of appearances.

"Approach."

The torchlight dropped from her face and lit the path she was to follow.

"What time is it?" she asked when she reached the man who'd challenged her. It was just after 1am, he told her. He didn't have an accent. Sienna had been expecting a Swede but the man sounded Britannic. He noted her confusion and reassured her.

"Seven years ago, I was standing where you are," he said, urging her to follow the track until she found a set of steps carved into the cliffside.

His disclosure excited Sienna. His very presence proved that there was life after Orkney. What's more, if he was willing to risk it and return to help others, it must've been worth fighting for. Sienna wasn't sure she would be brave enough to do that. Once she was gone, she would stay gone. She never wanted to see this place again but it inspired her that others had the courage and were prepared to gamble everything.

The stone steps were slippery and invisible against the black of night. But another torchlight beckoned her down so she felt her way to the bottom until her feet sank into pebbles.

There were around twenty people down here, most of them Cans and a couple dressed in black fleeces and wearing Smart Glasses. A launch had been pulled ashore but Sienna could see no signs of the main boat it had come from. It was too dark and was at anchor without its lights blazing away.

One of the traffickers approached Sienna when she joined the party.

"Wrist," he said without ceremony.

Sienna offered him her wrist. He held a magnetic key to her bracelet and removed it with the click of a button. Easy as that.

"You have a key," she said in wonder, having assumed they would have to use bolt cutters or an angle grinder to take them off.

"Friends in high places," the trafficker laughed, slipping Sienna's bracelet into his pocket and trudging down the beach. Indeed, Assirem must have supplied the key but where was she? Sienna assumed she would be here but she wasn't. That was a relief. The violations she had suffered at her hands had been an excessive price to pay but it was over now. All that was left was for her to find Jonas and Malek and for the three of them to hand over the gold.

As if on cue, Jonas emerged from the crowd. He was

smiling with excitement and hugged Sienna instinctively. She embraced him in return although she would have rather waited for once they were at sea.

"You've got it?" she asked, miming what she meant when he didn't hear.

"Three ounces," he confirmed. "I can't believe it. Thank you."

"No, thank you," she said, embracing him again while looking back up at the cliffs for signs of Malek.

"Don't worry, he'll be here."

But Jonas's confidence seemed misplaced because soon enough the traffickers began inviting Cans to step forward. The launch was only big enough to take six at a time so Sienna hung back to give Malek every chance. The first party set off, along with three traffickers, chugging out to sea while the last trafficker stayed on the beach in the vanguard.

The group waited anxiously for the launch to return. It seemed to take an age but finally, almost half an hour later, they heard it chugging back through the surf and mooring against the pebbles with a crunch.

"Okay, next six. Let's go."

The traffickers took the gold as they ticked each person off. Jonas watched in wonder. Siphoning must have been more rampant than he could've ever imagined. The next party climbed aboard and embarked upon the final leg of their journey with a helping shove.

Yet still there was no sign of Malek. He should have been here by now. The recycling plant was some distance away but he'd surely had enough time to make it. Had he got lost in the darkness? Had he been caught by Stewards? Sienna wanted to go up the steps and look for him but the trafficker was adamant. No one was to go wandering off in the dark. Not now they were underway.

She remembered how she hadn't been able to find the steps when she'd first arrived. How the long black coastline had all looked the same. If Malek was in the same position, they needed to send him a sign but the traffickers were adamant. They had a schedule to keep.

The yearning she felt to see Malek was the same she had felt for Kat. For Alicia. For Geri. Even for Julie. She'd always clung to people when she felt lost. It was a bad habit of hers but she told herself it was for the right reasons this time. She had to get Malek free. It was her fault he was on Orkney. Only she could set him free. And vice versa.

Of course, she had assisted in the cancellation of dozens of people while at Geniture. Hundreds even. More than she could bear to imagine. And she had done so diligently and efficiently because she had believed in the system. She had been a willing and effective part of it. The system could not have functioned without her. Her and hundreds like her. She was the system. But the system had lied to her. It had lied to them all.

No, that wasn't true. That was Sienna trying to mitigate again.

The system hadn't lied. It had merely reshaped the truth and Sienna had moulded herself to accept it. Because she had been a part of that truth. That glorious and wonderful truth. And all those who weren't, all those who had challenged the ideals or decried them as false were weeded out and dispatched to the hostels, the camps and the islands to cleanse the pure and inclusive narrative of New Britannia.

Sienna couldn't turn back the clock. She couldn't help those she'd condemned. That was her reality and her burden. It was also her penance. But she could help Malek. She could right one wrong. Earn his forgiveness. And in doing so, one day, many years from now, maybe she could even forgive herself.

But she was running out of time.

The launch returned and the penultimate six climbed aboard. That left just four of them on the beach. If Malek didn't arrive in the next thirty minutes, he'd be stuck here on Orkney.

Sienna waved one of the gold bars above her head, hoping it might glint against the starlight, but it was way too dark for that down in the shadows of the bag. The wind roared and the waves crashed yet nothing else stirred out there in the darkness. All too soon the trafficker took the gold from her and pointed out to shoreline.

"Your carriage awaits," he said, bowing with faux chivalry.

Sienna saw the launch bobbing through the breakers, empty but for the Valkyries who'd come to ferry them into the next life.

"We have to go," Jonas told her. "We'll use the other ounce in Sweden. It will help us when we get there."

The launch crashed up the beach and the vanguard pulled it ashore.

"Okay. Sweden next stop."

Two Cans climbed in, followed by Jonas, each handing over their gold as they stepped aboard. But Sienna hung back, desperately willing Malek to appear. He had to. He had to come.

She felt a hand on her arm and herself being pulled in the direction of the launch.

"It's time to go," the man said.

She stared up at him, catching a glimpse of her despair in his silver Smart Glasses. The Trafficker didn't need his night vision mode to see that something was wrong. She was distraught and broken, pleading for him to wait one more minute but he was determined to stick to the timetable, not least of all when those in the launch started shouting.

"We have to go."

Half stumbling, half dragged, Sienna was helped into the launch and the vanguard got ready to push them off. She felt the land slip away from beneath her and the bow rise against the sea when suddenly she heard it. A voice. A man crying in the darkness.

Sienna jumped up and almost fell overboard.

"Stop," she said. "He's there."

The traffickers looked at each other so Sienna pointed.

"He's on the beach now. Please, we have to go back for him."

For one terrible moment, she thought they weren't going to but at last, the rudder was turned and the launch headed back. Sure enough, there was Malek alongside the vanguard waving his arms about frantically. He'd made it. By the skin of his teeth, he had got here in time.

The launch crashed ashore and Sienna jumped out. She ran to Malek and leapt into his arms, crushing him with all of her might.

"I thought you weren't coming," she cried, so relieved to see him that she had been rendered blind to everything else.

"You can't get rid of me that easily," he smiled and they hugged on the shoreline, up to their knees in surf.

"Okay, lovebirds. Let's go," the vanguard said, directing them back to the launch.

Only now, with Malek by her side and her fears assuaged, did the scales slip from her eyes, helped in no small way when the vanguard slapped her on the back and said:

"It's okay, relax, we take care of our people."

37: WATER

It had started as a sick joke. A play on S Division's unofficial motto.

We take care of our people.

Sienna heard it from Verity Abebe at Windsor House. "Our people" had come to adopt a dual meaning. Primary, it meant fellow S Division staffers. To S Division, these were "our people". And S Division took care of its own. But a second interpretation came to mean Cans and *Rapists*. The enemies of New Britannia. These were also "our people". And it was S Division's job to "take care of them".

Some officers started saying it before eliminating a target. It was regarded in poor taste but not discouraged. That would have been bad for morale.

Sienna now saw what everyone else had missed. The last trafficker had stayed ashore to keep watch. He hadn't climbed into the launch to rejoin the main boat.

Because there was no main boat.

There was no Sweden.

These were not traffickers.

These were S Division, possibly rogue, certainly armed, duping desperate Cans into stealing gold for them. All that stuff about indentured servitude and five years of work? That was window-dressing to sell the scam. No one would have believed it if they'd promised puppies and kittens and happily ever afters. But a little more drudgery then freedom? Who wouldn't want that? It also explained the magnetic key. These pieces of equipment were guarded like magic Hobbit rings. They imprinted the number of the operator onto each bracelet and had to be registered within the system in which they functioned. No genuine Stewards would have handed theirs over to a bunch of Swedish pirates.

The more Sienna looked, the more she remembered her S Division training, particularly concerning cover stories and world-building, entrapment and counterinsurgency.

Everyone else was looking out to sea trying to spot the boat but Sienna was looking back at the ferrymen. More particularly, at the stun batons on their utility belts. There were coils of rope at their feet and lead weights too. Once they'd got beyond the shallows, maybe a mile or two, they would be beyond sight and sound of land. No one would ever know. Or see them again.

Sienna grabbed Malek and pulled him close.

"They're going to kill us. We've got to go."

Malek looked at her in shock, his eyes wide and confused. "What?"

"Now," Sienna shouted, grabbing Malek by the arm and a buoy that had lain by her feet, dragging both over the side as she leapt from the boat.

The bitter shock of cold knocked the breathe right out of her and the darkness disorientated her so that she couldn't tell up from down, heaven from hell. But the buoy did its job and took her back to the surface where she found Malek coughing and spluttering. She struck out for him and they came together, each grabbing the buoy in an attempt to keep their heads above the waves.

Voices in the darkness called to them and a torch beam searched the waters. But the launch's momentum and the headland currents had already put some distance between them. Now Sienna started to kick in a desperate attempt to increase it.

"What are you doing?" Malek spluttered, frozen in shock just moments after basking in the warm glow of freedom.

"They're dead. They're all dead," Sienna half-replied half-spluttered as a huge wave surged over them.

"Who?" Malek asked when they resurfaced.

"Everyone."

A terrible realisation now hit Sienna. This would include Jonas. He'd been so trusting they had led him right into it. But what else could she have done? She couldn't have warned Jonas and the others. They had no weapons to fight with and no defences against stun batons. They would have been shocked, trussed up and dumped overboard along with everyone else the moment they'd shown their hand. They had to go when they did, without deliberation, without warning. They had to catch the traffickers by surprise. To have delayed by even a second would have meant death.

"How could you know?"

Malek still clung on to hope. She had to be wrong. It had to be a misunderstanding. No one could be that evil. That avaricious. In a minute they'd be picked up and they'd all have a good laugh about this back in Sweden.

But she hadn't been wrong.

And when the first gunshots rang out, Malek knew it too.

"We're gonna kill you," came the accompanying threat. *"Dirty fucking Cans."*

The shots went well wide. Not even close. They couldn't see them. They were probably shooting at every wave that looked like a swimmer.

Torchlights and more bullets swept the water, several coming perilously close before sweeping wide again. Sienna and Malek were practically invisible in the inky black sea. The only thing that gave them away was the white buoy which they now relinquished. They carried on kicking, their clothes dragging at their limbs as they fought their way through the water but the strong current kept them afloat and powered them towards the coast.

After an exhausting struggle in freezing waters, Sienna felt her foot touch shingle. But she didn't have time to get a toe hold. The crashing waves dragged her headwards, over bruising pebbles and jagged rocks, cutting her hands and battering her legs. When it relinquished, the waters turned back and almost pulled her out again, but she clung on with every fibre of her being until she was able to crawl onto land. Malek was rolling in the surf, unable to stand and struggling to reach a footing but Sienna couldn't do anything for him, she was lame with fatigue and frozen to the core. After several torrents, the waves deposited him onto the pebbles and left him there gasping for air. Sienna inched her way across to help him out of the surf.

"Hide."

That was all she could say. Her mind was still swimming even though she was not and her mouth would hardly move. But they forced themselves to put one foot in front of another and staggered ashore to discover sheer cliffs barred their way on all sides. They'd landed in a rocky cove and there seemed no way up. Out there on the water, the launch swept backwards and forwards, directing its lights across the waves while a new threat sounded from above. The voice of the final 'trafficker', running along the cliff edge scanning the surf with his torch.

Sienna found a small fissure in the rocks, so tiny that it could not be called a cave, but she and Malek were able to squeeze inside.

Their hunters would be scanning with night and thermal imagers but after being in the water for so long, the escapees bore little heat.

They lay between the cracked rocks and the wet sand and

tried not to move. Tried not to scream. Tried not to breath. How long they lay there, huddled together for warmth and awaiting the inevitable, neither knew but they each drifted in and out of consciousness for most of the night until Sienna came to and realised it was dawn. At first, she couldn't move. She was paralysed with cold and her body was battered, but slowly she forced her limbs to comply until she was able to crawl out into the sun.

The launch was gone. As was the 'trafficker' above having assumed they'd drowned and given up. In the morning they would be indistinguishable from any other Steward, shocked and bewildered when twenty Cans were reported missing to Orkney control.

Sienna and Malek didn't have long. Just a couple of hours until the balloon went up. In this state, they would almost certainly be caught. And what then? Sienna could tell the authorities what happened, the conspiracy and the murder ring. But knowing S Division as she did, it would all be hushed up. A few bad apples, that was all.

S Division took care of its people.

Her jumpsuit was soaked through, filled with grit and as heavy as lead. She wouldn't get far in it. She tried to undo her buttons and untie her laces but her fingers wouldn't work. Malek came to her aid and they helped each other strip to their vests. Back in the fissure they dug a hole and buried their clothes in the sand. They were even colder now but at least they were lighter.

"We need to be quick."

Not far from here was St Ninians, a small settlement overlooking a sandy beach half a mile south. Sienna had passed it the previous night and remembered seeing washing on the line. If they were to have any hope of staying alive, they would need dry clothes.

They hurried through the early mists of dawn, picking their way around the coastline and finding a track up into the meadow. Breakfast was cooking in St Ninians but the settlement still slept. They took what they needed from the line and hurried away, dressing in the fields once clear. The only thing they couldn't get were dry boots so they were forced to wear their own, albeit with a change of socks.

"Where are we going?"

It was a good question but Sienna didn't have a good answer. She couldn't return to Cornquoy and pretend nothing had happened. Even if Sekhmet hadn't been in on the murder plan, she was still complicit and would kill Sienna to protect herself. Assirem would also try to silence her. And then there were the rogue Stewards who'd run the operation. There was no going back to the lives they had fought so hard to flee.

Likewise, they had very little chance of staying at large. They were alone on a small rocky island with no food or shelter and no way off. And before long, every drone on Orkney would be searching for them. Weighing up their options, Sienna saw that they really only had one chance.

"We have to go back to the Brough."

Malek thought it was madness but Sienna had a hunch. If the rogue Stewards were part of the search, the one place they wouldn't want scrutinised too closely would be the beach where it had all happened. Maybe they'd steer the investigation away from it. Say they'd cleared it. Perhaps that's where they stashed their launch. Either way, it a was rocky and isolated locale, probably the reason they had chosen it in the first place.

Sure enough, they found several small caves in the cliffs

near the Brough and were able to squeeze out of sight. A few hours later, they heard the buzz of a passing drone and a few hours after that, saw a ship on the horizon following the coastline. The long arm of S Division had indeed turned out but they had two things going for them. Firstly, when Cans had previously fled for 'Sweden', no sign of the escapees had ever been found. S Division would almost certainly follow the same protocol; a 48-hour intensive search before registering them as missing, presumed dead at sea. The second thing they had in their favour was their unencumbered wrists. So much of S Division's security relied upon the steel ID bracelets. Without them, they were invisible to the system.

As hungry as they were, they stayed put and counted off the hours by unpicking the high-vis stripes from their jumpsuits. The only other thing they could do was sleep. It helped pass the time and preserved their strength but for the most part, it eluded them, tormented as they were by hunger and thirst. On the second morning, they snuck up to the meadow and sucked the dew from the long grass. It wasn't much but it was better than nothing. The second day went slower and was beset by rain. They stayed in the cave to preserve their dry clothes but positioned shells to catch water.

Another drone passed overhead, this one scanning the bluff. Malek prayed to Panthea. He wasn't a believer but it was the only thing he could do. Sienna closed her eyes, listening for the pitch of the buzzing to change. She daren't look. Her hot head would have been spotted from above. Instead, she watched Malek pray and joined in with an *Ah-non* at the end.

The drone moved on and the night eventually came. They endured more hours of discomfort and bad dreams but at last, the third and final morning arrived. The search would be called off today. Malek was the first to wake. He sat in the cave and watched the sun peak over the horizon before shaking Sienna from her slumber.

"It's light. What do you think?"

"We wait."

It was still only about 5am. The search would progress for 48 hours. That meant drones would keep flying until 7am, the hour the Cans would have been reported missing. Until then, they had to sit tight. They had no way of telling the time. No way of knowing if it was safe. All they could do was watch the sun and make sure they didn't go early.

The morning felt different to the previous morning. Probably psychological. They felt freer. More alive than before. Alone. When finally they adjudged the hour passed, they crawled from their hiding spot and climbed up to the meadow. All looked quiet. Nothing in the air or out to sea. Just the wind and the waves and the ever-circling seagulls squawking from above. If their luck held, they would be able to go about the island with relative freedom.

But go where? And do what? That was another matter.

Sienna had the makings of a terrible idea but first thing was first. They were starved.

The mists had evaporated and the winds were light. Patches of blue sky followed them across the terrain as they snuck back to St Ninians, keeping to the hedgerows and watching for signs of movement. No one was home. The buses must have taken everyone to the plant. Only the cook would be there, gathering roots and fungi for tonight's culinary delights. They hid behind a stone wall several fields away and watched and waited. Jumpsuits blew on the line and a couple of optimistic gulls patrolled the picnicking area but nothing else moved amongst the shipping containers. They kept vigil for the longest possible time, holding their bellies but loathed to blow their cover, not after all they'd been through.

"It looks clear," Malek said, but just as they were about to go, a lone figure emerged from one of the containers. The shock almost poleaxed them but they squeezed behind the wall and held their breath, half-terrified that he was coming to confront them. But the man carried on by, oblivious to their presence, and disappeared across the fields as he scoured nature's larder.

Once gone, Sienna and Malek jumped the wall and sprinted to the settlement, quenching their thirsts in the barrels and gorging whatever dried foods they could find. They knew the theft would be noticed but cooks from rival settlements sometimes stole from each other. Cans were little better than rats, after all. And it wouldn't be reported. Cans did not talk to the Stewards. Not unless they could help it.

They took what they could and headed south, sticking to the beach as they crossed the isthmus and hurrying from shrub to bush.

"Wait, this is the road I came along," Malek said, stopping when he realised their direction of travel. "If we follow this road, we'll come to the recycling plant."

Sienna was aware of what lay ahead. Five miles up this road was Kirkwall Recycling Plant, the busiest and most industrious place on the island, home to the Stewards' barracks and the administration centre for the whole of the archipelago.

"That's where we need to go," she said without explaining. She hadn't told him why as she hadn't wanted to freak him out but her terrible idea lay in this direction. Now was the time to share it.

"We can't hide forever. They'll find us," Sienna said. "But I know how we can get off this island."

"By nicking more gold?" Malek demanded, having had enough of Sienna's plans for one week.

Sienna could scarcely bring herself to tell him. It sounded so ludicrous but the theory was sound, if somewhat fatalistic.

"No," she said, "by being dead."

38: DEATH

Cremations were outlawed twenty years earlier. The burning of the dead was a major pollutant. Cremating just one body required 2-3 hours of incineration at between 760-980 degrees Celsius, creating a carbon footprint of around 180kg, the same as a 600-mile car journey in an old petrol vehicle. Even with a drop in the population, there were still 50 million people in New Britannia. With a death rate of 1% per annum, the resulting cremations would pump out 88,000 metric tons of carbon dioxide each year.

Not a principle worth dying for.

More senseless was the waste. The average body contains a rich variety of nutrients; essential vitamins and minerals that could help replenish the land and propel the circle of life. Some viewed the disposal of these nutrient-rich sacks as an ecological crime, no different from food waste or fly-tipping. Therefore, Charity GoodHope ruled that only carbon-positive funerals would be permitted going forward, with woodland burials becoming the norm and agricultural liquidation and disbursement becoming the progressive choice for the truly committed. Where once, relatives would gather around a hole and lament as their loved ones were lowered into it, now they could congregate in a field and sing songs as they were blown out of a tractor.

Not ideal when the wind changed direction.

Sienna had tried to take in everything on her visits to the A.D. Unit. Every sign, every door, every switch and vent. Anything that could take her mind off Assirem's intrigues. It was during one such assignation that Sienna's eye fell upon the tags of the bags awaiting collection. The label said: 'Akran Forest'. She'd not heard of Akran Forest but all the bags were similarly tagged.

Sienna made a point of asking Sekhmet about Akran Forest but she'd not heard of it. "It's not on Orkney if you're looking for somewhere to hide," she laughed. "These rocks won't support a forest."

Which meant one thing. Akran Forest was on the mainland.

Getting into the plant was easier than getting out. Malek led the way, guiding Sienna along the coastline and around the perimeter. There was no barbed wire or locked gates to bypass. A few Stewards patrolled to dissuade malingering workers but otherwise, the plant was wide open. Everything was digital and the bracelets kept control. Sienna and Malek found somewhere to wait out the clock and closed their eyes.

Once dark, they crept into the plant and made their way past the maintenance shed and the chemical stores to the A.D. Unit. Again, access was unnervingly easy. Had they been wearing bracelets, any door they were not permitted to enter would have locked automatically upon approach but as they weren't wearing any, they could access any area they wished.

"This is what happens when you get too reliant on technology," Malek whispered as they pulled apart the frosted glass.

"Maybe you should apply as a security advisor?"

"I don't think so," Malek glowered, only too happy to

leave them with their Achilles heel. "They've probably got an app for it anyway."

The A.D. Unit was deserted. By the living at least.

The lights were off and the shutters were down. The Dignity Suite was silent for the night. Against her better judgment, Sienna needed to see the room for herself, her mind awry with memories of Alicia. For a place of such foreboding, the room itself was strangely sterile, more like a dentist's surgery than a chamber of death. The walls were painted a calming magnolia and adorned with mindful quotations stencilled in friendly fonts.

Peace is found in quiet minds

Pain ends but love is eternal

A raindrop falls for one precious moment but lives in the land always

There are no ends, only new beginnings

A padded surgical chair dominated the room, inclined to face a screen above. Straps hung from the arms and footrests and an assortment of spigots and valves protruded from the base. Tubes and cables would have normally run from these portals but none had been left overnight.

Sienna approached the chair and touched the upholstery. Her eyes welled and her blood rose. How many had lain here and slipped away? How many were yet to come?

"I found food," Malek said behind her.

Sienna turned, unable to stand this place another second, her eye falling upon one last quotation as she left.

Smile when you say goodbye and you'll always be remembered as smiling

Sienna wanted to trash this room but knew this would trash their hopes if she did. She wiped the tears from her eyes and left the suite, following Malek into an ante-room yonder.

They had a long journey ahead of them and very little strength to see them through. Malek had rummaged the cupboards looking for sustenance and he had hit the jackpot with a store of dried fruit, chickpea crisps and a litre of oat milk in the medical fridge. There was also tea and coffee, the herbal and turmeric varieties, and an entire apothecary of pharmaceuticals. They took what they needed without going overboard. It was one thing to rob their own but another to do it to Stewards. They could not let anyone know they'd been in here, as tempting as it was to burn the whole place down.

"Okay, let's go," Malek said, scared witless but knowing they were faced with no other choice. "Let's be dead."

He headed to the mortuary while Sienna ran one last eye over the drugs available. They might not always have access to food but a few amphetamines could help them paper over the cracks. She took a few from each vial, knowing she was running a risk but determined not to be caught wanting. The amphetamines must have been for the Stewards, to help them stay alert. The rest were barbiturates and neuromuscular relaxants, potions of 'dignity'. Sienna wanted to tip them away but knew she couldn't, not without alerting the Stewards to their presence, so she replaced the vials and joined Malek in the mortuary.

She found him gawping at the bagged and tagged bodies, afraid to go near them or touch anything. She threw him a biodegradable black sack and told him to try it for size.

"And find a bunk."

They cleared a couple of shelves so that they could lie together then got into their bags. They were already tagged 'Akran Forest'. All they needed to do was lie back and enjoy the ride.

"This is never going to work," Malek said, shaking his head as he zipped it up from the inside. The bags were airtight so Sienna advised him not to zip it all the way, not unless he was a method actor.

"Stay calm."

Neither slept. On cold steel shelves in the middle of a dormitory of the damned, it would have been impossible and both got up from time to time to stretch their legs.

When the technicians finally came, they almost caught Sienna and Malek by surprise. They heard the glass doors swish open and voices passing by outside. As quickly as they could, they laid down, zipped up their bags and played dead. They'd punched a few air holes into the underside of the bags where they were less likely to be seen and hoped that would be enough.

Now they waited.

Noises started next door and music began to play, ambient and hypnotic. The day's work had begun. Twenty minutes later, the first of today's clients was brought in. The technicians unlocked their bracelet, stripped them, bagged them and put them on the shelf behind Sienna. Thirty minutes later, they came in with their next customer and repeated the process.

Sienna and Malek could do nothing but lie in silence as the shelves filled up around them. There seemed no let-up, no pause. Sienna didn't even try to count. She didn't want to keep a tally. They weren't just numbers to her. These were people, with lives and families and dreams of their own. Now silenced forever. Once again, tears welled in her eyes but she was unable to wipe them away. She couldn't move. Even when the mortuary was quiet, she couldn't risk being seen.

She lost all sense of time and space and, at one point,

drifted off in a haze of suffocation. She came to with a start and tore open the bag from inside, coughing and spluttering for cold clean air. No one heard her and she resumed her deception before anyone did.

How long the day went on, she had no idea. But the mortuary was considerably fuller at the end of the day than when she and Malek had first arrived. Eventually, she heard a technician enter and start scanning tags. She had a sudden panic that he would find no details for her on the system. But the scanner beeped as normal and he moved on to the next tag without a beat. She was officially dead.

A short while later, she heard a whole new bunch of noises. They sounded like wheels on tiles coming and going. The dead were on the move. This was the moment she had been waiting for but still, nothing prepared her for the shock of being picked up and dumped unceremoniously onto a cart. A body lay beneath her and another was dumped on top before she was wheeled through the corridors, down a ramp and outside to a waiting transport.

It was sickeningly disorientating. The motion terrified her and made her nauseous but she could not move or tense. She remained as limp and absorbed the lumps when they came, finding herself piled into the back of the transport in the middle of a stack of others.

"That's fifty," she heard someone say. "How many are left?"

"Ten, I think."

"Send them tomorrow or we'll miss the ferry."

Sienna didn't want to miss the ferry. She didn't want to stay sandwiched between these corpses until the following morning. Equally, she wanted to know that Malek was with her but she had no way of finding out, not without giving herself away. She had to just lie there, as she had so many times over the last few days and pray that Panthea loved repentant Auditors too.

The doors shut and the transport moved away. It took in every bump and divot on Orkney, squashing her beneath the pile of dead and crushing her from above. It became harder to breathe but still she remained inert, so close to the end in every sense. She felt the transport pass through a checkpoint before the clank of tyres on metal told her she had boarded the ferry. The transport stopped and the brakes engaged yet it was another thirty minutes before they departed. Eventually, a gentle swaying informed her they were underway, followed by a heavy pitching when they got beyond the bay. She gagged, unable to keep anything down but fortunately, she had little to throw up.

She was about to unzip her bag when she heard a voice in the transport alongside her.

"Hey Theo, you there?"

She froze. It wasn't Malek. It had to be a Steward or an administrator. In her naivety, she'd assumed the transports would be automated like every other transport on the island, that no one would be riding with them. Why would they? There was no one to guard and nothing to steal. Why did they need to be chaperoned?

"I'm on the eight-thirty but we set off late so I might be closer to nine."

This could ruin everything. She had intended to climb out and jump the transport once clear of Thurso, make her way down the northeast coast and look for assistance. As reviled as Cans were, there were still some who were willing to help, particularly in the north where the Highland clearances had uprooted whole communities. In some Scottish towns, *Rapist* activity was rife, with vandalism, arson attacks and even assassinations. Security was tighter in the north but if she was going to find a sympathetic ear anywhere, it would be amongst the disaffected.

But how could she when she was not yet free?

"Just another load for Akran. What? Ha ha, yeah maybe. You never know."

Sienna adapted accordingly. The prospect of tackling this man made her sick. She was not strong enough and lacked the stomach for violence after what she had done to Bella. Besides, if it was a Steward, he would be armed and she would have no chance against a stun baton. But equally, she couldn't allow herself to be transported to Akran and planted in the soil without a fight. She had to try.

But she couldn't do anything until they had reached the mainland. That was the most important thing. Until then, she just had to sit tight and await an opportunity.

The crossing took almost three hours and Sienna felt every pitch and roll. At last, the ferry's engines roared into reverse and the thump of steel against concrete told her they'd reached the dock. Other buses and supply wagons moved off before finally, it was their turn. The transport started up silently, its electric engines barely audible above the rumble of rubber on steel. The ramp clanked as they disembarked and all at once they were on dry land. She was home.

The transport stopped at the port checkpoint and she heard muffled voices but couldn't make out what was said. Soon she was underway again and rolling west along the coastal highway.

She couldn't believe it. She had escaped from Orkney and had made it back to New Britannia. But none of this counted for anything if she couldn't escape the transport.

Moving as imperceptibly as she could, she found the zip and began to pull it down from inside. The rush of cool clean air almost made her dizzy with relief but now she could hear better too. Close by, just beyond her line of sight, someone was moving. She knew she had no choice. She had to silence this man, perhaps even permanently. She had done it before. She could do it again. It would leave her broken and damn her for all eternity but it was either him or her. She was not going back to Orkney.

But before she could free herself, a hand grabbed her bag and tore it open.

"We did it. We bloody did it."

It was Malek.

He was smiling.

He was crying.

And like Sienna, he was now free.

39: ANIMALS

Whoever had sailed with them had got out at Thurso. It had probably been a Steward or an administrator hitching a lift to the mainland. Sienna hadn't heard them get out but Malek had. She was so happy to be free that she couldn't stop crying, not until Malek pointed out that they weren't free yet.

The transport was running along the highway, blindly heading for its final destination. And theirs if they didn't alight.

They tried the back doors but there was no handle on the inside and they were magnetically locked from without. The grid at the front was welded in place and the windows were sealed.

"We'll have to smash them."

"They'll see when it gets to Akran."

"They'll have us if we don't."

They looked for something to break the glass with but there was very little to hand. No wrenches or fire extinguishers or anything hard. Malek used his plastic shank to dig at the window seal but it made little difference. The glass would not budge. With no other choice, Malek resorted to brute force, lying atop the bodies and kicking at the rear window with the heels of his boots. The pane cracked and the frame warped but it took six more minutes before the glass fell away. Even then, they weren't home dry. The hole was scarcely big enough to squeeze through and they were travelling at 50 mph. They couldn't just throw themselves out. The road was unyielding.

Sienna went first, crawling through the hole and clambering up onto the roof. She reached down for Malek, who was less sure of himself and slipped a couple of times, but after a little encouragement, they both made it out.

It was dusk. The sky was light but the land around them was turning black. The road stretched into the distance and sweeping moorland lay on either side. They passed no houses or buildings, just a few dilapidated telephone poles that had been left to rot, the ends of their wires hanging free from their defunct insulators.

Malek studied the terrain. They were two metres up and travelling too fast. If they jumped, they'd very likely break their legs or backs or both.

"We'll have to hang and roll," Malek concluded but Sienna had a better idea. She crawled across the roof and hung her legs over the side in front of the transport.

"Careful," Malek urged her. One bump and she would go under the wheels.

But there was a method to her madness and after a little kicking, the transport suddenly braked. Malek had to grab an air vent to prevent himself from being thrown clear but within a matter of seconds, they had come to a halt. The horn now sounded.

Sienna and Malek jumped to the ground and staggered back. The transport set off again into the twilight.

"It's programmed to stop for animals. I figured it would have sensors," Sienna explained.

They watched their ride disappear and knew they only had an hour or so to do likewise before the damage was discovered.

"We'd better get going."

They turned off the road and headed across the moors. If the Stewards suspected something, they'd send up drones to retrace the route so the more miles they could cover, the more acreage the drones would have to scan. They gulped a couple of amphetamines and didn't look back, hurrying through the grass and the heather as if chased by wild dogs, searching for the next piece of the puzzle. The next key to their evasion plan.

The evenings this far north were long and colourful. A hue of pink and yellow lit their path as they picked their way through the brush, heading up several peaks, passing lochs and wooded knolls before encountering a sight that took their breath away.

Sheep.

Thousands of them.

They covered the hillsides and stretched off as far as the eye could see.

The animals looked dirty and ragged, with most still wearing their heavy winter coats. Swarms of midges churned the twilight air while newborn lambs hurried between their mother's legs and mewed for milk.

They'd seen no animals until now. They were all here, congregated en masse in an undulating carpet across the high terrain. They bleated continuously and became twitchy when Sienna and Malek approached but they did not bolt. They just eyed them nervously, chewing the cud and backing away as these strange creatures passed through them.

This was what Sienna had been looking for.

This would help them clear their next hurdle.

It came soon enough.

"There," Sienna said, stopping and pointing down the glen in the fading light.

Malek saw it. A tiny pinprick of light crossing the moors they'd just crossed. It was below them for now but heading upwards towards their position on the rise. It would be over them soon, honing in on their heat patterns and reporting them back to the Stewards. There was no escaping S Division drones in the open countryside. Not unless you had a crowd of several thousand to hide amongst.

They dropped to their bellies and tucked in their limbs. From above, they'd be just another yellow blob, one of a multitude grazing upon this hillside. That was the theory anyway. Whether it worked in practice was about to be seen. But Sienna knew they wouldn't get far in the open if they just ran. S Division took care of its people. They had to vanish.

A whirling sound was heard over the bleating of sheep and some of the flock bolted as it circled, scrambling over Sienna as if she wasn't there. The drone zigzagged over the enormous flock, chasing it one way and then the next before drifting south into the night.

Malek looked up when it was gone.

"That was too close," he said, puffing out his cheeks when the danger had passed.

Except the danger had not passed.

It was only now approaching.

As the night grew black, Sienna and Malek elected to stay with the flock. The drone would likely circle back and they would be spotted out on their own on this cold night. They took another pill to keep themselves awake and used the lull in excitement to try to plan their next move.

Something had been niggling at Sienna. Something she hadn't understood but had retained just in case: the strange Network code that had been posted through her door just before the Guardians picked her up. Neither she nor Carl had recognised it but she had always held out hope that one day she might be able to decipher it to contact help.

She shared it with Malek, along with the story of how she'd come by it, including Julie's part in all of it. She figured they were beyond secrets now but it came as a shock to Malek nevertheless.

"Fuck," was all he said, neither confirming nor denying that his girlfriend was a *Rapist*. Perhaps he didn't know. Or perhaps he didn't want to say, still unable to completely trust the womxn who had destroyed his life, even if she was now risking all to give it back to him.

In the end, he focussed on the message, surprising Sienna when he said it meant something to him.

"It's a code."

"It can't be. Network codes are sixteen characters. It's too long."

"It's a code of a code," Malek said. "People use them when swapping dark net keys so the bots can't track them."

"How do you decipher it?"

Malek thought. "I've seen a few of these. They're like cryptic puzzles. Often, knowing who sent them is the key. A music fan might code one with music references or a 'tish head might include food references. There's usually an element of black humour to them."

"You can't say black humour," Sienna objected. "That's racist."

"Cancel me."

Sienna withdrew her objection and felt suitably sheepish. Much like those around her.

Malek continued.

"If you're saying *Rapists* sent it to you, then I would say these characters probably refer to something that's been cancelled in the past. What are the characters again?"

Sienna ran through them, segment by segment. NET.IP was a standard Network protocol so she started with the next segment.

"@PM40."

"That's easy. I've seen that one before. PM means Prime Minister. 40 in this instance it means 1940. So the code is asking, who was Prime Minister in 1940?"

Sienna didn't know. Few people did. History wasn't widely disseminated in New Britannia, except in terms of how shamefully people should feel about it.

"Hitler?" she guessed.

"Close. His name was Churchill. He knew Hitler but I don't think they were friends," Malek explained. "A net code starts with four letters so if we take his initials, Winston something something Churchill. I can't quite remember what his middle names are but basically it's WLSC. Like I say, I've seen it before. Next bit."

Sienna envisaged the code.

"VC43K9."

Malek thought about it but gave up when nothing occurred to him. "I don't know that one. Something to do with 1943 or 2043 but I don't know what. Next?"

"RD82>."

"Roald Dahl," Malek said without hesitation. "RD means Roald Dahl. He was a writer. Used to write kids' books until his stuff was classified as 'problematic'. Very toxic now."

Sienna knew of him. She'd even cancelled a teacher who'd been caught distributing his books. There was one about a fox who murdered chickens and another about a group of Jews who dressed as witches to poison children. Or something like that. She hadn't read it herself.

"Presumably, it refers to a book he published in '82."

"Which was?" Sienna asked.

Malek shrugged. "I don't know. But if we can get on the Network, I can find it out."

The last segment was GO84. Again, Malek deduced the initials referred to a person or place and the number a year but he couldn't think who or what.

"If we had a pair of Smart Glasses, I could look this stuff up," he said, qualifying his statement with: "And if I had a cheese sandwich and a bottle of beer, I could have a cheese sandwich and a bottle of beer, too."

Sienna smiled in semi-agreement. A cheese sandwich would have been nice but she would forgo the bottle of beer in light of all that had happened after the last bottle she'd had. Butterfly wings and all that.

The night was clear with hardly a cloud in the sky. The stars twinkled far above, oblivious to Sienna and Malek's problems as they waltzed their way through the timeless universe. A waning moon cast a silvery light across the flock but the land itself was black. Neither Sienna nor Malek could make out much, sat where they were on the ridge overlooking the valley. If the drone was going to circle back, it would come from this direction.

The sheep stirred uneasily, bleating and pushing each other as the night wore on while the cries of lambs grew ever more desperate. Even without the amphetamines, they would have had little or no chance of sleeping amongst this lot.

All at once, a portion of the flock bolted, bundling through their position before stopping sharply and doubling back.

"What's that about?" Malek asked.

"Something spooked them."

Malek looked to the skies but saw no signs of the drone.

"I don't think it was the drone," Sienna whispered.

All at once, the sheep ran again, screaming and bleating as they did. Sienna and Malek were pulled with them, keeping pace and staying with the flock. Without warning, it changed direction and Sienna was bundled over. Several hooves hit her in the back of the head and when she regained her footing, she found herself winded and struggling to keep up.

From out of the darkness, a shape flashed before her. It moved like lightning as it crossed her path. She baulked and changed direction, stumbling back in shock to find a small knot of animals who'd been separated from the main group. She had barely time to think when a second shape fell on one of the lambs. A terrible screaming rang out along with more frantic bleating and Sienna turned and ran, blind with panic and with no idea where she was going. She knew that she was in terrible danger and that something was amongst the sheep. Something quick and deadly.

The shapes merged on all sides, picking off the weak and

killing without mercy. The flock veered again and Sienna saw eyes glowing in the night ahead. She had nothing to defend herself with and no idea where to run.

"Malek!" she screamed, desperate and terrified as she braced herself for the killer blow.

"Sinny!" she heard him cry back. "It's wolves. Look out."

She had already guessed as much and wondered how she'd overlooked the danger. She had invested so much of her energy into escaping the islands and evading the Stewards that she had forgotten that nature would be waiting to bite her at the first opportunity.

She heard a vicious snarl and saw that she'd almost run into several wolves feasting on the remains of a lamb. They snapped at her challenge, presumably thinking she was trying to steal their carcass, so she turned and ran, screaming and hollering in the hope that it would confuse them.

She now found the flock and pushed her way into the middle, just as every other animal was attempting to. The sheep were desperate and panic-stricken, as attached to their precious lives as Sienna was to hers, pushing to escape the claws and bleating with unadulterated terror.

Another lamb screamed in the night. Another life cut short.

"Sinny."

Malek sounded way off. They'd become separated in the darkness and now she was lost.

"I'm over here."

"Where are you?"

She couldn't see and was reluctant to leave the safety of the flock, no matter how fervently they wanted her gone.

"Up here. Come on," he called and Sienna noticed the outline of a small tree against the night's sky. It looked a long way and she would have to leave the multitudes to make it. What did she do? She had two choices; either stay where she was or make a break for it.

"Now..."

She figured she hadn't got this far by playing it safe so she decided to run. The panic rippled through the flock and she saw that the wolves were closing in again. She had to take the opportunity and hope they chose another poor innocent to pick on. Just as she had done her whole damned life.

Sienna pushed her way through and broke into open ground. Savage barks and screams of terror rang out in the night. She ran as fast as she could, half-sprinting, half-stumbling as the ground attempted to upend her every step.

Malek screamed at the top of his lungs and shook the branches to guide Sienna towards his position. Sienna did likewise, swearing and screaming in the hope of unnerving the wolves. In the midsts of lambing season, there were easier palatable kills to be had than a wailing banshee with barely an ounce of flesh on her bones. At least, that's what she hoped.

"Go!" Malek urged her, watching the flock break apart beneath the glare of moonlight amid a dozen stalking shadows.

Sienna stumbled and landed hard. A searing pain told her that something in her knee had given way. It would have been so easy to give up now. To lie here and die and know that she had done all she could but she refused to accept defeat. She had to go on. She had to live. It was the only way of striking back at them. Forcing herself up, she pressed on, hopping and hobbling as best she could in the direction of Malek's cries.

She reached the base of the tree and jumped for the branches, tripping over the roots and landing painfully. A shape rushed towards her. A black hole in the night with two gleaming eyes. With no time to react, she scrambled at the trunk and grabbed hold of a branch. But she lacked the strength to pull herself up and hung in limbo knowing that she couldn't make it. Her hand was slipping and the ground swelled beneath her but before she lost her grip, she felt fingers at her wrist. A moment later she was plucked into the air, turning and spinning as her feet swung free.

A snarling gnash raged below her and she tucked her legs in, grabbing anything she could as she fought her way skywards and away from the snap of death. Malek helped her find a perch and they both held on. The tree felt puny once she was in its branches, little more than an aspirational shrub, but they were clear of the ground and surrounded by a thicket of thorny sprigs. They weren't quite beyond the leap of the wolves but there were readier meals to be had. The weak were always the first to go.

Sienna and Malek hung on for dear life, guarding their feet and watching the skies until the first rays of dawn appeared. The sun had never looked so beautiful as it rolled back the terrors of the night. The hillsides became green and the valleys pooled with mists like enormous goblets of broth. The sheep had moved away, converging on the next slope to seek comfort from one another and bleat for their dead.

"I don't see anything."

Sienna scanned the countryside and agreed with Malek. There was no sign of the wolves. They had vanished along with the shadows. All they'd left to show for their night's work were the remnants of several carcasses and the lamentations of the recently bereaved.

Birdsongs heralded the new day while the wind stirred the leaves. All was bright and beautiful. All creatures great and less so.

"I think we should find somewhere else to camp tonight," Malek said, numb with shock at all they'd come through.

If this was the price of freedom, it came with a heavy tag.

But it was a price Sienna was willing to pay.

40: ROOTS

A sharp pain shot up Sienna's leg when she put her weight through it. She'd torn a muscle or a tendon and now she could hardly walk. If the wolves or the drones came for her again, she'd be stuck. Malek used his plastic shank to fashion a crutch from a branch. It wasn't perfect but at least it bore her weight.

Despite the clearances, there were still people dotted throughout the Highlands. Most were in the employ of the Animal Sanctuary; gamekeepers, welfare officers and the like although there were also a few holiday cottages along the coast. The Animal Sanctuary attracted tourists in the summer months, city folks keen to see the hordes of emancipated livestock living blissful lives in peace and prosperity. Busloads travelled through the Sanctuary while drones live-streamed the herds from above for those who preferred to view their animals remotely. Sienna knew the closer they got to people, the more they risked but she also realised they wouldn't last long in the open. Not if the previous night was anything to go by. They had to find a vacant holiday cottage or a house undergoing renovations. Somewhere they could hold up for a few nights. At least, until she could walk again. They might even find food or a boat they could use. Anything to help them avoid the twin perils of man and beast.

They hobbled on after a breakfast of dried fruits and drier amphetamines. They were running low on both and would have to scavenge for this evening's meal if they were to eat again.

The ground was rough and the pain sapped Sienna's energy. Malek helped as much as he could but the going was slow and the terrain unyielding. It seemed to stretch away in open rugged splendour forever. They encountered more carcasses along the way. Old bones from previous kills, picked clean by birds and bugs.

They stopped by a loch to take on water and washed some of the grot from their necks. Sienna felt filthy but the water made her feel even more so. She wondered if she'd ever feel clean again.

They continued west, following the lie of the land through hills and glens. After a time, they descended into a valley and followed it north, eventually coming to a fledgling forest that had been planted along the banks of a bubbling burn. Thousands of trees stretched the length of the valley and swayed gently in the breeze. Some were saplings while others had begun to spread their branches. There was an artificial uniformity to them. Nature by AI. The forest had yet to claim the landscape for its own but the greenery was all around.

Malek stopped abruptly.

"What is it?"

They listened. There was a noise on the wind. A mechanical noise. Through the trees some distance away but it was enough to cause them to stop. They headed uphill, away from the forest, skirting the ridge to avoid whatever lay ahead.

Movement. It was still a long way off but Sienna saw something gleaming in the valley. They ducked and circled the activity, Sienna hobbling every step of the way, dragging her leg and wincing with pain. After twenty minutes, they came up to get their bearings and saw a work party operating a mechanical digger. Several lorries were parked nearby, some loaded with saplings, the others with –

"Oh shit."

Body bags.

"This is Akran Forest."

They'd walked right into it.

An S Division transport containing dozens of bags stood waiting to be emptied. Foresters in dirty overalls dragged one out and carried it between them. They dumped it into a hole and the digger fired up. One of the foresters fetched a sapling and the digger pushed the dirt in until there were just a few inches left. The forester finished the job with a shovel and stamped the earth down with his boots.

Sienna and Malek looked back at the valley they had just come through. The forest stretched for acres and was made up of thousands and thousands of trees, each serving as a marker to an assisted death. The setting was peaceful and the valley ardent but the sheer enormity of it was grotesque.

"So many."

"I don't care what happens to me," said Malek in open-mouthed horror, "as long as I never end up in this fucking place."

Was Alicia here? Interred alongside Mariatou, their respective trees destined to grow lush together in the coming years. Or was she part of a different forest? There were several projects in the north that Sienna knew of. New woodlands championed by Charity GoodHope.

Thousand of years ago, before the armageddon of agriculture, the forests of Britain had stretched from the south coast of England to the Highlands of northern Scotland in an almost unbroken Eden of flora. Creatures of all kinds had dwelled here and nature flourished. Then man had arrived and destroyed it all, as man had a tendency to do. Many years later, as part of her vision for New Britannia,

Charity GoodHope embarked upon the reforestation of these lands. She was determined to turn back the clock and restore this sceptred isle to a time when it had been truly great, yet she had been a little sketchy on the details. Had this been her grand vision all along? Her idea of saving the nation along with the environment? Napoleon had once described Britain as a nation of shopkeepers. Charity seemed determined to turn it into a nation of trees. Literally.

The saplings stretched away in an unbroken belt of regimented fauna. Life would eventually return and flourish here but it would always be tinged with death. Sienna had to get away. Right now. This instant. She couldn't be here another second.

Malek helped her to her feet and they hurried on, moving as quickly as they could as the digger clunked in their wake, the shovels scraped and the boots stamped to grow the forest around them.

Shortly before evening, they found the coastal road again. They followed it for a distance heading west, ducking whenever a transport approached and watching the horizon until they came to a small cluster of homes. They looked derelict with locks on the doors and shutters on the windows. There were bleached-out eviction notices pinned to the gates.

DO NOT ENTER

PROPERTY OF A.R.S.L.

BUILDING UNSTABLE

It was hardly the Ritz but it would have to do. They couldn't go on. Sienna had been hobbling all day and they'd barely covered ten miles. Neither had slept in 48 hours and their nerves were shredded with exhaustion. They needed to rest and they needed to do so somewhere safe. Somewhere they weren't going to get ripped to pieces in their sleep.

They checked the properties and found one cottage where the shutters had been pulled away. Malek peeled them back as Sienna slipped through, dropping onto the bare floorboards and almost succumbing where she lay. Malek dropped beside her and said he'd check the place out.

There was little furniture so they pulled down the tattered curtains that still hung in the windows and laid them out on the floor upstairs. They slept as soon as they closed their eyes, falling through their dreams and landing hard the next morning. Sienna woke first, her heart racing and her brow sweating. Malek was still asleep and all was quiet. Nothing stirred except for the wind in the guttering.

She went in search of a bathroom and found water still in the taps. It was cold but clean. She washed her face and wrapped a wet cloth around her swollen knee. Her leg had gotten worse for all her walking and she had to cling on to the sink, wincing whenever she tried to stand. The medicine cabinet was empty. No drugs or bandages left for their convenience. Downstairs, the kitchen cupboards were likewise bare but there were tins on the floor, their lids peeled back and their contents eaten. Some of them looked new; soup and beans and one of pineapple slices. Someone had been here. And recently.

She flicked the light switch. Nothing. The power was out and when she checked the fusebox, she saw that the boards had been pulled, rendering the solar panels on the roof useless. Still, it was worth checking the other houses. If they could find one with a working power source and an operational OS, they could access the Network and decrypt the cypher.

Sienna turned to hobble out when she stopped dead.

Standing in the doorway, staring open-mouthed in shock,

was a young teen. He was barely out of childhood, betwixt man and boy, but he was dressed like a soldier in camouflage fatigues and wearing webbing and a backpack.

She didn't wait for him to react. She lunged straight at him, ignoring the scream in her leg as she dragged him to the ground. It caught the boy cold and he flailed his arms but was unable to find a contact. Sienna, on the other hand, possessed an unerring accuracy and punched him in the face with two quick fists, bloodying his nose and splitting his lip.

"Dad! Dad!" he yelped in terror and Sienna knew she had only moments to react. She flung herself across the floor, stretching out one hand while gripping the boy's collar with the other. She had no weapons to hand, nothing to fight with, so she grabbed the only thing she could use.

The lid from one of the discarded tins.

Footsteps came fast and a man was shouting but Sienna was too quick. She had the serrated lid at the boy's throat when the man burst in.

"I'll slash his throat. I'll fucking do it. Don't make me do it," she screamed, ducking behind the boy to avoid the glare of the rifle that was now pointed at her.

"Let him go," the man shouted in horror, desperation and fear etched across his face. "Let him go NOW!"

"I'll kill him. Back the fuck off. I mean it."

But the man wouldn't back off. He was too frantic and the rifle shook in his hands as his son was threatened before him. If he could have got a shot off, he would've. But there was no way of shooting this awful hag without risking his boy. And the tin in her hand would have torn out his throat in a blink. He was frozen with fear.

"Put the gun down. Put it down now!" she kept shouting, the sharpened edge pressing ever deeper into the boy's soft skin to make him squeal in pain. Blood trickled between her fingers and Sienna fought to shut out her own humxnity as she did what she needed to do. Visions of Bella screaming came back to her and she almost vomited at the prospect of spilling this kid's blood but she knew she had no choice. When backed into a corner, there was only one way out.

"Drop the gun!"

As desperately as he didn't want to, and as helpless as it made him feel, the man saw he had no choice, not if he wanted his son back alive. Moving slowly, he lowered his rifle and set it on the ground.

"Now let him go," he pleaded, desperate to pull his child from her arms but wise enough not to try. "Please, don't hurt him."

Despite his compliance, Sienna wasn't about to throw away the only thing that was stopping this man from exacting swift vengeance. She had to stay the course. She had to be brutal. She had to think ahead.

And she had to kill them both if necessary.

But for that she needed Malek.

"MMalek! Get in here. Quick."

He was already awake. Obviously. The commotion downstairs had been loud enough to wake half of Akran Forest. He was confused but on high alert. He grabbed his sharpened shank and readied himself to propel all boarders but the commotion stayed downstairs. Now it was calling him. Urgently. And Malek knew he had no choice but to answer.

As cautiously as he could, he made his way downstairs towards the shouting.

Straight away he saw a man standing in the doorway. A big man in camouflage fatigues wearing a backpack and equipment all over his body with one important exception. He wore no Smart Glasses, no goggles or headset of any type. He looked like a throwback to another age but Malek didn't need to view his Network settings to interpret his status. He was upset about something. Very very upset.

The man saw Malek approaching and stepped back in readiness. He snatched something off his belt and held it aloft. A weapon of some kind to match the one Malek had in his hand. He looked at the puny plastic shank he was holding and dropped it straight away. This was a fight he couldn't win. Moreover, in his weakened state, it was one he could very easily lose.

But there was another way out.

"Let's talk this through," Malek implored.

The man stayed his hand and Malek wondered if reason had won the day until he saw the other mitigating factor. Sienna had squeezed herself beneath the kitchen worktop and was holding a second person before her, a child, using him as a shield with a sharpened edge at his throat.

He now understood the man's state and slipped in to place himself between them all, mitigating the threat to both.

"It's okay, no one's going to do anything stupid here, are we? We're just going to talk," Malek assured all, not sure who he was trying to impress upon the most. The boy's neck was pink with blood but it was just a nick. But one flick of Sienna's wrist and a deluge would pour forth.

Malek urged the man to lower his knife and advised Sienna to do the same.

"No one needs to get hurt today," Malek said. He saw that they had a big problem but accepted this wasn't the solution. Something Sienna had not.

"Get his gun," she shouted. "Get it now."

He'd already noticed the man's rifle by his feet but he knew the man wouldn't let him take it. He couldn't. To have done so would have been suicidal. This situation needed less drama, not more. But the omens were good. By laying his rifle down, the man had demonstrated a willingness to talk. Now Sienna needed to do the same.

"Sinny, let the boy go," he said, speaking to her gently. "Nice and slowly, let him up."

But Sienna clung on to him as she had clung on to life these past few months, with a precarious grip and a determination not to let go. Not for anything. Or anyone. She had to get away. She had to live. She had to fulfil her promise to Alicia.

"Sinny, I know you're scared but it's okay. We'll be okay. I swear."

The man saw the dynamic at work and sheathed his weapon. He held out his hands just as Malek was holding out his and tried to temper his tone to show Sienna he meant her no threat.

"I just want my boy back," he said as softly as he could. "Nothing more."

Malek urged Sienna to comply but the calmer their demeanour became, the more distressed Sienna grew. With her back to the wall, Sienna would fight. She could summon all kinds of strength and kick and gouge and bite and even kill. But Malek was asking her to do something more dangerous than that.

He was asking her to trust again.

And she couldn't do that.

She didn't have it in her. Not after all she'd seen and done, in the camps and before, in that darkness and distant memories she'd once called life.

"Sinny, you have to listen to me. It's not going to do us any good. Drop the metal. He's just a boy. He didn't do anything to you."

"But he will. That's what you don't understand. If I let him go, they'll kill us both."

The man edged forward, his hands stretched out in supplication.

"I won't. I swear on Panthea. We will just go. We won't say anything to anyone. We don't want any trouble."

But Sienna had heard too many lies for one life already. And she'd told a fair few herself. And the worst lies of all were always delivered with a smile.

"Get the gun. Get his gun."

But Malek could see only one way out of this mess. And that wasn't it.

"Are you with the forest team?" he asked the man, turning from Sienna to engage with him directly.

"What?" the man said, still too tightly sprung to hear at first. "No. I'm an Animal Welfare Officer."

"You look after the sheep?"

"And the cow, pigs, horses. All the animals."

He was here for work but had chosen this week of all weeks to bring his teenage son with him. It was a family calling and time to show him the ropes. They'd not worn their Smart Glasses because no Animal Welfare Officers did. They were of little use amongst the herds and distracted the wearer from the real footprints laid out in the land. The rifles were for protection. Lone wolves occasionally attacked people in these parts. As did poachers. And both had been seen near here recently.

Malek spoke of his and Sienna's journey, of how they'd come from the islands and all they'd been through. He confirmed that they'd seen wolves but no one else. He kept their trip through Akran Forest to himself and Sienna didn't contradict him. Some secrets were best left buried.

"I was a data engineer in my old life," Malek said with a disarming smile. "Which is about as far away from this as you can get. But Sinny here, she was more like you, I guess."

Malek turned to Sienna and knelt before her.

"She was an Auditor. One of those people who go through other people's lives looking for the worst in them." He inched closer, scarcely able to see her from where she was hiding but catching her eye all the same. "They'd dig and dig until they found something horrible, and if they didn't, they'd dig some more until they did. And then, when they'd finally got the goods on you, they'd say to themselves 'See, we were right, these people are no good' and they'd throw them to the wolves. Do your herds ever do anything like that?"

The man shrugged, unwilling to comment.

"Sinny, it's time to stop looking for the worst in people. I know it's got us to this point but it won't take us any further. Just let it go. What's past is past. Take a leap."

Malek might as well asked her to hug a wolf for all the sense he was making. This man, this man with his guns and knives and batons and anger, would no more let them go than he would a rat. Even if he didn't shoot them, he'd turn them into the Stewards and they would be sent back to the islands. The only thing stopping him was the serrated tin lid at his precious boy's carotid artery. She didn't need to trawl through his Network history to understand that.

Malek reached for Sienna's hand but she pulled it away.

"Don't," she warned him.

The man saw no other way. He realised he'd taken the wrong approach and sought to correct that. He stooped to pick up his rifle and worked the bolt to chamber a round. A . 303 cartridge now sat locked and ready to join the conversation.

Sienna saw him but she was too late to warn Malek.

"Behind you," she shouted.

Malek turned just in time to see the rifle swing in his direction. He had no chance to react and scarcely a moment to breathe but the rifle remained silent. Instead, the man raised the barrel to the ceiling and held out the stock for Malek to take.

"It's yours. Just let my son go."

41: SCARS

His name was Khalif and his son was Zain. They had Diversity Gradings of 21 and 16 but that seemed immaterial at this point. Khalif was the Animal Welfare Officer for the district and had been since the Sanctuary's inception. His family had come from North Africa several generations earlier and had heralded from herdsmen. Zain had grown up being told that animals were in his blood but when Sienna finally let him go, he examined his wound and saw only shame.

Khalif tended to his son with antiseptics and offered Sienna a wrap and a painkiller for her leg. She accepted the wrap but refused the painkiller, unwilling to take anything that might blur her senses. Khalif also produced a tub of falafel and offered them around. Once more, Sienna accepted but only after Khalif ate a couple himself.

"We were checking the houses for animals. They can get in but they can't get out," Khalif explained. "We had no idea you were in here. We weren't looking for you."

"How many are? Are they combing the area?"

"No one really. An appeal for information went out over the Network and the Guardians said a gang of saboteurs were operating in the area but there was no mention of Cans."

"Saboteurs?"

In truth, the authorities were still trying to figure out what had happened to the transport. A window had been broken and two bodies had been stolen but no one could understand why. Sienna and Malek had been reported missing from Orkney four days earlier along with twenty others but the two events went unconnected. As far as the Stewards and the Guardians were concerned, the transport had been targeted by bad actors on the mainland, possibly for organ harvesting or pagan rights. Drones were dispatched and Network movements were monitored but the culprits had disappeared.

"Are there roadblocks or patrols?"

"Not that I've seen."

This was promising. After so many missteps, they'd finally earned a little luck. Now they had to decide how best to use it.

"We need to get on the Network," Malek said. "To send a message and get help. We don't want to hurt either of you. We just want to get out of here." He was still holding the rifle but not at them. In truth, he wanted to put it down but he was worried if he did, one of the others would pick it up and that would end badly for all concerned. For the time being, Malek realised his were the safest hands.

Zain glared at Sienna and held his neck. His cut was sore and his pride was more so. The day had started out so brightly, wearing his cool camouflage gear and tracking the land with his dad, feeling tough and grown up. Then that stinking Can had grabbed him with her filthy Can hands and humiliated him, hurt him, drawn his blood and made him feel helpless. He'd wet his pants and now everyone could see. He hated Cans. This one in particular. They should all be shot. He would have gladly done so and no one would have blamed him. But his dad seemed intent on talking with them as if they were real people. Share their food even. Provide them with information. That wasn't right.

"There's no coverage out here," Khalif said. "Only in the towns. The Guardians ripped out all the receivers to stop smugglers from linking up. You'd need a 7G transmitter to patch in from here and even then, the signal's fuzzy."

Khalif had a 7G transmitter in his jeep outside but it was patched into the Sanctuary Security Hub in Thurso.

"What about Stewards?" Sienna asked.

"They've got their own system. I don't deal with them directly."

Sienna wouldn't allow Khalif to get his 7G set. All it would take would be a prearranged signal to summon the Guardians and that would be that. The miles they had come and the blood they had spilt would count for nothing.

"So how do we get a signal out?" Malek asked. But Sienna didn't know. At least, not in a way that was safe.

"Who are you trying to contact?" Khalif asked, qualifying this by insisting it was none of his business but perhaps he could help.

"We don't know," Malek shrugged. He admitted that they had a secret code they could not decipher and said it might put them in touch with some people who might be able to help or not. If they were willing. Or not.

"And that's your plan?" Khalif said.

"No. That's what we've got instead of a plan."

Khalif scratched his head and mulled something over. He

asked if they would allow Zain to step outside but neither Sienna nor Malek were willing to split their forces for the sake of privacy. The room was empty. It had once been a sitting room and the faint outline of furniture still stained the walls. But most of the fittings were gone, along with the people who had once called it their home. There was no hiding from each other in here and nothing to be gained from trying. Except mistrust. Khalif knew they couldn't sit around all day. The Cans were getting twitchy and a solution might eventually occur to them that would guarantee his and Zain's silence. His options were limited so he did what he had to in order to move things along.

He betrayed a trust.

"I have friends who might be able to help you. Get you away from here. Far away."

Sienna was instantly suspicious but her expression was nothing compared to that of Zain's.

"Dad?"

"We're Animal Welfare Officers, son. We're sworn to help all animals in need. Even those with two legs."

Khalif had no truck with the policies of the Polychrome Alliance. He'd seen too many people turn on each other over the years, friends and relatives swept away in the blink of an eye, lives ruined. This was why he preferred the north. The open countryside and the wild herds. Here there was real freedom and genuine humxnity. Neighbours looked out for each other. People got on. Few trusted the authorities. How could they, in a land scarred with derelict homes?

Khalif went on to describe how he knew someone who imported peanuts and exported vapes. The cartridges that were sold in New Britannia were considered Class A narcotics abroad, particularly those filled with high-grade synthetic Oxy,

Coca and Fent. Big money could be made from shipping them to the continent. And the desolate coastlines of the north provided an ideal launching site for smugglers. The local authorities were also willing to turn a blind eye. For a price. Khalif had no problem with free enterprise. Although he would have preferred Zain to have found out about it later when he was a little older. Zain was still so young. Still so idealistic. He didn't need to know where his dad disappeared off to every third Sunday of the month. Or how he'd afforded a licence to have four children on a humble AWO's salary.

"Where to?" Malek asked.

"Norway," Khalif said.

Norway wasn't quite Sweden but it wasn't New Britannia either. Norway marked the northern extreme of Gaultier's Federal States of Europe. It might not have been as close as France or as hard a border as Ireland but it still represented a frontier and would be patrolled as such. That said, it was heavily forested and the coastline was riddled with fjords. A smuggler's paradise. Khalif's people had been making the crossings for years. They knew every cove and inlet. They also knew a fair number of border guards who patrolled the coastline. The crossing would not be without its risks but where there was a will, there was a way.

"How do we know you're not lying?" Sienna demanded.

"The same way I know you're not going to shoot me," Khalif said. "I don't."

It seemed a fair point but Sienna felt the need to spell out her position so that there was no ambiguity.

"I won't let myself be taken again. And if I have to, I'll take as many of you with me as I can."

All eyes turned to Malik.

"I came with Sinny. Till death do us part."

It seemed, after all they'd said and done, Sienna and Malek had signed a contract after all, albeit, an unwritten one. Although these were often the most binding.

With no choice but to place their trust in Khalif, Sienna and Malek agreed to go with him. Sienna struggled to her feet but scarcely had the strength. Khalif helped her as far as the window. Deciding who went through first brought to mind the old farmer's dilemma about crossing a river with a fox, a chicken and a bag of grain but eventually, she allowed the fox to go first, assured in the knowledge that they still had his chicken in case he tried anything. But a dull thud and an anguished cry put paid to that theory and she turned to see Zain grabbing the rifle and firing.

The blast went wide and showered her with plaster but that was just to get her attention. Zain had slugged Malek from behind but he wanted Sienna to know all about it when he blew her filthy head off.

"Dirty Can. How dare you touch me?"

He cycled the bolt to chamber a new round and levelled the sights on her face. Malek was sprawled at his feet, his head sticky and his mind groggy. Sienna was too removed to get the jump on Zain again. All she could do was stare down the barrel and await the inevitable.

"Don't do it. Zain, no," Khalif shouted but Zain was deaf to his dad's entreaties. He wasn't about to allow his family to be held to ransom by a couple of filthy Cans. The very thought made his skin crawl. The teachers on his school platforms often spoke of the dangers of Cans with most of his class agreeing they were no different to cockroaches. His dad had tried to check his extremes, a habit that caused Zain to regard him as a reactionary, but he never dreamed he'd go so far as to collaborate with Cans.

"She's got it coming."

"No Zain, don't."

Khalif started to climb through the window but Sienna pushed him back. He wouldn't have made it anyway and would have only confused the situation. She hobbled towards Zain and appealed to him directly.

"I'm sorry I hurt you," Sienna said. "I was wrong to do what I did. I had no right."

This was good. This was what Zain wanted. It wasn't enough to stamp on slime, he wanted to hear it beg for forgiveness first.

"You have every right to be angry at me and I don't blame you," she said. "But know one thing, if you pull that trigger, you'll never be free of me. This is the face you'll see every time you close your eyes, in every nightmare and every vision. It will make you sick and you'll give anything to get rid of me but you won't be able to. I'll haunt your dreams and ruin your life. I know this because I still see the face of the womxn I killed."

This caught him off-guard and for a moment, Zain was impressed at having tangled with a real-life murderer. Of course, he considered the possibility that she might be lying but it played better in his mind if she were not. He wanted to know more and this was enough to stay his finger. Sienna sensed his hesitation and knew there was only one sure way to settle her debts.

"I marked your neck," she said, hobbling sideways and stooping to pick up the tin lid she had held to Zain's throat. "For that, I apologise." Before her nerves got the better of her, she drew the tin edge across her cheek, the one already scarred from the last time someone had pointed a rifle at her, spilling blood from nose to ear. The gesture was intended to placate Zain but it actually filled him with revulsion. She dropped the tin and felt her sticky face, looking Zain square in the eye. "But it's the scars we can't see that run the deepest."

The sight of the gore and Sienna's lack of reaction to the pain made Zain feel nauseous. The situation was disgusting and so horrible that he wanted no part of it anymore.

"Give me the rifle, Zain," his dad urged him from the window. "She won't touch you again."

This did the trick and the rifle completed its tour of all hands to end up back where it had started. Khalif took possession and weighed up his options. Sienna saw it in his eyes but he just puffed out his cheeks and looked to Sienna and Malek, both now leaking profusely all over the floorboards.

"Like I say, these old buildings; it's easier getting into them than getting out."

He spent the next fifteen minutes patching up Sienna and Malek and reassuring Zain with a few fatherly words before suggesting they got going.

The road was clear. Fewer than three or four vehicles ever rolled by here each hour but Khalif watched and waited to be sure.

"Let's go."

His jeep started up with the push of a button and they rolled away on a whisper. The rifle was stashed in the boot and Zain in the forward passenger seat but Khalif sat in the rear with his guests, leaving the AI system to see them home.

His wife worked remotely as a spiritual guidance counsellor and he had three other children, all of school age who were upstairs in the education room clicking away at various DOE links. She wasn't expecting Khalif back at this hour but he told his wife that Zain had been attacked by a wolf. This appealed to Zain's ego, particularly when Khalif went into lurid detail about how heroically his son had fought the beast off. In the meantime, he hid Sienna and Malek in his outbuilding at the end of their land. It was normally full of veterinary supplies and herd monitoring equipment but this week it also held 791 vape cartridges, his contribution to the local free market economy.

"Stay out of sight and I'll be back soon," he promised them. He thought about locking them in but realised this would breach their trust. Besides, if they'd managed to escape the islands, his shoffice was unlikely to present too many problems. Later on, he brought them a roll-out mattress each and blankets, water and snacks and Sienna and Malek made use of them all. Sienna even allowed Khalif to give her a shot of Ketorolac for her pain. But the most wonderful thing was Khalif's bathroom. He sent his wife and youngest children out of the house under some pretence and invited Sienna and Malek to use his facilities. This was as much for his benefit as it was for theirs as both stank worse than sickly goats and made him gag every time he went near them. He gave them clothes from his own wardrobe (minus any incriminating labels) and burned their once-pink jumpsuits. This was the second time a stranger had given Sienna clothes. The first had been the Cans in Woking when Geri had kicked her out. She couldn't remember their names. Martin and Chris? Another thing to feel bad about. Now a different stranger had supplied her with a different set of clothes in a different hour of need. Different people. Different circumstances. Yet the same simple gesture. She was grateful. More than she could possibly say. And almost too much for her to comprehend.

Khalif even allowed Sienna to use his clippers to trim her

hair. Several inches of auburn locks had grown back since she'd been shaved months earlier, leaving her looking like the unkept verge of a forgotten highway. Shaving around the sides and applying a little lipstick revived the parts of her that food and water couldn't reach. She felt humxn again. More than that. A womxn. It was an unfamiliar feeling, unnerving, and made her feel like an imposter in her own skin.

A different person.

A new Sienna, reborn with eyes wide open.

42: DECISIONS

They passed the days stocking up on food and rest. Khalif was a kind and considerate host but Zain stayed away, unwilling to assist and unable to do anything else after Khalif had taken him off-line.

Khalif also helped crack the Network code that Sienna had memorised. It took a great many attempts and some dark net searching but eventually they unravelled the cypher and accessed a page by inputting Sienna's username and some captcha questions that had been tailored to her.

To their surprise and disappointment, there was no magical rescue plan awaiting their initiation. Instead, there was a form with lots of questions relating to her job and cancellation experience: names, usernames, positions, dates, links, screenshots, complainants, informers, arguments and counter-arguments. There was also a box for additional information and a cursor that flashed in anticipation.

"They're compiling data," Malek concluded. "That's all they wanted. They couldn't help you but they thought you could help them."

"With what?"

"Feedback," Malek said.

As frustrating as this was, Sienna took consolation from the fact that she was able to make a contribution. As an insider and an outsider, with specialist knowledge of both Geniture and the camps, Sienna was able to write extensively about the process, with special reference to the A.D. Programme and the trafficking scams. If her warnings could help others avoid the same fate, then some good may come of her ordeal yet.

She signed off with a personal note.

Sienna Clay, formerly of Bedford, Woking, Camp 14 and Orkney Mainland. Escaped from all four together with Malek Smith 12/06/84. Awaiting embarkation to Norway. If you do not hear from us again, presume dead – sinnysinful2056.070

Malek was open with Khalif about what he had done to be cancelled. That was to say, not a lot. But he pitched it as a lesson from history, something Khalif could learn from and pass on. Sienna, on the other hand, was rather more reticent. She wasn't ashamed of her transgressions. Quite the reverse. It was that she had initiated the cancellations of hundreds of others, therefore she felt it would have been poor form to lament her own fall from grace. Sienna's emotions were in turmoil when it came to her misfortunes but she knew one thing; of all the Cans in all the camps, she had been the most worthy of banishment. She didn't like it. But she did have to live with it. Always and forever.

The day of the crossing arrived. Khalif came for them at dusk. He'd made sandwiches for the journey and packed medication and spare clothes.

"These guys I deal with, they're gangsters but they're no friends of the Polydollies."

"Do you trust them?"

"About as much as I trust any gangster. But you'll be okay.

I've vouched for you. They'll take good care of you."

His choice of words alarmed Sienna and it fell to Malek to explain why. Khalif understood and assured her it was no metaphor.

"They'll get you to Norway. You have my word. They won't double-cross you."

"How can you know?"

"Because I speak their language."

Khalif had donated his entire shipment of vape pods to cover their passage with the promise of another thousand when he received proof of their safe arrival. Sienna didn't know what to say but Malek did. He hugged Khalif and promised he'd never forget his kindness.

"Unless the Guardians pick us up, of course," Malek added, qualifying his position.

Under cover of eventide, Sienna and Malek climbed into Khalif's jeep and set off on the last leg of their journey. Sienna looked back at the house as it receded into the distance and saw a womxn at the window.

"Don't worry," Khalif said. "She will be praying for you."

They drove along the coastline for 45 minutes until they came to a small dirt track. They pulled off the road and headed to the banks of a great sea loch that opened up onto the northern waters. A figure stepped out from behind a stone wall and flagged them down with a torch. They slowed to a halt and wound down the window. A man looked in, scanning their faces with his torchlight.

"You're late," was all he said.

They started up again and drove the last stretch until they reached a small jetty. Several trucks were parked up and men stood watching and waiting. Khalif stopped and got out. Sienna slipped a hand into her pocket and felt for the scalpel she had taken from Khalif's supplies. Even with a concealed weapon, she would have stood little chance against so many but the blade wasn't for them. It was for herself. She was resolute in her mind. She would not go back. One way or the other, this was her last day in New Britannia.

Khalif returned and brought with him a handsome young man who looked barely out of his 20s. He looked an unlikely gangster with EarPods, flick-down Smart Glasses and easy manner. Perhaps that was why he was so successful.

"This is Tor. He'll take you to Norway."

"Tørvikbygd," specified Tor. "After that, you're on your own. And you've never seen us before. *Avtalt?*"

"Of course," Malek agreed. But Sienna was determined to get a little more for Khalif's money.

"We'll need a safe route to Sweden. And food and ID chips."

Tor laughed.

"Why not?"

He called to his colleagues in Norwegian and one of them came over with an envelope.

"For you, the VIP package."

It contained a GPS, two pairs of Smart Glasses and a wallet that held several hundred US dollars. She knew some parts of the world still accepted cash but she'd never seen paper money herself.

Khalif had taken care of everything else. It wouldn't have done to have dropped them off in some lonely fjord miles from anywhere and wished them a *bon voyage*. The GPS would get them to where they were going and the Smart Glasses and money would help them steer clear of trouble.

"Thank you," Sienna said, giving Khalif a grateful hug. "I don't know how to thank you."

"Don't come back," was all Khalif could say.

Sienna gave him her word and once they helped him unload his jeep, they said their goodbyes and followed Tor down to a dingy that was tethered to the end of the jetty. Sienna remembered back to the last time she'd stepped into a little boat but at least this time they could see where they were going. A silhouette bobbed in the middle of the loch. A trawler sat at anchor, its lights extinguished, its jamming equipment running to render it a silhouette on radar too. Tor signalled with a torch and the trawler reciprocated. A bell sounded and she heard the engines fire up.

"We'll get going straight away," Tor explained. "Summer evenings. The weather's good but too much light."

He wasn't wrong. A strange green hue hung in the sky. It had been pulsating all evening like an emerald kaleidoscope against a turquoise tide.

"The aurora," Tor said.

Sienna had heard of them but she had never seen them. They were beautiful but what did they portend?

Tor shook his head. "It's just a trick of the night. We make our own luck on this Earth."

Sienna couldn't disagree.

As they covered the short distance to the trawler, Sienna's hand stayed in her pocket the whole time despite Khalif's assurances. Ropes were thrown and cargo transferred. Tor's crew helped Sienna and Malek aboard and Sienna readied herself for the punch. If it was coming, it would be now. But she and Malek found themselves on deck without incident. The little dingy cast off and the trawler weighed anchor, engines growling as they circled out to sea.

"Stay up top until you find your sea legs," Tor suggested. "Most of you Brits get sick first time out. You can chunder over the side. No one has to clean it up. But don't fall in."

They found a spot against the stern. The deck was wet and waves were jarring, just like the seascapes Malek used to paint, but he felt no such inspiration. He looked back at the only land he had ever known as its dark contours slipped away without ceremony and ached with sadness. Sienna showed no interest. No regrets or bittersweet feelings. Her sole focus was the journey ahead and the dangers to come. They were heading into the FSE, a coalition of states dedicated to the eradication of progressive politics. Millions had been murdered in the name of orthodoxy. Sienna knew they would be dealt with swiftly should they be caught. Norway might have been a liberal outlier but it was still under the yoke of René Gaultier, the butcher of Brussels. Their journey had only just begun.

"Did you ever cancel someone you know you shouldn't have? Someone you thought didn't deserve it?" Malek asked after a time.

"I didn't cancel anyone. I just audited histories and gathered data. Congress sanctioned the cancellations," Sienna replied, persisting with her self-justifications.

"You were only following orders?" Malek suggested.

It was less of a cop-out and more of a barb and Sienna saw it for what it was. In a nation that prided itself on freedom, liberty and diversity, Sienna had lacked the courage to step out of the herd and face the wolves. She'd never questioned Congress. Never disagreed with their perceived wisdom. Never bucked the trend.

Not until it had impacted upon her own life.

Then and only then had Sienna's eyes been opened. It had taken the loss of everything she had known to acquire the one thing she had always lacked.

"I regret them all," she finally said.

In the quiet that followed, she remembered a passage from the Book of Miranda she'd heard during her brief flirtation with Panthea.

Let thee who is without sin point the first finger. For they are truly righteous and shall inherit the world.

She had believed it wholeheartedly at the time, just as she had believed in her own righteousness. Now she wondered how anyone could be without sin when the very nature of sin was objective. The old Gods had considered eating apples to be sinful. Eve taking a bite at a serpent's instigation was referred to as the 'original sin' and womyn were castigated by 'holy' men for millennia. Clearly this was nonsense, dogmatic prejudice designed to disenfranchise the 'weaker' sex and reduce them to chattel. But it had been held dear by scores of 'enlightened' societies for centuries.

Rami Jaffri's great-grandfather had committed a hate offence decades before Rami had been born (he was only following orders too). Rami had paid the price and been cast out. But had he been responsible for his forefather's actions any more than womxnhood had been for Eve's? Sienna could no longer conflate the two. But nailing Rami had felt good at the time. And Geniture's balance sheet had grown thanks to the efforts of E Division. As indeed it did with the Halliday brothers, Abby Grey, Charles Garfield and hundreds of others Sienna had audited. Including Malek Smith.

In her heart, Sienna knew that Karma had simply caught up with her. That her skewed morality was the reason her life had fallen apart. That she had run up a deficit during her time at Geniture that spiritually, she was unable pay.

She was, of course, entirely, hopelessly and completely wrong.

The universe hadn't cancelled her. And she hadn't brought her demise upon herself, either wittingly or unwittingly. She was simply a collateral casualty of a greater struggle; one that went on unseen outside of the corridors of power. She would never know it. And she could never know it. But seven months earlier, a meeting had taken place that would determine not only Sienna's fate but that of Bella Köse, Myrtle Moorcroft, Ignatius ZvzWoski and a dozen others at Geniture when Charity GoodHope had summoned her minister, Zaria Okello, to discuss a somewhat delicate matter.

*

"Thank you for seeing me at such short notice, Zaria. It is good of you to come."

"I am always happy to sit with you, Chairperson. And learn from your wise counsel."

Charity smiled up from her official Sofa of Office. She directed Zaria to the beanbag opposite and stared intently from behind her pinked-out Smart Glasses.

"It has come to my attention that Geniture is running an audit into the country lines meat trade."

"Geniture runs hundreds of audits every week, Chairperson."

"But not all with your personal oversight."

Zaria smiled uncomfortably. She shifted on her beanbag and played for time but Charity was waiting for an answer even though she had yet to ask a question.

"As Chief Executive Officer, I like to take a hands-on approach whenever I can." It was a political response and Charity treated it as such.

"Let us be frank. I don't think there is anything to be gained from playing these sorts of games."

Zaria agreed. She had little other choice. She had wanted

to delay this moment until her people had uncovered more evidence but Charity had forced her hand. So be it. Zaria could be frank when she needed to be too.

"As you know, in my capacity as your loyal Minister, I have overseen an extensive reorganisation of my department and, whilst cataloguing certain files, an interesting document came to light."

"Did it?"

"An old document. From before your administration. Something your predecessor commissioned when the nation adopted you into its care."

Zaria had spent many nights since the document had come to light imagining this moment. She had thought about how best to present it and what she would ask for it but it had never occurred to her how much she might enjoy it. Was Charity aware of the document? Possibly. Hence this hurried meeting. But like everyone that Geniture called upon, she must have assumed that her skeletons were safely locked away.

"Fawqiyya el-Abdulla was like a mother to me. It broke my heart when I learned of her treachery."

"Indeed," smiled Zaria. "Which is why I know in my heart that this document has to be a fake. And why I was so keen to take steps to prove it thus so that I might clear your name. You have my complete and utter discretion, of course."

It was near-impossible to sit on a beanbag with any sense of grace but Zaria, overweight as she was, struggled more than most, tumbling sideways when the bag shifted to dump her on the floor. Charity made no effort to help her. She just stared at Zaria floundering on her face and wondered how she could have possibly come by the document. Every copy had been deleted and every witness purged. How had this come back to haunt her now?

A PDF flashed in Charity's in-tray which included a cover page stamped: 'Strictly Confidential: For My Eyes Only' together with Fawqiyya el-Abdulla's authorisation code.

"It relates to a DNA test the former Prime Minister ordered some years ago. On a hair sample she took from you," Zaria said when she was finally able to right herself. "My reading is, she was keen to discover your ancestry and share your cultural heritage with the nation so that the people could celebrate your diversity."

This was laying it on a bit thick but Zaria was still smarting from having to sit on a beanbag and now looked to turn the knife.

"Picked up off the coast with no clue as to your origins. I guess it was only natural that Fawqiyya would want to learn about your family. And the foreign regime you were fleeing."

Charity didn't need to read the document. It contained a host of genetic markers, geographic percentages and heredity indicators as well as a family name picked out again and again – <u>Garfield</u>. Her father (Garfield's second cousin) hadn't been striving to reach Britannia. But to flee it.

"I'm sure there must be a perfectly reasonable explanation. But should this data ever come to light, I worry that it might affect the nation's morale."

Charity did not bother to feign surprise. She had learned that Geniture was investigating Garfield's genealogy after her Guardians had interviewed an Auditor. Her only surprise was at whose instigation the audit was being conducted. She had always regarded Zaria as a threat but thought she could clip her wings by bringing her into the Governmynt. She had subscribed to the old adage about keeping your friends close and your enemies closer but it seemed Zaria was intent on getting closer still.

"I will ensure that my Auditors and Stewards do everything in their power to protect your privacy but I'm afraid I cannot guarantee it. There are certain areas of authority outside of even Geniture's purview. If, however, in my role as a Minister, I was able to subsume responsibilities for the Guardians also, I have no doubt that I could easily manage these findings to your satisfaction."

Zaria had always been bold when it came to business. She was a shooting star, the youngest CEO of a blue chip company and the most popular Minister in the cabinet. She was also, in most people's eyes, the natural successor to Charity GoodHope for when the great womxn finally stepped aside. Perhaps sooner rather than later. But she had been a little too impatient. A little too ambitious. And she had overplayed her hand against an opponent she had severely underestimated.

Zaria may have been ruthless but Charity was the embodiment of righteousness, a virgin child of destiny entrusted with the salvation of her people by Panthea herself. And her 'loyal' Minister had revealed herself to be worse than Hitler. Worse than Gaultier. Worse than Churchill even. A hate-filled enemy of diversity, inclusion and progress. As were her Auditors at Geniture. Particularly those involved in undermining her position.

But Charity had taken steps. She had moved fast and made arrangements to kill the investigation, root and branch. She still had the power. And she was determined to keep hold of it for as long as she could.

"Why don't we discuss it at my country residence?" Charity suggested with one final smile. "We can go now. You can fly us there in that helicopter of yours. I'm sure we can find a solution that works for us both."

43: NORWAY

Sienna awoke to a flurry of activity.

Something was happening.

Something wasn't right.

She had been resting in the cabin below, trying to sleep without success. They'd been at sea for two days and thus far the journey had passed without incident. She hadn't been able to drop her guard but she had been able to disguise her paranoia enough to avert suspicions. While they were at sea, she was at Tor's mercy. It would not have done to have made him uneasy. Therefore, she had buried her fears, mixed in as much as she could, smiled when appropriate and did as she was told, all the time ready to lash out like a coiled spring at the first sign of provocation. The crossing was less than three days but the stress had taken several years off her life.

But it had gone smoothly. So far.

The coast was thirty miles away. The inlet they were steering for, straight ahead. There, they would follow the waterway through Norway's rugged interior for 60 miles and dock at Tørvikbygd, a tiny village nestled on the banks of the Hardanger Fjord.

But something had changed. Voices were shouting. Boots were thumping. Tensions were rising.

Sienna shook Malek awake and told him to grab something.

"What?"

"Something heavy."

She had her boots on and was already dressed when Tor came into the cabin. He stopped when he saw the scalpel in her hand.

"We've got to dump the stuff," he said, nodding towards the crates beneath the bunks.

"What's going on?" Sienna demanded.

"Coastguard. We have to hurry."

Sienna stood her ground. She had little alternative, having no room to back into, so Tor edged close keeping his hands in plain sight. His eyes never left Sienna's, not even to glance at the blade in her hand, as he dragged out the first of several crates before hurrying away.

"Please," he said, stopping at the ladder before climbing up on deck.

Malek looked at Sienna, an ungainly fishing weight hanging in his hand.

"What do we do?"

"Dump the stuff," she said, "but watch out or they'll dump us too."

They grabbed the remaining crates and carried them up top, dumping them onto the deck for Tor and his crew to dispose of.

Several miles astern was a fast patrol boat doing everything to live up to its name. Tor and his crew were running at full throttle but all they could do was delay the inevitable. They couldn't outrun the authorities but they could buy themselves enough time to ditch their payload. They broke open the crates and set to hurling their profits into the sea with remarkable stoicism.

"You win some, you lose some," Tor remarked, skimming the last of the Coca Vapes across the waves with a flourish. "Tomorrow is another day."

He now turned to Sienna and Malek, the last items on his action list and shook his head in apology.

"I'm sorry," he said, almost sounding as if he meant it. "I wish there was another way."

Sienna had been expecting this moment, armed herself

and prepared for it. She'd envisioned herself slicing the throat of the first man to touch her, followed by her own slender wrists, but now that it was here, it was harder to do than she had imagined. She wanted to survive. She wanted to go on and escape and live. Just as Alicia had urged. She wanted to choose life yet what alternative did she have? Even if she fought off Tor and his crew, the coastguard would be upon them in moments. She couldn't resist an armed boarding party with just a scalpel.

Malek swung his weight with some effort and shouted at Tor to stay back. But Tor didn't move. Neither did the men alongside him. Three men? Where were the rest?

All at once, Sienna received a blow to the back of the head and felt the deck rush up to greet her. Something fell on top of her and pinned her to the boards. She screamed and wailed and howled as the scalpel was prised from her fingers, vowing to bite the first person who got close enough and craning her neck to do so. More bodies jumped on top of her and Sienna struggled beneath them but ultimately to no avail. There were too many.

Malek was blaspheming off to her right, as were several Norwegian tongues, but nothing more happened. Sienna had expected to be bound and her body cast overboard into the bitter depths but instead she sensed Tor at her ear.

"Be cool, my dangerous friend. Be cool. We are not going to hurt you."

It seemed a curious assertion considering there were four people on top of her but Tor was calmness personified.

"You need to be cool, yeah. No stabbing. No cutting. No blood. Especially not your own. You'll be okay. You dig?"

With that, she felt some of the weight shift from her back though her hands were still pinned to the deck.

"Khalif told us what might happen if we ran into trouble. What sort of a tiger we were carrying, so I thought it best if we were ready. I hope you understand. We couldn't take any chances."

Tor now stood and spoke to his crew. They released Malek and helped him to his feet. Malek looked confused, not least of all when Tor offered him a shot from his hip flask, having first proved it was not poison by taking some himself.

"Skol," he said, before looking down at Sienna. "What about you, tiger? Are you ready to put your claws away?"

The last remaining hands released Sienna and she sprang to her feet without assistance. She backed towards the stern and scanned the deck, her eyes wild as she took stock of the situation. It still hadn't sunk in that Tor meant her no harm. Her fight-or-flight state was coursing through her veins and screaming at her to do either.

Malek moved to her side and helped her come down.

"It's okay. I'm here. We're here together." He touched her arm and she flinched, backing away a step or two.

"Listen to your friend," Tor advised. "Be cool. It's all good."

Tor's crew were equally placid, having stepped back to give Sienna her space, some nursing painful cuts and scratches.

"Khalif was right about you," Tor laughed and some of his crew smirked in agreement. Some but not all. It occurred to Sienna that the whole time she'd been amongst them, Tor and his crew had probably been as wary of her as she had of them. Their scuffle may have laid to rest one fear but it didn't alter the facts. There was an FSE patrol boat fast approaching and they were undesirable aliens from an enemy state.

But once again Tor flashed Sienna a youthful smile and held out his hands to placate her.

"Be cool," he advised her. "Be Norwegian."

*

Sienna sat in a grey interrogation room and stared at the grey table in front of her grey chair. A border officer in a grey uniform blended into a grey wall by a grey door and gave her grey looks.

Whatever the plan had been, it had quickly unravelled in spite of Sienna's coolness. The coastguard had boarded their vessel, Tor had tried to talk his way out of it but the ruse was up the moment they had spoken to Sienna – in Norwegian. Tor had offered some explanation for her lack of response but it hadn't worked. Malek had cracked and another man blabbed and suddenly they were in cuffs.

To find herself here, in this grim and sterile detention room, was more than she'd been expecting. She'd assumed a summary execution and an unceremonious splash would have followed but Gaultier's people clearly had other ideas. Torture, mutilation, sadism or spectacle? She could only imagine her fate, each guess worse than the last. But so far, nothing. She'd been looked over by a medic, given a shot of something and some 'paracetamols for her pain' and addressed in English but so far she had refused to break, clinging on to the hope that if she didn't say anything, they could not use her words against her. This may have been a forlorn hope but as a former Auditor, her mind still worked this way.

After a time, the door opened and two womyn entered. They spoke to the officer in Norwegian and he replied in kind. Despite not understanding the words, Sienna understood the subtext.

One of the womyn was around Sienna's age, with dark hair and blue eyes. She wore a black suit that sported a silver button, some sort of insignia of office. The other womxn was older but not by much. She wore a knee-length floral dress, the type the womyn of yesteryear wore, and had a faux maternal look about her. The yellow flowers on her dress stood in sharp contrast to their drab surroundings and made Sienna look away.

Neither wore Smart Glasses or headsets of any kind. Like the table before her, each was unvarnished and regressive.

"I am Anniken Stien, Operational Supervisor for Bergen Frontier Security. This is Katherine Jordahl, Special Assistant to the Department. Could you tell us your name, please?"

Sienna said nothing, remembering how her interview with Guardians Cabot and Rhys had gone months earlier, that terrible episode in which she'd misgendered Bella. That was where this had all started, or so she still believed. That had been the beginning of the end. In trying to talk her way out of a bind, she had instead talked her way into hell. She may have reached the end of the road but she was damned if she was about to make the same mistake twice. If they wanted to get her name, they would have to beat it out of her.

"Not even a first name?"

Sienna didn't flinch.

"How did you come to be on that boat? The captain said he picked you up at sea."

Again, Sienna said nothing. She just stared and gritted her teeth, frightened but defiant. She had come so far and seen so many things yet this grey room and these grey people would be the last she would gaze upon. Not even a mindful quotation to comfort her in her final moments.

"Is there nothing you would like to tell us?"

Neither yes nor no. Sienna refused to give them so much as an utterance.

"You don't need to be frightened," Stien said. "We're here to help you."

Weren't they always? The Guardians, the Stewards, the *Rapists* and all. Even Geri and Purdy, Carl, MUM, Panthea and her AI counselling bot. Everyone had always been so keen to help Sienna. It was a wonder she wasn't better set.

Stien produced a pad from her pocket and called up a page.

"Sienna Clay from Woking, New Britannia," she read. "Sent to the camps November sixteen for crimes unspecified and Orkney some time in March. Escaped last week together with Malek Smith and secured passage to Norway from Tor Karlsen."

Stien looked up at Sienna and saw the fear in her eyes, the dread and deep ingrained trauma, all she had been through and all she had suffered. Yet she also saw a cast iron strength. An unrelenting, unyielding and unbendable spirit that had been forged in the fires of adversity. At first sight, she was a slight girl, small and brittle. Most would have thought a stiff breeze would have knocked her over but this girl, this elfish pixie, had not only made it out of the death camps of Orkney, she had survived abduction, attempted murder, wolf packs and ostracism and was still ready to resist. Life had underestimated Sienna. She probably even underestimated herself. Stien wasn't about to do the same.

"Sienna, this is going to be very confusing for you but please try to take in what we're about to tell you."

Stien sat back and let her colleague take over. Jordahl placed a large tablet on the table and called up several albums before starting.

"I know how you must be feeling. Six years ago, I was sat where you were and terrified like you," Jordahl said, her accent unmistakably English, Yorkshire or Nottinghamshire or somewhere like that. Sienna was reminded of Alicia and her will almost crumbled. Almost.

Jordahl continued.

"Everything you know about Europe, particularly the Federal States, everything you've been told and brought up to believe, the wars and atrocities and barbarism and hate, none of it is true. It's a lie. It's *the great lie*."

She probably believes it, too, Sienna thought to herself. Everyone believes their own distortions. Every killer is the hero of their own narrative. Gaultier probably thought he was safeguarding the racial purity of Europe against the heathen masses, the traditional values and culture of an archaic and dying civilisation. But the fact remained. The seas lay empty. And the voices of the dispossessed had been silenced. These were realities they could not hide.

But Jordahl was adamant. "There are no killing pits in France. None in Italy or Germany either. It simply did not happen."

Throughout the centuries, the guilty had always denied their crimes but history has a way of unearthing the past. Sienna didn't know why this turncoat was trying to trick her but she refused to be blinded to the truth.

"I guess not," Sienna said, finally speaking, if only to show that she understood.

Jordahl nodded. "Well, we did say this wasn't going to be easy."

She slid the tablet to Sienna and invited her to see for herself. It contained hundreds of pictures, mostly featuring ordinary European street scenes and happy citizens going about their business, some of them from diverse cultures and pansexual communities. Sienna looked but it proved nothing.

Postcards from the East. Anything could be faked these days. Jordahl read Sienna's reaction and agreed.

"This isn't our proof. This is just an introduction to prepare you for what you're about to see. We need you to stay calm and try to open your mind. Yes?" Jordahl stood up and invited Sienna to do the same.

"What?"

"Nothing is going to happen to you. We're just going for a walk."

Stien saw the flash of panic in Sienna's eyes and knew she'd been conditioned to expect the worst. She must have thought this was it, that a firing squad or a gas chamber awaited her through that door so Stien moved to reassure her.

"You're not worse than Hitler."

Sienna glared at her.

"Malek says he's sorry. You're not worse than Hitler. He shouldn't have said it. And if you'll forgive him, he's ready to go to Sweden with you whenever you are."

Stien smiled but Sienna didn't. She was so confused. Frightened and desperate.

"Where is he?"

"Waiting for you."

They could have tortured or coerced Malek into confessing their names but of all the information they could have exacted out of him, these remarks seemed spurious in the extreme. On Orkney, Sienna had asked Malek to trust her. Now it was her turn to trust him, albeit his words. One way or the other, whatever was about to happen would happen with or without Sienna's consent. All she could do was what she had always done; hope for the best. And prepare for the worst.

Sienna stood and Stien added one caveat.

"You just need to give me your ankle," she said, pulling a steel bracelet from her pocket.

Sienna tensed but Stien assured her it was nothing.

"Every refugee gets one. Just until you're processed. We can't have you running around town when we want to talk to you."

But Sienna refused to be tagged. She'd been tagged once before. She wasn't about to allow herself to be tagged again. Jordahl patted Stien on the shoulder and told her to put it away.

"She'll be fine. She's not going to run. And if she does, she'll come back. I trust her."

Stien didn't share her colleague's optimism but Jordahl had better insight than she. Both had heralded from that insane island across the water. And both had broken free. Stien was happy to let her colleague take the lead. Just so long as she didn't have to run after anyone today. She had the start of a menstrual migraine coming on and too much work to get through. If only she could've had the day off.

"Let's go."

44: EPILOGUE

Outside, the air was warm and the sun shone like brushed gold. It was early summer in Bergen and the avenue trees were in full bloom. Hydrobuses cruised by and people hurried about their business. The buildings were different, colourful and Nordic, and the street signs were displayed in only one language but for what it was worth, Sienna felt she could have been at home.

"The hostel is up the street. You'll stay there while your asylum claim is assessed."

"Asylum?"

"It's a formality," Jordahl said. "We don't get many people from Britannia. From Russia and Turkey mostly. But not from there."

"We have lots we'd like to ask you," Stien added, keen to get started but aware that such things could not be rushed.

"All in good time," Jordahl said. "When she's good and ready."

Sienna noticed how closely Stien was sticking to her but Jordahl was happy to wander out in front and lead the way. She thought about running. Of course she did but she still had trouble walking, her knee not yet pain-free. Besides, where could she run? In a strange country, unable to speak the language, no money, no papers and no one to turn to. She was all alone and at their mercy. Yet mercy was what they'd shown her. Jordahl was right. What other choice did she have but to trust them? At least until she'd got things organised.

"How did you get here?" Sienna asked Jordahl, hobbling to catch up.

"Boat, same as you. Trying to get to Sweden," she laughed. "Paid everything I had and still didn't make it. Can you believe that?"

"Your name? It's not Britannic."

"No, I took my husband's name when we married," Jordahl explained, showing Sienna the medieval Norse ring on her finger.

Sienna tried not to react but was unable to help herself. The shackles of matrimony still enslaved womyn here. What manner of Gulag was this? Jordahl noted Sienna's reaction and smiled.

"It's almost as if I can read your mind," she said, wishing she could put an arm around her but knowing Sienna wasn't ready yet. "It's okay. You're going to see and hear a lot of strange things today. But they're all good. You're safe."

They walked on in silence, Sienna looking around, Stien watching her. Across the road, a family from the sub-Saharan strolled by pushing a pram. Sienna stopped and stared, almost unable to comprehend.

"You have Grade 20s here?" she said, having to guess at their number in the absence of visible metadata.

"Nope, just people," Stien said before Jordahl could.

"Gaultier allows them?" Sienna said, unable to tear her eyes off the family as they crossed the road unmolested and free.

"Ah yes, that's the other thing. René Gaultier is dead," Jordahl said, almost as an after-thought.

"What? When?"

"Ten years ago. He'd been out of office for about three years and just died."

"How?"

"Cancer. It was pretty quick."

This couldn't be true. Sienna knew it couldn't. She'd seen the news feeds. Watched the hate speech clips on the Network. The rallies he'd staged for his fanatical followers. The rhetoric and threats. Charity had denounced him only months earlier. She'd attended the October march to protest against his regime. How could he be dead?

"He was tough on controls and pushed through a lot of controversial legislation but he wasn't a tyrant. An asshole maybe but not a tyrant, and he was voted out in the end. Not like your glorious leader," Stien said, less than sympathetically. "It was all bullshit. Peddled by your Pollies and controlled by your Network and you people lapped it up."

Jordahl threw her a look to suggest she went easy today. It was Sienna's first time beyond the looking glass. Stien could do worse than cut her some slack.

"But the boats in the Channel? The migrants and the missing?" Sienna said, referring to the absence of refugees. If there were such freedoms in Europe, where had all they gone?

"They chose to make their homes elsewhere," Jordahl said as diplomatically as she could but Stien refused to sugarcoat it.

"You don't flee one crazy dictatorship for another one. And those that tried were stopped by your own navy in the name of rumour control. Most of the migrants who crossed the Channel in the last twenty years were all heading away from Britannia."

"That's not true," Sienna insisted. "Charity GoodHope fled the FSE. She was a refugee. She was a victim of the purges?"

But they had no time to get into that now. They rounded the corner and Sienna saw Malek sat on the wall outside the hostel, free and unfettered. She ran to him and they embraced, overjoyed and overwhelmed in equal measure. Malek had no guard to watch over him. Just a bracelet on his ankle and a tablet in his hand to help him catch up with the last twenty years worth of news.

"Are you okay?" Malek asked, smiling from ear to ear at seeing Sienna again.

She wasn't sure. She was so confused by it all, just as Stien had promised. It couldn't be true. Could it? How was it possible that an entire truth could be nothing more than a lie?

"It's not about truth and lies. It's about what you choose to believe," Stien said acerbically. She produced the bracelet again and this time Sienna allowed her to fit it. "It'll only be for a week or two," she promised. "For your own sake.

Welcome to Norway."

Across the street, Sienna noticed an enormous mural painted on the side of a building. It featured a womxn in what Sienna took to be traditional Norwegian dress warmly welcoming a small brown-skinned person of indeterminate heritage. It had obviously been painted across from the hostel to make newcomers feel welcome but this was not what had caught Sienna's eye. On the pavement directly below stood a small protest camp manned by a couple of middle-aged reactionaries, temporarily off the clock as they ate their lunch. Banners had been strung from the street railings and placards taped up declaring NORWAY FOR NORWEGIANS, NORSEMEN AND PROUD and YOUR COUNTRY NEEDS YOU – GO HOME.

Sienna couldn't 't understand it.

No one was moving in to arrest them. No one was gathering evidence to use against them. No one was even taking any notice of them. No police. No Guardians. No Stewards. None of the families out strolling in the sunshine. Not even Stien or Jordahl. Not until they saw Sienna and followed her eye.

"Oh them. Sorry about that," Jordahl apologised when she saw the unwelcoming banners. "This sort of thing shouldn't be allowed."

But Sienna wasn't so sure. Of all the things she had seen over the course of the last seven months, surely this was the most unsettling and yet the most reassuring. She sat with Malek on the wall outside their hostel and looked out upon this strange new world full of strange new sights and strange new people.

And marvelled –

– at the sheer diversity of it all.

A PLEA BY THE AUTHOR

I self-published Cancelled after many months of submitting it to agents and publishers. The vast majority never replied and those that did dismissed it with a cut-and-paste response. Not to sound bitter but unless you are represented by one of the big agencies, no traditional publisher will even look at you. And these days, it's harder than ever to get a literary agent if you hail from a lower socio-economic background (ie. if you're a pleb like me).

Therefore, if you enjoyed this book, please consider telling a friend or posting a recommendation on Facebook, X or TikTok, etc. Word of mouth is an author's best friend.

Secondly, please consider posting a review on Amazon or Goodreads as that could really help too. Your review could be as little as word but it could make all the difference. I will even thank your name to the acknowledgements page. Just drop me a line at the below address to let me know and I will add you when I update the files. Obviously, if you don't want to be named & famed, that's no problem either.

dannykingbooks@yahoo.com

WITH GRATEFUL THANKS

I offer my heartfelt thanks and appreciation to the following people for helping me research, edit and promote this book: Jeannie King, Tony Wilson, Matt Bunce, Carl Keszei, Lula, Alison Congalton, Mike Baker, Paul Melhuish, JS Clarke, Inja Crockett, fellow scribe, Carl Jason Randall (author of '51 Mosquitos' and 'Cockney Runts'), Lindsay Stone, Yan Pugh-Jones and Luke Sherwood for his *Basso Profoundo* review. I would also like to thank The Libertarian Futurist Society for nominating this book for the 2025 Prometheus Award. And lastly, I am compelled to thank my daughter Scarlett for coming into my office and asking if she could be thanked in this bit as well.

Thank you one and all.

BOOKS BY THE SAME AUTHOR

THE UGLY SISTERS

When Cinderella danced with Prince Charming at the Great Ball, the entire Kingdom was taken in by her beauty. Almost. For there were two who could see past her delicate charms and into the avarice of her cold dead heart. And for centuries they were vilified for it. Everybody knows the story of *Cinderella*. But this is the story of Marigold and Gardenia Roche – better known as *The Ugly Sisters*. And it is no fairytale.

"I grabbed this book on a freebie, expecting a short fun read, but was stunned when it turned out to be a full-length novel that's absolutely brilliant. Great fun, very easy to read thanks to the excellent writing, and a totally unexpected take on a very old fairy story. Plenty of twists and turns, thoroughly believable characters and wonderfully enjoyable. Highly recommended" – Verified Purchase, Amazon

THE MONSTER MAN OF HORROR HOUSE

John Coal is a creepy old man who lives at the end of the street. All he wants out of life is to be left alone but the neighbourhood kids take great delight in tormenting him morning, noon and night. Unable to go to the authorities, John has no choice. He must convince these malfeasants that he is not a man to be trifled with. He must convince them that he is, John Coal – The Monster Man of Horror House.

"Storytelling at its best" – Verified Purchase, Amazon

SHORT-LISTED 2017 Vincent Price Horror Awards

THE MONSTER MAN OF HORROR HOUSE RETURNS

John Coal is back in this second anthology of horror tales. Fresh from the carnage of the first book, John and his ward, Rachel, flee north, away from the authorities and into the Scottish wilderness. Here they will encounter phantoms and fiends, demons and the damned, all of whom would be well-advised to avoid John Coal – The Monster Man of Horror House.

"I couldn't put this down, I read the whole series in two days and nights!! A fantastic and addictive series" – Verified Purchase, Amazon

CURSE OF THE MONSTER MAN OF HORROR HOUSE
A monstrous scarecrow, a hellhound train, killer crustaceans and a celestial game of chess are just some of the horrors awaiting us in this third and final instalment of terror tales, as told and lived by accursed John Coal – The Monster Man of Horror House.
"I don't know why I like John Coal so much. Dudes a bit of a coward, and not very brave even when he talks big, but his horribly cursed life is a very interesting tale indeed" – Verified Purchase, Amazon United States

THE NO.1 ZOMBIE DETECTIVE AGENCY
The world has been overrun by zombies. Mere pockets of humanity remain. Cities lay in ruins. But none of this can stop Jake Trundle from solving the biggest case of his career because Jake is dead too. And somewhere deep within the recesses of his rotting mind flicker the embers of the last case he was working on before the world turned to hell. Now he is compelled to solve it for all eternity. He doesn't know why, he doesn't know how, but he's going to solve this case anyway. Even if it kills him all over again. Jake Trundle is a zombie. But he was a detective first. And nothing can take that away from him. Not even death.
"Blackly comic and frequently haunting, Trundle is an entertaining take on the Private Eye trope" – Verified Purchase, Amazon

THE HENCHMEN'S BOOK CLUB
Mark Jones is a henchman for hire. He guards bunkers, patrols perimeters and spends much of his working week getting knocked out by Ninjas. This is his job. Still, for every hour under gunfire, there are weeks of sitting around in monorails watching scientists scurry by so Jones starts a book club. It was only ever meant to pass the time. It was never meant to save the world.
"One of the best ripping good yarns I have come across in quite a while" – The Literature Professors' Book Club

THE BURGLAR DIARIES

A small-time housebreaker takes us on a tour of the side streets and back alley of his local manor and shares his thoughts on life, love and larceny along the way. #1 bestseller (independent publishers) and *Big Issue In The North* pick-of-the-month book (March 2001). It's fairly safe to say, this book would not be published today. Buy it to find out why.

"One of the few writers to make me laugh out loud. Danny King is brilliant at making you love characters who are quite bad people" — David Baddiel

WINNER of the 2001 Amazon Bursary Prize

THE BANK ROBBER DIARIES

A bank crew is forced to adapt when their leader goes to prison. Gangsters, mobsters and shysters compete to blow each other away in this rip-roaring tale of over-the-counter enterprise.

"Low on morals but big on laughs. If you can thieve one, go for it" – BBM

THE HITMAN DIARIES

Ian Bridges works his own hours, has a job he's good at and earns great money. But he's not a happy man. He longs to meet that special lady to share his success with but the women he meets usually end up dead. Still, not to be deterred, he's determined to find true love. Even if it means death to every woman in London.

"King's humour is as black as Donald Rumsfeld's heart" – Maxim

Adapted into two separate short **films**, both of which can be streamed **FREE** online (details in the FILMS section).

THE PORNOGRAPHER DIARIES

Godfrey Bishop works for a porn magazine. He talks to the models, reads the sex letters, organises photoshoots and even gets to direct the action. He has, according to his friends, the best job in the world. But Godfrey has a problem. He hasn't been with a girl himself in over a year leaving him a frustrated wreck. Throw in a twelve-girl orgy, an outraged feminist, an obsessive stalker and a naked run from the police and you have "an amusing, if thoroughly filthy, ride (The Leeds guide).

"King's filthiest and funniest novel yet" – Buzz Magazine

The stage show adaptation ran for four weeks at the 2007 Edinburgh Fringe Festival. Script available.

THE PORNOGRAPHER DIARIES (the play)
The complete text for the stage adaption of the novel of the same name. It includes a list of cast needed (two male, one female), a stage layout and a list of furnishings and props (minimal). Theatre companies are welcome to license the text in order to perform the place. Contact details are provided within.

"Maintains the pace and energy of the book – a difficult trick to pull off... pardon me" – The Stage

"Watching a woman in the audience who looked like Mary Whitehouse chortle along to every cock, tit and fanny joke was worth the admission price alone" – Broadway Baby

"Entertains and succeeds despite its subject content" – Festival reviewer

MILO'S MARAUDERS (book 1)
Darren Miles has been in and out of prison since he was 15. Now aged 27, he is released from his latest stretch and returns home vowing to go straight. But things aren't that easy. His girlfriend has dumped him, he can't get a job, he has no money and the police are waiting for him to slip up again. What chance does a guy like him have?

"A snappy, slangy novel that morphs heist caper with black comedy and crawls inside the criminal mindset" – Buzz Magazine

MILO'S RUN (book 2)
Milo has finally scored some real money: a hundred grand in used notes and it's all tax-free. However, if he ever hopes to spend a penny of it he'd better keep running before the law catches up with him. Milo has a 30-second head-start, a stolen car and absolutely no idea where he's going. All he knows is that he can't stop... not for a minute... not even for a second.

"A nerve shredding page turner" – The Big Issue in the North

SCHOOL FOR SCUMBAGS
Teenage delinquent, Wayne Banstead is expelled from yet another school and finds himself in a special academy for 'misdirected boys'. It plays host to the worst of the worst, the cream of teenage offending. The teachers have their work cut out. But far from rehabilitating them, the teachers seem more intent on teaching their pupils how to make crime pay. With careful tutoring, Wayne and his classmates are about to take a step up into the big leagues. But in the big leagues, the big boys play for keeps.

"The perfect antidote to Hogwarts" – The Sport

BLUE COLLAR

Catford brickie, Terry Prior, wakes up in a strange room next to a strange girl and has the strangest feeling they were meant for each other. But this is obvious to all. Terry is a full English with builder's tea type of guy whereas Charley is more Eggs Benedict and Earl Grey. She is posh, she is wealthy and she is gorgeous. Which means she is way out of Terry's league – or so everyone thinks. When gastro-pub meets local boozer and white-collar meets blue, Charley and Terry's love is built on the shakiest of foundations.

"This book reads like a dream" – The Sunday Express

SHORT-LISTED for the 2010 Melissa Nathan Award for Comic Romance

MORE BURGLAR DIARIES (book 2)

Following on from Danny King's best-selling debut and based on the BBC comedy series, Thieves Like Us, narrator Bex takes us on another tour of Tatley's rooftops and drainpipes, and through more lock-ups, cock-ups and jobs as he recounts More Burglar Diaries. Featuring an introduction by the author, a full novelisation of all six episodes and an all-new and final adventure for literature's least likely heroes.

"Danny King is an urban philosopher with a touch of comedy and tragedy. A very very funny book" – Verified Purchase, Amazon

INFIDELITY FOR BEGINNERS

Static caravan magazine editor, Andrew Nolan, is going nowhere. Other people in faraway places fight in wars or rescue toddlers from burning buildings but not Andrew. He just writes about caravans. And static caravans at that. To escape the drudgery, Andrew loses himself to his daydreams, imagining zombie Armageddons, deep-sea space aliens and the sexual intrigues of his friends and co-workers. However, one such daydream begins to take on a very real shape when his attractive assistant, Elenor, begins making eyes at him. Or is she? Is it all in his imagination or is Elenor really laying it on a plate? It's not easy for a complete novice like Andrew to tell.

"Has a more serious undertone than the previous books but still witty and a great read, hard to put down. I'm definitely a Danny King fan" – Verified Purchase, Amazon

EAT LOCALS

In a quiet country farmhouse, Britain's vampires gather for their once-every-fifty-years meeting. Others will be joining them too; Sebastian Crockett, an unwitting Essex boy who thinks he's on a promise with an older woman; a detachment of Special Forces vampire killers who have bitten off more than they can chew. And a couple of serial killers who are about to get a taste of their own medicine. This is going to be a night to remember for most. And for some, it will be their last. The official novelisation of the cult movie starring Charlie Cox, Mackenzie Crook and Freema Agyeman.

"Lashings of sardonic humour abound in the prose as well as the dialogue, with rapid-paced plot and action. And an extra star for the backmatter, where King describes the experience of writing a film and how no-budget filmmaking works" – Verified Purchase, Amazon

THE EXECUTIONERS (written as DM King)

Britain reinstates capital punishment for the crime of murder. Third to hang is notorious killer, Jammal Grey, aka the Dulwich Ripper. Three weeks later, the daughter of DCI Bowman – the man who caught Grey – is murdered in a copycat killing. Who could have done this? And why? Bowman knows who. And he knows why. Because the Ripper is still out there. The wrong man was hanged. And now he must hunt him down all over again before more women start to die. And the shocking truth is revealed.

"Brilliant read" – Verified Purchase, Amazon

AMY X AND THE GREAT RACE

What the remote island of Pompolonia lacks in size, it makes up for in tradition. Each year a Great Race is run, from the white sands of Octopus Bay, up to the volcanic lake atop Mount Pomp. All islanders aged 12 are compelled to race. The winners always come from one of the seven Great Houses and this year will be no different. The King's own daughter is set to take part. And win. The outcome is assured. But somebody forgot to tell Amy X, a Lowland waif so poor that she can't even afford a last name. Amy has her own dreams and they are every bit as precious as any Princess's. For one hundred years the great families of Pompolonia have had it all their own way. But this year, a scrawny girl with no name and no shoes will give them a real run for their money.

WINNER 2016 Story for Children Prize, Wells Festival of Literature

AMY X AND THE PRIM & PROPER PRINCESS SCHOOL
The King's Academy for Personal Excellence is a remarkable school and the only academy in the world with a perfect 100% exam pass rate. Most Pompolonians learn only bottle making at Pomp Comp but those destined for higher things can enjoy the finest education money can buy. This term a new student will be inducted. Amy X has been awarded a scholarship and she is about to discover that all knowledge comes at a price – especially to those who can least afford it.

SHORT-LISTED for the 2017 Story for Children Prize, Wells Festival of Literature

AMY X AND THE TERRIBLE TYPHOON
Amy X is set to go where no Lowlander has ever gone – somewhere else. But a terrible storm blows in to sink her ship and she is washed back to the shores of Pompolonia. She has only been gone a few short hours but it is not the island she left behind. Homes have been smashed. Families are scattered. The Kingdom is in ruins. But Princess Honor plans to rebuild the Kingdom in her own glorious image – with no expense spared. She will "Make Pompolonia Great Again" and every islander is pressed into service. But one young girl refuses to "do her bit". Another storm is brewing. Pompolonia had better take cover again.

DATING BY NUMBERS (written as Kim_89)
Kim finds her cosy life has been turned on its head after a long-term relationship ends. Quiet nights in with Steve have become quiet nights alone. Dinner for two has become pudding for three. And sex has become something she only hears about from friends. To shake things up, Kim throws herself into internet, speed and blind dating, meeting charmers, Dahmers and creeps along the way. Craig_47, Rick_8, Philip_ 93, David_121, Tim_56, Eben_2 – it's not easy to keep count when they all want one thing. A funny and sexy odyssey through shark-infested waters of the dating game. The names in this book have been changed so that the stories needn't be.

"I loved this book. It's a fine piece of writing. It's very honest and down to earth. It was so funny in places. I laughed out loud much to the amusement of my family" – Verified Purchase, Amazon

FILMS BY THE AUTHOR

I have also written a number of films, most of which are available to stream on Amazon, YouTube and other such platforms.

WILD BILL
Feature film

An ex-con is released from prison and returns home to find his teenage sons fending for themselves on an East London estate after their mother abandoned them. Bill must step up and be the best father he can if his boys are to escape the same cycle of crime and punishment that brought him down. Directed by Dexter Fletcher. Starring Charlie Creed-Miles, Will Poulter, Liz White and Andy Serkis.

"Everything that's good about British filmmaking" – Daily Mail
"Brilliant gangster drama. Hugely entertaining" – Sunday Express
"Gripping, intense and with a razor-sharp wit" – The Sun
"Great film" – Heat Magazine

BAFTA NOMINEE, Outstanding Debut 2013
WINNER Writers' Guild (GB), Best First Film 2012

Stream via Amazon Prime, Google Play, Hoopla and Plex. Also intermittently available on Netflix.

EAT LOCALS
Feature film

A group of vampires gather for a summit meeting to discuss feeding quotas and induct a new member only to be attacked and sieged by special forces. Blood, gore and dark comedy ensues. Directed by Jason Flemyng. Starring Charlie Cox, Freema Agyeman, Mackenzie Crook, Robert Portal and Ruth Jones.

WINNER British Indie Film Festival, Best Director 2017
NOMINEE British Independent Film Festival, Best Film 2017
NOMINEE Silver Méliès, Best European Film 2017

Stream via Amazon Prime, Google Play, Tubi, Plex and Apple TV. Intermittently shown on Legend (freeview 41, freest 137, Virgin 149, Sky 148)

THIEVES LIKE US
A six-part BBCThree series based on The Burglar Diaries. Written by Danny King. Starring Tom Brooke, Fraser Ayres & Gary Beadle.

"Good comedy that needs more publicity (10/10)" – IMDb reviewer
"Better than the promos led me to believe (8/10)" – IMDb reviewer
"Best British comedy in years (8/10)" – IMDb reviewer

Not seen on British television since 2007. However, four of the six episodes have been uploaded onto YouTube (not by me, I should add). Search for 'thieves like us sitcom' and you should find them.

RUN RUN AS FAST AS YOU CAN
Short film – 16:31mins

Five children are chased through the woods in the fading light. Who is after them or for what purpose is unclear. All that is obvious is their fear at the thought of being caught. A relentless chase with a meteoric twist for young and old alike.

WINNER Los Angeles Film Awards 2017
Stream FREE: https://vimeo.com/217200224

LITTLE MONSTERS
Short film – 4:31mins

Katie is scared of the monsters under her bed but she needn't be. Not when there is so much more to be frightened of. Directed by Simon Harris. Starring Dexter Fletcher and Polly Polnnick.

WINNER London Short Film Festival, Best Horror Short
Stream FREE: https://vimeo.com/334917788

SEVEN SHARP
Short film – 6:01mins

Dan is mad at Louise. They are late for dinner with Jimmy and Becky and Louise hasn't even got her makeup on yet. Why can't she be on time for something just once? Directed by Roque Cameselle and Andrew Turner. Starring Josephine Wynne-Eyton, Kirsten Buchanan, Coque Varela and Andrew Turner.

WINNER Focus Wales Best Short Film 2019
Stream FREE: https://www.youtube.com/watch?v=D2TFsqj805E

THE HITMAN DIARIES
Short film – 9:09mins

Based on The Hitman Diaries, Daniel Caltagirone takes the first couple of chapters and adapts it to film. Directed by Mark Abrahams. Starring Daniel Caltagirone, Ella Smith, Sarah Manners and Johnny Harris.

Filmed as promo short to attract investment for a feature version.

Stream FREE:
https://www.youtube.com/watch?v=m8ov7l5WxL4

ROMANTIC
Mini-feature film – 23:54mins

Russian filmmaker, Constantine Tupitsyn takes my novel, The Hitman Diaries, condenses it into a 24-minute mini-feature and sets it against the snowy streets of Perm. Directed by Constantine Tupitsyn. Starring Constantine Tupitsyn, Oksana Ermakova, Kristina Utkina, Ekaterina Kharina, Semyon Tomilin, Anna Noskova, Aleksey Krasnov, Dmitriy Mikhaylov and Olga Kel.

A great effort by Constantine and the crew. This film was made with sticking plasters and love but only the love is visible onscreen.

Stream FREE: https://www.youtube.com/watch?v=vJXZG7of5PM

CHARACTERS

Main Characters
Sienna Clay	Auditor / sinnysinful2056.070
Geri Hussein	AI writer / girlfriend / hardcorebaby.2058.17

Geniture Personnel
Zaria Okello	CEO
Bella (Ben) Köse	Sector 4 Supervisor
Myrtle Moorcroft	Head of X Division
Ignatius ZvzWoski	Head of I Division
Verity Abebe	S Division Steward

Geniture Structure
X Division	Investigative and Interpretative
I Division	Tip-offs and information
V Division	Truth and Dissemination
G Division	Genome and DNA
E Division	Economic and Administrative
S Division	Security and Safety
Congress	Fortnightly sanction meeting

In Charge
Charity GoodHope	Chairperson of New Britannia
Zaria Okello	Minister For Survivors
Unnamed	Minister For Respect
Fawqiyya el-Abdulla	Ex-PM (*nee* Felicity Wilberforce-Jones)
René Gaultier	President of the FSE

Cancelled Characters
Rami Jaffri	Great-Grandson of Clive Cooper
Clive Cooper	Policeman 1977
Halliday Brothers	Sons of transphobic mother
Charles Garfield	Ex-Butcher (veganking2025.1008)
Abby Grey	TERF sports campaigner

Friends
Purdy and Diego	Geri's friends
Fuzz and Aurora	Geri's friends
theoneandonly2060.663	Grade 20, Geri's friend

The Hub
Malek Smith	Data Analyst (databoy2062.11)
Julie Adamski	Product Manager (trulyjulie2064.332)
Anita Xeno	Lunch friend

Other Characters
tigereyes2049.4	Username at bus stop
ramjamdingdong2036.1	Man in club
spongecake2038.69	Beer thief
darkmatter2021.407	Guardian Informer
Investigator Cabot	surreyguardian.637
Guardian Rhys	surreyguardian.444

Historic Characters
Milly Main	Vegan influencer
Warrant Officer Saguna Singh BC	Hero of Shetland
Captain Maïmounatou Mekongo BC	Hero of Orkney
Trinity Dhaliwal	Designer of MUM
Kensie Tyne	AI writer and Naturalist
Paula	Rape Counsellor
Maya Deshpande	Rape victim
Jaya Deshpande	Journalist / sister of above

Camp 14
Doctor (*Cuntface*)	Overseer
Alicia	Friend /mentor (Mansfield)
Kat	One-time partner
Farahnoush	Can denied food at farm
Mariatou	H.A. Programme user / Doctor
Petula	Transwomxn
Tilly	Runaway

Camp Orkney
Braided officer	Spokesperson upon arrival
Christ-like officer	Fitz Kanu
Jolyon Romero	Spokesperson at Cornquoy
Sekhmet Krol	Cook at Cornquoy
Nora	414 work bench
Wojciech	Ejected newcomer
Jonas	Gold smelter / escapee / Linksness
Malek Smith	Escapee / Greenigoe